MW01154243

JENNY POX

by

J. L. Bryan

Published July 2010

www.jlbryanbooks.com

Cover design by Phatpuppy Art (phatpuppyart.com)

Jenny Pox © 2010 Jeffrey L. Bryan

All rights reserved.

For my family

<u>Other Books by JL Bryan</u>:

Tommy Nightmare (the sequel to *Jenny Pox*)

The Haunted E-book

Dark Tomorrows (short stories)

Helix

Mid-Afternoon

Dominion

CHAPTER ONE

Jenny sat in the red dirt and played with a plastic dinosaur. She liked the front yard, with all its mysteries--the high clumps of weeds, the big fallen-over tree trunk shaggy with scrub growth, the shiny bottles and cans Daddy left everywhere. She liked all the funny pieces of machinery and broken furniture around the shed. People brought things to Daddy's shed, and he fixed them, sometimes. Daddy was a Handy Man, except when he was Drinking.

Jenny heard a funny, shaking noise, like one of the old rattle toys in her room. It was from somewhere near the fallen tree. Maybe on the other side of it.

She crawled on the sandy, oil-stained dirt, through high weeds. She startled a chipmunk near her knee and he skittered away from her. She giggled at the funny little striped creature.

The rattle sounded again and she crawled to the tree. She turned and crawled along its length, stopping every foot or so to poke her fingers into the weeds and ivy that had grown over the fallen tree's bark. She pulled aside stringy plants to peer into dark places under the tree, and she squinted her eyes to peer into knotholes.

She found the place where a narrow, weed-choked gully had washed out underneath the trunk, creating a kind of dark cave underneath. She leaned her face in close, cupping her hands around her eyes to try and shield out the sun. She couldn't see anything, but she heard the rattle again, longer and louder this time, from the darkness right in front of her nose. It was in there somewhere.

She reached her hand deep into the gully, pushing and tearing through thick weeds. The rattling grew louder. She touched something cool and muscular. It pulled away from her fingers, and now the rattle went crazy. She reached her arm all the way into the narrow gully, up to her shoulder. Her fingers brushed the mysterious muscular thing again, and again it pulled back. She pawed around in the dirt. She could hear it rattling, but she couldn't find it again.

She wondered if it had moved all the way to the other side of the tree. Maybe she could find it over there. Jenny drew her hand out of the gully. She scrabbled up onto the trunk, which was nearly as high as she was, clawing her way to the top with her fingernails and toenails. She leaned out over the other side of the tree, looking among the weeds and brown bottles, her bare feet dangling in the air behind her.

She tilted forward until her head was almost upside down, her thick black hair hanging down like streamers. She watched it emerge from the gully. Triangular head, black eyes. Its head looked like her dinosaur toy. Its body looked like a living piece of rope, unspooling from underneath the trunk to slither off through high weeds and towards the woods, where Jenny wasn't allowed to go. Its long body kept coming out and out, and Jenny snickered. The creature was just so long, it was almost silly.

Its skin was olive, with pretty black diamonds all over its back. Jenny reached down and ran her fingers along it as it passed. It writhed at her touch and gave another long rattle. She wrapped her fingers around its body and picked it up to play with it, thinking it would be a good friend for her dinosaur. And she liked that rattley sound, it was like whispering, like telling secrets.

Its head arched up and twisted around to face her. It opened his jaw and hissed, revealing huge fangs.

Jenny shrieked and tumbled backward off the fallen tree. One hand tightened its grip on the ropey creature, while her other hand grabbed uselessly at the air for something to stop her fall.

She landed hard on the dirt, flat on her back, dragging the long creature over the tree with her, and its long body landed across her stomach. It was thrashing hard and rattling faster, and she could see the rattle now, a fat cone of shell-like rings at the tail end.

She lifted the creature's long belly off her with both hands. The fanged head raised up, dripping fluid from its teeth, and then swooped towards her bare, dirt-crusted left foot. She cried out as the head struck her ankle.

But it didn't bite her. Instead, its head slid off her leg and into the dirt, and Jenny held her breath and watched it, keeping herself very still. The creature didn't move again.

Along the segment of the snake's body that drooped between her hands, its scaly skin had busted open all over and dark blood seeped out. The blistering infection spread out along its skin in both directions from her hands, towards its head and towards its tail. All her fingers felt sticky and gross.

Jenny dropped the snake in the dirt and crawled over to the tail end. She tapped the rattle, but the snake didn't react. She picked up the rattle end and shook it, and it made the funny sound. She giggled.

Excited now, her fright already fading, Jenny jumped to her feet and ran toward the front porch, dragging the long dead snake behind her. She stopped at the porch steps and shook the rattle again.

"Daddy!" she called, not sure if he were awake yet. "Daddy daddy!"

Daddy didn't answer. She went up the three steps and through the open front door.

Daddy was snoring on the couch, in front of a heap of shiny silver cans and an overflowing ashtray on the coffee table. Jenny grabbed his arm—careful to touch only the sleeve, not the skin—and shook him.

"Daddy! Toy!" she screamed at his heavily stubbled, drooling face. She shook the rattle at him. "Daddy!"

"Wha…?" His eyes eased open, bleary and unfocused.

"Toy!" Jenny gave the rattle a good, hard shake to really make her point.

Now Daddy's eyes snapped open wide and she could see all the little red veins in them. He smacked Jenny's hand, hard, slapping the snake rattle out of it. The snake tail flopped to the floor while he snatched Jenny up onto the couch, putting her behind himself and away from the new toy. The shock of the slap wore off and bright red pain flared up to replace it, and Jenny started crying.

Daddy looked along the length of the snake. Its head lay just inside the front door.

"Did you kill it, Jenny?" he asked. This only made her cry harder. She'd thought the snake was more of a toy than a live animal.

Daddy chucked an empty beer can at the snake. The can struck the creature's body, then rolled across the floor and stopped against the far baseboard, where it would remain for several months. The snake didn't respond to this insult.

"Stay here!" Daddy said. He stepped over the snake's body and crossed to the fireplace, where he fiddled with the rack of fireplace tools. Jenny saw his right hand, the one that had slapped the rattle from her. He had only touched her for a second, but that was enough to give him bleeding blisters all over his palm.

He took the fireplace shovel, walked to the snake's head, and stabbed down through its neck. The shovel bit into the hardwood floor. He scraped the snake's head forward, separating it from its body. Dark blood leaked onto the dusty floorboards.

Jenny drew her knees to her chest and kept sobbing. She felt guilty. She'd made Daddy mad. And she felt bad for the snake. She shouldn't have touched it.

Daddy scraped up the snake's head onto the shovel and carried it outside. Then he came back for the body.

He looked at Jenny and sighed. He looked tired, and a little pale and sick. Jenny couldn't stop crying.

"Gonna be okay, baby," he said. He ran to the kitchen and washed his hands, and poured some of the icky brown stuff for scrapes onto his open sores, the sores he'd gotten from touching Jenny. He sighed in relief. "You just stay where you're at and don't go nowhere. Stay!"

He went into the back of the house, where the bedrooms were, and returned wearing a long-sleeve orange Clemson shirt and cloth gardening gloves. He shook out his red cloth mask and slid it down over his head. It had only two tiny holes for eyes, and one tiny hole over his mouth. It was his Cuddle Mask.

He helped Jenny put on her own fuzzy pink cotton gloves. Then he shook out her little yellow Cuddle Mask and slid it slowly down over her head, taking care not to tangle or pull her hair. He straightened the mouth hole so Jenny could breathe, and then the eyes holes so Jenny could see.

Now he could pick her up and set her in his lap. He wrapped his arms around her and she buried her face in his shirt, listening to his heartbeat, smelling his stale sweat. Her sobbing finally began to subside.

"See, Jenny?" He rubbed the back of her head, through his glove, through her mask. "It's okay now. That was a diamondback rattler, a big one. You got to stay away from snakes, especially the rattling kind. Okay? They're poisonous."

"What's poze-nuss?" Jenny asked into his chest.

"When something bites you and it makes you sick. Some things are poisonous if you just get too close to them. Like poison oak."

Jenny lifted one small, fuzzy-pink-gloved hand and looked at her fingers.

"I'm poze-nuss," she said.

He took a long, deep breath. He kissed the mouth hole of his mask against the crown of her mask.

"You ain't poisonous to me, Jenny."

"Yes I am! I'm poze-nuss all over!"

"You just got to stay careful."

"Never touch people," Jenny whispered quickly, like a student who'd learned by rote.

"Not with bare skin," he said. "And never, ever play with snakes!"

"Never play with snakes," Jenny repeated, adding this one to her catalog of "Nevers." Like: Never touch people. Never talk to anybody but Daddy.

Daddy lifted her from his lap and set her down beside him on the couch. He picked an open beer can from the table and shook it next to his ear. A little liquid sloshed inside, so he drank it down. Then he lit one of his Winstons.

"I wish your momma was still alive," he said. "I don't know what the hell to do with you. Little snake-killer."

CHAPTER TWO

With her dad's guidance, Jenny managed to make it through kindergarten and the first two months of first grade without a big incident. Jenny kept herself apart from the other kids, never touched them with bare hands, avoiding their hands and arms if they reached toward her. As long as she didn't talk to people, and refused to play any games at recess, most people would just leave her alone.

It hurt to watch other kids play sports, or just thoughtlessly bump into each other in the hallway or lunchroom, and give each other high fives or hugs. She was different. No other kids made people sick just by touching them. Jenny kept a wide space around her and stayed quiet and wary at all times.

The incident happened in early October. Jenny was in her usual place at recess, on the little sloping hill by the playground, where most people only went for a quick break in the shade. She sat cross-legged in dirt and pine needles and watched other kids play freeze tag.

When two squirrels chased each other around a tree above her, Jenny started watching them instead. She loved how careless they seemed, even running at breakneck speed along a high electrical wire or hurtling from tree to tree, always landing in the right place without any effort. Once, in the thick woods around her house, she'd seen a squirrel leap from one treetop, sail across twenty or thirty feet of open space, and land in the lower limbs of a distant tree. The squirrel hadn't even stopped when he landed, just kept on running.

She'd been watching squirrels a lot more since she learned they could do stunts.

The three girls that approached her were the ones that "owned" the big wooden bench in the corner of the playground. If they weren't playing with the other kids, they were on the bench, braiding each other's hair, whispering, or doing those games where girls sang a rhyme while clapping each other's hands.

The three of them whispered and snickered as they passed the freeze-tag game, heading straight for Jenny. Jenny pretended not to see them coming. She closed her eyes and hoped they would go away, but she heard their shoes crunch through the pine straw and stop right in front of her.

Jenny opened her eyes. The three girls stood over her, looking down with their arms crossed. They wore bright, wide smiles. It was a look that would grow ever more familiar to Jenny in the coming years of school, the one that was extra friendly and sweet to hide the cruelty lurking behind it.

They were Cassie Winder, a short, freckled, red-haired girl; Neesha Bailey, a black girl who was really into pink camouflage pants; and the leader, Ashleigh Goodling. She was the daughter of Dr. Goodling, the preacher at the white Baptist church. Ashleigh stood a few inches higher than anyone in class, and she was the only one who was already seven. She stared at Jenny with her gray eyes, which were the color of rainclouds and impossible to read. Like the other two girls, her hair was twisted into three or four giant braids, which they'd given each other.

"Hey, Jenny Morton," Ashleigh said, with a too-wide smile. "Whatcha doing, Jenny Morton?"

Jenny just looked back and kept her mouth shut. She felt suspicious, and a little panicked, and didn't have any idea what to say.

"Why you always up here alone, Jenny Morton?" Ashleigh asked.

"I don't know," Jenny said.

"You think you're better than everybody?"

"No."

Ashleigh planted her hands on her hips and leaned forward, putting her eyes closer to Jenny's. "You think you're so great. Then why's your hair so stupid and weird, huh?"

Cassie and Neesha snickered behind their hands.

"Do you cut your own hair, Jenny Morton?" Ashleigh asked.

"No. My daddy cuts it."

This was too much for Cassie and Neesha, who burst into laughter. Ashleigh didn't laugh but wore a small, tight, satisfied smile.

"Y'all go away," Jenny said.

Ashleigh's smile vanished all at once. Her eyes narrowed, and her voice became low and hissy.

"You don't tell me what to do, Jenny Morton! My daddy says your daddy's just a dumb drunk redneck and he shouldn't even have a kid!"

Jenny's face turned hot. Jenny was stunned at how the words felt, like a hard slap deep inside her face, the pain not instant but suddenly appearing a few seconds later, then spreading fast.

"Well," Jenny said, "My daddy says your daddy's nothing but a carnie-booth crook!" Jenny wasn't entirely sure what it meant, but she was pretty sure she got the words right when it came to her daddy's opinion of Dr. Goodling.

"Everybody likes my daddy!" Ashleigh said. "That's why everybody gives him money. Everybody likes my mommy, too. You don't even have a mommy. Prolly cause you're so ugly! She died cause you're so ugly!"

"Shut up!" Jenny screamed.

"You shut up!" Ashleigh countered.

"You're stupid!" Jenny said. "Leave me alone!"

"Leave me alone!" Ashleigh mocked Jenny's voice, but made her sound extra scared. Her two friends laughed behind her.

Jenny's fingers dug into the pine needles beside her, looking for a rock, but instead she found a large pine cone with a lot of pointy tips. She picked it up, reared back, and threw it as hard as she could at Ashleigh.

It struck the dead center of Ashleigh's face, between her gray eyes, prickers jabbing her forehead and upturned nose. Ashleigh just looked shocked at first, but then her face reddened and she shrieked.

She jumped on Jenny, knocking the smaller girl onto her back in the pine straw, then started slapping her with both hands, back and forth, again and again.

"Stop!" Jenny screamed. Her hand flailed out and found Ashleigh's face, and she raked her fingernails across it.

"Ow!"Ashleigh seized a fistful of Jenny's hair and pulled hard, ripping strands out by the roots. Jenny grabbed one of Ashleigh's big braids and yanked it, making her scream again.

A sudden shaking, coughing fit ripped through Ashleigh. Ashleigh kicked away from Jenny and rolled over to her hands and knees. She crawled away, wheezing, struggling to breathe.

Neesha and Cassie stepped in front of Ashleigh to protect her, as if they expected Jenny to continue the fight. Instead, Jenny crawled back from them, stood up, and then backed away some more.

She watched Ashleigh coughing on her hands and knees, and she felt fear deep, deep inside her gut. She'd broken the biggest "never" of all--never touch another person.

Then she realized that the rest of the class had abandoned their games of freeze tag and kickball. They all stood on the edge of playground, watching and pointing at the fight on the slope while jabbering at each other. Mrs. Fulner, the first-grade teacher, made her way through the crowd of kids.

"Just what on Earth are you children doing?" she demanded.

"Jenny Morton hit Ashleigh!" Cassie said.

"Oooh…" Ashleigh groaned. She lay on the ground now, hands covering her face.

"Is this true, Jenny?" Mrs. Fulner asked.

Jenny couldn't think of what to say to make all the trouble and attention stop. So she stuck with what she knew: mouth closed, eyes on the ground, until they left you alone and went away.

Mrs. Fulner eventually did turn away, to check on Ashleigh.

"Ashleigh, honey?" She stood over the girl. "Sit up. Let me see you."

"No," Ashleigh groaned.

"Ashleigh, up, now!" the teacher snapped.

Ashleigh sighed. She rolled up to a sitting position, and she dropped her hands from her face.

Mrs. Fulner, and most of Mrs. Fulner's class, let out a pained gasp. Jenny felt a sickening, falling sensation.

A thick red rash of swollen pustules covered Ashleigh's face, hands and arms. One big bump high on her cheek burst and leaked a fat teardrop the color of Elmer's Glue.

"Ewwwwwwwwwwww!" a dozen kids squealed from the playground.

"She's got chicken pox!" a boy yelled from the back.

"It's from her!" Ashleigh screeched, pointing at Jenny. "She gave me pox!"

"She gave you <u>Jenny</u> pox!" Cassie said.

"Jenny pox!" one kid shouted, and others took it up: "Jenny pox! Jenny pox!"

"Don't be ridiculous!" Mrs. Fulner said. "Ashleigh, let's go visit the nurse, honey. I'll call your mother." She walked Ashleigh up the gravel path to the school building. She reached out a hand, nearly touched Ashleigh's shoulder, then thought better of it and pulled back. The teacher shot a glare over her shoulder at Jenny.

The crowd of kids chanted "Jenny pox! Jenny pox!" until Mrs. Fulner and Ashleigh were inside the building. Then all of them turned their heads and stared at Jenny.

"What?" Jenny asked.

The whole class ran away from her, screaming, to the other side of the playground.

CHAPTER THREE

When Jenny heard the crash, she was alone at her house, working at the little foot-powered potter's wheel she'd bought secondhand from Miss Gertie's Five and Dime. She'd paid for it herself, with money saved from her after-school job at the library. The wheel occupied the corner of the dining room, which she and her dad never used for dining. The dining table itself was invisible under heaps of scattered hand tools, assorted junk her dad was supposed to repair, and mail no one had ever opened.

Jenny could spend hours sculpting clay. She loved the rich hues and textures, the way it turned warm and fleshy and pliant the more you worked it with your fingers. It was satisfying to turn the raw shapeless clay into something useful and beautiful. Jenny could touch plants without killing them, but clay was the closest she could come to touching skin.

She'd only had the wheel for six months, and already 'Miss Gertie' (actually, Rose Sutland) was selling some of Jenny's creations on consignment at the Five and Dime. Jenny had just finished her junior year of high school, so she was finally on summer vacation and had plenty of time to make more.

The crash came from the side of the house, where the metal trash cans were stored. The sound broke a deep silence, startling her. She'd been so absorbed in the new flowerpot, she hadn't even noticed the record player had long ago finished Side 1 of Patsy Cline's "Sentimentally Yours."

It was ten o'clock at night, and her dad wasn't home. She didn't expect him anytime soon. He'd found some work repainting an old house in town, so he'd probably stopped by McCronkin's for a drink or ten.

Jenny lifted her foot from the pedal and let the wheel spin to a stop. There was another crash. It definitely sounded like a trash can. Probably a possum or raccoon scrounging for a bite. Her dad must have forgotten to bolt the trash enclosure again.

Jenny swung through the kitchen for a broom and then walked out onto the screen-walled back porch, which faced the heavy woods behind the house. Her father had built the porch before she was born. Most of the old house had been built or rebuilt by his hands at one time or another.

The night was hot and sticky and full of buzzing insects, but very dark, lit only by shafts of moonlight through the tall pines. She wished the exterior lights on the side worked, but they'd been defunct for years. If something wasn't used much, her dad had a tendency to put off repairing it, possibly forever.

Jenny looked out through the porch's screen wall, but even if she could have seen anything in the thin moonlight, the house blocked her view of the trash enclosure. She went to the screen door, lifted the hook from its eyehole, and pushed it open.

She cautiously descended the stairs to the yard, holding the broom out before her like a weapon. She crept past the thorny tangle that had once been a flower bed and looked around the corner of the house.

She held back a gasp. She'd expected a small scavenger, but the creature rooting in her garbage was much bigger then a possum. She couldn't see it very well. She tried to remember if coyotes were aggressive, or easy to run off.

Her dad had built the trashcan enclosure out of mismatched fence pieces, with a metal "ROAD CLOSED" traffic sign for a roof. The gate was from a child's wooden playpen, complete with a row of colored sliding rings on a crossbar and a smiling sun painted at the corner. The gate was open now and the creature hunkered behind it ripping open a white kitchen bag.

As her eyes adjusted to the moonlight, she realized that it wasn't a coyote, but a skinny mongrel dog with wild, matted fur. The dog was tearing apart the Hardee's take-out bag Jenny's dad had brought home. There wasn't anything in it but empty ketchup packets and greasy napkins.

The dog wouldn't find much to eat in their garbage. With her dad's uncertain, off-and-on income, they couldn't afford to waste food.

Jenny went back inside. Her pantry didn't contain much that was good for a dog, mostly grits, cereal and soup, but she did find a can of Chef Boyardee beef ravioli. She popped it open, dumped the ravioli into one of her early, misshapen clay bowls, and warmed it in the microwave.

Back outside, the dog was still at his hopeless rooting. Jenny stood by the corner of the house, well away from him, holding the warm bowl.

"Hey, doggie," she said.

The dog jumped, took one quick look at her, and ran into the woods. His head bobbed up and down like a galloping horse. By the sound of it, he didn't go too far into the woods before he stopped. Jenny hoped he was watching her.

She placed the bowl on the ground where the dog had been, near the scattered spill of garbage. She walked back to the corner of the house, squatted to the ground, and made herself as small and unthreatening as she could.

"Come on, doggie," Jenny said, in a high baby-talk voice. "It's gonna be okay!"

She heard a little pawing in the woods, and then the dog whined. He could probably smell the heated ravioli floating in meaty red sauce.

"Gonna be okay," Jenny tried to assure the dog.

After another minute, the dog finally crept out of the woods into the moonlit yard. He kept his head low and looked at her warily, his big black nose snuffling the air. He step-hopped over to the bowl, and now Jenny saw why he walked so awkwardly, head bobbing up and down, body rocking from side to side. He only had one front leg. The other one was just a three-inch stump.

"Oh, baby," Jenny said. "What happened to you? Were you chasing cars?"

The dog lowered its snuffling nose to the ugly makeshift dog bowl and sniffed the ravioli. He slurped it all down in less than ten seconds. He continued the licking the bowl for a minute to search for any trace of sauce. Then he knocked the bowl over and licked the underside for a while, just in case. As her eyes adjusted more to the moonlight, Jenny could actually see his ribs outlined against his skin.

Jenny watched the stump leg to see if the injury was recent or old, if the dog needed emergency care. It didn't seem to be bloody, or wet, or dripping. She didn't have a way to take him, anyway, since her dad was still out with the truck.

When the dog was finished, he turned his head at Jenny and wagged his tail.

"No," Jenny said. His tail stopped wagging. "If you eat more now, you'll get sick. You go on, now. I'm too dangerous to you."

The dog lowered his head, hop-stepped toward her, and gave another wag.

"I'm serious," Jenny said. "You'll die if I pet you. You'll get the Jenny pox."

The dog took another tentative hop-step toward her. Clearly he couldn't be reasoned with, so Jenny stood up on her tiptoes, raised her arms above her head, and shouted "Go!"

The dog flinched, then streaked away into the woods.

Jenny awoke early the next morning and made her dad's favorite hangover breakfast: one tall glass of milk, one over easy egg on toast, one mug of extra-strong black coffee, with a little space left in it so he could add a shot of whiskey when she wasn't looking.

"How's the painting job?" she asked as they ate.

"Ugh." He shook his head. "Paint fumes. I'm not looking forward to the rest of the day."

"Which one are you painting?"

"One of those big old places on Magnolia. Ripping down kudzu and poison ivy all over it. House hasn't been used since the 1960s. I guess Mr. Barrett thinks he can clean it up and sell it." The Barrett family owned the Fallen Oak Merchants and Farmers Bank, and with it half the decaying properties in town.

"Who's gonna buy it?" Jenny asked. "Can't nobody in Fallen Oak afford one of those big places, and nobody rich is gonna move here."

"Who cares? A fool's money spends as well as anybody's. And I got to get on my way." He drained the coffee, to which he had, of course, added that crucial dash of cheap whiskey when she'd looked away.

She stood up with him. "Can I ride to work with you and borrow the truck today?"

"It's almost out of gas."

"I'll put some in. I have money."

Her dad jingled the keys to his ancient Dodge Ram truck.

"Maybe you better drive," he said. "I'm gonna nap on the way. I still got a little drunk left in me from last night." He hadn't shaved or showered, but Jenny supposed that didn't matter too much for house painting work.

Jenny navigated the big old truck into town. It was big and hard to turn, but she was a an old pro at steering the clumsy thing around, since she'd never driven anything but the Ram.

She dropped him at a decaying mansion on Magnolia Street with wraparound porches on the bottom two floors and a balcony on the narrow third floor. Magnolia was once the center of town society, ages ago, when it was home to large landowners, cotton brokers, and horse and cattle traders. Most of those families were gone now, or still here but broke, like the Blackfields clinging to their one dirty gas station on the south end of town.

The Mortons were a little like that, too. Jenny's great-great-grandfather had owned hundreds of acres of farmland around Fallen Oak. Her late grandfather, and now her father, had sold off the good fields bit by bit in order to survive. They were now left with twenty-five acres of brambles and woods on hilly, rocky land that was no good for farming. Jenny was determined not to lose what remained.

She passed through the town square, which centered on a green lawn with a bandstand. In the afternoons, the courthouse overshadowed the green. Whoever built the courthouse had clearly expected Fallen Oak to grow into quite a city. It was two stories high, brick, with a row of fat white columns out front supporting a triangular pediment, like the front of a Greek temple. On the pediment, the sculpted frieze depicted farmers bearing corn and cotton towards the central figure of Justice, blindfolded and holding her scale high.

Wide brick steps led from the sidewalk up to the front doors. Big, gnarled old oaks flanked the steps. Supposedly, a slave had once been hung for sorcery on the largest tree, back in the 1700s, generations before the courthouse was built.

The bottom floor of the courthouse held the courtroom, the police department, the town jail, and the mayor's office. The upper floor was mostly storage.

Also facing the grassy square were the Fallen Oak Baptist Church where Ashleigh's father Dr. Goodling preached, and the Barretts' bank, and a two-story brick building with a few shops and a lot of vacancies. Dusty FOR RENT signs hung inside whitewashed windows. Jenny parked in front of an empty shop.

Miss Gertie's Five and Dime occupied a space near the end of the building. A clump of bells and chimes jangled as Jenny pushed open the glass door.

The interior of the store was beyond dusty, and so cluttered it made Jenny's house look organized. The store had racks of old romance novels, outdated calendars, antique tables and chairs shoved together so tight you could barely pass, wind-up clocks, creepy china dolls, creepier nutcrackers that looked like soldiers with giant teeth, typewriters, gas lanterns, faded postcards, an overcrowded clothing rack, a disused wood-burning stove that now stored handkerchiefs and embroidered linens. A bookcase near the front window displayed Jenny's bowls and flowerpots, along with assorted hand bells, Christmas ornaments, picture frames and collectible salt and pepper shakers.

"Ms. Sutland?" Jenny called out.

Eventually, Ms. Sutland emerged from her back office, while positioning her rectangular-framed glasses on her nose. She was in her eighties and walked slowly, one arthritic hand trembling on the brass duck-head topper on her cane. Every day she pulled her white hair into the same loose and sloppy bun, with hair spilling out in every direction.

"Is that little Jenny Morton?" She may have smiled a little, somewhere within the cobweb of wrinkles on her face. "Wouldn't you like some iced tea?"

"No, thank you, ma'am," Jenny said. "I'm just—"

"Hard candy? I may have licorice. Let me check…"

"No, thanks, Ms. Sutland—"

"How are your mother and father, dear?"

"My dad's fine, thanks," Jenny said. It was pointless to remind Ms. Sutland that Jenny's mother died when Jenny was born. The elderly lady would try to comfort her as if it had just happened, as if Jenny had ever known her mother.

"Hm. I suppose you're just visiting for your money, then, aren't you?"

"Money?" Jenny asked. "Did somebody buy one?"

Ms. Sutland shuffled to her mechanical cash register. She might be fuzzy about the world beyond her shop, but when it came to inventory, her mind was razor sharp. "Two little flowerpots and that lovely mixing bowl."

"Wow!" Jenny said.

"I shouldn't say, but all three went to Mrs. Barrett. She said she'd like more of them."

"Really?" Jenny was stunned. If Mrs. Barrett was a fan of her work, there was money to be made. Jenny and her dad were desperate for it.

"I told her it was a South Carolina girl made them," Ms. Sutland said. "Didn't tell her it was anybody here in town."

"That's fine, Ms. Sutland. I'd rather she just buy them all through your store." Jenny didn't bother pointing out that ladies in town probably wouldn't buy the pottery knowing it was made by crazy, white-trash Jenny Morton.

The bell on Ms. Sutland's cash register clanged as she opened the drawer. She fished out four twenties and passed them into Jenny's brown-gloved hand. Jenny accepted them gratefully. She had expected to spend money at the Five and Dime, not receive it. This was a huge amount all at once.

"Thank you!" Jenny said.

"Oh, my pleasure, dear. Would you like an iced tea?"

"No, thank you, ma'am. I actually came for a new pair of gloves. These are wearing through." Jenny looked at the clothing rack, with its careless mixture of coats, hats, ties and dresses. Jenny's favorite shelf displayed gloves and scarves.

"I'm so glad you reminded me, dear," Ms. Sutland said. "I don't know where my mind is today. I found these for you in the back room." She placed a heart-shaped candy box trimmed in bits of pink satin and yellowed lace on the counter. She lifted away the lid.

Jenny leaned over to look inside. The old candy box held a pair of very delicate white gloves made of lace and ribbon, laid out on a silk handkerchief. They were something a lady might have worn to a Magnolia Street wedding, many decades ago.

"Those are beautiful," Jenny breathed.

"I knew you'd like them, with you wearing them gloves all the time."

Jenny pulled the brown cotton glove from her right hand and reached into the box. She touched the lace gloves gently with a fingertip, feeling the soft, almost ethereal lightness of them, the incredible attention and work that had gone into them. Finally, she forced herself to pull back and hurried to replace her brown glove.

"Only…" Jenny said, "They're too nice for me, Ms. Sutland."

"Impossible, dear."

"I need thicker gloves. I would just tear those up."

"I understand." Ms. Sutland sounded a little sad. She replaced the lid and moved the box under the counter. "You need something to protect against the sun, don't you? Ghostly little girl. You must burn like a lobster."

"Yes, ma'am." Jenny smiled at her. Ms. Sutland never gave any appearance of knowing that Jenny Morton, around town and especially around school, was "Jenny Mittens," the freakish loner who wore gloves and long-sleeve shirts every day no matter the heat. Ms. Sutland never spoke of it, and Jenny was grateful.

"Jenny Mittens" wasn't as bad as her horrible elementary school nickname, the awful "Jenny Pox." No adult had believed Jenny was capable of giving Ashleigh Goodling a sudden outbreak of running sores and swollen pustules just by touching her. Eventually, the kids grew up and stopped believing what they'd seen, and over the years the tale of "Jenny Pox" had gone the way of cooties, the boogeyman, and the neighbor who hides razors in apples on Halloween. The frightening girl with a wicked supernatural power had become merely the scrawny, friendless "Jenny Mittens," who wore gloves all the time and dressed in a lot of her deceased mother's old clothes. You avoided Jenny Mittens because you despised her, not because you feared her.

As far as Jenny could tell, "Jenny Pox" was long forgotten, and she could not be happier about that.

Jenny picked out cheap gray gloves and paid for them out of her new pottery money. As Ms. Sutland rang them up, Jenny apologized for not buying the fine white pair.

"Never you mind about that," Ms. Sutland said. "I'm just glad you didn't buy these at the Wal-Mart like everybody else."

"I never go to Wal-Mart," Jenny said, and it was true. The Wal-Mart over in Apple Creek, fifteen minutes away, was always crowded and full of running children that could bump into you. Jenny never went anywhere more crowded than the Piggly Wiggly, and even that was almost too much. Even with gloves and a full set of long clothes, Jenny lived in fear of touching somebody.

"I'll tell you what, dear," Ms. Sutland said. "I'll just hold these gloves for you. When you meet that special fella, you can wear them to your wedding."

The unexpected comment triggered every awful thing Jenny knew about her future: that she would never be married, never have children, never even kiss a boy. All of that meant touching. She bit back a rush of tears and hurried to the door, but she didn't open it. She stared at what was happening outside, thinking that life got worse all the time.

Two cars had parked at the grassy square, a sapphire blue Audi Roadster convertible with the top down, and a red Ford Ranger truck with yellow-flame racing stripes. She recognized them both on sight, but especially the convertible. It belonged to Seth Barrett, technically Jonathan S. Barrett IV, of the Merchants and Farmers Bank Barretts. Seth had attended a private Christian school, Grayson Academy outside Greenville, all the way up to high school. Then his parents had moved him to the public Fallen Oak High School with all the other kids in town.

Jenny was in the same grade as Seth but had never spoken to him. One fact summed up all she needed to know: he'd been Ashleigh Goodling's boyfriend since freshman year.

And there was the wretched, horrible, beautiful couple now, Seth and Ashleigh, walking hand in hand from the Audi convertible, over the sidewalk and onto the green. Several yards ahead of them were the other members of Ashleigh's lifelong inner clique: Neesha

Bailey, with her boyfriend Dedrick Moore, and Cassie Winder, with her boyfriend Everett Lawson.

Seth was the star running back on the Fallen Oaks football team, Dedrick the huge center lineman, Everett the wide receiver. The three boys spread out across the green and tossed a football. Jenny's eyes were fixed on the girls arranging their picnic blanket on the corner of the green closest to the Five and Dime.

She looked with envy on the girls' summer clothes, spaghetti straps and bare bellies, shorts and open-toe sandals. They were nearly naked in the scorching June heat, while Jenny was forever doomed to jeans, long sleeves and gloves anytime she left the house. If she stared at Ashleigh long enough, she could work herself into a hot hatred of the girl. She hated how Ashleigh casually blew her parents' money while Jenny had to work hard to help her dad get by. She hated Ashleigh's big suntanned boobs that wanted to pop out of her halter top, her long legs and perky round ass that boys openly drooled over (and Ashleigh, goddamn her, was <u>still</u> the tallest girl in school). Jenny was always the color of notebook paper, and her scrawny body was all flat surfaces and straight lines.

What Jenny really hated, of course, the fuel for the rest of it, was that Ashleigh was the one who made sure everyone remembered Jenny Mittens was a repulsive nobody, to be scorned at all times.

"Is there trouble with the door, dear?" Ms. Sutland asked from her counter. "Do I need to have your daddy come fix it?"

"No, ma'am. I was just, uh…"

"Out with the sheep, gathering wool," Ms. Sutland chuckled.

"Yes, ma'am."

Jenny looked at the girls outside. There was no way to avoid them. Her dad's truck was in plain view, right across the street and less than thirty feet from Ashleigh and friends.

Jenny wished Ms. Sutland a nice day, took a breath, steeled herself, and opened the door. The clump of bells and chimes sounded extra loud to her.

She hung her head forward and let her long black hair shield her face. She kept her eyes on her tattered tennis shoes as she walked to the old Ram.

"Hey, Jenny Mittens!"

Jenny looked up, and immediately wanted to kick herself in the ass for it. She should have ignored them, climbed into the truck and left. Instead, she was looking across the street, right at Ashleigh Goodling's cloudy gray eyes. People said Ashleigh's eyes were exotic and beautiful. Jenny knew that if she had eyes like that, people would call them hideous and bizarre.

"Whatcha doing, Jenny Mittens?" Ashleigh yelled. "Shopping for gloves?"

Cassie and Neesha laughed. The boys were either out of earshot or too busy to pay attention. Jenny actually wished the boys were closer. Ashleigh was at her most vicious when alone with her two best friends. The more witnesses, the sweeter and more innocent Ashleigh became. In front of a crowd, she was downright adorable.

Jenny felt her cheeks burn. Her humiliation was all the worse because she had, in fact, been shopping for gloves, and now carried the gray pair in one of her brown-gloved hands. She laid the new gloves against her hip to hide them, then opened the truck door and climbed inside.

As Jenny backed up and straightened out on the road, she glanced at the green again. Neesha and Cassie were talking animatedly to each other, Jenny Mittens already forgotten. Ashleigh, though, was ignoring her friends and watching Jenny drive away, her face placid and expressionless, her gray eyes inscrutable.

When Jenny parked in her red dirt driveway, something blurry darted from the front yard and into the woods. Jenny smiled.

Jenny carried in the groceries she'd bought at the Piggly Wiggly and unloaded them in the kitchen. Her pottery money had allowed her to buy bread, milk, cheese, tissue-thin Carl Buddig ham and turkey, and some fresh fruit. She'd also picked up a can of dog food.

She carried the dog food outside and stood over the clay bowl she'd used for ravioli the previous night. She tapped the dog food can and whistled towards the woods.

"Come on, boy," she said. "It's gonna be okay, now. Just bringing you a snack!"

There was some movement in the area where the running blur had disappeared, several yards into the woods. The dog wriggled out of the underbrush and rose up on his three logs, watching her nervously.

"Stay," Jenny said. She popped open the can and poured chicken and gravy into the bowl. She backed away to the corner of the house, saying "Stay...stay...stay..."

When she was safely away from the food, Jenny squatted low near the ground and called out in a high, encouraging voice: "Okay! Okay!"

The dog looked between her and the food bowl a few times, then hop-stepped his way out of the woods to the food. He sniffed it, then chomped it down. He watched Jenny warily as he ate, as if expecting a trap. Jenny understood how he felt.

In the daylight, she could see the dog clearly. He was some kind of mix, with a lot of bluetick hound; she could tell by the floppy black ears and speckled body. He was shaggier than a bluetick, though, and little jowly. His amputated leg looked healed, not a new injury at all, which relieved Jenny. He seemed to have adapted to three-legged walking as well as he could.

"Okay," Jenny said. "If I'm really the best you can do, then you can stay. But there are rules. Don't touch me—that's for your own safety. And you can't stay in the house, because you might get too close to me. And I can't ever pet you—" Her voice broke a little as she said it, and in her mind she flickered back to the white lace wedding gloves. She fought the sudden unexpected tears, and swallowed them back. "But my dad can touch you," she said. "If you want. Okay? And if you ever find a better place, you should run away to there."

The dog wagged his tail as she spoke, which made him rock a little bit on his front leg.

When she stood up, he raced into the woods as if someone had fired a starting gun.

"Good boy," Jenny said. "Keep away from me."

And finally, after holding it inside all the way from the Five and Dime, she broke down and let herself cry.

CHAPTER FOUR

On the first day of her senior year, Jenny stepped off the school bus with her head already lowered, long hair hiding her face, hoping only to get through the day without being noticed. Everyone else on her long rural bus route was a freshman or sophomore. Most of the older kids either had a car or had a friend who did.

She gripped the straps of her backpack extra tight. The first day of every year terrified her.

She headed straight for the bright orange double doors, not looking right or left. She had to dodge little knots of students that gathered to chat around the outdoor picnic tables. She glanced at the mural on the front of the school: "Sonny" the Porcupine, the Fallen Oak High mascot, charged down a grassy field dressed in a helmet, football locked under his armpit. Rival school mascots, including a bear and a gamecock, were skewered on Sonny's quills, having apparently been foolish enough to tackle a gigantic porcupine.

When Jenny made it inside, she faced a major obstacle. Ashleigh Goodling stood with Cassie, Neesha and other girls from the varsity cheerleading squad in the center of the main hallway, right where it intersected the English and Social Studies hall. There was no way to get anywhere in the school without passing them, unless Jenny wanted to turn back and go around the outside, which would only call attention to herself.

Ashleigh, like her friends, was dressed in new clothes and shoes for the first day of school, and all of them looked carefully made up and manicured. Ashleigh had added dark lowlights to her puffy blond hair. Most of the girls in school would have the same within two weeks.

Jenny felt stupid in her mother's long-sleeved polka-dotted blouse, the cuffs tucked into her gray gloves, which had grown worn over the summer. She hoped Ashleigh and her friends were too busy for her.

Jenny approached the intersection, feeling her stomach knot itself up. She saw what the girls were doing now, greeting people from the flow of foot traffic, occasionally stopping to hug or to peck a cheek, while giving some kind of full-color paper flyer to everyone who passed.

She stayed close to the wall and held her breath as she swerved wide around the knot of people. It was easier than she expected to go unnoticed past the cheerleaders, since lots of people, especially boys, were crowding in on them, eager for anything these girls might be giving away.

Jenny managed to slip past them, but when she looked back, she saw Ashleigh staring right at her. Ashleigh's expression was neutral, but her eyes narrowed just a little when Jenny met her gaze. Then Ashleigh snapped her head away with a flip of her golden hair, and squealed an excited greeting at some approaching boys.

Jenny hurried down the main hall, towards the next intersection—then saw she wasn't free yet. Seth Barrett was there, with Everett Lawson the wide receiver, and a gaggle of underlings from the freshman and JV teams. They were pushing smiles and more full-color flyers on everyone who passed. Jenny sighed and moved to cut around them.

"Hey!" Seth Barrett stepped in front of her, blocking her way. She slowly raised her eyes from the ground to meet his, and she gave him her coldest, most hateful stare, imagining her blue eyes were pieces of arctic ice. He was handsome, of course—Ashleigh had very high standards—and his dazzling smile looked almost genuine. Jenny had learned what that look meant, though, the smile that was so ready to become a mocking smirk.

"What?" Jenny snapped. She imagined her voice cracking like a whip, slapping him out of her way.

"Vote Ashleigh Goodling for senior class president." Seth's smile didn't waver. He held out one of the flyers, and Jenny finally had a look. Her upper lip curled.

Along one side, it showed a full-length picture of Ashleigh in her cheerleader uniform, her leg kicked high as if the picture just happened to be snapped in mid-cheer, which just happened to reveal one long, tan leg, and just a peek of yellow bloomers under her khaki skirt. Under this was a caption that said LEADERSHIP, referring to the fact that Ashleigh was already captain of the varsity cheer squad.

Along the opposite side were three smaller pictures of Ashleigh. One was black and white and showed Ashleigh in glasses and ponytail, pencil in hand, reading a textbook. It was captioned: HARD WORKER. The next showed Ashleigh coaching little kids at her church youth group, and was captioned: DEDICATED TO THE COMMUNITY. The last one showed Ashleigh two years ago, giving a speech on the bandstand in the town square. That had been part of her successful campaign to ban *Harry Potter* books from the Fallen Oak school library. The caption for this: GETS RESULTS.

Jenny looked from the flyer to Seth's stupid wide smile. She scowled.

"Fuck you," she told Seth.

His smile twisted down into a hard scowl. Jenny knew that move, too. It was what Ashleigh did, right as she shifted gears from teasing to insulting. Seth had probably learned it from her.

"Hey, what's your problem?" Seth snapped.

This brought Everett Lawson's attention around, and he slapped Seth's shoulder. Everett smirked at Jenny under his camouflage cap.

"Oh, what's the matter, Jenny Mittens?" Everett asked. "Wearing your gloves too tight today?"

"Shoot, it can't be her bra," said one of the JV players. He was a junior, a fat kid with an uneven flattop haircut. "She don't hardly need one with them pancakes." Then he lay his hands flat on his chest and swiveled from side to side, sticking out his tongue as if trying to lick his own nipples. This had all the JV players dying with laughter, and Everett and Seth started laughing, too.

Jenny stalked away down the science hall, where her locker was located. Sheets of bright poster board were mounted on the walls above the lockers, with blown-up pictures of Ashleigh and words written in stenciled marker, outlined with glitter, urging VOTE FOR ASHLEIGH and ASHLEIGH FOR PRESIDENT.

Jenny put her lunch in her locker, then closed the locker door and leaned her forehead against the cool metal, eyes closed. There was no way she could survive another year.

Jenny trudged through her classes, ignoring the overheard whispers asking why "Jenny Mittens" was there. In previous years, the school had placed her in honors classes because of her high grades, but there were no honors classes for seniors. Instead, seniors took Advanced Placement courses aimed at gaining early college credit. Since Jenny had no plans to go to college, she was taking general studies level classes.

She just wanted the diploma to make her dad happy, to convince him he'd done a good job raising his daughter on his own. If not for that, she'd have dropped out last year and gotten a full-time job. Failing that, she could at least make and sell a lot more pottery without school getting in the way. She was growing very skilled with clay, and had even treated herself to a few sculpting knives and little bamboo cutting and trimming tools to help develop her craft.

She grew vegetables in the yard, and she made her own clothes out of her mom's old clothes and things she bought cheap at thrift stores. She didn't need much money.

So, while the honors, college-prep kids had gotten used to her and learned to ignore her presence in class, she was a novelty to some of the general studies kids. All day, she heard them whispering the usual rumors about why she wore gloves, including that she'd been in a horrible fire that ruined her hands, or that she was obsessively afraid of germs. Jenny never argued against the rumors, since all of them were better than the truth.

The worst class, as always, was P.E. It was the only one where you couldn't get by with just sitting in a back corner staring at your textbook. It also brought a huge danger of physical contact with others, especially when dressed in the required gym clothes.

Worse, Ashleigh and Cassie were both in her P.E. class this year, so avoiding Advanced Placement hadn't even allowed Jenny to escape Ashleigh. There were also, of course, several of Ashleigh's suckers-up, girls who gravitated toward her in the locker room as they dressed out, wanting to be part of her conversation, in her orbit. Jenny picked a locker in back and stayed there while she changed clothes, well away from the crowd around Ashleigh.

Ashleigh and Cassie were snickering about Brad Long, the debate club geek who was challenging Ashleigh for class president. The other girls fell over themselves to laugh at Ashleigh's jokes. Occasionally, another girl would throw in a comment, and occasionally, Ashleigh would favor such a girl with a smile.

After a minute, Ashleigh turned to look at Jenny.

"What's wrong, Jenny Mittens?" she asked, and the rest of the class turned to stare at Jenny. "Are you still too good for the rest of us?"

Jenny said nothing. She had already changed into her long-sleeve t-shirt and long shorts—really, a cut-off pair of sweatpants—and now held her P.E. gloves in one hand. Jenny used friction-grip batting gloves for her gym classes.

Jenny scowled, and the suck-up girls laughed.

"Coach Humbee wanted me to tell you something," Ashleigh said. Humbee was the head football coach, a balding man with a gigantic beer gut. He was also their PE teacher. "He says no gloves allowed in PE this year."

Most of the girls laughed. Jenny had a few things she wanted to say back to Ashleigh, but she kept her mouth closed. Escalating it would just bring more attention, and with it the risk of touching. It would probably be teasing, aggressive touching, and Jenny would have a hard time not infecting anyone.

Jenny looked at Ashleigh, who wore a tight, satisfied smile. Then Jenny just stared at the floor, and eventually the girls lost interest and went back to dressing out and chattering among each other.

Jenny strapped on the gloves anyway, though Humbee always yelled at her about them. Getting yelled at was better than accidentally killing the other girls while playing basketball or volleyball. Even if they maybe deserved it, just a little.

She closed her locker and hurried out to the gym. Twelve years later, and she still had to deal with Ashleigh on the playground.

When she got home, Jenny ran to her room and stripped off the too-hot polka dot blouse and jeans, and then peeled away the gray gloves and threw them on the floor. She changed into a light sleeveless t-shirt and her favorite cutoff jean shorts, relieved to finally let her skin breathe. Her hands were wrinkled like prunes from the sweat inside her gloves.

She went back outside and whistled toward the woods.

"Rocky!" she called. It was what she'd been calling the three-legged dog, because of his swaying, rocking walk.

A brief howl responded, the hound's usual way of communicating, but it didn't come from the woods. Jenny turned toward the shed. Rocky emerged from the scrapwood doghouse she'd built him, wagging his tail. The doghouse was up on blocks, just inside the shed, with its doggie doorway facing outside to catch some breeze. When winter came, she would move it to the back of the shed and turn it around to block that same wind.

Bits of ripped cloth and cotton stuffing were scattered around inside the shed now, the remnants of a toy squirrel she'd made him from scraps of brown cloth.

Rocky step-hopped toward her and let out another quick bay. He was still almost as skittish as he'd been three months ago and didn't even let Jenny's dad pet him. Jenny was glad. If Rocky wasn't so people-shy, she would have to get rid of him to protect him from her. As it was, she'd learned she could run around in light clothes, and even free of her gloves, without any fear that Rocky would brush against her hand or bare leg.

"Come on, boy! Let's go for a run!"

Rocky wagged faster. Jenny stretched her legs a little and took off into the woods, following one of the foot paths that wound through her family's land. Rocky chased her. He was incredibly fast despite his missing leg, and sometimes ran laps around Jenny— now behind her, now way ahead, now running parallel to her through the woods.

The running cleared her mind, burning up so much energy she couldn't think. It was the best way to wear out the anxiety and fear that always threatened to fill her.

She and Rocky ran through the woods climbing ridges and steep hills until the sun was gone.

CHAPTER FIVE

The student council elections were on the second Friday of the school year. Before school that day, Ashleigh Goodling called a special breakfast meeting at her house. Attending were Cassie, her campaign manager; Neesha, who was running for the class historian office (on the "Ashleigh ticket," as Ashleigh thought of it) and also Ashleigh's boyfriend Seth, who could be useful in his way. Plus, she might be able to fit in some make-out time before school.

They sat at the long table in the high-ceilinged dining room, looking out through the giant picture window towards the duck pond in the back yard. Over coffee, juice and bagels, they reviewed Ashleigh and Neesha's speeches, to be delivered to the senior class later that morning.

"I don't think you have anything to worry about," Seth said after their second pass through Ashleigh's speech. "Nobody's going to pick Brad Long over you."

"Almost nobody," Ashleigh said. "I want a landslide. I want him to feel stupid for even running against me. But you're right, Seth. We should focus on Neesha. She has two challengers for class historian."

"Rob Pirkle from A/V club is no challenge," Neesha said. "I'm more worried about Wendy Baker."

Ashleigh looked at the flyers made by Neesha's competitors. Rob Pirkle, like Brad Long, was a nobody, the kind of dweeb who always ran for office despite being way too unpopular to have a chance. She touched the other flyer, with the smiling photo of Wendy.

"She's about middle-class popularity," Ashleigh said. "And a French horn player. That's why we need to worry. The band, the drama types, art club, and the random dorkers. We have to outflank Wendy there. Cassie?"

Cassie opened a Trapper Keeper with CAMPAIGN written on the front in heavy black marker. She fished out a printed page of text and laid it on the table.

"What's that?" Seth asked.

"Wendy Baker's speech for today," Cassie said.

"About time." Neesha grabbed it and started reading.

"Sorry, Neesh," Cassie said. "Wendy only finished it last night."

"How'd you get it?" Seth asked.

"Wendy's little brother is a freshman," Cassie told him. "And a real horndog, it turns out. Easy mark."

"Really, Cassie?" Ashleigh teased. "A freshman?"

"Oh, please, like I had to do anything. Just a little…" Cassie traced her fingertips slowly down Ashleigh's arm, and fluttered her eyelids. "'Oh, Billy, we should hook up sometime…'"

The girls broke down in laughter.

"Okay," Neesha said, thumping the copy of Wendy's speech. "She's proposing some kind of collaborative thingy, where the band, the choir, drama club, everybody gets together to put on a big spring musical. Everybody can contribute. The art club, the A/V club, everybody has a role."

"That's a good idea," Cassie said.

"A big coalition," Ashleigh said. "Neesha, who's going first?"

"I'm first for the historian candidates."

"Great," Ashleigh said. "So add Wendy's idea to your speech, but make it better."

"Like a movie instead of a play!" Cassie said.

"Or something so big they have to use the stadium instead of the cafeteria," Ashleigh said. "Whatever. Just bigger, better."

Neesha opened her laptop and began editing her own speech.

"You girls are so bad." Seth gave all three his most dazzling, knee-weakening smile.

"You're as bad as us." Ashleigh stood and stretched. She was still in her white silk pajama pants, with a Superman tank top.

She dropped into Seth's lap and kissed him a few times, letting him slip in a little tongue. He rubbed her calf through the thin silk pajamas, and then his fingertips crept in toward her thigh.

"Hello, Ritz-Carlton?" Neesha said. With her thumb and pinkie, she imitated a phone by her ear. "This is Ashleigh and Seth, and we need to get a room."

"Good idea." Ashleigh hopped off Seth. "Let's go up to my room. You can use my printer while I get dressed."

As they climbed the stairs, Seth whispered, "Your room? Won't your dad get pissed?"

"Oh, yeah. And he's in his upstairs office, too. Not far away at all," Ashleigh said. She stopped two stairs above Seth and turned to face him. She hooked her thumbs inside the waist of her pajama pants, and then pulled the front of the pajamas out and away from her, as if she was about to slide them down and flash him. If he'd been standing on the same level as her, instead of two stairs below her, he could have just looked down and seen everything. "We would be in so much trouble if he saw me doing this."

Seth gaped at her tanned belly with hopeful eyes, mouth wide open, like a dog presented with a rare steak but told to sit. Boys were really so simple. Ashleigh could tell she'd totally blanked out his mind—that, despite his usual brash confidence and his gorgeous smile, he was really her bitch.

"Take it off, baby!" Cassie called down from the top of the stairs.

Ashleigh saw hope bloom fresh in Seth's eyes, and a very obvious boner sprouted inside his khaki shorts. She tugged the pajama pants down just a little, letting him see more of her hips, but nothing too important.

He reached a hand toward her crotch. She slapped it away and released her pants, which snapped back into their proper place.

"Bad boy," Ashleigh teased. She held up her left hand and wiggled her third finger, the one with the silver abstinence ring. "We got rules around here, you know."

Then she turned and went up to join her friends, wiggling her rear end ever so slightly for Seth's enjoyment (or, perhaps, his suffering). She enjoyed enticing him to the brink of madness, knowing he could have any girl in the school, but instead was her own little slave. And well-trained, too.

Upstairs, she sent Seth to help Neesha port her laptop to Ashleigh's printer in the little sitting room off Ashleigh's bedroom. She asked Cassie to help her get dressed. Seth was clearly disappointed, and would rather have been part of the dressing-Ashleigh project than the speech-printing one, but he did just as he was told.

Soon, Ashleigh stood in front of the full-length mirror in her walk-in closet, with Cassie standing behind her and evaluating. Ashleigh wore a black blazer with matching slacks, and a gray blouse that perfectly matched her eyes, which had taken ages of internet shopping to find. A cross pendant hung from a thin gold chain around her neck, pointing down at the modest cleavage revealed by the blouse.

"What do you think?" Ashleigh asked.

"Could be sexier," Cassie replied.

"This isn't sexy?"

"The slacks look great back here." Cassie patted Ashleigh's ass. "But they won't see that on stage."

"I'm not going for obvious sexy," Ashleigh said. "More like restrained, professional sexy. Like you're trying so hard to hold the sexy in, but it keeps slipping out. Mixed signals, you know? You want to get them hard, but you want them to feel guilty about it, too."

"Then this looks perfect. You're a genius, Ashleigh."

"That's right." Ashleigh plucked a pair of black high heels from the shoe wall, but didn't put them on yet. "Let's go to school."

Outside, Neesha and Cassie sped away in Cassie's red Mazda. Seth cranked his Audi convertible, but then they idled in the driveway. He gave her a questioning, hopeful look.

"Are we ready, or…?" he asked.

"One more thing." Ashleigh wrapped her fingers around his head, gripping his strawberry blond hair, and pulled his face to hers. Ashleigh was tall enough to kiss a boy dead-on, without reaching or stretching. At five-ten, she actually looked down on many boys in her class. She'd made her unusual height into an attractive asset, instead of whining about it and slouching and trying to downplay it like some girls would.

She let Seth reach into the top of her blouse, even into her bra, and grope around in there. She felt distracted and a little bit nervous. Senior class president was one of the last big check boxes.

She'd started in ninth grade, when she'd not only been elected freshman class president but also founded the Future Leaders of America club, which invited businesspeople and local politicians to give talks about how to succeed. She'd been president of that club ever since, growing it to seventy members so far.

Her sophomore year, she'd started a chapter of the national, youth-led Cool Crusaders ministry at her church, for kids 12-18. She'd taken the idea for their first big project from the Cool Crusaders website: campaigning to ban the *Harry Potter* series from the school libraries on the grounds that it promoted witchcraft. Ashleigh didn't really believe *Harry Potter* had an evil influence, and actually liked the books personally, but she also liked organizing the kids, having them write letters to church leaders, newspapers and radio stations. She liked convincing the Women's Steering Committee at her church to support her. She even got herself elected President of the 'Christians Act!' student prayer group in school, to enlist more kids.

They'd given out anti-*Potter* pamphlets all over town, at church, the county fair, the Wal-Mart. They held protests. They were opposed by the school librarian, the school principal Mr. Harris, some English teachers, and a few members of the school board. Eventually, Ashleigh was invited to a Christian radio station in Greenville, one that half of South Carolina could hear. She told the talk show host lurid stories about how Satan worship was really popular among the kids, because everybody wanted to be like the students at Hogwarts. How it involved lots of drugs and sex. And, of course, how the kids were brilliant at hiding the devil worship from their parents. She even took calls from listeners.

Afterward, Ashleigh and Cassie and Neesha rolled on the floor of Cassie's room and laughed until their throats ached.

After that media attention, Ashleigh's crusade was joined by Cassie's father Mayor Winder, the County Commissioners, and even State Senator Rutherford "Randy" Hoke. They pressured the county school board until they caved, Ashleigh won, and the books were removed from both school and public libraries. Then everybody in town knew Ashleigh was a force to be respected, on her own terms, not just because her dad was the white preacher.

Then last year, she'd become the first junior in the school's history to be elected captain of the varsity cheerleading squad, a job that always went to a senior cheerleader. This was helped along by some incriminating photos of a few of the senior girls, which Ashleigh had arranged, and which those girls were very eager to keep secret.

This year, Ashleigh was once again varsity cheerleader captain, president of the Future Leaders of America, president of Christians Act!, editor of the yearbook, and on track to becoming class valedictorian. All she needed to cinch the perfect Georgetown application was to win today's election.

"Stop," Ashleigh said. She pulled Seth's hand from her blouse, then adjusted her bra and shirt. "Drive, or we'll be late for school."

The senior class met in the cafeteria first thing in the morning. Student council candidates, and Mr. Harris the principal, sat on plastic chairs on the raised stage at one end. The A/V club had set up the podium, microphone and speakers. The rest of the senior class and several teachers sat at the cafeteria tables to watch the speeches.

Ashleigh kept a cheerful smile as she listened to the other students give their halting, nervous speeches. There were three candidates for class treasurer, and Ashleigh's chosen was Bret Daniels, a linebacker and friend of Seth's. She made a big show of smiling at him in apparent admiration while he gave his short speech in a flat monotone.

Neesha gave her speech for the class historian position. She proposed a spectacular spring musical that would incorporate all the various creative clubs, a big stadium-sized production the town would never forget. Wendy Baker looked shocked, then horrified, then sick to her stomach as she listened to a larger and more elaborate version of her own big idea.

When it was finally her turn, Wendy stumbled through the first two sentences of her speech. Then she burst into tears and ran sobbing out of the cafeteria. Ashleigh watched with a look of concern on her face as Wendy ran away.

The spring musical itself would never happen, since it sounded like a huge, lame waste of time to Ashleigh. She couldn't see how such a thing would fit into her own plans. But the point was to shepherd her people through the election.

Mr. Harris announced the presidential candidates. Brad Long did what stupid debate club kids always did—talking way too fast, with too many big words. He got a smattering of applause as he sat down.

Ashleigh, the incumbent from last year, cleared her throat into her fist and approached the podium. She adjusted the microphone height—she was taller than Brad, so this brought a few laughs. Then she looked up and beamed a smile at the eighty-three kids in her graduating class.

"Hi, I'm Ashleigh Goodling, and I'm running for president." This brought some applause and whistles. Nobody had whistled for Brad Long. Ashleigh looked out on the crowd. For a moment, she met the evil blue eyes of Jenny Mittens, the bitch who looked like a skinny corpse with a bad, self-administered haircut and horrible clothes. And the gloves, of course. An arc of hate crackled momentarily between them, like electricity leaping from one pole to the next, and Ashleigh quickly shifted her gaze to more pleasant people.

"I want to say something before I start," Ashleigh said. "Wendy Baker's out of the room now, but I just wanted to say that stage fright is not easy. I'm dealing with some right now." She got laughter out of that. "When I was a kid, I struggled with it a lot, giving talks at church, and other places. It's something you learn to deal with. But it's hard, and I hope nobody makes fun of her about it. Can we agree on that?"

This brought a murmur of agreement, and all the teachers smiled at Ashleigh. Then Cassie's boyfriend Everett, probably prompted by Cassie, shouted "You said it, Ashleigh!" which made people laugh.

"Okay, now for my speech," Ashleigh said. She'd practiced it so many times that she didn't really need the note cards in front of her. "We've been together a long time, haven't we? Most of us have gone to school right here in Fallen Oak since kindergarten. And this is our last year together, y'all. And that's actually pretty sad when you think about it.

"All of you know who I am, and I know each one of you. I know people say things about me. I've heard some of that, and I'm sure you have.

"People make fun of me for being the head cheerleader. But to them I say, excuse me for having a little school spirit, and trying to make things fun for everybody. I think we should all have a good time at our games, and support our team. That's just how I feel.

"They laugh at me for starting the Future Leaders of America club. Well, I just personally think it really does matter that you and I learn all we can, so we can build an even better, more powerful America tomorrow, when it's our turn to run the world. You don't have to agree with me, but those are my values.

"They laugh at me for being so busy with church. Well, I'm sorry, but I happen to believe in spirituality, and in giving back to the community. I just think it's right. It's important to me, and it's hurtful when people make fun of me for that.

"They laugh at me for wearing my abstinence ring." Ashleigh held up the ring finger with the silver band. "Okay, that's fine. I just think it's important to have self-respect, and to respect your own body, and not let people take advantage of your feelings. You know, it's easy to fall in love and easy to get hurt, and easy to screw things up for yourself. I think abstinence is about responsibility and making the right choices for the future. I don't insist everybody does it. I don't make fun of people who don't choose abstinence. So why make fun of me just for my personal choices?

"So, you don't have to agree with everything I stand for," Ashleigh said. "But remember, this is the year that counts. Senior year. Student council is responsible for homecoming, and most of all, prom. These are the memories that will last our whole lives. You want responsible people to make sure they turn out great, and you know that my friends and I are the people who can take care of all that, and do it in a way that makes everybody happy." This was a little over the line, since candidates weren't supposed to endorse other candidates, but what was Mr. Harris going to do, disqualify her?

"So, please vote for me, Ashleigh, for president. And I'll take care of everything."

The cheer squad, football team, prayer club and Future Leaders all stood to applaud her, as she'd personally, secretly asked them individually to do. Most of the class followed the trend. Ashleigh looked carefully among the crowd. Jenny Mittens was still seated, of course, looking at her own shoes. A few other kids, mostly friends of the other candidates, stayed in their chairs and looked morose.

The whole "Ashleigh ticket" won the election in a landslide.

CHAPTER SIX

The Saturday morning after the election, Ashleigh and friends were back at school for cheer practice while the football team scrimmaged in their practice jerseys. It was Labor Day weekend. The day was hot and sticky under the scorching blue sky.

As they drove away from practice, a light drizzle began to fall. Ashleigh was riding with Seth in his convertible, and she had been looking forward to letting the hot day blow dry her hair, shirt and shorts. She sighed as Seth put up the roof. He needed a blow dry himself. Dirt and grass stained his practice uniform, and his strawberry blonde hair was damp and reeked of sweat from hours inside his helmet.

Up ahead, Cassie and Neesha rode with Everett and Dedrick in Everett's red Ranger with the stupid yellow-flame decals. The plan was to drop the girls at Ashleigh's so they could clean up, change into bathing suits, and fill Ashleigh's picnic basket with sandwiches and snacks. The boys would change out of their pads, possibly shower (one could hope) and round up some beer and pot for the night. Then they were meeting everybody at Barrett Pond, the town reservoir. The afternoon and night would be all about swimming and getting totally hammered.

But right now, while they were alone, Ashleigh needed to talk with Seth.

"What are you doing about your SAT?" she asked him.

"What?" Seth asked back, without turning his head from the road. An obvious delaying tactic. He played his stupid Mos Def CD at ear-splitting volume.

"Are you practicing for the SAT yet?" Ashleigh shouted, letting a little shrillness creep into her voice as she turned down the stereo. "You don't have much time left!"

"Oh, that," Seth said. "Yeah, totally. I'm starting on that next week."

"You should have been doing it all summer," Ashleigh snapped. "I kept telling you—"

"I said I'm going to work on it!"

"You'd better," she said. "You're not getting into Georgetown with your scores from last year."

"Not everybody can get a perfect SAT score like you, Ashleigh."

"Maybe not, but your score has to come up. It just takes practice, like football."

"Yeah." He watched the road quietly for a minute. "What if I don't get into Georgetown?"

"Then we go to NYU," Ashleigh said. "I have to be in the center of things, where the action is. How many times do I have to tell you--"

"And if I don't get into NYU, can we just go to Clemson instead?"

"*Clemson?* I know you're kidding. Tell me you're kidding, Seth."

Seth shrugged. "My dad went there. Turned out okay for him."

"Okay? Seth, just running your family's little toy bank in this shitbox little town is not okay. My life is going to be about way more than what's okay. I am not spending my life at the Eldrid Country Club, drinking mimosas and spitting out babies." This was a direct swipe at Ashleigh's own mother and her friends.

"I know, Ashleigh. But my parents spend a lot of time in Florida, too. They've got a boat. That wouldn't be so bad, would it?"

Ashleigh gripped the armrest, her knuckles whitening as her frustration mounted into fury.

"I am going to Georgetown for undergrad," she said. "And you are coming with me. Do you understand?"

"Hey, I know, believe me," he said. "Maybe there's a short-bus school for me near there. We can still get a place together or something."

"No. I need you by my side, shaking people's hands. It's all about who you meet in those schools." Ashleigh reeled in the anger and put on her sweetest smile. She rubbed his thigh through the grass-stained practice pants. "I just want what's best for us. I know you can go far if you just try. I have faith in you."

"I am trying." Seth stomped the accelerator, obviously wanting to cut this conversation as short as possible. Soon they tailgated the red Ranger. Everett apparently took this as a challenge or an accusation of being a slowpoke, and the truck surged ahead, drifting into the other lane at the next tight curve.

"Okay, we talked, and you're going to do it this week." Ashleigh gave him another big, winning smile. "Now, let's not worry any more tonight. I just want to get wasted."

"That's my girl." Seth put one sweaty, muscular arm around her shoulders and pulled her close. His speedometer needle sailed past ninety as they rocketed down the empty country road.

The same Saturday, Jenny sat alone at the spot she'd cleared on the dining room table. She was poking her new sculpture with the sharp end of a toothpick, trying to imitate Rocky's speckled fur pattern. The sculpture was about a foot tall at the head, and maybe eighteen inches long, with the tail curled alongside his body, since she couldn't figure out how to make it stick out behind him without falling off. She'd made his three legs and the stump leg, his head, his body, but it needed a ton of detail work, especially around the face and paws.

Though it was getting to be afternoon, she could hear her dad snoring back in his room. She'd eased his door most of the way closed, but hadn't closed it all the way for fear the click against the jamb might wake him. He'd gotten into a bad whiskey drunk last night, crying and rambling about Jenny's mother, as he sometimes did. Jenny preferred to let him sleep it all off, because he got difficult when he was drunk. Or hung over.

Finally Jenny grew tired of the silence—she preferred to play her mother's old vinyl records when she worked with clay. Jenny stood and stretched her back and arms. She'd been hunching forward for too long.

She wiped the clay smudges from her hands and changed into her most lightweight shorts and tank top, since it was another scorching day out. She bound her hair into a ponytail and put on her favorite broken-down sneakers.

Outside, she saw Rocky dozing in the shade of a big, gnarly old oak shaggy with moss. She whistled and he jumped awake, up on his feet, wagging his tail.

"Hey, Rocky," she said. "Want to go for a run?"

He dashed to their usual starting place at the trailhead, his tail swishing vigorously, and bounded away before Jenny got there. She stretched her legs a couple of times and started jogging.

Her senior year was two weeks down, forty to go, or thirty-seven if you subtracted winter and spring breaks. Ashleigh was class president, of course, after a speech where she pretended to be some kind of victim. As if anyone ever dared to pick on Ashleigh Goodling. And when Ashleigh told people to be nice to Wendy Baker, Jenny had seethed. Ashleigh was probably behind Wendy Baker's sudden meltdown. It was her style, and it cleared the way for her friend Neesha. It was all so petty. Who cared about student council, of all the ridiculous things to care about?

As Jenny warmed up, she put on speed. Despite all the cool green shade surrounding her, humidity had already soaked her in sweat. Rocky bounded in and out of sight while she traveled deeper into the woods.

Jenny tried to make herself feel better by telling herself she'd done the best she could, under the circumstances. Between taking care of her dad and getting all the way through school, she'd done okay. She hadn't given anyone else Jenny pox since Ashleigh in the first grade, which represented a huge achievement, though one that nobody but her dad knew or cared about.

The cheering up did not happen. She'd been alone all her life, would be alone all her life, and the best she could hope for was to not accidentally kill anybody along the way.

Jenny was thinking about suicide again. Such thoughts rolled in a few times a week like storm clouds, casting darkness over everything in her life. A cold, lonely existence didn't seem worth the fight of staying alive. All her hopes were negative. She hoped she didn't infect anyone. She hoped nobody harassed her too much at school. She hoped her dad didn't die anytime soon—he was nearly fifty, drank and smoked a ton, and spent more and more time looking at old photographs of Jenny's mother. His will to live didn't seem very strong. It was ironic, in a way, because the only thing that kept Jenny from killing herself was knowing how much it would hurt her dad. They both kept themselves alive and miserable for each other's sake.

Light rain began to fall through the treetops, sprinkling cool water on her. It invigorated her, and instead of turning back toward the shelter of her house, Jenny pressed onward and ran harder.

Rocky bayed and howled somewhere off to her side. She saw him charging through the woods like a dog on a mission. Ahead of her, a plump wild rabbit emerged and zigzagged across the foot path. Rocky broke out of the underbrush in hot pursuit and chased the rabbit into the woods on the other side of the path.

"Leave him alone, Rocky!" Jenny called without breaking her stride. Being mostly bluetick hound, Rocky obsessed over anything that was furry and roughly the size of a raccoon. Jenny was glad he could occasionally feed himself this way, but today, she was in no mood to see the chubby little rabbit torn apart. But then, Rocky's chances of actually catching the rabbit were slim. With his missing leg, he wasn't really a great hunter, which was why he'd been starving when Jenny found him.

Jenny pushed herself harder, hoping to burn away the burgeoning depression that wanted to suck her down. The rain grew heavier, pattering on thousands of leaves overhead. The rabbit crossed the path again, heading in the opposite direction now, with Rocky only a couple yards behind.

"Rocky, come on!" Jenny gasped for air, her legs muscles burning. "Leave him alone!"

Rocky had no interest in her opinion. Rabbit and dog rushed on through the woods.

Jenny crested another of the rolling hills, wishing it would rain harder, not just this teaser rain. Only a few drops actually made it all the way through the canopy to tantalize her skin.

Up ahead, past the next hill, she could see a big gap in the trees. That would be a meadow, where she could do a couple of laps while the cold rainwater soaked her. If Rocky flushed the rabbit out into that meadow, the rabbit might even lose the chase.

Then she crested the hill and realized she'd gotten turned around while running. The gap ahead wasn't the meadow she was thinking about. This gap marked where the foot path intersected Esther Bridge Road.

Rocky loped right towards the paved road, his face cracking through underbrush. The rabbit spurted from the underbrush and onto the widening path. It sprinted towards the road with Rocky close behind.

"Rocky, no!" Jenny yelled. She didn't hear any cars coming, but people drove fast on Esther Bridge. "Rocky, stop! Stay, Rocky, stay, stay!"

But Rocky had a nose full of rabbit and no ears for her. Jenny reached her top running speed as she pounded down the hill after them, leaning into the sprinkling rain, burning up the last reserve of energy in her scrawny body.

She had no idea what she would do if she caught up to Rocky. She hadn't brought any gloves, and couldn't touch him without giving him Jenny pox. Still, she ran hard after him, calling his name.

The rabbit scrabbled out onto the blacktop, hopped halfway across it and paused for two seconds. Then it hopped the rest of the way across and dove into a ditch on the far side of the road. Rocky's claws clattered on the blacktop as he ran into the road.

Jenny recognized the truck, the red Ranger with blazing yellow stripes. Everett Lawson. He was streaking along at about a hundred miles per hour.

She reached the edge of the road just as the front grill smacked into Rocky. The dog gave a sickening, heart-wrenching yelp as the impact knocked him off his feet. He did a three hundred and sixty degree spin in the air, and then landed with a whump on the side of the road a few feet from Jenny.

"No!" Jenny screamed as she ran to him. "Rocky!"

Everett's truck raced around the next curve and out of sight, not even slowing to see what he had hit.

Jenny knelt in the dirt next to the pavement, her heart whamming against her ribs. Rocky lay on his side, not moving. Along his side, blood seeped out into his fur in three different places. He wasn't dead, not yet, but he was hyperventilating and gasping out bloody, foamy saliva onto the pavement. His lower jaw looked loose and badly angled, as if one of the hinge joints had been shattered. His body lay in the roadside weeds, but his head was still on the pavement, where another car could come at any time.

Jenny tried to look in his eyes, but they'd rolled back into his head.

"Rocky!" she screamed. She waved her hands uselessly in the air above him. She couldn't do anything, not even move him back from the road. No gloves, not even any sleeves to pull over her hands. Even her shirt was too small and thin, with too many little moth holes, to be of any use.

Stupid, she thought. She should always carry gloves in case Rocky needed her. Why had she never thought of that? She seized big handfuls of her hair and pulled, screaming her anguish and her frustration.

"Oh, no, Rocky," she said. "Oh, no, please, Rocky, I love you, please don't…

The dog's breathing slowed. He puked some foamy, pink liquid out his broken jaw.

"No, Rocky, please, I love you so much, please don't…"

The engine of another car approached and Jenny felt a tiny, irrational ray of hope. Someone with a car was coming, someone who could touch Rocky without killing him, someone who could take him to the veterinarian.

Then she saw the blue Audi convertible, its top closed against the rain, and her heart sank. Nobody was less likely to help than Ashleigh and Seth. Still, she jumped up and down and waved her arms overhead. If they helped Rocky, she didn't care what they did to her the rest of the year. She needed her dog.

The Audi passed her by, slowing only when it approached the curve ahead. She felt sick.

Then the car slowed even more. It pulled off on the side of the road and parked. The driver's door opened and Seth Barrett stepped out. Ashleigh did not.

"Hey, what's wrong?" Seth asked Jenny.

What Jenny meant to say was thank you for stopping, my dog is hurt bad, please take him to the vet and I will do anything for you. Instead, what came out was:

"Your stupid redneck friend Everett just ran over my dog!"

"Oh, wow!" Seth slammed his car door and jogged across the street towards her. Jenny watched his approach warily, not sure whether to feel hopeful or more afraid. She looked towards the Audi's passenger door, but as far as she could tell, it wasn't opening, Ashleigh wasn't getting out.

When Seth reached her, Jenny became sharply aware of how exposed she was, bare legs, bare shoulders, bare arms and hands, a thousand places Seth could brush against her. He was only wearing a short-sleeved t-shirt and football pants that came down to his knees. Jenny folded her arms and stepped back.

"It's Rocky," she said, choking back sobs. "Can you take him to the vet in your car? I don't have a car."

"I don't think he would make it to the vet." Seth dropped to one knee by the dying dog. One of Rocky's paws kicked out and clawed up dirt in a wild spasm, and then it was still.

"Wow, he's really hurt," Seth said. He seemed genuinely concerned, but Jenny didn't trust that for a second. She kept glancing at the car, waiting for Ashleigh to come out and somehow make it all worse. Ashleigh was probably laughing at Jenny's suffering right now.

"Hey, Rocky." Seth poked his fingertips at Rocky's speckled, bloody mess of a belly. Rocky let out a small, high-pitched, gurgly sound, which might have been a yelp if he'd had the strength.

"He doesn't like to be touched," Jenny said.

"Oh, he doesn't like to be touched, huh?" Seth lay his hands on Rocky's side. "Let's see!"

Then Seth pressed down hard on Rocky's broken ribs with both hands.

"Stop!" Jenny screamed. "What the fuck is wrong with you?"

Her hands clutched at the air. Only a lifetime of deeply ingrained avoidance kept her from grabbing Seth's hands, or more likely, punching him in the nose as hard as she could. There was also that small, evil voice in her head, the one that said this was probably best for Rocky, it was probably best his suffering end quickly. Hot tears were rushing down her face, dripping from her chin, and she couldn't stop them.

Seth leaned forward and bore down with all his weight on the dog. Jenny thought she heard something pop deep inside of Rocky. The dog let out a strangled whimper, and then blood mixed with bile gushed out of his mouth.

Jenny couldn't watch, couldn't look away, couldn't move. It was all too shocking. She could almost hear Ashleigh's wicked laughter from inside the Audi. Of course Ashleigh was here, on the worst day of Jenny's life, to drive the knife extra deep and give it a twist. What were the odds of them showing up right now? Jenny would never win the lottery, but she'd probably get struck by lightning.

As much as she'd hated them, Jenny would never have believed that Ashleigh and Seth were so sadistic and full of hate for stupid little Jenny Mittens that they would even punish her dog. They were sick, warped people.

Then something clicked in Jenny's mind. She was going to kill them all. Rocky first, to end his pain. Then Seth. Then she'd walk over to the Audi, smash the window if need be, and kill Ashleigh Goodling. A calm clarity fell over her. Jenny imagined a swarm of black flies crawling inside her hands, willing it to be the deadliest, fastest-killing strain of Jenny pox that she could muster.

Jenny raised her bare hands. They felt sweaty, and prickly, and highly contagious. Inside herself, Jenny felt very cold.

Seth pushed his hand up along Rocky's body, applying pressure the whole way. He lifted Rocky's battered head, forced the dog to close his broken jaw, then clamped his hand around it, squeezing hard, as if trying to choke Rocky on his own tongue. Rocky gave a weak, wheezing snort through his big black nose.

Jenny knelt by Rocky and extended her hands towards him. She took a deep breath.

Seth released the dog and tumbled backwards into the high weeds, out of Jenny's reach.

Jenny heard a pathetic little whimper. Rocky's nose was twitching in the blood-moistened earth. Then his eye rolled, and she could see his pupil again in its proper place.

Rocky lifted his head from the ground and twisted it back to sniff at the big patches of blood on his side. He looked at Jenny. Then he rolled onto his belly, and rose unsteadily from the ground, first planting his front legs, then pushing his body up with his hind legs. He shook himself as if he'd just gone swimming in the creek and wanted to dry off.

The dog sniffed at his own body, his own blood, for a long time, while Jenny just watched. She couldn't even feel shock anymore. She was a complete blank, unable to think at all.

Rocky swiveled around to look at Seth, who reclined on his elbows, eyes closed. Seth's perfect, suntanned, acne-free skin had gone as pale as Jenny's, but with an unhealthy gray tinge. Rivers of sweat poured from his scalp, over his face and ears, and his whole body was trembling.

Rocky, in the ultimate uncharacteristic move, bounded over to Seth, opened his mouth, and lapped at the boy's face with his tongue. Seth didn't open his eyes, but slowly raised one hand and patted Rocky around the head.

"Good boy," Seth murmured. His voice sounded a mile away.

Rocky froze, as if suddenly self-aware and shocked by his own behavior. He jumped and ran away along the foot path, back toward the woods. Then he got distracted by his own tail, which he chased around like a puppy.

"What?" Jenny said. It was all she could say. She looked at Rocky's enthusiastic prancing, then at Seth, who now lay on his back with his eyes closed, hands behind his head, as if he meant to take a nap right there on the side of Esther Bridge Road.

"Seth!" Jenny finally managed to say. The name was not so hateful in her mouth as it used to be. "Seth, what did you do?"

"What?" Seth didn't open his eyes.

"You know what. My dog. Look, he's okay!"

Seth half-opened one eye and turned his head toward the woods. Then he closed it and laid his head back on his hands.

"Yeah," Seth muttered. "Guess it looked worse than it was."

Jenny gaped at him. It took her some time to gather up more words and put them in order.

"But…I saw the truck hit him. Everett's truck. It just happened. He was dying."

"Nah." Seth raised one hand, weakly, and attempted a dismissive wave. He still didn't open his eyes. Apparently he had Jenny's same trick, just keep your eyes closed and don't say much, if you want people to leave you alone. "Guess the truck just grazed him a little. He'll be fine."

Jenny watched Rocky sniff around the underbrush, then hoist his leg to pee on a white birch. That was when she noticed the other thing.

"Seth," Jenny forced herself to speak the unbelievable words. "My dog only had three legs. Now he has four."

"Really?" Now Seth opened his eyes, finally looking interested, and eased up to a sitting position. He linked his arms around his knees and watched the dog.

On Rocky's new front leg, a wide band of hairless scar tissue marked where the stump had ended and the new part of the leg began. Besides that, Rocky looked fine. Better than Jenny had ever seen him, in fact.

"How long?" Seth asked.

"What?"

"How long since he lost the leg?"

"No idea. As long as I've known him. Months, at least. Maybe years."

"Jeez," Seth breathed. "No wonder he sucked so much out of me."

Jenny snapped her head around to look at Seth. "You did it. You fixed him. You can heal with your touch."

"What?" Seth leaned back on his elbows again, and suddenly seemed very interested in a patch of colorful wildflowers on the ground. "You're crazy. Nobody can do that."

"Seth, I'm not stupid."

Seth sighed and looked up at her again.

"You can't tell anybody," he said. "You have to promise. Seriously. Okay?"

"I promise, Seth. I can keep secrets better than anybody."

"Nobody knows, and I don't want everyone treating me like some kind of weird freak or…" His voice trailed off as he looked at her.

"I know." She tucked her hands into her armpits and pinned them there with her arms. She had a dangerous urge to throw her arms around him and kiss him on the mouth. Not that she would follow it—the last thing she wanted was to give him Jenny pox. It helped to know Seth wouldn't be interested in kisses from someone like Jenny Mittens, anyway, even if she wasn't fatally poisonous. She remembered how close she'd come to killing him and Rocky both, and she shuddered.

"Thanks," he said. "It's just really important nobody finds out."

Jenny glanced towards his car. "What does Ashleigh think about it?"

"She doesn't know!" Seth said. "That's what I'm telling you. My parents don't even know. Nobody. Except you."

"Ashleigh isn't in your car?"

"No, I just dropped her off at her house. I'm alone."

"Then you're safe," Jenny said. "I won't tell."

Seth pushed himself to his knees, then to his feet, struggling for balance like a tired old man instead of a varsity athlete. Jenny steadied him by laying a hand on his back, which was safely covered by his shirt. His back muscles felt warm and taut to her. Jenny pulled away quickly and stepped back.

"I have to…meet my friends." Seth staggered a few steps toward his car, then stopped and leaned over, hands on his knees, to catch his breath and his balance.

"You look wrecked," Jenny said. She was thinking of her dad trying to walk when he was plastered. He would get belligerent and insistent on driving somewhere, and she usually ending up driving him there so he didn't crash and die. She'd been doing that since she was thirteen. "Should I drive your car for you? I'll take you wherever you want. I can walk home from anywhere."

"Oh, no. I don't need Ashleigh asking why I've got Jenny Mittens driving my car."

Jenny had been immune to that nickname for years, but for some reason it stung when Seth said it now. He noticed the look on her face.

"I'm sorry," he said. "That's what everyone calls you. It just kind of slipped out." He glanced at her hands. "Hey, where are your gloves?"

Jenny shook her head and smiled at him. She avoided his question. "You save my dog's life, you can call me anything you want. Call me stupid redneck skank if you want."

"I wouldn't call you that!" he said.

"Ashleigh would. I think she has. It's so hard to keep track of everything she calls me."

"Ashleigh…" Seth stood up, stretched, and lifted the car keys from his pocket. "I gotta go get weed for the reservoir."

"The what?"

"For…Barrett Pond. I don't usually call it that. The whole Barrett thing gets old around here. Barrett Avenue. You know."

"Everyone calls it Barrett Pond."

Seth looked at her for minute. He was getting his color back.

"You can come if you want," he said. "Beer and swimming. Good times."

"Uh, no…" Jenny tried to imagine Ashleigh's face if Jenny actually showed up with Seth. It would be an ugly night. "No, I should probably stay with my dog, make sure he's okay. You know."

"I understand." Seth tossed his keys in the air, caught them. "Okay, then. I'll see you later, Jenny."

Jenny smiled. He smiled back, holding her gaze for a long moment.

"Keep that dog off the road," he said. He staggered across the road.

"Thank you, Seth!" she called after him.

"Forget it happened," he replied. "I'm not kidding."

Jenny watched him climb into his car, close the door, start the engine. She waved as he pulled onto the road, until he was out of sight.

She followed the foot path back into the woods, where Rocky lolled in the shade.

"Hey, Rocky, want to go home?"

Rocky sprang up on all fours with his tail wagging. He turned and ran up the trail, eager to race her home.

CHAPTER SEVEN

On the last Thursday in September, Ashleigh called a special girls-only meeting of the Cool Crusaders. About forty girls from the middle and high school showed up in Activity Room B in the church basement. They ate cookies, chips and sodas provided by the Crusader girls on the Hospitality Committee, while a Jars of Clay CD played over the sound system, until Ashleigh announced it was time to start.

Ashleigh stood at the whiteboard at the front of the room, purple marker in hand. She'd already written "Cool Crusader Girls Rock!!!" in her big, flowery handwriting, all across the top of the board. She smiled as the group sat down in the rows of plastic chairs pulled together by the Hospitality Committee.

"Hey, what's up, y'all?" Ashleigh asked. "Are we having some fun tonight?" The younger girls cheered. Ashleigh encouraged the older girls to carpool the younger ones to meetings, since it made them feel special to be picked up by juniors and seniors at home, rather than dropped off at church by their parents. Parents seemed to like it, too, since it made things easy on them.

"Ladies, we've accomplished so much in this town, and I want to thank you all for being part of this group. We've worked against witchcraft, we've encouraged kids to be more religious, we've even showed adults like Principal Harris a thing or two." The girls who'd been part of the anti-*Harry Potter* campaign applauded and whistled. "And I think we should be very proud of ourselves. Why don't you give yourselves some applause, just for being here?"

The girls clapped and cheered for their own wonderful selves.

"This year, the national Cool Crusaders ministry in Sacramento is focusing on a very major subject: teen abstinence. First, who here has signed the Crusaders Abstinence Pledge?" She raised her left hand and tapped the silver band with her thumb.

About half the girls raised their left hands, wearing the same ring.

"Is that all?" Ashleigh put on a look of dismay. "What are the rest of you thinking? Don't you want to commit yourselves to doing the right thing?"

Some of the other girls nodded.

"Good." Ashleigh winked at Shannon McNare, a junior who held a stack of Cool Crusader Abstinence Pledge certificates, printed from the Cool Crusader website on canary paper. Shannon passed them out, while another girl passed around a plastic cup full of pens.

"Shannon is our Abstinence Coordinator. Each of you should sign the Pledge and give it to Shannon, along with fifteen dollars cash. I'll mail it all in, and you'll get your own abstinence ring in two to four weeks. Just ask your parents for the money. Believe me, they'll pay up for abstinence." The girls laughed.

"I want every one of you to sign this pledge and turn it in to Shannon by the beginning of the main Cool Crusaders meeting next week. This is important, because we're going to have a special mission next week. I want each of you to pick out a boy Crusader, and next week we're going to break out into pairs, boy and girl, to talk about abstinence, why it's important, and all the temptations involved. I expect each of you to get your boy to sign the Pledge and order a ring."

Many of the girls, probably a majority of them, looked horrified at the idea. She tried to calm them down. "Now, I know this may sound challenging, but it is a challenge, to build your courage and confidence as a woman. We ladies have to be leaders on this issue, and trust me, boys will listen if you tell them you want to talk about sex." The looks of fear turned to laugher. "Teens leading teens—that's the whole point of Cool Crusaders. And I want every Cool Crusader in this church, guys and girls, wearing an abstinence ring to the Halloween Lock-In.

"Now," Ashleigh said, "Let's hear some reasons we are committed to abstinence." A few girls raised their hands. Whatever any girl said, Ashleigh wrote it on the whiteboard, approving of all suggestions. She made a long list of bright purple words like GOD, PURITY, PARENTS, PREGNANCY, HEALTH, OUR FUTURE, and SELF-RESPECT. When the group was all tapped out, Ashleigh gave them a big smile.

"These are all great reasons," Ashleigh said. "I'm glad everybody's so fired up on this subject. Now, there's one thing nobody mentioned, one you may not know about. And this one is a very big secret." Ashleigh looked at the closed door, as if expecting spies and eavesdroppers. "I don't want any of you talking about it outside this room. Raise your hand if you promise to keep this secret."

Every girl raised her hand.

"Okay." Ashleigh used her stage-whisper voice, the one that made a whole crowd feel like Ashleigh was taking them into her confidence, cutting them in on the real dirt. It was almost magical, the effect that voice had on a crowd. "Here's the secret, and I want you each to think about it. Every guy you meet—except maybe in your family—all of them want to have sex with you. They've all thought about it. They might be thinking about it right now."

Some of the girls, especially the middle schoolers, looked at each other with big, frightened eyes. There was much whispering and gnashing of teeth, and Ashleigh waited for all of them to finish.

"It's really all they think about," Ashleigh said. "Studies have shown that if a guy looks at you, he's probably imagining you and him having sex together. They can't help it, that's how God made them.

"But when they see this," Ashleigh tapped her thumbnail against her abstinence ring, "It means they can't have what they want, because you're devoted, and not just some slut." Some girls giggled. "It makes them respect you. And, listen, it makes them want you even more. Think about the last time you wanted something you knew you couldn't have—like an expensive pair of shoes your dad wouldn't buy for you. Didn't that make you want it more?"

Several girls nodded, and there was more whispering.

"Now—and this is the other part of this secret—the more you make a boy want you, without letting him have you, the better he will treat you. He'll buy you things, take you places, do what you tell him, and stand up for you and protect you. The more you make them want it and don't give it, the more control you have. Abstinence isn't just saying 'no.' Abstinence is power."

Ashleigh let that sink in a minute, then asked if there were any questions. A freshman girl, Erica Lintner, daughter of the town police chief, raised her hand.

"I like 'abstinence is power,'" she said. "Maybe that could be like our saying, or our, whaddya call it…"

"Slogan?" Ashleigh suggested.

"Yeah!" Erica said. "Our slogan."

Ashleigh pretended to consider this very carefully. "Hmm. 'Abstinence is power' as the slogan for our campaign. I think Erica has a great idea. What does everyone else think?"

Lots of girls hurried to agree with Ashleigh. Erica beamed, clearly very proud of herself.

"So here's what we're doing," Ashleigh said. "Each of you write your top three picks for your boy 'abstinence buddy' on the little heart-shaped pieces of paper Shannon is passing out. Shannon and I will go through them, and by the time you leave tonight, you'll know who your buddy will be."

This led to tremendous chatter. A sophomore raised her hand.

"Can it be a boy you have a crush on?" she asked.

"Of course," Ashleigh said. "Any boy you'd like to talk about sex with."

Another girl, a very dorky bucktoothed sophomore named Veronica Guntley, raised her hand. She spoke very slowly when Ashleigh called on her.

"I was thinking," Veronica said. "When you say all the guys want to have sex with us, well, does that, well, does that include Principal Harris? And Coach Humbee? And the dentist? Or Dr. Goodling? Or what about--"

"How dare you?" Ashleigh asked in a low, hissing voice. She stalked toward Veronica, and other girls shifted their chairs away to leave Veronica isolated in the middle of the room. "My father is a man of God. He is anointed!"

Ashleigh was looming over Veronica now. The younger girl had scrunched way down in her seat, staring at her hands, her face bright crimson and very close to tears.

"God's ministers are not like normal men," Ashleigh said. "God's blessing changes them and makes them holy. What is wrong with you, Veronica? Why are you having these thoughts?"

"I'm not!" Veronica wailed.

"I think you've made your thoughts clear to the group, Veronica. I want you to apologize to me for making accusations about my father, and to all the girls for trying to ruin this meeting."

"I'm sorry!" Veronica cried. "Everybody, I'm sorry! I didn't mean it. Please, Ashleigh, please don't hate me!" Veronica buried her face in her hands and sobbed. Ashleigh let her do that in front of everyone for a couple of minutes. Then Veronica asked without looking up, "Do I have to quit the Crusaders now?"

Ashleigh waited a long pause, then said, "Veronica, stand up."

Veronica stood, crying hard, her whole body shaking.

Ashleigh placed her hands on both of Veronica's hot, slick cheeks, and curled her fingers around to touch the back of Veronica's neck. The gust of power rose in her, the secret thing that only Ashleigh had and nobody else, and it ran like an electric current out through Ashleigh's fingers and into Veronica's skin. Veronica's trembling slackened.

"It's not Christian to kick people out just for being dirty and sinful," Ashleigh said. "You just need to learn to control yourself better. That's what this abstinence campaign is all about. We can work out your problems together. So no, I'm not kicking you out of the Crusaders. Not tonight."

"Oh, thank you!" Veronica threw her arms around Ashleigh's waist. Ashleigh tried not to look grossed out when the girl buried her snotty, wet face in Ashleigh's breasts. Ashleigh returned the hug, smiling to hide her revulsion. The girl's nose was really dripping.

"I love you, Ashleigh!" Veronica cried.

"We all love you, too, Veronica," Ashleigh said. "Right, everybody?"

The rest of the girls applauded or shouted that they loved Veronica, too, and a few of them got up to hug Veronica. Ashleigh touched several of their bare arms or faces, spreading the energy around. She couldn't help it. The energy gushed out of her whenever she touched another person. Sometimes, Ashleigh wished she could keep it inside.

After her encounter with Seth, Jenny had trouble concentrating on anything. Her mind kept drifting to Seth, how kind he'd been to her, talking to her like she was a normal person. She thought back, and couldn't remember having trouble with Seth until he started going with Ashleigh freshman year. Even when Ashleigh spread the rumor in tenth grade that Jenny's doctor made her wear gloves because she was addicted to masturbation, Jenny didn't remember Seth talking about that. And everyone had been talking about that for a couple of months. Maybe Seth wasn't so bad, but had a bad influence on him from Ashleigh.

For the first time, Jenny attended the school football games on Friday nights, dressed in long sleeves and a pair of tan-and-yellow Porcupines gloves from the school spirit catalog. She sat among parents instead of students, since there was a lot less jostling and touching, and a whole lot less interest in picking on Jenny Mittens.

She liked watching Seth take the ball and crash his way down the field. It also thrilled her when the Porcupines switched to defense, because then Seth would go to the sidelines, take off his helmet and splash water on his head. She liked to watch that. She also liked watching him help his teammates, in a secret way only Jenny knew about.

During the first game, Porcupine quarterback Tycus Williams had been sacked hard in the second quarter and twisted his ankle. He'd limped off the field leaning heavily on Coach Humbee, while the crowd applauded politely.

On the bench, Seth slung an arm around Tycus and talked to him, gesturing toward the cheerleaders. Tycus laughed, and Seth touched the back of Ty's head and whispered something in his ear. Tycus nodded and grinned. After halftime, the quarterback was in the game again, repaired and full of energy, and led the team to victory over the Barlowe Bears.

Seth did the same for any injured player on his team—shaking their hands and gripping it while he spoke to them, or giving a playful noogie, or leaning his forehead against the injured boy's under the pretense of giving him an up-close pep talk in the noisy stadium.

Jenny liked the games because she could watch Seth for hours and get away with it. She couldn't approach him at school, with Ashleigh and friends close by and always ready to tear Jenny apart. At the games, she could at least look all she wanted. The only sour notes came at halftime and the end of the game, when Ashleigh would push herself against Seth to kiss him, and his hand would slide down toward her khaki skirt. For all of Ashleigh's religious posturing, when she'd become cheer captain, the cheerleaders' skirt hems had risen by several inches, and their tops had shrunk to leave their stomachs bare.

After the games, Jenny would go for a walk in the woods by her house. She would end up sitting on a certain large boulder in one of the little valleys that dimpled the hilly woods. Lying on the flat top of this boulder, her head against smooth stone, she would think about Seth.

In her mind, she replayed the time he'd stopped to help Rocky, but she made things happen differently. Instead of driving away to meet Ashleigh, he took Jenny's hand and led her into the woods. He pushed Jenny against a massive, gnarled old tree, and kissed her, pushing his tongue deep into her mouth. His lean, strong body pressed against the front of her, while her back rubbed against the rough bark. Then he would take the straps of the tank top she'd been wearing that day, and slide them down along her shoulders and arms, pulling her shirt down and turning it inside out at the same time. Then he laid his warm, healing hands on her bare chest.

Usually, that was all Jenny could take. She would lie on her back on the big rock, breathing hard, feeling ashamed of herself. Then she might go again, making Seth do different things in her imagination.

She'd heard the word "crush" before, but never realized it was something so powerful it filled your head and body, and made it hard to eat and sleep. She felt extra stupid because she was probably the hundredth or thousandth girl to crush on Seth Barrett.

She could not have set her sights any higher. But she couldn't help
it.

Jenny also harbored another, less physical fantasy about
Seth. She imagined that after she discovered his healing power,
Jenny had eagerly spilled to him about her own awful power, the
Jenny pox. In her fantasy, Seth was totally understanding and happy
to finally be with someone like him. He said he could love her even
if he couldn't touch her. That was the truly dangerous fantasy,
Jenny knew, the one that could only cause profound grief and
suffering—but again, she couldn't help it.

She started jogging through town late at night, when she
wasn't likely to encounter anyone as long as she stayed away from
McCronkin's Irish Pub. Fortunately, Rocky had lost all taste for
paved roads and wouldn't go near one, so she didn't have to worry
about him, but she did have to run alone. She never worried about
getting attacked when alone at night. Nobody had ever tried
anything like that, but if they did, she would just give them a quick
and horrible death.

Jenny lived south of town, and Seth lived on the east side.
For a week, she jogged past Barrett House every night on
reconnaissance. It loomed on top of a hill, surrounded by a tall,
spiked wrought-iron fence that dated back to the Great Depression.
White brick columns topped by stone lions flanked the front gate.
Through the gate, you could see some of the three story stone and
brick house, which looked very old, much hidden behind huge
ancient trees thick with Spanish moss and purple wisteria. The
driveway was brick and ended at the house with one of those hey-
I'm-rich turnarounds with a fountain and garden in the center island.
Vines had overtaken the fountain and much of the garden. The more
she jogged past Barrett House in the moonlight, the more it looked
like the country retreat of a crumbling dynasty, from a kingdom
gone to ruin.

She never saw Seth outside and didn't pick up any clues
about how to talk to him without his friends around. She'd
considered slipping a note in his locker or backpack, but with
Jenny's luck, Ashleigh would find it first. She'd considered calling
him at home, but the number was unlisted. Anyway, that seemed
awkward, since he hadn't given Jenny his number, and Jenny didn't

have much practice talking on the phone, aside from bill collectors threatening to shut off the power. All her thoughts led to dead ends.

Strangely, her inspiration eventually came from Ashleigh Goodling.

CHAPTER EIGHT

Ashleigh sprang up on her long legs, high into the air, and swatted the ball as hard as she could over the net. On the other side of the court, the ball cracked into its intended target—the center of Jenny Mittens' stupid, ratty face. Jenny cried out and fell to one knee. She covered her face with her batting-gloved hands. The ball skittered out of bounds, a point for Ashleigh's team.

"Oh, gosh!" Ashleigh said. She covered her mouth with her hands. "Did I hurt you, Jenny Mittens? Are you bleeding? Are you crying?"

"Nice save, Jenny Mittens," growled a girl on Jenny's side.

Coach Humbee sat on the indoor bleachers. He looked up from the sports section of the South Carolina newspaper *The State*. He glanced briefly at Jenny Mittens, then at Ashleigh Goodling, then went back to reading.

A sophomore girl entered the gym and showed the coach a slip of paper. Humbee nodded and pointed to Ashleigh.

The girl ran over, smiling at Ashleigh with all her teeth, and held out the note to her. Ashleigh did not move to accept it.

"Yes?" Ashleigh said, raising one eyebrow.

"Uh, hi, Ashleigh Goodling! Uh, Principal Harris wants to see you."

Ashleigh rolled her eyes. She knew what this was about. She took the note and glanced at it. The sophomore girl bobbed on the balls of her feet, awaiting instructions from Ashleigh.

"Oh, great," Ashleigh sighed. She waved to Coach Humbee, who waved and nodded back. Ashleigh headed for the gym door, the anxious sophomore in tow.

"So what's it like being the president?" the sophomore gushed. She was clearly awed at actually having a chance to talk to Ashleigh.

"Fantastic." Ashleigh crumpled the note and threw it in the wastebasket as they left the gym.

The receptionist, Ms. Dottie Langford, who displayed plush and porcelain kittens on her desk, smiled when Ashleigh arrived. Ashleigh complimented her shirt, with its embroidered image of a basket of kittens. Mrs. Langford buzzed the principal, proudly announced Ashleigh's arrival, and sent Ashleigh into the principal's office.

Principal Harris was a reedy man, with much bald on his head and a salty, peppery moustache. His glasses magnified his eyes so much that he looked like a cartoon character when he was wearing them. The effect was especially noticeable when he was trying to be serious. When Ashleigh entered, he removed his glasses and pinched the bridge of his nose.

"Close the door and have a seat, Ashleigh," he said.

Ashleigh lowered herself into one of the chairs across from him.

"Goodness, you look exhausted, Principal Harris," Ashleigh said. "Are you ill?"

"No more than usual." He replaced his glasses, and his eyes doubled in diameter. "Ashleigh, we have a problem."

"You have a problem, sir?"

"We do. You and I. And I'm sure you know why."

"I don't know what it could be, Principal Harris."

"This abstinence program?"

Ashleigh cocked her head and looked puzzled. "I don't understand, sir. Christians Act! got written permission from you to promote abstinence at school. I thought everyone agreed it was a good idea." Since there was a large membership overlap between Cool Crusaders at church and Christians Act! at school, Ashleigh had naturally used the flagpole prayer group to carry the campaign into school.

"We did give you permission to put up some posters encouraging abstinence. We are not opposed to that."

"Then what could the problem possibly be?" Ashleigh asked.

Principal Harris stared at her in disbelief for a minute. Then he said, "Let's have a look. These are examples I personally removed this morning." He placed a stack of four full-color, glossy posters on his desk. Neesha had done the photography, since she had the equipment and the talent.

The top one depicted two students, a boy and a girl, in bathing suits by the pond behind Ashleigh's house. The boy had his arms around the girl's waist. Both of them were soaking wet. The caption read: ABSTINENCE IS POWER.

"What is this about?" he asked.

"Clearly, it's about how couples must work together and agree on abstinence, even though they're tempted," Ashleigh said. "I mean, obviously."

"And what about this?" Principal Harris slid the top one aside, revealing a portrait of Neesha's boyfriend Dedrick, shirtless to show off his muscles, his underwear slung very low, his pants even lower, his belt unbuckled. He made a 'peace' sign, his head slung back. Again, the caption: ABSTINENCE IS POWER.

"Or this?" The next picture depicted senior Ronella Jones, topless, her back to the camera. She wore tight, low-slung jeans, and had Egyptian hieroglyphs tattooed on her lower back. The picture had the slogan ABSTINENCE IS POWER.

The final picture showed Alison Newton, a senior cheerleader, with her jeans unzipped. She covered her panties with both hands, as if saying "No." ABSTINENCE IS POWER.

"Ashleigh," the principal said, "What on you Earth made you think these would be acceptable?"

"Principal Harris, I think I understand kids today better than you," Ashleigh said. "They know sex is tempting. If we don't admit that, then they won't believe the rest of our message. You know?"

Ashleigh considered reaching out to touch the principal's hand, infect him with some of that special Ashleigh-energy, but she never used it on him. Principal Harris was too much fun to torture.

"And how would I explain to parents why my hallway looks like an Abercrombie and Fitch catalog?" Principal Harris asked. "Why we have pictures like this of their children?"

"Just send them to me, and I'll explain," Ashleigh said.

"I want them all taken down. Today."

"Principal Harris?" Ashleigh drew herself up to her full height in the chair. She gave him a sweet smile. "Do you want people thinking you're opposed to teen abstinence?"

"I am not opposed to—"

"Do you want people in town asking why you're so anti-abstinence? Do you want people at church wondering why you encourage premarital sex among your students?"

"I certainly do not—"

"Do you want this all over the media? I can go back on the True Word Radio Hour any time I want."

"Ashleigh, don't be ridiculous—"

"What about parents calling you at home all night? Death threats on your front door? I can make it all happen again, Principal Harris. You saw how wild they got over kids and witchcraft. Now imagine it's kids and sex."

Principal Harris glared at her now, his jaw flexing as if chewing an extremely gristly piece of meat.

"Okay, I get it," he said. "You want me to oppose you. You want another media storm, with innocent little you as the victim again."

"Not at all, Principal Harris. That's silly."

"Why do you do these things, Ashleigh?"

"Because I care so much about the community, Principal Harris."

"I'm not sure I believe you," he said.

"Then think of it this way." Ashleigh stood and stretched her hands high over her head, as if cramped from two minutes of sitting down. She tried to be a little seductive about it, letting her gym shirt crawl up her stomach, and Principal Harris averted his eyes and scowled at the floor. "I'm graduating this year. You decide if you want peace and quiet, or if you want to go to war with me. Personally, I like war."

He looked up at her again, undisguised hatred on his face.

The bell rang. Ashleigh gathered the confiscated posters and rolled them together.

"I have another class," she said. "I'd better get out of these sweaty gym shorts, don't you think, Principal Harris?"

"Go." He spoke through clenched teeth.

She opened the door and stepped into the reception area, leaving it open behind her. Then she turned back and sang out, "Good-bye, Principal Harris! I'll return these posters to the hall! Thank you!"

The principal didn't respond. Ashleigh winked at Mrs. Langford.

"Oh, would you like a lollipop, dear?" Mrs. Langford said.

"Oh, gosh, thank you, ma'am. Lime, please."

Mrs. Langford passed her one from a kitten-shaped glass bowl.

"Have a nice day, dear!" Mrs. Langford said. As Ashleigh stepped into the main hall, she heard the receptionist mutter to herself, "Such a sweet young Christian lady."

In the hallway, Ashleigh saw two boys from Christians Act! and gave them the posters. She told them to hang them prominently in the main hall, right away.

The rest of the abstinence posters stayed where they were, displayed up and down the main hall.

In the locker room, Jenny splashed handfuls of cold water onto her face where Ashleigh had slammed the ball into it. She rinsed the blood from her nose, but it was still swollen and tender.

When the bell rang, Jenny moved slowly, letting the rest of the class leave ahead of her. As she left the locker room, she looked over at Coach Humbee on the bleachers. As far as she could tell, he remained absorbed in his newspaper.

Jenny bent down, plucked the crumpled note from the trash can, then hurried out the gym door. She concealed the note in her fist as she jogged along the gravel path to the main school building.

She was alone on the path when Ashleigh Goodling returned from the principal's office. Ashleigh had a bright, triumphant gleam in her eye and walked with a little extra bounce, obviously fresh from some victory or other.

Jenny kept her eyes on the ground and tried to avoid her, but Ashleigh, dozens of feet from any witnesses, couldn't resist. She pulled the green lollipop from her mouth and sang a verse from an old song, one Cassie had invented when she was nine years old. There was a hand-clap game that went with it, which had been quite a hit in Jenny's fourth-grade class.

> Jen-ny Mit-tens,
> Drownin' kittens,
> She's so stupid,
> So says Cupid…

A deep, primitive anger rose in Jenny, and she fought to squelch it. She didn't dare do or say anything, especially not with the filched note burning in her fingers like contraband. She kept her eyes down as Ashleigh passed by. Behind her, Ashleigh cackled as she opened the door to the gym.

Inside the main building, Jenny ducked into a bathroom stall and locked the door. The girls in the next stall were sharing a cigarette, and she held in her urge to cough. She spread the note out between her fingers.

It was 5" x 8" paper, torn from a pad. The Porcupines logo and the school's address and phone number were printed in brown and yellow on the top. Mrs. Langford had written in all caps: ASHLEIGH GOODLING TO PRINCIPAL'S OFFICE ASAP.

Jenny folded the note and zipped it into an interior pocket of her bookbag. It was just what she needed, the magic ticket that gave any student the power to pluck another out of class, since Mrs. Langford foisted the notes onto any kid who happened by in the main hall whenever she needed one delivered. Jenny began to sweat nervously as she made her plan.

She splashed more cold water on her swollen nose and went to fourth period.

She sweated and worried through the rest of her classes. She knew her intentions, had known them from the moment she'd picked the note from the trash. Now the audacity of it frightened her. She could get in a lot of trouble. She also knew that if she didn't do it today, if she slept on it, she would definitely change her mind.

When the bell rang to end sixth period, and the kids headed for the front doors and parking lot, Jenny walked to the school office. Mrs. Langford looked at Jenny like she was a slimy slug discovered on the shower wall. When it came to popularity, the teachers and staff had a funny way of taking on the kids' opinions. Especially Ashleigh's opinions.

"Yes?" Mrs. Langford asked.

"Uh, hi, ma'am," Jenny said. "Uh, can I get, I need to, how do I get some transcripts? My transcripts? For college?"

Mrs. Langford sighed and rolled her eyes. She swiveled to the big gray filing cabinet behind her and opened a drawer. Jenny's gaze darted to the desk, and she spotted the 5" x 8" notepad with the Porcupines logo.

"We send them to the schools directly," Mrs. Langford said as she rummaged through file folders. "If we give them to you, they're no good."

Jenny reached for the pad, and the cuff of her glove caught on the ear of a porcelain kitten. The kitten spilled over and clanked into the kitten-shaped glass candy dish.

Mrs. Langford looked back over her shoulder and hissed. Jenny pulled her hand back.

"I don't remember offering you candy!" she barked.

"Sorry, Mrs. Langford."

"That's impolite. Candy's for my glycemics."

"I didn't know that. I'm sorry."

"Little thief." She turned back to the file drawer. "How many forms do you need?"

"Just one," Jenny said.

"Feeling confident, are we?" Mrs. Langford reached into a folder.

Jenny leaned over the desk. A pen lay across the pad, and it would roll off if Jenny didn't move it. She picked up the pen. Mrs. Langford was shaking one form out of a shrink-wrapped pack. Jenny took the pen in her index finger and thumb, then scooped up the notepad in her three remaining fingers, holding it awkwardly against her palm. She panicked immediately. The pad was too big for her jeans pocket, and if she unzipped her bookbag, the sound would draw Mrs. Langford's attention.

As Mrs. Langford began to swivel back to face her, Jenny put her hand with the notepad and pen behind her. She needed more time, so she used her other hand to flick the little porcelain cat that had fallen over. It skittered across Mrs. Langford's desk, and Mrs. Langford watched it with a scowl. It was enough time for Jenny to cram the notepad as far as it would go down the back of her pants. She didn't know what to do with the pen, so she shoved it down next to the notepad, and grimaced as she poked herself in the ass.

When Mrs. Langford looked up, Jenny was still adjusting her shirt. Mrs. Langford gave her a scowl as she stood up the little porcelain cat, which was posed in a paw-licking gesture.

"Let my things alone!" Mrs. Langford said.

"Sorry, ma'am," Jenny said. "I knocked it over, and I was trying to fix—"

"Just keep your paws to yourself!" Mrs. Langford held out the transcript form. "Where are you applying?"

"Uh… Harvard," Jenny said. She felt herself sweating all over, and worried that Mrs. Langford would see the look on her face, or her wobbling legs, and know that something was up. The notepad felt huge against her back.

"Harvard?" Mrs. Langford looked Jenny up and down as Jenny leaned very carefully forward to accept the form. A little sneer crept into her upper lip. "Good luck on that, sugar."

"Thank you, ma'am." Jenny stepped backwards from the desk, scared to turn around. Mrs. Langford turned her attention to her computer.

Jenny pivoted quickly around. Her backpack hid the notepad from behind, she hoped, but the fatal side view would make Jenny's theft apparent. She quick-marched to the door, reached to open it— but then it swung in toward her.

Principal Harris nearly collided with Jenny. He stepped back, smiling down at her. "Oh! Excuse me, uh…" His eyes fell on her gloved hands, and his smile faded. "Oh. Jenny." He stepped back, turned aside and gestured for her to exit.

Jenny emerged carefully from the door into the hall. If she walked straight out, he would get a clear view of the notepad jutting up from the back of her pants. So Jenny turned sideways as she walked, keeping her front to him. Then she made a kind of silly grand gesture of a wave for the principal to go on by her, as if she were somehow holding the door for him, which she wasn't. There was no rational reason for Jenny to not just step away and walk on down the hall. This was awkward and weird even for her.

Principal Harris just sighed, shook his head, and walked into the office.

Jenny hurried down the hall, toward the exit, the notepad slapping her back with every step. It rode up as she ran, threatening to fall out and smack the linoleum floor.

She waited until sixth period the next day, a Thursday, to put it into action. She knew Seth had English as his last class, because she was in Social Studies on the same hall. So Jenny cut class, something she'd heard other kids talk about, but had never dared to attempt herself. The teachers took attendance, didn't they?

Jenny waited in a bathroom stall until all the doors closed and the hallways fell silent. Then she took a breath and stepped out. She paused to look at herself in the mirror. She'd woken up early and spent almost an hour trying to figure how to braid her hair, which left her feeling exposed and vulnerable all day, and she wasn't entirely convinced it made her look better. She wore an old Swiss-dot black that had probably been made sometime around 1960, and a very thin sweater over that to cover her arms. She also wore her good black gloves and shoes.

She'd purchased concealer and inexpertly dabbed it on her swollen, discolored nose, where Ashleigh had slammed the volleyball into it. She wasn't too impressed with those results, either. The only thing she was really happy with was her dark purple lip gloss.

She looked both ways as she stepped out of the bathroom. Nobody. Her heeled shoes clomped and echoed very loudly as she walked past the office, turned down the English/Social Studies hall, and approached the door to Mrs. Peckering's room. Jenny looked in through the narrow, prison-style window at the AP English class. Seth was there, but so were Ashleigh, Cassie and Neesha. This would be tough.

Jenny took a deep breath, willed her heart to stop beating so hard, and opened the door.

Mrs. Peckering was busy scribbling on the chalkboard and talking about Beowulf and Grendel. She sighed when she saw Jenny Mittens, and her shoulders slumped, annoyed at the interruption.

"Yes?" Mrs. Peckering said.

Jenny couldn't summon the courage to say a word. She trudged into the room, eyes on the carpet, not daring to look toward the students. She stopped when she reached Mrs. Peckering, and she held out the note.

Jenny had gone through eleven sheets of Mrs. Langford's notepad paper before the one that Mrs. Peckering now took from her. It read, in all caps, SETH BARRETT TO PRINCIPAL'S OFFICE ASAP, in what purported to be Mrs. Langford's blocky handwriting.

Mrs. Peckering pointed at Seth and curled her finger for him to come.

Seth stood up. "Should I bring my books?" he asked.

Jenny waited for Mrs. Peckering to answer, but then realized Mrs. Peckering was staring impatiently at Jenny.

"Uh…yeah. I think so. Yeah. Yes." Jenny nodded her head a couple dozen times before stopping. Her legs and her guts felt like quivering goo. She could not believe she was doing anything like this.

"Aw, too bad." Seth grabbed his backpack and made his way up through the rows. Jenny slumped a little, her eyes on the floor.

"Get going, both of you," Mrs. Peckering said. "The rest of us are busy learning."

Seth gestured for Jenny to go first out the door. Jenny smiled as she passed him. Behind Seth, Ashleigh saw Jenny's smile.

"Hey, Seth," Ashleigh said. "Don't catch Jenny pox."

Normally, any joke from Ashleigh, no matter how poor, would get laughs from at least some quarter. This time, there was silence, except for a nervous attempt at laughter by Cassie. When she realized nobody else was going to join, Cassie started clearing her throat, as if she'd really meant to do that instead.

Something vague stirred in their memories, something deep and dark from long ago. Jenny could see it in their faces, and she felt it in herself. The words had not been spoken anywhere outside of Jenny's mind in ten years. Only Seth, who'd been at Grayson, looked genuinely puzzled by Ashleigh's comment.

"Close the door behind you," Mrs. Peckering said. Then she turned back and resumed writing and talking, and the students picked up their pens, and the moment was gone.

Seth closed the door behind him.

In the empty hall, he smiled at Jenny.

"So Mrs. Langford grabbed you this time," he said.

"Huh?" Jenny said. She'd had all kinds of plans about what she would say at this moment, but now every single one of them vanished from her brain. She was all jittery nerves and raw, conflicted, dangerous feelings. "Oh. Yeah, yep."

Seth turned and started walking. Jenny walked alongside him, smiling, then hiding it, then trying nervously to smile again.

He glanced around the hall, then leaned toward her.

"How's Rocky?" he whispered.

"He's really good!" The words rushed from Jenny's mouth, and she felt relieved to have something to talk about. "Yeah. He's so fast now. And hates any kind of road."

"Good for Rocky." They walked quietly for a little bit. "How are you? Any little aches I can take care of?"

"Oh." Jenny didn't dare try to stumble through an answer to that.

They were approaching the office door. Seth reached for the door handle. At the last second, Jenny realized what was happening and seized his hand in her black glove.

"Wait!" Jenny whispered. "The principal didn't really send for you. I made the note. It's fake."

Seth's eyes did one complete orbit while he processed this.

"Why?" he asked.

"Oh. I thought you might want to, you know, skip out of school early?"

"With you?" Seth asked.

Jenny hesitated before answering: "Yeah. With me."

"Oh, wow." He looked at the principal's door. "But I have football practice after school."

"Oh." Jenny said. "Okay." Her eyes went to her shoes. She felt stupid (so said Cupid). Of course Seth had practice.

"But that doesn't really start until 3:30," Seth said. "So that's like two hours. Where are we going?"

Jenny considered his words carefully, not sure he'd heard him correctly. He sounded like he was saying yes.

"Uh," Jenny said. "What do you think?"

"I don't know," Seth said. "This is your prison break."

"There is this," Jenny said. "This big rock in my woods. It's bigger than a house. Sometimes there's a stream, if it's been raining. I could show you. If you want to see that. It's just a rock, but really big. You can climb up and sit on it and everything."

"You want to go to your house and show me your big rock?"

"And Rocky," Jenny said, feeling stupid again. "So you can look at Rocky and see how he's doing. That's what I meant to say."

"I'd like to see Rocky," Seth said.

"And we can smoke, if you want. I have some homegrown."

"Sold!" Seth grinned. He looked at the office door again, and his eyes widened. "We have to go! This is worst place for us to be right now."

They slipped out the back door of the school and went around the long, less traveled way to the parking lot. Seth tossed both their backpacks into his trunk and opened her door before hopping in on the driver's side.

He cranked the engine and retracted the roof. Jenny ran her fingers along the smooth gray interior.

"Won't Ashleigh be waiting for you?" Jenny asked, then wanted to kick herself.

"She drives herself," Seth backed out, then drove for the exit. She looked back nervously at the school's rows of dark, narrow windows, and felt very exposed in the convertible. She hoped nobody saw them.

Jenny had spent too much time thinking about taking him out of class, and not enough planning for what would happen after that. What was she going to do with Seth? What did she expect from him? What did he expect from her? What was she thinking?

When they arrived at Jenny's, she didn't want to take him in to see her cluttered house. Her yard was bad enough. He stood in her red dirt driveway, looking around at the house, the shed with all the old advertising signs tacked to it, the completely mismatched, random lengths of fencing in the yard, the scattered pieces of automobiles, dishwashers, refrigerators.

"Is your dad an artist or something?" Seth asked.

"Totally," Jenny answered. Rocky bounded out of the shed, ducked back when he saw Seth, then crept back out shyly, tail wagging. He must have recognized Seth, because he didn't bark, but he didn't get close enough to let Seth pet him.

"He looks good," Seth said. He pointed at the hairless band of scar tissue. "I guess that won't grow back."

"It's okay, I don't think that bothers him. Anyway, I've been looking into this stuff—Rogaine? Heard of it?"

Seth laughed and shook his head. "I can't do cosmetic healing, sorry. Injuries only."

"Wait here." Jenny hurried inside. She removed the cigar box from under her bed and quickly rolled a thick spliff for them to share. The weed was from the patch her dad grew for a little extra side income, since side income was all he had. It wasn't grown on their land, of course, but a couple miles away, on unused, overgrown land owned by the bank. She realized that, technically, it was grown on land owned by Seth's family. This struck her as funny, but she couldn't tell Seth. She wasn't about to narc out her own dad.

She held up the joint when she returned outside.

"The trail's this way," she said. Jenny led him into the shadowy woods. The woods were still green and alive in September, but here and there you could see something gone brown and dry, the early flickers of fall. It was still hot enough that the cicadas filled the trees with their buzzing songs.

She took him along the path full of honeysuckle and wild blackberries. It was the long way, going around the first two hills instead of over them, but it was the prettiest.

"So," she asked, "Are you going to be like a doctor or something?"

"Not you, too," Seth said.

"What?"

"The doctor thing. I tell people I want to do maybe physical therapy. So, you know, I can put my hands on injured people and heal them and get away with it. But then everybody hears physical therapy and says I should be a doctor. My parents, my family…Ashleigh, Ashleigh's parents…"

"That's a lot of opinions," Jenny said.

"Yeah!" Seth said. "And I want to say, look, I'm really not all that good with the science and math, you know? Or school in general. I don't even think I'd make it into medical school. And why should I spend twelve years on that when I'm not really using medicine to heal people? Just seems like a waste."

"You should do what you want to do," Jenny said.

Seth laughed, then stopped walking and looked at her.

"What is it?" Jenny said.

"Nobody ever says that," Seth said. "Here, let me give you something." He reached his hand toward her face, which was horribly, dangerously bare, with all her hair pulled up and pinned in place. The rest of her was still covered. She'd thrown off the high heels but still wore the stockings, even though they would get destroyed by this walk.

She realized he intended to touch her and heal the volleyball bruises around her nose, and she gasped. She stumbled back, off the trail, over a log and into the underbrush.

"Whoa!" He stepped forward and extended his hand. "I didn't mean to scare you. Sorry."

Jenny looked at his bare hand, and her fingers twitched in her gloves. She reached out and took it. He helped her up, taking her under one arm, and she quickly slipped away from him.

"You can't touch me," she said, and she felt her heart splinter as she said it aloud. "That's the only thing. I can't explain why, right now. Okay?"

Seth looked at her a minute, then frowned and nodded.

"Okay. I understand why."

"You do?" Jenny felt a little panicked.

"It freaks you out, doesn't it?" he said. "Knowing that healing energy comes out of me. It's scary. Scary to me, sometimes."

"Yeah, okay," Jenny said. It actually wasn't a bad excuse, for now. "Just for now, okay? Maybe I'll get used to it."

"Right," Seth said. "Actually, that's kind of a relief."

"Really?" Jenny felt more than a little disappointed.

"Yeah." They started walking again. "Because I can't turn it off. It's always flowing out of me whether I want it to or not. Not just my hands. Everywhere."

They made brief eye contact, then both laughed nervously and looked away.

"So people always want to touch me," Seth said. He grinned, and looked relieved that he could actually talk about it. "Think about it. Headache, stubbed toe…bruises…anything. If you shake my hand, it goes away. Hug me and you'll feel totally recharged. Kiss me—" Seth broke off and laughed nervously again. "So, nobody really knows why, they just know they feel better when they touch me. And that drains you, all day long. I have to eat tons of sugar to keep up."

"That's crazy," Jenny said.

"So, if you don't want to touch me, that's actually great," Seth said. "That makes you one of my favorite people to hang out with."

Jenny laughed and felt strange, warm, gooey things inside her belly.

The big rock was nestled at the bottom of a little valley. The easiest way to get on top of it was to follow the path up the closest hill, in which the rock was embedded, and then climb down to it. The hardest way was to walk to the bottom of the valley, then climb the flat face of the rock, using little nooks and cracks as finger and toe holes.

Jenny took him the hard way, letting him see how nimbly and easily she could scale it. She looked down and watched with a smile as he followed, struggling to find the handholds and footholds. When he reached the top, she gave him a hand and helped up him the pebbly slope to the flat plateau on top of the rock.

Rocky scampered around in the bottom of the valley, which was apparently full of wonderful things to smell. His tail whipped back and forth as he snuffled through dead leaves.

There was an open space in the canopy above the rock that let the thick yellow afternoon sunlight through. Seth stood in the shaft of light as he looked around, taking in the woods, and it turned his hair a blazing red-gold color.

"So this is your big rock," he said.

"This is my big rock," she agreed.

"These woods are all yours?"

"Yep. They're all full of rocks like this. You can't do anything useful with these woods except hide in them."

"That's pretty useful," he said. "I like hiding."

Jenny realized he was still holding her hand, and she looked down at it, feeling self-conscious. Who was forgetting to let go? Was it her fault?

Seth followed her look to their hands. He rubbed his thumb on the back of her glove.

"Gloves," he said. "I should wear gloves to block people off. That's a great idea." He released her gloved hand, then plucked at the sleeve of her sweater. "And sleeves all year. If I dressed like that, people couldn't drain me all the time."

Seth looked into her eyes. Jenny froze and didn't dare say a word.

"You have it," he said.

"What?"

"The touch. The healing thing." He waved his open hand and wiggled his fingers. "You have it, too. And you figured out how to hold it in. That's why you wear gloves. That's why they call you Jenny M—"

"I know what they call me," Jenny whispered.

"But you have it, too. Like me."

"No," Jenny said.

"Then why the gloves?"

Jenny took a breath. It was dangerous to tell him. He was very close to Ashleigh. But he was trusting Jenny, and that made her want to trust him. He couldn't be such a bad person, if he could do things like heal Rocky.

"I don't have it," she said. "I have something else."

"What?" His smile was beautiful to her in the sunlight. "You already know mine. That's not fair. Rocky wants you to tell me." He nodded at the dog, who was sniffing around a rotting tree stump.

"I'd better start this." Jenny lit the joint with a match and took a couple deep pulls to soothe her nerves. She'd never told anyone about it. Only her father knew. The kids in her first-grade class had outgrown believing in the supernatural, and the parents and teachers had never believed about Jenny pox. And anyone else who'd ever known about it was dead.

"It's called Jenny pox," she told him.

"What Ashleigh said in class today? Everyone kind of freaked out a little bit, didn't they?"

"You didn't go to our elementary school." She passed the joint to him, and he took a deep pull.

"Nope," he said, while holding his breath. "Grayson Academy. *Virtus, honor et ducatus.* Chapel on Sunday and no girls." He blew out a long blue plume of smoke.

"I gave it to Ashleigh when I was a kid," Jenny said. "By accident. Mostly. She was attacking me and I hit her with my bare hand."

"What happened?"

"She broke out with infected blisters on her face, in front of the whole class. She never told you about it?"

"No, I'd remember that," Seth said.

"Everyone called it Jenny pox. That's when I got into gloves." She waved her gloved hand with a sarcastic smile. "I hoped people forgot about it. I think Ashleigh remembers, though."

"Are you sure it came from you?" he asked. "Have you ever infected anybody else?"

Jenny took the joint back from him. "I don't know if I should tell you."

"Maybe Ashleigh was just sick," Seth said. "Maybe it wasn't you."

"Okay, listen," Jenny said. "But you can't tell anyone. I shouldn't tell you." She took another drag. "I just have poor decision-making skills right now, and I blame that on my drug use. So listen. I infected my momma when I was born. She died."

"I'm sorry, Jenny. I didn't know that."

"You ever hear about the doctor's office burned to the ground over in Millwater?" Jenny asked. "About eighteen years ago?"

"I don't think so."

"Good," Jenny said. "That's where I was born. My momma went into labor and that was the nearest place. I infected the doctor who delivered me. He died the same night. And the nurse who helped him, she died. Everybody who touched me. My daddy saw it happen, and he figured out not to touch me with his bare hands."

"Are you serious?"

"My daddy—well, the whole doctor's office caught fire and burned to the ground somehow. I mean, everybody was dead anyhow." Jenny made herself shut up. She shouldn't have told anyone about that. Her father had burned down the office to hide what had happened to the doctor, the nurse, and Jenny's mother, just to protect Jenny. It was a deep secret, one her father still worried about coming back to haunt them. It was the last thing she needed to be sharing with Ashleigh's boyfriend. She couldn't understand why she was trusting him with all of this, but she couldn't help talking to him about it. She'd been holding it back all her life, and he'd somehow opened up the floodgate.

Seth lay back on the rock and looked up towards the clouds. He smoked the joint and thought about this.

"Man," he said. "I thought mine was crazy."

"Yours is easy," Jenny said. "I can't touch nobody. You get diseased. If I hold on too long, you die."

"That sucks," he said. "That really, really sucks." He looked at the joint they'd been sharing. "Uh, are you sure this is safe? I won't get sick?"

"It's not contagious," she said. "It's only if I touch you. Like yours. It's an energy."

"You can have the rest, though." He handed it back to her. "I mean, I do have practice. I think. Isn't this a weekday?" His eyes were bright red, and he seemed confused.

Jenny stubbed it out.

They lay on their backs and looked up at the circle of bright afternoon sky beyond the shadowy trees. He was more than a foot away, but he felt dangerously, deliciously close to Jenny, close enough she could feel his body warmth and hear him breathing. Warblers sang in the trees above them, and a woodpecker clattered away in the distance, high enough to echo across the woods.

"So that freaked you out, didn't it?" Jenny asked after a few minutes.

"Nah," Seth said. "That doesn't scare me. I heal diseases all the time. And I never get sick."

"I don't, either!" Jenny said. "I've never been sick."

He rolled on his side to look at her. "I've never even had a zit. Or a bruise."

"I've had bruises." She looked back at him, enjoying the excuse to study his face. "Never zits or blackheads or anything."

"I know. You've got a beautiful face," he said.

She laughed and rolled back to face the clouds. So did he.

"I'm really sorry about the Jenny pox," he whispered.

"Me, too."

"I have to get to practice soon."

"I know."

After a while, Jenny showed him the way back.

CHAPTER NINE

On Saturday, in the media room at Ashleigh's house, Ashleigh sat in one of the hanging sky chairs and tapped at her Blackberry. Seth was sprawled on the couch, trying to enjoy the movie *Grandma's Boy*, if only Ashleigh would stop interrupting.

"Okay," Ashleigh said. "Let's co-ordinate our schedules." She reached out an empty hand and snapped her fingers.

Seth rolled his eyes and dug into his pocket for the Blackberry she'd bought him last year. He handed it over. Ashleigh began typing on it.

"So that's dinner with my parents Thursday—just come over after practice, you can shower here." She winked at him.

"I could just shower in the school locker room," he said.

"Don't be gross. Game Friday, then Saturday, we chaperone the Halloween Lock-In…" Her thumbs flew as she typed.

"Nah," Seth said.

"What's that?" She looked up.

"I don't want to do the lock-in."

"What are you talking about?"

"Come on," Seth said. "Halloween's on a Saturday night this year. And we're seniors. I don't want to waste it at church with a bunch of kids again. Think about it."

Ashleigh frowned, and a single wrinkle appeared on her forehead.

"But the lock-in needs chaperones," Ashleigh said.

"You have plenty of seniors," Seth said. "You don't have to go. Just turn it over to that Darcy Metcalf girl or something. She'd do it. I want to do something fun."

"The lock-in is fun!" Ashleigh said. "We've got a dance room this year, a haunted maze—"

"The lock-in is fun when you're fourteen," Seth said.

"We had a lot of fun there when we were fourteen," Ashleigh said. "Well, I was fifteen. The first time we kissed. Remember those kissing games at five in the morning?"

"Yeah. Now I want to do something new."

"Seth," Ashleigh said. "We always do the lock-in."

"That's kind of my point."

"Seth." She put her hand against her forehead. "I need to be there."

"I'm not going," he said.

"Seth!" She glared at him. "What is wrong with you?"

"I can't enjoy Halloween?"

"And just what would you rather be doing than spending the night with me?" she asked.

"I still want to go to some haunted houses," he said. "Some churches even do them, you'd like that."

"I'm not doing that," Ashleigh said quickly.

"I know, because you're a scaredy-cat."

Ashleigh smiled and left her chair. She sat beside him on the couch and reached toward his hand. Something about the gesture creeped him out, and Seth scooted back out of her reach.

"Seth!" she said. "What's your problem?"

"I told you."

"Come on, Seth." She slid toward him and reached for him again, and again it struck him as strange. Maybe he was just extra aware of people leeching off his energy, after his conversation with Jenny.

He got off the couch and stood up, escaping Ashleigh's hand.

"Seth! Come back here!"

"No." He crossed his arms.

"Seth!" She jumped up and reached both hands toward him, and he used a hanging chair as a shield.

He didn't know why he was freaking out, but he suddenly had the very strong idea that Ashleigh had figured out a way to control him through pulling out his energy. Or something like that.

Maybe she didn't even understand it herself, just knew that it involved touching him. Or maybe he was paranoid.

"Why are you being a freak?" Ashleigh said.

"Last year, I spent the whole night sticking kids' hands into spaghetti and telling them it was gorilla brains. And we had to clean up after that one guy that puked. And there was the girl who wet her sleeping bag—"

"But we could have fun together," Ashleigh said. "And Cassie will be there."

"We've done your thing for three Halloweens. I want real fun, not sitting-in-the-church-basement fun. I'm going to do my thing. Get pissed off if you want."

"Seth, come here and let me touch you." Ashleigh spread her arms wide, and pushed her chest forward.

The back of his neck prickled. How many times did she touch him during a typical day? Hundreds?

"Why?" he asked.

"Because I want to make you feel better." Ashleigh slowly unbuttoned her shirt, revealing a scarlet bra underneath. "Don't you want to feel better, Seth?"

"Why would that make me feel better?" he asked.

"Seth!" Her hands fell to her sides, leaving her last button still in place. "You asshole!"

"Why would it? Why do you want to touch me?"

"Why would you even ask me that?" Now there was a cold, calculating look on her face. She was studying him with her unreadable gray eyes.

"You're not going to change my mind," he said.

"Maybe I will." She unfastened her last button, shrugged her shirt to the floor. She approached him, eyelids lowered, lips pouting. "You know, my dad's busy at the church. We have the house by ourselves."

"I have to go, Ashleigh."

Her face turned to a hard scowl. Her voice became strangely low and husky, and throbbed with anger. "Then go! Get the hell out of my house!"

Seth left the room, went down the hall, down the front steps, to the front door. As he opened it, Ashleigh ran out onto the landing above, now wearing only her underwear.

"Don't even think about coming back until you apologize to me!" Ashleigh screamed down at him.

"Okay," Seth said. He walked out the front door, and he left it wide open behind him.

Jenny's dad had a few odd jobs in town, so Jenny spent Saturday organizing and scrubbing the house. She called her dad on his cell phone and asked him to buy some new cleaning supplies at Piggly Wiggly, because she was using up all they had.

Jenny scrubbed everything in the kitchen and both bathrooms, then worked her way up to organizing the junk in the living room, dining room, the laundry room, the front and back porches.

She got absorbed in the work and lost track of time. By the time her dad arrived home at midnight, she was sitting on a folding chair in the front yard, exhausted and sweaty, looking at all the weeds and machinery pieces.

He parked the truck slantwise, then stumbled out, clutching his flask in one hand.

"Whatcha doon, sugarbeet?" he asked her.

"I'm just thinking," she said. "We should get rid of all this junk."

"T'ain't junk," he said. He took a swig, then gestured around with his flask. "Lots of them good, scrappy parts in there. Don't know what I need til I need it."

"But we shouldn't leave them out here like this," Jenny said. She looked toward the shed, but that was already full and cluttered itself. "What if we build a new shed?"

"Nother shed?" He looked off into the space between the shed and the house, as if imagining it. "Oh, yeah. Take some doing, but we could put it up."

"It doesn't have to be a whole shed," Jenny said. "Just a roof to keep your stuff out of the rain. And some tall fencing so company can't see it."

He took another swig and pondered this. "We got company coming?" he asked.

"Maybe," Jenny said.

"Friends of yours?"

"Yes."

"Aw, good for you, Jenny." He stumbled towards her and reached out his arms to hug her.

"Daddy, no!" Jenny skittered back. "I ain't covered up!" She was dressed lightly, in old, moth-eaten clothes that left her arms and shins bare.

"Oh, sorry, honey." He tried to drink from his flask, then turned it upside down and shook it. Empty. He dropped it in the dirt and staggered up the porch steps. "All right then. Going in."

"Good night, daddy."

"Night."

Jenny walked to the shed and turned on the electric lamp hanging from a roof beam. She found a pencil and paper and sat at the workbench, one of the few surfaces her dad kept clear. She designed improvements for the house, starting with a fence from the house to the shed. They could move all the front yard junk behind that, and then be free to work on the yard itself. Then they could build additions onto the shed, extending it behind the fence.

When she was sure her dad wasn't coming back, she took out the roach of the joint she'd shared with Seth. It had been almost intimate, both of them touching their lips to it, back and forth. The closest she could come to kissing him.

She'd figured out long ago that her body's castoffs—her hair, her spit, her blood—weren't contagious. It was only her live, skin-to-skin touch that was dangerous. The Jenny pox wasn't a virus, but more like a dark energy that flowed out from her, inspiring disease in others. The opposite of Seth.

She lit the roach with a match and held the smoke in her lungs, imagining traces of Seth mingling with her. She listened to Rocky snoring in his dog house, and smiled.

The next day, she woke up early and resumed her cleaning binge, and she didn't worry about keeping quiet for her dad's sake, and he managed to stay asleep anyway.

The phone rang around one-thirty, and she let the machine get it. Jenny never answered the phone if her dad was home. On the old answering machine in the living room, which ran on giant orange cassettes that were no longer manufactured, she heard her dad's recorded voice, saying to leave a message. Then it cut off as the caller hung up.

A minute later, the phone rang again. This time, he left a message after the beep:

"Hey. This is Seth Barrett calling for Jenny. Um, you can call me back at—"

Jenny ran to pick up their one house phone, also in the living room.

"Hey, Seth!" she said.

"Oh, good. What's up?"

"Um. Nothing." Jenny couldn't think of anything to say. She should try to be funny? Or clever? Or cool?

"So, what are you doing for Halloween?" he asked. "Do you want to hang out?"

"Doing?" Jenny felt herself blush. Her brain was not working for her. She struggled to remember an article from the one issue of Cosmopolitan she'd read at the library, when work was slow one day. She was supposed to act like she had a lot of other engagements and pretend to be unavailable. She wanted to smack her forehead—she shouldn't have picked up the phone.

"I'm hitting some haunted houses," Seth said. "They do one in this old warehouse in Vernon Hill that's supposed to be really scary. I've never been able to go. Do you want to come with me?"

"On Saturday?" Jenny asked. "This Saturday?"

"Yeah, Halloween. And there's a big field party over in Barlowe that night. You can go in costume, or—"

"Okay!" she heard herself squeal. Shit, she thought. So much for being unavailable.

"Yeah?"

"But Barlowe?" Jenny asked. She felt a twinge of distrust. "Aren't they your big enemies?"

Seth laughed. "Right. Anyway, they have better parties than Fallen Oak."

"I don't know, Seth."

"About which thing?"

"A party?" That word made Jenny anxious. "That's a lot of people to bump into."

"Oh, the touching," Seth said. "So wear a costume. Gloves, masks, hats—Halloween's the perfect time for people like us to go party." People like us, Jenny thought, and her heartbeat quickened.

"Are your friends going to be there?" Jenny asked.

"Maybe some. Definitely not Ashleigh or Cassie. They're doing the lock-in at church all night."

"Wow!" Jenny said, then felt like a nerd. She lowered her voice a little, trying to sound like a normal human being. "I mean, okay, I guess that's cool."

"I wanted to hang out with you instead."

"Oh." Jenny was glad he couldn't see how hard she was blushing, or how she kept twisting back and forth on her heel like a freak, wrapping the phone cord thick around her fingers. "Okay, Seth."

"What are you going as?" he asked.

"Going? As?"

"For Halloween."

"Oh! A costume." Jenny's mind was a complete blank. "I'm still thinking about it."

"I haven't picked one, either," Seth said. "Ashleigh usually buys it and gives it to me. She always wants it to match her costume."

"But Ashleigh's not coming," Jenny said. "So you can wear what you want."

"Yeah," Seth said. "I need to shop."

"Me, too."

"Tomorrow after school?" he asked.

"Don't you have practice?"

"Nah. Humbee's out of town 'til Thursday. Nobody's going."

"Okay," Jenny said. "Tomorrow."

She held onto the phone for a long time after he hung up.

On Monday, the Leadership Committee of Christians Act!—Ashleigh Goodling, Cassie Winder, and Darcy Metcalf—met with Principal Harris in his office. His magnified, giant eyes looked incredulous behind his glasses throughout their presentation. He made no move to touch the written proposal or the pen they'd laid on his desk.

"So, if I understand correctly," the principal said. "You're no longer content with just hanging those awful and inappropriate posters all over my halls. You want to make a video, and then show it to all classes on Friday. You want me to allow that?"

"Yes, sir, Principal Harris," Darcy said. She was a chunky girl who wore big, ridiculous folk art earrings, and she was very serious about her Christian groups. Ashleigh and Cassie had allowed her into Leadership Committee because she was a hard worker and earnest enough to take on all the boring stuff, like setting up the stupid pamphlet table and collection cup at the flagpole prayer.

"Statistically," Darcy continued, "The rate of risky behavior among teens rises sharply around the, quote, party holidays. It is crucial to get the abstinence message across just before Halloween weekend. Unfortunately, most of these teens will not be at safe places like the church lock-in."

"Yes, Darcy, I appreciate that." Harris focused on Ashleigh. "And do you have this video here to show me?"

"Oh, not yet, sir," Ashleigh said. "We're still putting it together now."

"But you would have it by Friday?" he asked.

"Yes, sir. Even if we have to work all Thursday night to get it done."

The principal sat back in his chair. "You want me to sign off, sight unseen."

"Oh, we assure you, Principal Harris, it will be high quality," Cassie said. "Neesha is very talented. You see her posters around school."

"You're going to have the same girl in charge of this video?"

"Yes, sir," Cassie said.

"And will this video be similar to the abstinence posters you've put up?"

"Oh, yes, sir," Ashleigh said. "It's all part of the ABSTINENCE IS POWER campaign. So if you'll just sign off on that proposal…"

Principal Harris barked out a laugh. "You really expect me to sign this?"

"Please," Ashleigh said. "We need to use the A/V equipment."

"Ashleigh, ladies, it horrifies me to think what would be on that video." Principal Harris reached past the pen and grabbed a fat black permanent marker. "You've pushed me enough. You are not going to make an explicit video with my students and show it in my school. Here—" He wrote the word REJECTED across the proposal and signed it. "—here is my signature." He shoved it back across his desk and it tumbled into Ashleigh's lap.

Ashleigh and Cassie stood. Darcy, after a confused few seconds, joined them.

"I think you may regret this, Principal Harris," Ashleigh said.

"I could never regret saying 'no' to you, Ashleigh," Principal Harris said. "Abstinence is power, am I right?"

Darcy gasped. Ashleigh stood, tucked the rejected proposal against her chest, then turned and led the way out of the principal's office. Darcy was the last to leave, and she looked very upset.

They walked out into the hallway, Ashleigh and Cassie cool, Darcy acting like a spaz.

"What was that?" Darcy said. "You said you would stand up to him, Ashleigh!"

"It's fine, Darcy," Cassie said.

"Fine? But he rejected it! There's no, we can't, we won't get to make the video!"

Ashleigh patted Darcy's neck, discharging a little energy into her. Darcy immediately chilled out and gave Ashleigh a gummy smile.

"Don't you worry your pretty head," Ashleigh said. "The video has already been made, and we will get it out there. We didn't really need the school's outdated A/V crap. We used the church's."

"Oh!" Darcy giggled. "I should have known to trust you, Ashleigh."

"Yes," Ashleigh said. "Now, run off to your little class."

When Darcy was away, Ashleigh turned and looked at the poster hanging in front of them, the one of Alison Newton with the open fly and the teasing, two-handed rejection.

"Tell the Special Activities Committee to make all these posters disappear today," Ashleigh told Cassie.

"He didn't order us to do that," Cassie said.

"I'm ordering," Ashleigh said. "But let them think it came from the principal. Tell them wait until after school, so nobody sees them doing it. This is a secret action."

"Sounds good," Cassie said.

"I want every single poster brought to my house," Ashleigh said. "Right away. Tonight."

"Are we getting into the second part already?" Cassie asked.

"Why not?" Ashleigh waved the rejected proposal. "We got all we needed from the first part."

CHAPTER TEN

Monday afternoon, Seth took Jenny shopping in Apple Creek, which had an actual indoor mall with a whole store devoted to costumes, masks and party supplies. The store was packed with Halloween shoppers. Jenny had prepared herself with her usual long sleeves and gloves, and also tied a dark scarf as a kerchief around her head. Still, she felt nervous and guarded near so many people, especially with all the running kids, who occasionally whacked face first into her black jeans.

"What kind of stuff did Ashleigh make you wear?" Jenny asked as they looked across a wall of masks.

"You know, couples' costumes," Seth said. "Robin Hood and Maid Marian. Beauty and the Beast—"

Jenny's laughter rang across the store, turning heads.

"What?" Seth said.

"Oh," she said. She held up a finger, still laughing, trying to catch her breath. "You were serious."

"Hey, I kind of liked the Beast," he said.

"Right. Look, you be what you want to be. But I'm going as a vampire."

"Where's that?" Seth looked at the rack of costumes.

"I just made it up. But I can get some clothes for it at the thrift store. You know, the Five and Dime?"

Seth shook his head.

"How do you not know about the Five and Dime?"

"Not that into shopping, I guess."

"Okay," Jenny said. "But I want to use that for my cape." She took a black cloak with a cowl from the rack. "And this." She grabbed a large make-up kit, with putty and dye for making your own designs, and latex for sealing it. "This is perfect. I don't want to be one of those stupid sexy vampires. I want to be an ugly rotten corpse kind of vampire."

"That sounds cool. I think I saw a coffin full of fangs over here."

Jenny stopped at a display of mannequin heads wearing wigs.

"What kind of hair would a zombie vampire girl have?" Jenny asked.

"Green," he said.

Jenny smiled and lifted a glittering, kind of punkish green wig from a head. She tossed it on and looked at herself in the mirrored wall.

"It would look good with this." Seth gave her a giant tube of green glow-in-the-dark face paint.

"I'll be a glowing green zombie vampire," she said.

"I'll do that, too, if you can do my make-up," Seth said.

"Yeah, I could sculpt something horrible from your face."

"Thanks," he said. "This'll be my best costume since Oscar the Grouch in fourth grade."

For the lock-in, Ashleigh told the Hospitality Committee she would bring the punch herself, at her father's request, since there had been problems in the past with kids spiking it.

Ashleigh and Cassie drove all the way to Greenville to visit an organic herb shop that had the ingredients she wanted. She'd read about them in a book that claimed to tell the ingredients of witch's spells. They included ginseng, cinnamon, clove, a certain chili pepper, and some things that Cassie had to read to the clerk from a list.

On Saturday, Ashleigh mixed these in with two big cans of Hawaiian Punch. Then she reached her left hand into the punch bowl. She imagined her special energy pouring out through her, into the liquid. She stirred the bowl for an hour with her bare hand.

It had taken most of another hour to scrub away the red punch stain.

Ashleigh and Cassie were going as angels, with robes custom-made by the lady who did alterations and tailoring for Ashleigh and her parents. They wore luminous white make-up, with some gold and red coloring at the eyes and lips, matching the ribbons in their hair. And of course, feathered wings from the costume shop in Apple Creek.

She didn't know what Seth's problem was, but she couldn't really blame him for skipping the lock-in. None of the guys were doing it. The senior chaperones were mostly female, and the one senior guy that was volunteering, Larry freaking DuShoun, wasn't the type who had anything better to do. If Seth wanted to go to some stupid haunted house with his buddies, she supposed she could let that go.

But he'd been a real dick about it. And he hadn't let her touch him, that was the disturbing part. Like he knew about her power. He must have noticed how she just touched people and got what she wanted. How people responded to her and obeyed. That was Ashleigh's secret, and she didn't want anyone to know it, especially not a dumb boy like Seth. She didn't know how to handle somebody waking up and realizing Ashleigh's enchantment— nobody had ever done that before.

The Crusaders and their invited friends gathered at the church as they finished up their trick-or-treating around town. Ashleigh's father made an appearance, dressed as Zorro, and tossed out handfuls of candy to the teenagers, while telling them to have fun and stay out of the haunted parts of the church. He raised his own key to the church, and with a great flourish, locked them into the building from the outside.

Ashleigh had a complete set of keys to the building, and could let them out in case of an emergency, but they always pretended there was no way out. Ashleigh had possessed a complete set of keys to the church since sixth grade, when she had swiped her father's long enough to get them copied at the hardware store. That was how she'd been able to sneak a few kids into a church attic at a lock-in years ago, when Ashleigh had started the Halloween tradition of playing spin the bottle in the early hours of the morning, after the chaperones had gone to sleep.

Of course, she was too old to play that now, and as a chaperone, it was her duty to pretend she didn't know about it. It was going to be a pretty boring night for Ashleigh. Good thing Cassie was here, with two bottles of wine for when they "went to sleep" on their sleeping bags in a Sunday school classroom upstairs, where they would be away from the noisy kids.

"Everyone!" Ashleigh tried to speak over the din of costumed teenagers crowded into the church lobby. The other chaperones started clapping their hands for attention.

"Everyone," Ashleigh said. "Before we get started, I want to thank the Hospitality, Decorating and Activity Committees for all their hard work this year. This will be the best Halloween lock-in ever!" A lot of kids applauded. Others pushed impatiently at the double doors to the church basement. "We have a few rules, for those of you who are guests or haven't come to our lock-in before. Stay downstairs, the upper floors are off limits. Most areas you aren't allowed are locked anyway. Second, respect church property: no breaking, vandalizing or stealing. Duh. Third, no fighting, no kissing, no inappropriate behavior. Fourth, any problems or questions, come to a chaperone. Chaperones, raise your hands." Ashleigh, Cassie, Darcy Metcalf, and the gawky Larry DuShoun raised their hands.

"Now," Ashleigh said. "We always start with a prayer. So everybody take the hands of the person to your right and left." Ashleigh took Cassie's hand with her right, and some freshman guy in an insect costume's hand with her left. As she spoke, Ashleigh imagined her energy, her special power, coursing out not just into the people she touched, but through the entire crowd, hand to hand. She pushed it out as hard as she could, and she felt the crowd charging up.

"...help us to remember that being young is a fleeting, special time," Ashleigh was saying. "And this time will fade soon into the hard and cold life of adulthood. Let's celebrate the magic while we have it. Amen."

"Amen," the other kids said. Ashleigh signaled to Darcy, who nodded and unlocked the basement doors. She and Larry, the only male chaperone, led the horde of excited young people downstairs, nearly getting trampled in the process. Cassie hung back with Ashleigh, as did the freshman bug-boy, who still hadn't released her hand.

"Everything okay down there?" Ashleigh asked him.

The boy moved closer, his eyes big and glistening behind his yellow bug-goggles. "I like you," he whispered.

"Well, aren't you sweet?" Ashleigh tried to pull her hand free. She'd pumped a lot of Ashleigh-power out through this one, probably overloading him. He'd have a crush on Ashleigh for years. "Go on down with the others. You don't want to miss the fun."

"I'd rather stay with you," he whined. Cassie snickered.

"I'm too busy chaperoning," Ashleigh said. "Go on down with the others, I promise you'll have fun!" When he didn't let go, she added, "Maybe I'll hang out with you later. But only if you leave me alone right now."

The boy pouted, but he finally released her and trudged to the stairs.

"New boyfriend?" Cassie asked.

"Shut up," Ashleigh said. "He might be an improvement. At least he showed up."

"No big deal, about Seth," Cassie said. "Everett never comes."

"Seth does. Ever since I invited him freshman year."

"And now it's senior year." Cassie took Ashleigh's hand and smiled. Cassie was always touching Ashleigh, unconsciously sipping energy out of her. It got annoying. Now Cassie was pulling her to the stairs. "Come on. Let's go supervise."

They descended to the basement hallway, where there was a snack table with bowls of candy corn, orange cupcakes topped with plastic spiders and ghosts, and Ashleigh's huge bowl of red punch, to which she'd added ginger ale to make it fizz. Some partygoers were already dipping out cups of punch, while others were in a hurry to see the attractions.

Activity Room A had become "The Monster Maze" built of room dividers, large cardboard panels, and bed sheets. People had to find their way in the dark, through twists and turns among glowing spiderwebs and skeletons, and spooky music and sound effects, ending at the "Devil's Throne Room." Here, a sophomore boy dressed in a devil mask sat on an elevated chair under red light, welcoming the lock-in guests to an eternity in Hell. Then they escaped through a very narrow passage (two mattresses on their sides, in wooden frames, pushed close together) and out of the room. Cassie stood at the entrance door, daring the teenagers to take their "abstinence buddies" into the scary maze.

Activity Room B was the "Nightmare Nightclub," which Ashleigh had neglected to clear with her dad, or mention to him. A junior girl named Brenda Purcell, in a Bride of Frankenstein costume, played club music mixed with Halloween sound effects—groaning ghosts, clanking chains, howling wind. People could dance in there, and rest on cushions scattered along the walls if they got tired. Room B was Ashleigh's responsibility.

Larry DuShoun supervised Activity Room C, "Ghoulish Games," which included the games like bobbing for apples, and a series of boxes into which you'd reach your hand to feel things. Larry, in his scarecrow costume, would intone that you were now touching brains, eyeballs, intestines. Last year, Ashleigh had stuck Seth with that room.

Room D was split by a room divider: girls' sleeping bags on the left, boys' on the right. Darcy would sleep among the girls, and Larry among the guys, to deter any funny business in the early hours of the morning.

It didn't take long for Ashleigh's magic punch to cast its spell. Within an hour, there were kids coming out of the maze holding hands, their masks askew and makeup smeared. Many ended up in the dance room, either dancing much closer than Dr. Goodling would have approved, or openly making out on the cushions along the walls. Darcy complained about this outbreak of inappropriate, sinful behavior, until Ashleigh held her hand for a couple of minutes to dope her up.

"Wow, they didn't even wait for the chaperones to go to sleep," Cassie whispered, just after they checked on the maze, where the devil was locking lips with an elf girl. They stepped into the hall, and Cassie looked at the punch bowl. "What did you put in there? Ecstasy?"

"Just love, Cassie."

"Can I try some?" Cassie grabbed a cup, but Ashleigh took it away.

"No punch for us," she said. "But we need these cups. Let's go upstairs and open that wine." Ashleigh looked down the hall and motioned for Darcy Metcalf to join them.

"Do we have to bring her?" Cassie whispered.

"Don't worry," Ashleigh whispered back. "I'm pretty sure she's a lightweight."

Cassie sighed. "Okay. What about Larry Douche Long?"

Ashleigh looked into the games room. Larry DuShoun was kissing a junior girl in a cat costume. Kissing was doubly against the rules if you were a chaperone.

"Larry's doing fine," Ashleigh whispered.

"Hey, what's going on, my ladies?" Darcy asked.

"We're taking a break," Cassie said. "Come with us."

"Now? But, but—" Darcy sputtered as she looked around. "We can't leave now! The kids are out of control." Her voice dropped to a whisper. "Some of them are kissing with their tongues!"

Ashleigh put a hand on Darcy's arm and squeezed. Darcy's pupils dilated and she melted against Ashleigh, leaning her head on Ashleigh's shoulder. Ashleigh cast a look of disgust at her, and Cassie laughed.

"Come on, dear," Ashleigh said, nudging Darcy off her. "Let's go have a cup of wine. It'll be fun."

"Okay," Darcy whispered.

They went upstairs to the Sunday school classroom where Ashleigh and Cassie had laid their sleeping bags. Cassie unzipped her small suitcase, grimaced at Darcy, and picked the cheaper of her two bottles. She uncorked it and poured generous drinks into the plastic Jack-O'-Lantern cups.

"Wait," Darcy said. "We're not allowed…"

Ashleigh soothed her with another touch on the arm. The girl was turning into a real drain. "Do it for me, Darcy."

Darcy accepted the cup.

"To the most successful lock-in ever," Ashleigh said, and all three touched cups and drank.

Soon, Ashleigh and Cassie were giggling, while Darcy lay on her back, eyes closed, and moaned about being dizzy. Eventually, she was snoring.

Ashleigh popped open the second bottle and poured.

"To best friends," Cassie said.

"You said it." Ashleigh tapped her cup to Cassie's, and they drank.

Later, Ashleigh and Cassie slipped out into the hallway, wearing jackets, carrying their cups with them. Ashleigh unlocked the door to the narrow, winding staircase that led to the belfry under the church's steeple, where the bells rang on Sundays and holidays. They giggled more as they climbed, unsteady on their feet.

Ashleigh unlocked the trap door at the top and they emerged into a very cool early morning. They looked over the edge at the town. At three stories, the church bell tower overlooked everything.

"To Fallen Oak!" Cassie raised her cup, and Ashleigh repeated the toast, adding, "May it rot in Hell!" They broke down into laughter, falling on each other and sloshing wine.

When they recovered, Cassie looked out again at the rooftops.

"You know," she said, "We really rule this town. I mean, people do say that, but also it's true."

"I know," Ashleigh said.

"I mean, everybody looks ups to ush. Up to us. Everybody wants to be us." Cassie dropped to a conspiratorial whisper. "And they're scared of us."

"Yeah," Ashleigh said. "But who cares about this stupid little place? There are cities out there. Whole countries. We have to think bigger, Cassie. This is just the beginning."

"Just practice," Cassie whispered. "For when we do it for real."

"You know, I have a secret power," Ashleigh said. She took a deep breath. Her drunken mind, out of some stupid feeling of camaraderie with Cassie, and maybe tired of keeping it all secret, was about to make her spill.

Then Ashleigh's cell phone rang somewhere in her jacket. She fumbled around the pockets until she found it.

"It's Neesha," she told Cassie.

"Neesha, Neesha. Why does Neesha get to party with the boys on Halloween?"

"Duh," Ashleigh said. "My dad doesn't like black people in his church." Ashleigh clicked the green button. "Hey, girl, what's up?"

"Ashleigh," Neesha said. "Are you sitting down?"

"Sure." Ashleigh was actually leaning over the railing, looking down at the church roof.

"You are not going to believe what I just saw," Neesha said.

CHAPTER ELEVEN

Jenny and Seth put together their costumes at her house. Seth dressed in a natty old-fashioned tailcoat from the thrift store, looking very gentlemanly until Jenny used putty, latex and dye to sculpt his face into something green and rotting, with open bloody sores and cuts. She thought to herself that she could have done that without make-up—all she had to do was remove her rubber gloves and touch his face.

Seth admired his horrible face in the mirror, then popped in his fangs.

"I vant to zuk your blood." He waved his black-gloved hands above his head as he tried out his awful Transylvanian accent.

"You vish," she replied. She wore a lacy dress gone very yellow, with gauzy sleeves she'd made herself to cover her upper arms, black mesh stockings inside high black boots, and the cape and wig from the costume store. She would have virtually no skin exposed tonight, and that relaxed her a little.

She sculpted her own zombie-vampire face in the mirror, while Seth watched with admiration, until he got bored and started rolling a joint from her stash.

When Jenny finished her make-up, she peeled away her rubber gloves and put on the white lacy gloves from the Five and Dime. She unrolled them to her elbow. Ms. Sutland, delighted to see Jenny with a boy, had given her the gloves for free. She'd also had more pottery money for Jenny. Since Seth had insisted on paying at the mall, Jenny paid for everything at the Five and Dime. She didn't mention that a lot of the money actually came from Seth's mom.

Now the two of them stood in front of Jenny's mirror, with rotten faces and prominent fangs. Jenny had even covered her neck with make-up and latex, so there was nothing left exposed to the touch but her black-shaded eyelids and lips. If nobody touched her there, she would be fine.

"We really look like we just climbed out of our graves," Seth said. He took her white-gloved hand in his black one.

"And we've been in there a long time," Jenny said.

He chuckled around his fangs. Jenny drew the black hood over her green wig.

"Ve should drive a hearse," Jenny said.

"Ve haff only my car. Ve shall listen only to dead musicians."

"Vonderful," Jenny said. "Ze best kind. Ze night is ours, my love." Their eyes met in the mirror, and he squeezed her hand a little tighter.

They kept the top on Seth's convertible to protect their makeup. At the end of October, it was getting a little chilly, anyway.

They hadn't planned to stop at the "House of Hell" put on by the Presbyterians in Apple Creek, or even known about it. Seth saw the sign by the side of the road and insisted on checking it out.

They were admitted in groups into an old barn, which had been divided into rooms with small raised stages. Groups walked together from room to room, and were told to stay behind the ropes. Jenny and Seth were admitted in alongside a family with four children.

The door closed behind them, and they stood in darkness for a minute while voices whispered hurriedly somewhere to their side. Then a single spotlight fell on a two-foot-high stage, which was separated from the audience by a length of rope. A teenage girl reclined in a hospital bed onstage. She had something the size of a basketball under her hospital gown, making her bulge as if pregnant. Her bare legs had been taken from some department store mannequin—her real lower half was somewhere under the curtained hospital bed.

"Oh, I'm tired of being pregnant!" she said. "I want an abortion!"

"Did somebody say 'abortion'?" The spotlight was replaced with lurid red lights mounted on the far wall. Three people in devil masks and doctor's coats ran towards the girl waving pitchforks and hacksaws at the girl's swollen belly. She screamed and pressed down on it, and blood spurted out between her legs.

"Gross!" Jenny said.

The two parents shushed her. Their kids were gaping, and one of the boys looked ready to cry.

A sheet dropped between the audience and the performers. In the red light, on the sheet, devil-shadows waved their pitchforks around. The girl screamed and the devils laughed.

Eventually the lights went out, and the door to the next room opened. It was an extremely dull morality story about drugs, so bland, even when the devils showed up, that it washed out some of Jenny's horror at the first room.

In the third room, the scene opened with two boys lying in a bed. One put his arm around the other.

"Stop it, Peter!" the second one said. "How many times do I have to tell you? The Bible says it's wrong!"

"But it feels so good, Jim!" the first one said. "You'll like it if you try it."

"But it's a sin, Peter!"

"Just try being gay with me! You can always change your mind later!"

"Oh! Okay!" The boys pulled the blanket over their head and rolled around under it. "That feels good, Peter!"

Jenny giggled, drawing angry looks from the family, who seemed to be taking it quite seriously.

"Sorry," she whispered. Beside her, Seth was shaking, trying to hold in his laughter.

Predictably, devils ran out and snatched the blanket from the bed. They attacked the boys with whips and paddles.

"Ow!" yelled Jim, the unfortunate sucker who'd given in to temptation, as a devil paddled his behind. "That hurts! It hurts so bad when you're being gay!"

Peter sat up, now wearing devil horns himself. "Oh, it'll hurt a lot more...down in HELL!"

Jenny's laughter must have echoed through the barn. Seth broke down along with her.

"Y'all be quiet!" the mother shouted. "I want my boys to see this!"

They apologized to the lady and stumbled together into the fourth and final room. This one was pitch black, and extremely hot wind blew from it, probably from space heaters. Recorded screams and cries filled the dark room. A red light clicked on—a flashlight with a gel lens, held under the face of another guy in a devil mask.

"This is the fate of all doomed souls!" the devil said. "The final destination, the end of the line, the last stop on the track—"

Jenny and Seth were still trying to hold in their snickering from the last room.

"Learn ye well these lessons, those who still live!" The devil approached them now, waving his pitchfork around for emphasis. "The wages of sin is death!"

"That feels good, Peter!" Seth whispered out of the side of his mouth, and Jenny burst into fresh laughter.

"Okay, come on," the devil said to them. "I'm trying to teach these kids a serious lesson here—" He turned and pointed his pitchfork at the family, and Jenny saw that he actually wore a full red suit, complete with a pointed tail that hung from his butt and jiggled when he talked. At that moment, it was just the icing on the cake, and Jenny collapsed against Seth, laughing.

"Enough! That's enough!" the devil said, and now the three kids were laughing, too, at the devil's tantrum. "Guys!"

More devils came into the room from the other stages. Jenny and Seth were escorted out of the House of Hell, even ushered past the smiling people at the exits offering pamphlets on how to avoid the horrible fates you'd just witnessed.

Out in the parking lot, the mother of the four kids yelled at Seth and Jenny as they passed on the way to the car.

"We was trying to teach our children!" she screamed. "We hope y'all proud of yourselves! Your fault if they turn out butt-humpers!"

They hurried into Seth's car and locked the doors. He drove away, leaving the angry family far behind.

"That was totally romantic, Seth," Jenny said.

"Sorry."

"The audience was the scary part."

"So now you're ready for the real one in Vernon Hill," Seth said.

"Will this one actually be scary?"

"Supposed to be the scariest one in the state."

"Who said that?" Jenny asked.

"The sign advertising it."

The haunted house in Vernon Hill looked much more promising, a large old grain warehouse with a long line of people waiting to get inside. The line moved slowly, it turned out, because each couple or small group was allowed to enter separately.

"Good luck," breathed the skull-faced monk who took their cash. "Follow the ghostly glowing trail…it's your only hope if you want to survive."

He opened the door, and they entered the dark, narrow passage inside and followed the strip of glowing green tape on the floor, which was the only lighting. The door closed behind them, with the sound of squealing rusty hinges, a loud slam, then cackling laughter. Screams and undecipherable, wailing voices echoed from the darkness around them. Jenny and Seth saw each other as floating, disembodied zombie-vampire faces. If it weren't for their glowing green makeup, they wouldn't have seen each other at all.

The glowing strip of tape led them around a corner into a room lit by two stained-glass windows (or plastic, electric-powered imitations). They glowed onto a coffin on an elevated platform draped in dark purple. Velvet ropes kept Jenny and Seth from going too close.

There was a rusty scraping sound, as the lid raised just a few inches.

"Join me," a voice whispered softly from inside. Then a few pale fingers wriggled out of the slightly open coffin. They weren't rotten zombie fingers or pointy vampire fingernails, just normal fingers of a normal person.

"Join me," it whispered again. "It's so cold when you're dead."

Jenny drew closer to Seth. This was actually creeping her out.

There was a hiss right behind Jenny, and a rush of cold compressed air blew on the back of her neck, puffing up her green wig. She screamed and jumped against Seth, who laughed.

They left the room and followed the glowing tape into some kind of psychotic surgeon's operating room, hung with musty green hospital curtains. The surgical lights shown at crazy angles and cast huge, twisted shadows. The surgeon stood at the head of the table, in a blood-splattered surgical mask and smock, gleefully waving a scalpel and a meat cleaver. He cackled maniacally. Jenny thought the laugh had to be a recording, since no one could keep that up for hours.

On the operating table, among buckets and basins filled with gore, were two severed arms and one severed leg jutting up through the table, waving and wiggling around. They occasionally lunged at the surgeon, who struck back with the big cleaver. One arm grabbed the doctor around the throat. As Jenny and Seth leaned forward to see what would happen, a live head sprang up, screaming, from the bloody basin closest to them.

Jenny grabbed onto Seth again, or maybe he grabbed her this time. She was pretty sure he'd screamed when she did, too.

She kept close to him as they stepped through an open surgery cabinet, which led them to the next section of hallway. They heard whispering as they drew close to a barred door. When they reached it, a man with crazy hair and stitches all over his face jumped out against the bars. His arms were bound in a straitjacket.

"You gotta help me!" he whispered. "I don't belong here! I came in for the tour five years ago, and I've been a prisoner ever since. Help me! Come back!"

Around the next corner was a very rickety-looking wooden staircase, under dim, swampy lighting. A sign beside the staircase read: "The Cursed Covered Bridge – Do Not Enter!" The glowing tape led right up the steps, to a black-curtained doorway at the top.

"Ladies first," Seth said.

"Funny," Jenny said.

Seth went ahead of her. Each step gave a different creaking or cracking sound as you put your weight on it, and actually sank a little bit. It felt like the whole staircase would collapse at any second. Even the handrail wobbled.

At the top, they passed through the strips of black curtain and onto the covered footbridge.

It was just wide enough to walk single file. The roof, walls and floors all looked like they were made of old, rotten boards, with lots of knotholes and broken slats. The sound of a roaring river, and even the smell of dank moisture, rose from underneath the bridge. A very small amount of pale light shone in through the knotholes in the roof.

Seth held her hand behind his back as she followed him. Jenny kept her feet on the glowing strip of tape, drawing her shoulders in and avoiding the walls as much as she could. She knew that scary faces or pictures would pop up in some of the "broken" gaps in the walls, but there were way too many for her to guess where.

As they edged forward in the dark, more sounds joined the running water—splashing sounds, then groans. They were soft, complaining groans at first, then louder and angrier the further Seth and Jenny walked into the bridge. Jenny was beginning to think nothing would pop up at all, when a cold, wet hand seized her boot around the ankle.

Jenny screamed, and the groans rose louder, and were joined by shrieks and howls. Voices roared all around them. Strobe lights flickered through the holes in the roof. Then the whole bridge tilted to the left, throwing Jenny and Seth against the wall. Wet, decayed zombie arms reached through the left wall, pawing all over both of them.

The bridge tilted the other way, and they fell against the opposite wall, where more zombie arms grabbed at them.

"Come on, Jenny!" Seth grabbed her by both hands and pulled her up. The bridge rocked from side to side as they ran. Zombie arms reached for them from both walls and the ceiling.

They burst through the shredded black curtain at the end and stopped to catch their breath in the dark corridor beyond.

"This one," Jenny gasped, "Is much scarier."

They made their way through the rest of the haunted house, and Jenny only screamed one more time, when they were walking through a room full of spiderwebs, and a bunch of fat, bristly, wriggling, battery-powered spiders on strings had dropped from the ceiling, landing all over her.

They passed through a cemetery filled with dry ice fog at the back of the warehouse, through a gate, and they were outside. Jenny was still shaking when they reached his car.

"What did you think?" he asked.

"That was awesome." Jenny grinned around her fangs.

"You screamed a lot."

"You screamed more!" she countered.

"So we're going to that party," Seth said. "Unless you're too scared."

"Why should I be?" Jenny asked. "I'll be the scariest thing there. Even if I didn't have a costume, I'd still have Jenny pox."

It was a twenty-minute drive to Barlowe. Whatever they passed, Seth told her it was haunted. According to him, they passed a haunted barn, a haunted cow pasture, a haunted Waffle House, a haunted Department of Motor Vehicles.

When they reached Barlowe, Seth stopped at a railroad crossing, even though there was no train coming. He looked up and down the tracks.

"What are you doing?" she asked him.

"Just watching for the ghost train," he said. "This railroad is haunted."

She snickered and punched him in the arm.

The farm outside Barlowe had dozens of cars and trucks lined up in the front field. They followed the dirt road to park with everyone else. Then they walked towards a distant barn illuminated by firelight, from which they could hear old Metallica songs, played very inexpertly by a live band without anything electric. They crested a rise in the field and saw the band was set up in the back of a truck. At least a hundred people were dancing, or drinking from a keg at the front of the barn, or hanging out by a bonfire. Nearly everybody was costumed, so the crowd was a weird mix of aliens, gorillas, hoboes, superheroes, ghosts, a mummy, and lots of girls who'd managed to find or make skimpy, revealing costumes, whether they'd dressed as cats, fairies, or nurses.

"See?" Seth said. "Barlowe parties much better than Fallen Oak." He led the way into the crowd.

Seth high-fived a werewolf and a cowboy bandit, who pulled down his kerchief to show Seth his face. The bandit commented on how much the Fallen Oak Porcupines sucked, and Seth responded by insulting the Barlowe Bears. It seemed good-natured. Then the werewolf looked at Jenny.

"Who's your date?" the werewolf asked Seth.

Jenny wanted to open her mouth and correct him, tell him they were just friends, Seth had a girlfriend elsewhere.

"This is Jenny." Seth introduced her to the Barlowe kids.

"You like cider, Jenny?" the cowboy asked. "We got two full kegs over by the barn. My cousin's band sucks, but they get better if you drink."

"I like cider," Jenny said, though she'd only had the nonalcoholic kind.

"Then have your boyfriend take you over there and get you some."

"Yeah." The werewolf smacked Seth's elbow. "Go put some in her."

Seth grabbed two plastic cups from a sleeve and pumped them full. Jenny discovered she liked this kind of cider, too—it was sweet, and you forgot there was any alcohol in there.

Seth introduced her to one person after another. Jenny didn't remember their names, but she would always remember how it felt, being treated like a regular person among regular people. Nobody from Barlowe High had ever heard of Jenny Mittens. Here, she was just Seth's date, Jenny, and some of the Barlowe guys even tried flirting with her when Seth wasn't looking. She felt like she wore a disguise much deeper than her costume.

She drank more cups of cider, embracing the warm, glowing buzz it gave her, ignoring Seth's warnings to slow down. She even joined the dancing crowd in front of the stage for a little while. Even with her layers of costume, she was nervous with so many people moving so fast around her, and she quickly retreated.

Jenny was pouring her fifth or sixth cup of cider when Neesha and Dedrick approached her and Seth at the keg. Neesha was dressed as a go-go dancer with a giant rainbow wig, while Dedrick was the movie monster Candyman: black trenchcoat, hook hand, plastic bees glued to his face.

"I must be drunk already!" Neesha said when she saw Jenny and Seth. "Cause I think I'm seeing Seth Barrett with Jenny Mittens at this party."

"Guys, you know Jenny Morton." Seth put an arm around her shoulders, and Jenny felt absurdly protected by it.

Dedrick looked her up and down, raised an eyebrow at Seth, and swigged his cider.

Neesha stepped toward Jenny. "Jenny Mittens, Seth might be slumming with you tonight, but he will be right back up Ashleigh's ass tomorrow. Trust me. I've seen it plenty of times."

Jenny knew exactly what Ashleigh would have said in Jenny's situation. Emboldened by the cider, and Seth's arm around her, she said it aloud, even imitating Ashleigh's haughty, condescending voice: "Oh, look at you, Neesha. No wonder Ashleigh calls you 'the ugly one.'"

"She does not call me that!" Neesha charged at Jenny, but Dedrick restrained her.

Jenny let Seth take her arm and lead her away from the brewing fight. She sipped more cider as Seth led her around behind the barn, to a quiet area away from everyone. There was a wooden trailer half-filled with hay bales. Goats in a pen munched on grass, and one of them watched Jenny and Seth with curiosity. Overhead, the night was clear, and she could see a hundred thousand stars. The barn helped to block out a terrible rendition of "Enter Sandman."

Leaving the crowd made Jenny aware of just how drunk she was. She never drank. Now she felt exuberant, her stomach warm, her head floating like a big, smiling cloud, all her worries erased.

Seth boosted Jenny up onto the hay trailer, then climbed up to sit next to her. From this higher vantage, Jenny saw people in costume making out by the barn's back door, and against a fence, and in the field of puffy white cotton beyond the fence.

"Don't let Neesha bother you," Seth said.

"Who?"

Seth laughed. Jenny drained her cup and looked at him. She was feeling dangerously bold, overflowing with courage. It wasn't a familiar feeling, but she could certainly live with it.

"Seth," she whispered, "I've been thinking about you."

"What kind of things are you thinking?" Seth grinned.

"You said you weren't afraid of me because of your power."

"No. I'm not afraid of you because you're too cute to be scary."

"But I was thinking, what if you're right? I spread disease and you heal. So what if yours cancels mine, and we can touch?"

"Let's try it," he said.

"This is serious," she said. "You could get hurt. Or die."

"But if we can touch, that means we can make out, right?" he asked.

"Maybe."

"You want me to risk my life for maybe?" He grinned.

"No, forget it." Jenny made herself breath. The world was starting to swim. This was a bad idea. "It's too dangerous."

The tall, broad-shouldered werewolf stumbled around the back of the barn, and then puked noisily against it. He saw Seth and Jenny, raised his fist and cried "Seniors! Woo!" Then he staggered back to the party, shouting "I'm empty! Time to reload!"

"I want to try," Seth said. "You're the only person who can help me understand what I have."

"Are you sure?"

"Yeah. Let's do this."

Jenny scooted away so she could turn and face him.

"Take off your glove," she said.

"Do I get to tell you what to take off?" Seth pulled away the glove and held up a bare hand.

"Maybe next time." Jenny carefully removed the lacy white glove from her arm. Her heart pounded. It felt like she was about to lose her virginity. "Just one fingertip. For one second. Okay?"

"Okay, Jenny."

"Hold still." Jenny had to close one eye to focus on his finger, since she was seeing double. She reached her hand towards his. With a huge mental effort, fighting eighteen years of repression, she touched the tip of her finger to his. She felt a burning sensation at the contact, and quickly pulled away.

"Does it hurt?" Jenny asked. "Do you have the pox?"

"I'm fine." He smiled. "See? Told you I can't get sick."

"Do it again," she said. This time, Jenny laid her palm flat against his. She held it for one, two, three seconds, and then she couldn't bear it and pulled away. She stared at his hand, waiting for the sores to appear, the corruption to spread through his skin.

Nothing happened.

"One more." Jenny pressed her hand against his for five seconds, then ten, long enough to spread an infection deep into him. Every passing second made her more anxious, and she exhaled when she pulled away.

"What do you want to try next?" Seth asked. "Our feet?"

"Seth," Jenny said. "I can touch you."

"I told you."

"No, but I really can." She stripped away her other glove, and his, then laced their fingers together. It was a new sensation: human skin, not her own. It felt warm and soft, like good clay she'd been kneading for a long time. She trembled. "You're really okay."

"Are you? You look a little sick."

"I'm definitely not." Jenny ran her fingers up and down his arm. Worlds of new sensation opened to her. "I want to touch you so bad."

"I think I can deal with that."

She lay her hand on his cheek, where the latex had begun to peel. She pulled away strips of it, then stroked his bare cheek. His skin was soft, but a little grainy where he was starting to get stubble. She delighted in every texture. Touching him drowned out her other senses.

"You face feels nice," she said. She peeled off more strips of latex and makeup.

"Thanks."

"You touch me."

Seth peeled away lumps of latex and putty, and then touched the bare half of her face. His fingers sent shivers down to her feet and back up again.

Jenny's hands circled around Seth's face, to the back of his head.

"Seth—" she said, and then he kissed her. She held his head there and kissed his mouth over and over, as she'd imagined doing just after he healed her dog. Their fangs clicked together each time. The tip of his tongue slipped into her mouth, and Jenny wanted to scream with delight.

"Get rid of these." He pulled the fangs from his mouth. Then he pulled the fangs from hers, and she kissed his fingers as he did it. Then they were on each other again, Jenny kissing him hard, Seth's hands inside her cloak, all over her dress. She wanted to take off the dress and discover how his hands felt on her naked body.

"Seth," she gasped when she stopped for air. "We could do anything." Her voice dropped to a low, drunken whisper. "We could have sex."

116

Then she turned, leaned over the edge of the hay trailer, and puked out a huge amount of apple cider. It splattered on her dress and boots, and some of it got on Seth.

"Uh," Seth said, "Maybe not tonight."

Seth pulled into Jenny's driveway at three in the morning. He opened her door, helped her to her feet, then guided her slowly toward the front porch. Rocky gave a welcoming yowl that made Seth jump.

The porch light flickered on, and Jenny's dad came out. He hadn't shaved in days, and was drinking a tall Pabst Blue Ribbon. According to Seth's father, he was the best mechanic, repairman and general contractor in town, when he wasn't drinking.

"Jenny!" he said. "Where you been?"

"Uggh," Jenny said. Seth helped her onto the first step.

"She's not feeling great," Seth said.

"Wonder why that might be." Jenny's dad looked warily at Seth, and at Seth's car, as he stepped down to take under her other arm, so they could both walk her up the stairs. Seth noticed how carefully the man avoided Jenny's bare hands and head.

"This way." Jenny's dad led them into a living room that seemed cluttered and low-ceilinged to Seth. They lay Jenny on the couch. "You need anything?" he asked her. "Water?"

"Uggh," Jenny replied. "My stomach is…haunted…"

Her dad looked over at Seth. "Let's you and me go outside."

Seth followed him to the front porch, where he lit a Winston and hacked a couple of times.

"What did she have tonight?" he asked.

"Just apple cider," Seth said. "Lots of cider."

"No liquor? Pills?" He eyeballed Seth. "Coke?"

"No, sir," Seth said. "Just cider, I promise. I tried to make her slow down—"

"All right. And just what do you mean taking my daughter out someplace to get her drunk?"

"It was just a Halloween party. She wanted to go."

"Your daddy in town, son?"

"No, sir. He's in Florida right now."

"What I figured. You had my little girl up at your house?"

"No, sir. Just a haunted house and a party."

"Well, Jonathan, you sure are lucky. You coulda got yourself killed tonight."

"I wouldn't hurt Jenny." Seth wanted to tell him not to call him Jonathan, because he hated being called that, but he was pretty sure this wasn't the time to mention it.

"She mighta hurt you." Mr. Morton shook his head. "Now, Jonathan, I been around this town a while, and I understand some things. Like I understand if a Barrett boy goes around with a girl from the south side of town, he's only looking for fun. I happen to know your daddy some, which is why I ain't running you off with my twelve-gauge. Yet."

"Yes, sir," Seth told him. "I want you to know I really do like Jenny. A lot. I'd like to keep seeing her."

"It don't matter. Your family wouldn't stand for it. You gotta know that."

"I don't care what my parents think," Seth said.

"That's easy for a boy to say. Your parents got plans for you, and sooner or later you'll fall in line. That's what Barretts do."

Seth felt a flash of anger, but kept quiet. He didn't want to get any further on her dad's bad side.

"Now, I'm saying this for your sake and hers," Mr. Morton continued. "There's no good can come of you two running around. Somebody's gonna get hurt. Wish it weren't true, but that's how it is. So maybe it's best if you just get back in your fancy little Roadster there, Mr. Jonathan Seth Barrett the Fourth, and head on back to that house your great-granddaddy's bank built, and don't bother Jenny again."

Seth glanced in at Jenny, asleep on the couch, her face still zombie-green with the makeup. Then he walked down the porch steps. He stopped and looked back at Jenny's dad, intending to say something daring about how he wasn't going to let anyone stop him from seeing Jenny. But the older man just looked at him coolly, and Seth's nerves withered.

"Go on, now," he told Seth.

Seth climbed into his car. Rocky gave a sad yowl at Seth's departure, and Mr. Morton looked toward the shed.

"Coulda sworn that dog was three-legged," Jenny's dad muttered, and he stomped out his cigarette butt. "Getting old."

Seth backed out of the driveway, and he went on.

CHAPTER TWELVE

"I don't trust him," Jenny's dad told her.

Jenny was still lying on the couch where she'd slept all night. She wrapped an arm over her face to block out the hateful sunlight, of which there was far too much roaring in from the window.

"He's okay, Daddy," Jenny said. "Don't you work for Mr. Barrett sometimes? They're good people, right?"

"Too good for us, Jenny. Whatever he tells you, he's gonna be gone next year, and he ain't coming back for you. He'll meet all kinds of fancy girls off at school and marry one. I seen generations of Barretts in this town. I know."

"But that's a whole year away!" Jenny said. "Who cares?"

He sighed. "That boy's going to want things from you. You understand that, right? Things you can't give him without killing him."

"Daddy!" She almost told him about Seth's healing touch, how he had the opposite power from her, making him the only person who could touch her. But she'd promised Seth to keep his ability a secret, and so she kept her promise.

"It's true," he said. "And I worry what you might do to him on accident. And what would happen to you after that. We're lucky nobody ever tracked us down, after that night you was born and I had to burn down that poor doctor's place. Jenny, we kept this thing secret a long time. If we don't, they'll come after you."

"Who?"

"We been through this. People would panic. They might come and lock you up, away from everyone. Maybe kill you. Maybe use you for a weapon. I don't like the sound of any of that."

"What difference would it make?" Jenny snapped. "I'm already away from everyone. I never once felt normal until last night. And now you want to take that from me, too."

"I don't want to take nothing from you," he told her. "I'm thinking about your safety. And if you don't care about that, think about the boy's safety. And think about how his family's gonna react. Think what the town's gonna say."

"I don't care about any of that! And there ain't no town left to have an opinion. Daddy, this is my life. And I like him a lot."

"You don't think it hurts me to say this?" he asked. "It hurts me plenty. I wish you could do what you want. I wish you could go and date boys like a normal girl. I wish you could get married, have normal life…" His voice broke. He stopped and cleared his throat. "And Jenny, if you're going out, don't go drinking. You might stumble up, touch somebody—"

"Oh, please!" Jenny forced a laugh. She opened one eye, and sure enough, he was sitting in his recliner, can of Pabst in his hand. "You're really going to lecture me on drinking, while you sit there getting drunk?"

"I'm talking about careless." He walked into the kitchen and started banging things around. The sounds scraped across Jenny's brain, driving her headache deeper into her skull. "You ain't like other kids," he continued. "You got to be real careful—"

"I know!" Jenny screamed. "For the hundred millionth billionth time, I know that! That's all I ever think about. Do you have any idea what it's like for me, every second I'm alive?"

"To be honest, Jenny, I really couldn't imagine."

After a few minutes, he brought her a plate with his own favorite hangover food, toast and overeasy eggs, black coffee. He set it all on the coffee table in front of her. The eggs looked like they were sweating grease onto the plate.

Jenny ran to the bathroom and threw up again.

Ashleigh's cell phone woke her with its incessantly cheery ring. She and Cassie had barely managed to stay awake as they sent the younger kids home from the lock-in. They'd driven straight to Ashleigh's house in Ashleigh's caramel Jeep, and had collapsed on her bed without bothering to remove their costumes or make-up. Cassie still slept beside her, undisturbed by the ringing phone, her arm draped over Ashleigh's stomach, face nuzzled against Ashleigh's, sucking the intoxicating energy from Ashleigh even in her sleep. Ashleigh shoved her away, and Cassie rolled aside without waking.

The phone stopped ringing, but started again by the time she dug it out of her overnight bag. It was Seth.

"What do you want?" Ashleigh snapped.

"We need to talk, Ashleigh," he said. He sounded very serious. She didn't like the tone.

"That's right, Seth. I've got a couple things to ask about what you did last night."

"Now," Seth said. "I'm in front of your house."

Ashleigh hung up and ran to look out the window behind her bed, which looked out onto the driveway and the cobblestone walkway in front of her house. Seth was out there leaning against his car.

"Shit!" Ashleigh smacked Cassie's leg, and Cassie jumped.

"Ow!" Cassie rubbed the red patch where Ashleigh had slapped her. "That hurts! Bitch."

"Get up. Seth is here."

"Here? Now?" Cassie sat up, rubbing her eyes and yawning. "What time is it?" she asked through her yawn.

"Almost twelve." Ashleigh recoiled when she saw herself in the mirror. Her hair jutted in every direction. Her face was still stark white, and the smeared gold and red glittery makeup around her eyes and mouth looked more like a melting clown than any kind of angel. This would never work for a confrontation.

"Want to clean up first?" Cassie stood behind her, not looking much better, her angel wings bent.

"We don't have time." Ashleigh would have been happy to make Seth wait an hour or more, but she was pissed off and in a hurry to put him in his place. She walked into the bathroom. "Just fix the makeup and gel down the hair for a minute."

Ashleigh worked on it, covering everything with white and then refreshing some red on her lips. When it was Cassie's turn, Ashleigh grabbed her cell phone and queued up the picture of Seth kissing Jenny Mittens, so she could whip it out at the proper dramatic moment, preferably when Seth denied everything.

The image made her ill. Even the follow-up pic, of Jenny yarfing on herself, was cold comfort. Why did Seth have to choose the most horrible girl in school? It was very inconsiderate of Ashleigh's reputation. He could at least have shown taste.

She looked out the window again. Seth stood by his car, arms crossed. There was something she did not like in his pose. Something defiant.

"He's going to break up with me," she said.

"No way," Cassie said. "Not for Jenny Mittens. You're crazy."

"Look at him. He's not crawling over for an apology. He's ready to fight." Ashleigh glared at him. "I do not get dumped. Especially not for her."

"So dump him first," Cassie said.

"No way. Have you seen our selection of boys in this town?" Ashleigh asked, and Cassie snickered. "Besides, if I drop him now, then Jenny freaking Mittens will have him. That cannot be allowed. Imagine what people would think of me?"

"So the plan is…"

"Recapture him. Make him forget her." Ashleigh was staring holes into Seth's form below.

"How do we do that?" Cassie asked.

"Just trust the master," Ashleigh said. "All you need to do is answer the door."

Ashleigh went down the back stairs, because the big front stairs in the foyer could be seen from the tall glass windows around the front door. Ashleigh's house was full of open spaces, two-story rooms, and giant picture windows. Even the staircases jutted out way out into empty space before finding their way back to the floor.

Seth preferred to hang out at her house, instead of his, because hers was full of light and air. Seth's house was like a musty old tomb. You felt underground even when you were upstairs. Ashleigh liked that Barrett House was huge and full of expensive things, and that everybody called it Barrett House as if it were some important historical site. But she hated to be there, especially after dark, especially when there was nobody else in the house but her and Seth. If Ashleigh ever married Seth, that house was headed for some major renovation. Ashleigh would take down all the creepy-dead-ancestor pictures, to start with, and put up something nice, like a collection of ornate mirrors, or maybe a fancy painted portrait of herself.

Ashleigh crept through the dining room and waited behind the folding slatted doors, which opened onto the side of the foyer.

Cassie walked down the front stairs, taking her time, looking annoyed, making sure there was plenty of opportunity for Seth to see her and get focused on her, if he was looking into the house through the front windows.

As Cassie reached the foyer floor, Ashleigh stepped through the dining room doors and into the front corner of the foyer. She slid along the wall until she was beside the front windows, as far as she could go without Seth seeing her.

Cassie opened the front door.

"Come inside!" she called to Seth, who remained out on the cobblestone walk. He hadn't even come up the stairs to the front door.

"Tell Ashleigh to come out," Seth replied.

"Not happening," Cassie said. "We look like crap."

"I don't care."

"It's not about you. Do you want to come in or not?" Cassie said. "Because I'd really like to take a bath and go back to sleep. So just get out of here. We don't want to see you, and I don't feel like listening to you two fight anyway."

From her position just inside the front window, with her back against the wall, Ashleigh heard his shoes clomp across the cobblestones and up the stairs. Cassie stood aside to let him in.

"Where is she?" Seth asked. He was looking up the front stairs. Ashleigh crept up behind Seth and laid her hand on his bare neck. She willed her energy to flow strong and bright, then imagined arrows tipped with sharp red hearts striking all over his body.

The muscles in his back relaxed and he slumped as the defiance drained from him. Seth turned to her, his eyes half-closed, his mouth drooping in a goofy, drugged smile. She laid her hands

124

on both sides of her face. She had him, but now she had to keep him.

"Ashleigh," he sighed. "You're so beautiful."

"I know," Ashleigh said. "But what do we do about you? I mean, Jenny Mittens? Really, Seth? Why her?"

"I…" Seth's eyes shifted away. He worked his mouth slowly, and he looked like he was struggling to remember something important. "I…think…I like…Jenny…"

"Sh." Ashleigh covered his mouth. "You can apologize later. I'm just glad to see you. You missed a crazy night at the lock-in." Then she kissed him, pushing her power into him through her tongue. She turned her upper body a little from side to side, rubbing her tits on his chest. His hand slid around Ashleigh's waist and squeezed her ass through her gown.

As they kissed, her hangover dissolved and she felt fresh and awake. He always had that kind of effect on her, one of the main reasons she wanted to keep him. You could see people light up when he shook their hands. She suspected he had a little of her kind of power, though obviously much weaker, and he was too dumb to put it to use effectively. For that, he needed Ashleigh's guidance and direction. Ashleigh found him very useful. Trained properly, he could be a powerful servant, maybe even in a husband sort of role.

"Seth," she whispered. "I love you. How could you ever want to be with anyone else?"

"I couldn't," he whispered back. He cupped her breasts with both hands, and her nipples hardened inside her bra. Ashleigh was ashamed to think how much she wanted him back. He was the only boy she couldn't dangle on a puppet string, taking or leaving according to her whim. He had the irritating effect of actually making her crave him.

Ashleigh slid her hand down his stomach, to the front of his jeans. He was already stiff, but she made him long and hard with a little caressing.

"Do you want me to play with it?" she whispered against his mouth. She didn't wait for an answer, but found the zipper and slowly drew it open. Then she reached in and her fingertips touched him. She charged him with her special energy there, and he gasped. He kissed her harder, crushing her lips back against her teeth.

Ashleigh wrapped her fingers around it and pulled it out where she could see it. She stroked her fingertips along it, like petting an animal, then scraped it a little with her fingernails, which made him gasp again. She found herself getting wet and hot while she did it, and cursed herself. She was the seducer, not the victim, she reminded herself.

She wanted to really blow Seth's mind, break down whatever thoughts he had of (*that bitch Jenny Mittens*) wandering away from her. She never did more than this for him, using her hand. She wanted to give him more than that now, but she'd never put one in her mouth before, and she wasn't going to start today just to make a defensive move against pathetic little Jenny.

"Cassie, come here!" Ashleigh held out her hand.

Cassie stood by the open door, chewing her lip and watching them. Now she gave Ashleigh a confused, worried look, but she took Ashleigh's hand. Ashleigh poured energy into her, and imagined three arrows with red hearts thunking into her back.

Cassie's breathing quickened and her palm sweated against Ashleigh's. Cassie looked into Ashleigh's eyes, lovesick, then at Ashleigh's large breasts, then at Seth's bare cock.

Ashleigh laid her hand on the crown of Cassie's head and pressed.

"Get down there," Ashleigh said. Cassie sank to her knees on the foyer's blond hardwood floor. Ashleigh let a current of desire form between Seth in her left hand and Cassie's head in her right. Ashleigh pushed her head forward, making her take Seth in her mouth. She pulled Cassie's head by the hair, then pushed it forward again. She repeated this until Cassie was doing it on her own, Seth's hand gripping her red hair.

"Don't I always make you happy, Seth?" Ashleigh whispered. "No one else treats you like this." She started kissing him again. He pulled upward on her gown, and Ashleigh helped him, lifting it until he could lay his hands right on her breasts. He found her left nipple and squeezed and rolled it between his strong, warm fingers, and Ashleigh cried out. She was going to lose her mind if she didn't do something.

She grabbed Seth's hand and slid it down her belly and into the front of her panties. She occasionally made him do this, though she really didn't think he was very good at it, and preferred doing it

126

to herself while watching herself in the mirror. Right now, she wanted him to do it to her, clumsy fingers or not.

She positioned his fingers and moved them in little circles to show him what she wanted. It felt good, using his fingers like little tools she controlled. It felt better then letting him do it himself, and she continued it her way for minute before she let him take over.

She leaned forward, into him, and heard herself sigh. She pushed her tongue deep into his mouth. She slipped one hand under his shirt against his back, keeping him intoxicated with her touch. Her other hand found its way to Cassie's head to keep her in the energy circuit. Cassie made choking, gagging sounds as Ashleigh shoved her forward, gasped for air as Ashleigh pulled her back.

Ashleigh felt Seth's body shudder, and she held Cassie's head in place, making her swallow everything, keeping her there until Seth was done. Ashleigh suddenly yanked hard on Cassie's hair as her own hips jerked forward, and she came against Seth's fingers. Cassie screamed in pain.

Ashleigh sighed and leaned against Seth, wrapping her arms around him. Cassie slowly stood, wiping her mouth with the back of her hand, face flushed, dark green eyes glittering.

"See, Seth?" Ashleigh said. "I'm the best."

"You are," he whispered. His eyes were closed.

"And you'll never talk to Jenny Mittens again."

"Never," he agreed.

"Wait, I didn't get a turn yet." Cassie leaned herself into Seth's other side and kissed him on the mouth. She moved Seth's hands onto her chest.

"Don't be a whore, Cassie," Ashleigh said. She heard a car engine in the driveway. "Go play with your own boyfriend. Anyway, my parents just got home from church."

Jenny had never looked forward to school before. Monday morning, she slid down the window on her bus to breathe the cool, bittersweet scents of autumn. She admired the passing trees in their gradual, temporary dying, the sunset hues in all the leaves. She wondered how she might sculpt an autumn tree, the crooked branches, the rich colors. The trees could make you sad and hopeful at the same time. You knew winter was coming, but you knew it came every year, and it passed and there would be spring again. All the dying should make you appreciate life more, Jenny thought. Knowing she could kill any living thing with a touch, Jenny saw life as dangerously fragile (except sometimes her own life, which until now had seemed cursed and painfully long). The fall trees were living expressions of that, and it was her favorite season.

Jenny climbed off the bus with a smile on her face, and even kept it on for anyone she passed. Most people looked at her, saw her gloves, and then looked away quickly—or, pointed and started whispering and snickering to each other.

She breezed in through the front door and bobbed along in the stream of students until she saw the giant mitten. She stopped in the middle of the hallway and stared at it with growing disbelief. Other people flowed around her, some grumbling at her to move out of the way.

It was a big red mitten, made out of posterboard and hung over the hall like a banner. The words were in stenciled Magic Marker:

MANY MITTENS!
Give back this holiday season!
Donate old MITTENS, gloves, hats & scarves
to needy children!
MANY MITTENS provides for their winter!

Sponsored by Fallen Oak Student Council
Ashleigh Goodling, Senior President

Jenny felt like she'd been punched in the gut. As she walked further into the school, she saw more hanging posterboard mittens. Some said: DONATE TO GET YOUR NAME ON A MITTEN! with an example of a smaller mitten made of construction paper. The examples all read: JENNY DONATED MITTENS! Strings of blank construction paper mittens, all different colors, were hung along each of the side halls, waiting for the names of students and teachers to be written on them.

She noticed more of the kids looking at her and pointing or snickering, like the people outside. She was hearing "Jenny Mittens" a lot. The mitten posters naturally spurred talk about her among people, giving older ones an excuse to point out to younger ones the strange girl who always wore gloves, and stir up the various wild theories about why she wore them. Ashleigh had found an innocent way to surround Jenny with a very unwelcome kind of attention, all over school, from now until Christmas break.

Jenny wondered if Many Mittens was even a real charity, or something Ashleigh had created just for this prank, just to torment Jenny. "Many Mittens" even rhymed with "Jenny Mittens." That little touch had probably been Cassie's idea.

She'd expected repercussions for dating Ashleigh's boyfriend, but had not expected them this fast. It was only the night before last that Neesha had seen them together. Ashleigh must have been planning this already, Jenny told herself. Ashleigh hadn't really come up with the idea, and recruited people to make and hang the mittens, all in one day. If she had, then Ashleigh was much more frightening than Jenny had thought.

She stopped by her locker to trade out a couple of textbooks and drop off her lunch. She closed the door and tried to calm her stomach, which was knotty and goopy in anticipation of seeing Seth. His locker was her next stop.

She had no idea what would happen when she got there. Did going on a date and kissing automatically make you somebody's girlfriend? If so, did throwing up afterward cancel it out?

She didn't have any experience, and didn't have any friends to ask. She thought she understood romantic things well enough when she read them in books, but people in books made a lot more sense than people in real life. With real people, it was all odds and ends, and all you got was what you overheard, and it didn't sound all that much like what happened in stories. And people who had relationships talked about them in a language that was a little alien to her, since Jenny didn't have any of the experiences that their words described.

But now she walked with her head up and her hair back, feeling proud of herself in a way that was almost silly. She could be part of humanity now. She could touch, and be touched, and she could fall in love and be married and maybe even have children, because now she had Seth. The dark, lonely part of her life was over.

She turned the corner, and stopped in the middle of the hall for the second time that morning. Seth was there, surrounded by his friends. He had an arm around Ashleigh's waist, and was kissing her mouth hungrily.

Neesha spotted Jenny first. She smirked and winked at Jenny, then reached over to tap Cassie on the elbow. Cassie turned away from her boyfriend Everett and followed Neesha's gaze to Jenny. Cassie laughed and alerted Ashleigh, who turned from Seth to give Jenny a tight, satisfied little smile. Ashleigh even put her hand under Seth's chin and turned his face toward Jenny. Seth wore a blank expression, as if he didn't recognize Jenny at all. When Ashleigh lowered her hand, Seth started kissing her cheek and neck.

Jenny realized everyone had been right. Seth wasn't going to leave Ashleigh for her. Why would anyone abandon the pretty, popular girl for a sad little nothing like Jenny? She had been incredibly stupid (so said Cupid).

She turned and bolted down the main hall, and didn't stop running until she was in a bathroom stall, door locked. She leaned against the handicap rail, shaking with angry sobs, covering her mouth with a blue-gloved hand to muffle the sound. Out there, the whole school was laughing at her, for one reason or another. They'd gotten her again.

Obviously, Ashleigh had put him up to it, told Seth to ask Jenny out, to trick her and smash Jenny to pieces in one unspeakably horrible moment. He was her minion, sent to break Jenny's heart for Ashleigh's amusement.

She waited through the homeroom bell, and through the bell to start first period. Then she eased open the stall door an inch to make sure she was alone. She went to the sink, removed her gloves and splashed cold water on her face. She looked at herself in the mirror. Stringy, pale, hopeless Jenny Mittens, whom nobody liked, but everybody liked to hurt. She'd opened herself up to Seth and told him everything, and he'd betrayed her. She would never make that mistake again, with anyone.

Jenny went to her locker, took out her lunch, shoved her backpack inside, and slammed the door. The sound echoed up and down the empty hall. She headed for the nearest exit. The

slamming locker attracted a boy in an orange hall monitor vest who
ran after her and demanded her hall pass. She advised him to go and
fuck himself. At that moment, she would have killed anyone who
stood between her and the door. The monitor kid unknowingly
saved his own life by stepping aside and letting her out.

She walked into town, no longer drawing inspiration from
the colors of fading leaves, no longer feeling like she'd found the
place in the world where she fit. She wandered away from the
school, with no particular destination in mind. She eventually
walked to the town square and sat on a bench. Absentmindedly, she
took a few small white bites from the plump apple she'd brought for
lunch. She wasn't hungry. She only ate it because it was in her
hand. Her taste buds weren't working, and the apple pieces felt like
shredded paper in her mouth. She stopped eating, and let the few
bites she'd taken out turn brown.

From where she sat, she could see the cream-colored church
capped with its ultra-cutesy little bell tower and steeple, the tall
stained-glass mosaic windows, the perfectly kept flower beds. And
she could see the bank, dark and solid with its brown brick and its
stone trim, another cornerstone of the town. The church and the
bank, Ashleigh and Seth.

She felt like she'd lifted a little corner of a veil, and
discovered how she lived in a world that would be shaped by a
parade of people more powerful than her, people who would never
treat her like a human being. She'd always imagined life would get
better as she grew older. She would get wiser, discover things,
make friends, find the way to her own happiness and out of the
misery.

Now she realized it wouldn't happen. She'd been born
cursed and would die cursed and never understand why. There was
nothing to hope for, no happiness ahead.

She left the bench and walked slowly across the green
square, still holding most of the apple in her hand. She walked
down the alley alongside the church and glanced behind her to see if
anyone was watching. There was nobody. Even on Monday
morning, downtown Fallen Oak was a corpse.

There were three stained-glass windows on this side of the
church, each of them narrow, rectangular and two stories high.
They were just colored diamond patterns, not pictures like in some

churches. She knew these had been added as part of Dr. Goodling's renovation when he took over the church, before Jenny was even born.

Jenny stopped at the first of the tall windows. She took careful aim with the apple, then hurled it with all her strength. It struck dead center, shattering an entire pane of colored glass, most of which landed inside the church. Only a few jagged blue fragments were left clinging to the edges of the pane.

A burglar alarm erupted inside the church and echoed across the square. Jenny smiled as she walked away, her back to the courthouse and the figure of Justice.

Seth called her late Tuesday night, after midnight. When she heard him on the answering machine, she told herself she wouldn't pick up. Then she went into the living room to hear his voice. Then she picked up the phone before he finished his short, please-call-back message.

"What is it?" she asked him.

"Jenny! Hi!" he said. He sounded so cheerful that she wanted to strangle him immediately. "Are you okay? I haven't seen you at school."

"I was there a little bit on Monday," she said.

"Are you sick?"

"Yeah."

"Can I help?"

You could sound a little bit ashamed, Jenny thought. "I doubt it," she said. "What do you want?"

"I'm so glad I got you," he said. "I need to talk to you. Can I come over, or is it too late?"

"It's too late, Seth," Jenny told him. "Maybe Ashleigh's available."

"That's what I need to talk about. I'm having a serious problem with Ashleigh."

"You were getting along okay yesterday."

"That's the problem, Jenny. I really like you. I shouldn't even say it, but I really like you a lot. Didn't we have a good time Saturday?"

Jenny waited a long time, not even sure how to answer.

"It was okay," she finally said.

"Oh. Anyway, so I went to Ashleigh's house on Sunday, because I was going to break up with her. She's been creeping me out anyway, and I realized that I wanted to be with you—"

"And you changed your mind," Jenny said.

"You don't understand," Seth said. "She does something to me when I see her. It's how she touches you—"

"I really don't want to hear this." Jenny tried to sound strong and angry, instead of verging on tears. "Why are you calling me? What else does she want you to do to me?"

Seth paused a long time. "Nothing, Jenny. She hates you. She wants me to stay away from you."

"Then why don't you leave me alone?"

"Jenny, I think she's like us. With the touch. My healing and your...um, Jenny pox?"

Jenny hissed involuntarily, as if she'd been wounded, when he said that last word.

"Only, listen, I've been thinking about this," Seth said. "When she touches, she spreads love. Or something like it. Desire. That's her thing. Maybe there's someone else out there, a fourth, spreading the opposite of love, you know, hate or fear or whatever."

Jenny actually started to believe him for a minute. And she realized that she wanted to believe him, because it meant he hadn't tricked her, it hadn't really been another scam by Ashleigh, and Seth really liked her. For a moment, she let herself believe it. Then she remembered her promise to herself, not to trust anyone, and a lifetime's worth of carefully constructed shields and walls went up.

"Seth, look," Jenny said. "I know she put you up to this. Ashleigh doesn't have any special power. Just money, tits and an endless supply of bitch."

"She didn't, Jenny. This is the important thing. She did something to me on Sunday—her and Cassie both--and I only just recovered from it. I've been in dreamland for the last three days. It's hard to explain. It's like really, really good drugs."

"I'm glad she made you happy," Jenny said. "I have to go."

"Jenny, wait! I'm weak against her. I need your help. Please."

Again, Jenny was tempted to believe him. And again, she was not going to be suckered, especially not by Ashleigh and her pathetic followers.

"Seth, I can't help you," Jenny said. "You have to make up your own mind."

"But I don't control my mind when she's around."

"Next time, try." Jenny hung up the phone.

CHAPTER THIRTEEN

For Thanksgiving, Jenny baked a turkey breast in the oven, since there was no reason to waste a whole turkey on just two people. She also made stuffing from a box and cornbread from scratch while her dad cooked turnip greens with fatback. They ate at the kitchen table, while her dad stole glances over her shoulder to check the football scores on the TV in the living room. At least he'd turned down the volume for dinner. Jenny helped herself to a can of Pabst and drank that with her turkey.

Her dad told her how Mrs. Lawson's cat had gotten into a paint tray while he was renovating her garage, and left paw prints all over the garage floor in a shade that Lowe's called "Sunspot Yellow." Mrs. Lawson had decreed the paw prints adorable and wanted to keep them, so he hadn't needed to clean up the floor. But she did make Jenny's dad wash the paint off her cat, a much more difficult task.

Jenny told him some of the positive comments about Jenny's work Ms. Sutland had passed on from customers. They talked about the little wood-fired brick kiln they were building in the back yard, and Jenny's plans to take the pottery around to more stores in other towns.

When they moved on to the pecan pie, which her dad had made, a somber look appeared on his face. From his tone, Jenny could tell that he'd been putting this off the whole meal.

"Jenny," he said, "What are you thinking about doing when you finish school?"

Jenny took an extra long time chewing her bite of pie.

"Nothing," she said.

"What do you mean?" For some reason, he looked a little hurt.

"I can't go to college and I can't move to the city," she said. "I can't be crammed in with all them people. It's best I stay here in Fallen Oak, where everybody avoids me anyway. I can just get a job around here."

"They ain't no jobs around here, Jenny," he said. "Ask anybody. Lots of folks looking, too."

"So I'll keep taking the hours I can get at the library, and I'll make more things to sell. Ladies in town like my flowerpots, so ladies in other towns might, too."

"You're not going anywhere? You're just going to stay in Fallen Oak?" He gave her a weak smile. She could tell he wasn't very happy.

"I was planning to stay right here, if that's okay. Or were you gonna rent out my room?"

"No, this is your home, Jenny. But you ought to get out and see a little of the world when you're young. You can tell the folks who've hardly ever left town. There's something off about them.

"When I got out of high school, me and a couple buddies just got in a truck and drove west. Made it clear to Texas before we run out of money, and ended up taking six months to make it back. I guess Sammy never came back at all. Married that girl and moved to Oregon instead. You ought to at least do something like that, Jenny, travel around and see some things."

"But I don't have friends, Daddy. Too dangerous, remember? Just like you taught me." She stood up, her eyes stinging a little, and took their plates to the sink. "I don't want to talk about this no more."

She turned on the faucet and began scrubbing dishes so she couldn't hear him if he tried.

Later, a few of his buddies from McCronkin's came to watch football in the living room, drinking and smoking and yelling at the TV, since McCronkin's was closed Thanksgiving. They were in their late fifties and sixties, working guys like her dad who were alone for the holidays, divorced, widowed, or just plain never had anybody. Though her dad wasn't quite fifty, he looked shockingly like them, going gray and his face worn down with care, just reaching for that next drink to get you through that next hour of being alive and alone. She tried to imagine herself at his age-- probably alone in this same house, probably not even noticing it was a holiday. She couldn't even have a bunch of cats to keep her company.

Jenny went into her room and played a scratchy record by June Carter and Johnny Cash, while rolling herself a Thanksgiving joint on the faded, water-damaged album cover. June and Johnny looked young and full of life in the old pictures. She remembered how they'd been towards the end, old and worn out but still in love with each other. How Jenny cried when June Carter died, and how Johnny couldn't live without her and went to join her. It had been an epic tale of love and loss to Jenny, who'd still been young, but had grown up listening to the old records all her life. The records, along with some clothes and a vintage sewing machine, were her mother's legacy to her.

A framed picture of her mother hung on the wall of Jenny's bedroom. It was just a snapshot, Miriam in a cowboy hat and sleeveless checkered shirt, maybe twenty-two years old. She held a bottle of Bud Light high in the air like a trophy, and a big, open smile like she was cheering. She had Jenny's black hair and blue eyes, but somehow it was all much prettier on her mother, in Jenny's opinion. In the picture, she was surrounded by friends at McCronkin's, which must have had a younger, wilder crowd back then.

Jenny didn't know if she believed in heaven, or the afterlife, or anything like that. She found it hard to believe in a God who would pick Dr. Maurice Goodling as his spokesperson. Or take Jenny's mother away the moment Jenny was born. When she was a little girl, she liked to pretend her mother was an angel looking out for her. Now she wondered whether the woman would care at all about the child who'd killed her.

Jenny put the joint in her jacket pocket and tiptoed out the back door. She whistled, and Rocky trotted along with her into the woods, where enough leaves had fallen to let big patches of sunlight through. She made her way to her boulder and climbed up to her spot. She struck a match, got the weed burning, then lay on her back and smoked.

She looked up at the sky, which was clear of clouds and full of a gorgeous sunset that was starting to burn out into purples and blacks. She thought about Seth, lying beside her right here. Was it really possible that their time together was fake?

Ashleigh couldn't possibly have been responsible for the rabbit, for Rocky dashing out into the street, for Seth stopping to heal him, for Seth's immunity to Jenny pox. All of that was beyond Ashleigh's capability, unless Ashleigh was some kind of witch. Those things had been real, not Ashleigh's manipulation.

But Seth chose Ashleigh, Jenny reminded herself. There was no point in smashing up her own heart by thinking about him, and about things that could have happened, had almost happened, if only the world had been slightly different.

She smoked her joint, watched the remaining leaves rustle in the wind and spin down around her, and tried to empty her mind.

Ashleigh sat at one of the rectangular tables in the town library and studied the Napoleonic Wars for her AP World History final. She enjoyed reading about the little general who had seized control of Europe, making every royal family pee their thrones.

The library itself was small and occupied the bottom floor of an office building. The upstairs were shared with a lawyer/realtor (Dick Baker, The Attorney/Realtor You Trust, said his advertising over toilets around town) and Dr. Carson the dentist.

There were free-standing bookshelves to supplement the shelves lining the walls, and four tables with hard plastic chairs. There was also a miniature table and chairs in the corner that served as the children's section. The librarian sat at the checkout station reading *Anna Karenina*, coughing and squirting her throat with cherry Chloraseptic, the smell of which filled the room. It was raining and thundering outside, and the library smelled like mildew and sick children.

Ashleigh despised the public library—not only was it cramped and smelly, but you could also run into Jenny Mittens there, shelving the books for what had to be a pathetic amount of money.

Ashleigh was only here to keep watch on Darcy Metcalf, who studied at another table. Darcy was not only her pet religious busybody, the one Ashleigh could stick with the tedious jobs. She was also Ashleigh's main competitor for the title of class valedictorian. Ashleigh did not intend to lose that competition.

Ashleigh stood and stretched, as if taking a casual break. A couple of geeky sophomore boys at the library's two computers eyed her as she did this, and Ashleigh smiled at them. You never knew who might be useful. She walked past the two boys, winking at the marginally cuter one, who looked like he might suffer a stroke in response. She stopped at Darcy's table.

"What's up, Darcy?" Ashleigh gave her a big smile.

Darcy shook her head and leaned back. "Calculus is killing me. I feel like I've been faking it all semester. I know what equations to plug in, but it's like I don't really understand what's going on. Don't you hate that?"

"Yeah, I'm dying for finals to end," Ashleigh said. "I need a Christmas break."

"Me, too!" Darcy gave her a big, stupid smile, as if they were bonding over this rare trait of preferring vacation to school.

"To be honest," Ashleigh dropped her voice to a low whisper. "I need to talk to you about the Crusaders."

"Oh!" Darcy laid down her pencil and straightened up in her chair. "What is it?"

"Well..." Ashleigh glanced around with a reluctant expression, then sat in the chair next to Darcy and spoke in an even lower whisper. "Darcy, who is your abstinence buddy?"

Darcy drew in a sharp breath. Ashleigh knew the answer already—Darcy didn't have one. Like more than a dozen other girls, Darcy had been too shy or unwilling to actually approach a boy to talk about abstinence. She'd skipped the meeting where girls and boys were paired up to discuss their values about sex. Ashleigh had not bothered any of the other girls who didn't participate, but Darcy didn't know that.

"I don't have one," Darcy confessed in a low, shamed whisper. He eyes dropped to the open pages of her AP Calculus book. "I'm sorry, Ashleigh. I messed up."

"Why not?" Ashleigh asked, in her most chipper and innocent voice. "You know, it's very important to have somebody

you can talk with, especially with all the temptation out there. I
wish I could be that buddy to everyone all the time, but I just can't,
Darcy."

"Ashleigh…" Darcy's lip quivered. "It isn't a problem for
me. Guys don't try things, so there aren't temptations." She took off
her glasses and rubbed at her wet eyes. She made herself return
Ashleigh's unwavering smile. "Sorry, Ashleigh. I didn't mean to be
a spaz."

"Oh, no, you're not a spaz," Ashleigh said. She laid a hand
on Darcy's and looked her in the eye. "I think I know just what you
need. A date."

"I don't know. Maybe after finals—"

"I'd say this is an emergency, Darce. I had no idea about
your problems with boys," Ashleigh lied. "Listen, Darcy. I am a
total matchmaker. Any guy in school, I can get him for you.
Whoever you've fantasized about. Just give me a name. Anybody
but Seth, naturally."

Darcy snickered and blushed at the word "fantasized."

"Come on," Ashleigh said. "It's okay to tell me."

"It's stupid."

"Nothing's stupid. I can make anything happen."

"Okay." Darcy glanced around, as if either the librarian or
the sophomore boys would be interested in Darcy's secret crush.
"What about," and now she leaned to whisper right in Ashleigh's
ear, "Bret Daniels?"

"Really?" Ashleigh considered it. Bret was handsome
enough, in that dark hair and brown eyes sort of way, and had that
loud animal stupidity some girls took for confidence. He was dull,
but not hopelessly stupid. Ashleigh had encouraged him to become
treasurer because he needed to pad his college application, and she
knew he'd be too indifferent to oppose her on student council. He
had also slept with at least fifteen girls Ashleigh could name.
Ashleigh would barely need to use her power, just point him in the
general direction of Darcy's underpants.

"Stupid, huh?" Darcy asked.

"No way. That's easy, he's a friend of mine. I will
definitely set you two up. And I promise to act like it was all my
idea. That's not really lying, because it is kind of my idea, isn't it?"

"Yeah! Okay, right after finals, this Friday!"

"Sure. But you want to meet him and kind of hang out before the vacation. Trust me, the psychology will be all different if you wait."

"But I have to get an 'A' in Calculus or my whole GPA is wrecked," Darcy said.

Ashleigh pretended to give this some deep thought. Then she said, "I know! He's in my history class. I'll have him come study with me tomorrow night, and you'll be here. I butter him up and then I bring him over. Library romance, Darcy!"

"I don't know." Darcy looked very nervous. "That's a lot to think about…"

"So don't think about it, do it! That's what life is about, Darcy." Ashleigh rubbed Darcy's mousy, frizzy hair and cupped Darcy's face in her hand. "Let me do this for you. Please. All you ever do is work. It's your senior year. Don't you want one nice memory?"

"Okay, Ashleigh." Darcy gave a slackened, dopey smile.

"Good! Perfect! This will be so great, Darcy!" Ashleigh managed to squeal.

The librarian shushed them, then coughed and spurted more Chloraseptic.

The next day, as promised, Ashleigh told Bret Daniels to meet her at the library. He'd had other plans, but Ashleigh was holding both his hands when she asked, and she kissed him on the cheek, and that was that.

She waited outside and approached Bret while he was still in his car, a very old, very avocado-colored GTO. She handed him a cut-glass bottle of some expensive tequila, which she'd swiped from the copious liquor cabinet at Seth's house.

"What's this for?" he asked.

"Just thanking you for all your help on student council this semester," Ashleigh said. "I know you didn't really want to do it."

"Nah, you made it easy, like you said. Wanna do a shot?" He patted the wool-coated passenger seat of his GTO. "We can go for a ride if you want. I know this place with a nice view of the lake—"

"No, that bottle's for you, for later. May as well leave it in your car," Ashleigh said. "Come on, I want to get ready for this test, and I'm already sick of studying."

Darcy was inside, at the first table, punching rapidly on her big Texas Instruments graphing calculator. As Ashleigh had recommended, she dressed in a tight, low-cut shirt. Darcy had protested she was too fat to wear such things, and Ashleigh had replied that if she showed enough cleavage, Bret wouldn't look much further.

Ashleigh gave her a friendly wave as she led Bret to the last table, near the back.

Ashleigh and Bret actually did study history for about twenty minutes, to brush over a couple of dates and names Ashleigh was unsure about. For the most part, she absorbed history without any effort, soaking up all there was to know about wars, emperors, dictators, how to conquer and rule. It delighted her to study things like that. After Ashleigh was through studying for history, she made her move.

"See that girl over there?" Ashleigh whispered to Bret. When he turned to look at Darcy, Ashleigh wrapped her hand around his wrist and pumped the Ashleigh-energy, and she imagined stabbing him in the chest with a heart-tipped arrow.

"Darcy Metcalf?" he asked, with a husky note of admiration in his voice.

"Yeah," Ashleigh whispered. "Want to hook up with her?"

"Oh, yeah. I never saw how hot she was before." Judging by Bret's past conquests, this put Darcy below a very low bar.

"That's right," Ashleigh whispered. "She fantasizes about you. She told me. You could probably nail her tonight if you feel like it."

"Yeah," Bret said. "Good idea."

"Come on." Ashleigh took his hand and led him to Darcy's table. "Hey, Darce, got a sec?"

Darcy looked up with terror on her face, clearly too nervous to speak. Ashleigh put a hand on her shoulder and rubbed her fingers against Darcy's neck. She poured energy into both Darcy and Bret, letting herself be the connecting wire.

"Have you two met?" Ashleigh asked.

"We've had classes together." Darcy smiled up at him. He looked down the front of her shirt. Ashleigh felt the charge sinking in on both sides, the growing mutual attraction between them. She visualized each of them getting struck with a dozen of her imaginary heart-tipped arrows.

"Why don't you invite him to sit by you?" Ashleigh suggested to Darcy.

"Oh, yeah." Darcy gave one of her goofy, repellently gummy smiles, reeking of Listerine. She pulled out the chair next to her. "Bret, want to sit with me?"

Bret did, very much.

As they started talking, Ashleigh slipped back to her table. She switched to studying for her AP Biology final, which she really did need to do. When she looked up again, they were talking with their faces close together, their hands on each other's arms and legs.

The next time Ashleigh looked, they were kissing, Bret's hand way up inside Darcy's thigh. The librarian was either too absorbed in Tolstoy to notice, or too apathetic to say anything.

When Ashleigh looked up a third time, they were both gone. She gave a tight, satisfied little smile and went back to studying. Finals began tomorrow. It was no time to goof off.

The next day, Darcy didn't make it to school until two of the three exam periods were over. Her hair stuck up in clumps, she wore yesterday's dirty clothes, and she reeked of tequila and sweat. At one point she was leaning against her locker, crying hard, knowing her GPA was blown. Darcy was too busy with her meltdown to notice when Ashleigh passed by, so Ashleigh didn't stop or say anything to her. She snickered at the grass stains on Darcy's jeans and the little twig snarled in the back of her hair.

Ashleigh aced her own exams, that day and the next.

CHAPTER FOURTEEN

In the days leading up to winter break, Jenny kept the kiln in her back yard smoking. She was pushing to get more pottery out in time for Christmas shoppers. She brought them down to the Five and Dime about two weeks before Christmas. While she was there, she shopped for a gift for her dad. She browsed through the secondhand coats, looking for something she could tailor and embellish with new buttons and bits of fabric. Old Christmas carols played from a cassette, and the whole store smelled like the plate of homemade sugar cookies by the cash register.

Jenny gave Ms. Sutland a Christmas card she'd made from stationary and scraps of lace and ribbon. While Ms. Sutland oohed over it, Jenny noticed a collection of snowglobes now on display on the front shelves, near her flower pots and mixing bowls.

"When did you get these, Ms. Sutland?" Jenny asked.

"Somebody dropped off a whole box," Ms. Sutland told her. "Just in time for the season, too. Do you like them?"

"Yes." Jenny shook one that held a little cottage with bright yellow windows. A snowman drove a sleigh in the cottage's front yard. It was lovely and silly at the same time. Another globe had a big orange Siberian tiger stalking among fir trees hung with wrapped presents. It would be a perfect extra gift for her dad, since it looked like it could be the Clemson tiger.

Jenny brought both the snowglobes to the counter, and then added the natty brown overcoat she'd picked out for her dad.

"That coat's awful big for you, Jenny," Ms. Sutland joked.

"It's for my dad." She gave the tiger snowglobe a shake. "This one, too. The other snowglobe is for my room."

"And what about your little boyfriend?"

"He's not my boyfriend. We just had one date."

"That's a shame." Ms. Sutland placed the two snowglobes into a paper bag. "It didn't look like a first date to me. It looked like you two had been together for ages, when you were shopping for Halloween."

"Well, he went back to his old girlfriend, so…" Jenny shrugged and took out her money.

"And you're just going to let her do that to you?"

"Let who do what?" Jenny asked.

"The other girl." Ms. Sutland rang up the sale. "You're going to lie down and let her take him back?"

"It's his choice," Jenny said.

"And it's your choice what you do about it. If it's something you want, it's worth fighting for."

"What if he doesn't want me?"

"I saw how he looked at you, Jenny." Ms. Sutland gave a wry, wrinkled grin. "He wants to be with you, even if he's too dumb to understand that. Sometimes a man needs a woman to show him the way. Lots of times, to be honest."

"But she's too pretty," Jenny said. "And she's popular, and—"

"Don't go doing her work for her, now," Ms. Sutland scolded Jenny. "You take the fight to her. Maybe she wins, maybe not. But don't let her beat you in your own head."

"Okay," Jenny said, but only to hurry along the conversation, which was growing uncomfortable and embarrassing. She reached for the overcoat, but Mrs. Sutland held onto it. Her green eyes, a little cloudy with age, stared intently into Jenny's.

"Now you listen to me, Jenny," she said. "You won't regret trying, win or lose. But you will regret not trying. Next thing you know, you'll be a lonely old lady who don't stop talking about the one that got away. Then no one will want to have tea with you."

Jenny took all this in, remembering the lonely future she'd imagined for herself on Thanksgiving.

"But what could I do?" Jenny whispered.

"That's for you to figure out, Jenny. I don't know what you kids are about these days, with all your funny shoes and hair. All I can say is do it soon, because time moves a lot faster than a youngster like you would believe. Day after tomorrow, you'll be my age, looking back on your life instead of ahead to it. Trust me on that, Jenny."

Jenny nodded. "Thank you."

"Don't forget to take a cookie."

Jenny picked out an angel-shaped sugar cookie with gold and red sprinkles. She thanked Ms. Sutland for it, and bit its head off as she walked to the door. It was soft and delicious.

"Merry Christmas, Jenny!" Ms. Sutland called after her. "And tell your daddy I said the same to him."

"I will, Ms. Sutland. Merry Christmas." The cluster of bells jangled as Jenny pushed the door open into cool, crisp air outside.

"Jenny!" Ms. Sutland called after her. Jenny turned back to see the elderly woman's impish grin. "One more thing. Be spectacular. Make the boy see how foolish he was to walk away from you."

Jenny brought two cardboard boxes of decorations down from the attic. She hung a strand of fat colored lights across the front porch and a wreath on the front door. Inside, she set out what they had on tables and countertops—a Rudolph figure with a light-up nose; a Santa Claus in his sleigh with his boots propped up, taking a nap; a little nativity scene Jenny had made many years ago out of popsicle sticks, cotton balls, and pipe cleaners. There were some ornaments, including a big plastic snowflake frame with an old picture of both her parents, but they never put up a Christmas tree because her dad said it was a waste of a living thing. So Jenny hung ornaments on the walls and from the ceiling instead.

She tacked the big plaid stockings to the mantle, one labeled "Jenny" and one labeled "Daddy," both labels drawn by her with glue and glitter. She decided to make one for Rocky, too.

As she decorated, she turned over in her mind the things Mrs. Sutland had said to her. Jenny couldn't really believe that the time she and Seth had spent together was really just an act, put on by Seth while he tricked her. On the other hand, she found it even more difficult to believe that Ashleigh, too, had an unusual power, one that made people feel love. It sounded like a lot for just one little town way out in the country.

While Ashleigh did seem to wield some kind of power over Seth, Jenny didn't see any reason to think it was supernatural. The real explanation was probably a lot more down to earth, and could be found inside Seth's boxer shorts.

Mrs. Sutland had a point. Boys could be stolen, and stolen back. It happened in movies all the time. If what Jenny had seen in him was even a little true, he might be worth one more try.

She wouldn't see him until school started, which was two weeks (an eternity) away. She could call him and invite him over, give him one more chance, but that didn't seem like the best way. It was the opposite of spectacular.

Ms. Sutland's advice inspired Jenny's crazy idea. Each year, the Barretts had a lavish Christmas party, attended by all the big people in town and guests from all over the place. Their house would be open, and Seth would be home, and Jenny would have her chance to be spectacular.

The Mortons weren't invited, naturally, but Jenny knew the date of the party—this Saturday, a little more than a week before Christmas. She knew that because her dad was at Barrett House right now, helping to install new lighting and make some fixes before the big event. If Mr. Barrett was in from Florida yet, he'd send her dad home with a big bottle of good Scotch.

Jenny went into her dad's bedroom closet and found her mother's jewelry box on the back shelf. Jenny hadn't opened it in years. She blew dust from the hand carved roses on the lid, then gently raised it up.

She saw her mother's wedding ring, gold-plated with a microscopic diamond. She touched it briefly, felt a rising sense of loss, and quickly turned her attention to the other compartments. She found what she was looking for, the silver necklace with sapphires, and the matching earrings. Jenny lifted these out, admired them for a little while, then carried them into the kitchen. She cleaned them until the silver glowed and the sapphires twinkled like tiny blue stars.

She returned to the closet and took down one of her mother's two good dresses, the one that wasn't her wedding gown. This dress was a shade of blue her mother had clearly chosen to match the sapphires. All the blue was aimed at bringing out Miriam's eyes, the same eyes Jenny had inherited.

Jenny spread the dress and jewelry across her bed. She would need to spend time at the sewing machine, bringing the dress in to fit her, and she saw a couple of alterations that she thought would improve it. The dress dipped down in the front, and way down in the back, so she'd need something extra to protect people from her skin. And she would need shoes, since her feet were two sizes larger than her mother's. But she could make it work.

When her dad arrived home, Jenny asked him a lot of questions about his day, pretending she was just interested in how the inside of Barrett House looked, which was a frequent topic of gossip around town.

"Got the inside all squared away," he said. "The problem's outside. That damned fountain. Every December, I'm out there scraping away ivy and trying to get that pump going again. And every year this pipe or that pipe's clogged or broke."

"What about the security guard?" Jenny asked. "Does he have a booth?"

"What do you mean?"

"Isn't there some guard or somebody checking invitations? Making sure nobody sneaks in?"

"Not that I know of. They don't have no guard booth, Jenny. Where'd you get that idea?"

"I always imagine one inside that gate," Jenny lied.

"They usually got valets to park the cars," he said. "I guess they feel safe enough just having Chief Lintner at the party."

"What kind of food do they have at their parties?" she asked, then listened indifferently while he speculated at length about the caterers and the open bar.

Later, Jenny went outside to start her regular jog with Rocky. She stopped and considered the old Dodge Ram for a minute. It was mammoth-sized, noisy, and stained with years of mud and rust. Jenny imagined herself driving up to the front door of Barrett House and handing her keys to the valet. The old truck wasn't exactly going to make the impact she wanted. She thought this over while running through the woods with her very fast, very four-legged dog.

The next day, while her dad was at work, Jenny opened the drawer in the end table by the couch. She pulled out the spiral-bound notebook full of yellowed paper that her dad had long used as his personal phone and address book. She flipped through carefully, trying not to rip the stiff old paper. It was somewhat alphabetical. It took her a long few minutes to find the number she wanted: Merle Sanderson – Home.

Merle was around sixty-five years old, one of the men who'd come to the house on Thanksgiving to drink and watch football with her dad. He was a heavyset guy with a big gray walrus moustache, who lived alone way out on Hog Willow Road, except for his five adopted stray mutts, each of whom, he liked to claim, had moved in under false pretenses.

Merle had once owned the garage in town where Jenny's dad had worked, in those old days when Jenny hadn't been born yet and the town was much busier. The garage hadn't survived the slow, constant drain as more people moved away over the years, taking their cars and their money with them.

Now Merle did the same work out of his house, and he was known for all the old cars parked every which way in his yard, most of them up on blocks. He didn't have many neighbors, just the McNare farm, and their house was far away from his.

Jenny steeled herself and dialed his number.

"Y'ello?" he answered.

"Hey, Mr. Sanderson," Jenny said. "It's Jenny Morton. Darrell's daughter."

"Well, hey there, Jenny." Merle's voice was full of concern. "Is everything all right? Your daddy okay?"

"Oh, everything's fine, Mr. Sanderson. I just was going to ask you a question, if you have time."

"I surely do. And nobody's hurt? Nobody in jail?"

"No, sir, nothing like that."

"Oh, all right. Then what's on your mind, Miss Jenny?"

"I was wondering, if I could ask…You see, I was needing a car for a little bit, and wondered if you had one I could rent. Just for a night or so."

"I sure don't," he said.

"Oh."

"I would not take a penny from your hand, little girl. Have your daddy bring you up and you can borrow it, free and clear."

"Really?" Jenny was completely surprised by the offer. "Oh, thank you, Mr. Sanderson! That's so generous!"

"Shoot, that ain't nothing. I still owe your daddy his last paycheck from sixteen years ago. Come by any day but Thursday, that's the Colombo marathon on the TV."

"Oh, we will! Thank you so much!"

"Wait until you see the car, before all that," he said. "Anything else I can do for you?"

"You've done a lot! Thanks!"

"All right. Call and let me know when you're on the way. I'll clean her up for you."

"You don't need to do that!"

"Bye, now." He hung up on her.

"Why you borrowing a car from Merle, again?" Jenny's dad asked as he drove along Hog Willow Road, which was just an unlined strip of blacktop surrounded by low farmland and pasture.

"Because there's this fancy dress party Saturday night," Jenny said. "It's the whole senior class, so I guess they figured it was easier to invite me than leave me out." She felt awful lying to her dad, but he would never knowingly allow her to crash the Barretts' party, much less help her do it.

"You could borrow the truck Saturday night," he said. "Just drop me at McCronkin's. I'll get a ride home."

"That's the thing, Daddy. I just thought it would be fun to show up in my own car. People kind of laugh at me when they see me driving this."

"I didn't know that," he said. "Why would they do a thing like that?"

"I don't mind it, really," she said. "They'll laugh at me for anything. I just thought—since it's in front of everybody at once—"

"And you just called him up and asked to borrow a car?"

"No, I offered to rent and he said I could use it free."

"See, that's just the kind of thing put the garage out of business," he said. "Merle's too generous with folks, and the garage was always in debt. Did you know he still owes me my last paycheck from sixteen years ago?"

Merle Sanderson's place looked a lot like theirs: way out from town, close to nobody, but with a front yard full of automobiles instead of appliances. The house had peeling paint and looked like it was leaning a little bit to one side.

Merle walked up the dirt driveway to greet them, rubbing his hands on a black-stained hand towel that had once been yellow.

"I'd shake your hands, but I don't recommend it," he said. A layer of dark grease coated his face and shirt. Jenny beamed at him, relieved she wouldn't have to risk one of her awkward, ducking hugs where she spent all her time trying not to kill the other person.

"Good to see you, Merle," Jenny's dad said. "I appreciate you helping out my baby girl—who, by the way, did not say a thing to me before she called you."

"Headstrong." Merle smiled and winked at Jenny. "Just like her mother."

"Thank you," Jenny said, and both men laughed.

"Come on over here, Jenny. See what you think." He led them to a long, boxy, two-door car, which was a dark red-brown color, except for the daisy yellow passenger door and the primer colored trunk lid. "She's mostly a 1975 Lincoln Continental, with other things there and here. Actually a pretty nice car. Worked on it off and on the last ten years. Wouldn't take her mudding, but she'll putter along fine on the road."

Jenny barely heard him. She stared at the car for a long minute, then leaned in the open driver's window to check out the interior. The seats had been upholstered with a ridiculous cheetah-print pattern, the front and rear dash with fuzzy white shag carpet, now faded and moth-eaten.

"—needed a new transmission, all of it," Merle was telling her dad. "Never did fix up the interior, still smells like that marijuhwana—"

"I love this car," Jenny announced as she stood up. "Can I really borrow it?"

"Why don't you climb on inside and see if it fits?" Merle asked. He opened the door for her, then closed it behind her when she slid into the driver's seat.

She admired the old-fashioned dashboard, all knobs and needles and vinyl paneling. The seat covers did smell like the ghost of water bongs past. She put her hands on the wheel, and Merle handed her the keys.

"Give her a crank," he suggested.

Jenny carefully inserted the key into the steering column. She put her foot on the brake and turned the key. The car grumbled for a few seconds, then coughed its way to life. She revved the engine.

"Well, lookie that," Merle said. "I finally made the interior look pretty."

Jenny blushed.

"You think you can handle that car, Jenny?" her dad asked.

"Oh, yeah." Jenny felt giddy, like she was buying the car, not borrowing it for a couple of nights. "This is great."

"Tell you what," Merle said. "I'm spending Christmas with my sister's family in Pensacola. Why don't you keep her on through the holidays? I'll be gone before you bring her back, anyhow. Won't be here to take the keys."

"Do you mean it?" Jenny asked.

"All the same to me," Merle said. "Just be careful. And don't be driving it drunk. Back seat's big enough for you lay right down and sleep it off."

"I won't," Jenny promised.

"All right," Merle said. "Now, let's go see if we can find her a back tire, and take her down off that jack."

CHAPTER FIFTEEN

The gate at Barrett House was open, guarded only by the stone lions perched on their columns. Jenny eased the Lincoln through onto the long brick driveway. It was as wide as a boulevard and lined with huge ornamental dogwood trees, each tree filled with glowing webs of tiny white lights. As she drew close to the house, she passed the cars already parked along the driveway—new cars, some of them Mercedes and Cadillacs, nearly all of them black. The old Lincoln wouldn't fit in, but she was glad not to be arriving in the rusty Ram.

She reached the big turnaround, and got an up-close view of Barrett House. Her first impression was of a mausoleum, all stonework and dark brick, like the bank in town. Tall but narrow windows on the first floor looked out on the world like suspicious eyes. The windows on the upper two floors were larger, but not by much. The third floor was completely dark, so the house faded away into the night above.

She pulled up at the front, where a young man in a tuxedo emerged from the columns of the semi-circular portico jutting out from the house. The portico was topped with curving wrought-iron balustrades on the second and third floors, accessible from the house through narrow arched doorways.

Jenny didn't know what to do, so she waited. The valet grinned and opened the door for her. He was cute, only a couple of years older than her, with longish dirty blond hair.

"Hi," Jenny said. "Do I just leave the keys in here for you?"

"That will be fine, ma'am." He took her hand, which was sheathed in a long black glove, and helped her out of the car, not that she really needed it. "I think this is my favorite car tonight," he whispered to her.

"Thank you." Jenny looked toward the double front doors, which were propped wide open. Light and warmth rolled out from the inside, along with the sounds of murmuring voices, clinking glass, live musicians playing a slow instrumental of "Hark! The Herald Angels Sing." A sudden fear struck deep into her. She didn't belong here, and she would no doubt be ejected on sight.

Jenny watched the valet climb into her car and give her a thumbs-up before driving away. She gathered her sheer black wrap closer around her shoulders as if it would give her protection. Keeping her eyes straight ahead, Jenny walked uninvited through the doors of Barrett House.

The first room was two stories high, an entrance hall with a wide, curving staircase that hugged its way around the wall, lit by a huge chandelier and scattered lamps and candles, but it still managed to feel dark and oppressive. The walls were heavy wood paneling, black or a very deep brown. There were thick rugs on the parquet floor, thick embroidered draperies around the windows. A few middle-aged people in suits and cocktail dresses held a low conversation near the steps.

Paintings looked down on her, generations of Barrett men, most of them wearing dour expressions and severe black bankers' suits. The oldest was a man with a huge white beard, dressed in a Confederate officer uniform, seated by a table with a stack of leather-bound books. A grim-looking woman in a dark, big-skirted antebellum dress and much jewelry stood behind him with one hand on the back of his chair. Nobody in any of the portraits looked very happy, but Jenny supposed that was the style in those days. Now, you were always supposed to lean your heads together and pretend to be deliriously happy whenever anybody snapped a picture.

A massive granite chimney dominated the front room, reaching up two stories and presumably on through the third floor and roof. One thick log burned inside the fireplace. The fireplace and chimney gave the house an even heavier, almost medieval atmosphere, with the raw firelight and the smell of wood smoke.

A young woman in a black and white catering outfit offered to take Jenny's wrap, and Jenny declined. A young man in a similar outfit passed through the room carrying a tray of glasses with red wine, and he swerved a little to offer Jenny one. She gladly accepted.

There were three tall, arched doorways leading out of the front room, their heavy oak doors propped open. Straight ahead, the receiving hall shrank into a dark central hallway that burrowed away under the stairs. To her left and right were huge lighted rooms where people gathered in little groups, drinking wine and eating hors d'oeuvres from the caterers. The live music sounded from the door on her left.

Each of the heavy oak doors was reinforced with iron bands and a big brass lock. The doors were all propped open for the party, but clearly the whole house could be locked down if desired, like a castle under siege. Or a prison.

The young woman noticed her confusion and said, "The ballroom's to your left. Dining room to your right. Are you sure I can't take that for you?"

Jenny shook her head and walked toward the ballroom. She felt unsteady in her new high heels--Jenny was more of a sneakers girl. The heels clacked and echoed on the dark wooden floor, sounding loud to her ears, despite the string and bell music tinkling through the house.

She entered the ballroom, another dark-paneled space with another chandelier, crowded with scores of people. There was a large, empty dance floor in front of the quartet. A thirteen-foot Douglas fir strung with gold and red beads and miniature white lights stood in the corner behind the band. Most of the people were on this end of the ballroom at little clusters of tables and chairs close to the bar. The crowd was much older than Jenny, and many silver heads turned to evaluate the young lady who'd entered the room alone, the men with curiosity, the women with suspicion.

Jenny felt terribly exposed. Her habit was to look down at her feet and let her hair shield her face. Now she forced herself to look back at everyone, even raising her chin an inch. She gripped her slender little black purse (one of her mother's) tightly in her fingers, but she tried to keep her nervousness hidden.

Jenny had, after much effort, managed to tailor the dress to fit her without ruining it in the process. She'd driven to Apple Creek to buy the shoes, and the gauzy black material for the wrap, which she'd made herself. She'd also purchased make-up and perfume, which had been the hardest part. She must have spent an hour in the cosmetics section at Belk, looking at catalogs, studying herself in the mirrors, sniffing little scent testers. A friendly lady at the glass counter had offered to apply the makeup for her, and Jenny regretted having to say no. It would have made things much easier.

All of that had cost most of her savings. She'd cut her own hair, as always, but this time did it very carefully, following some magazine pictures, instead of just hacking off anything below her shoulders. She made a pin for her hair, too, with live mistletoe braided, twisted and glued into a spiral shape. The small green and white plant didn't match the rest of her outfit, but she liked it.

Jenny gave her best smile to the people looking at her. This seemed to break their interest, and they turned their attention back to their own little groups. Her worst, most paranoid fear, that someone would immediately point at her and yell that she didn't belong, or that she would be thrown out on sight, faded away. Thank God, she thought, that people were so self-absorbed.

She moved deeper into the room, trying to look casual and very much not an intruder, hoping to get lost in the crowd. She recognized people here and there. There was Mayor Hank Winder and his wife, Cassie's parents, who owned a timber processing center somewhere down the road. Police Chief Lintner was there, talking with Dick Baker, a lawyer and real estate agent known for his bathroom advertisements. Dick Baker was the father of poor Wendy, the girl who'd run offstage in tears during her failed bid for student council. There were plenty of people Jenny didn't recognize at all. Maybe they were from outside Fallen Oak.

Jenny reached the open, unpopulated expanse of the dance floor, crossed along the edge of it, then walked back along the opposite wall, still looking for any sign of Seth. Instead, she found herself moving right toward a knot of four people, and she went into a panic. It was Mr. and Mrs. Jon S. Barrett III, both of them looking salted and ruddy by long exposure to the sun. Jenny remembered that they stayed in Florida for months at a time. Graying, balding Mr. Barrett had the broken-capillary red nose and cheeks of a serious drinker, like Jenny's dad, and held a glass of whiskey, while most of the guests had wine. He and his wife dressed in dark, formal clothes that looked like they had grown organically out of the mansion around them.

She imagined them pointing at her, demanding to know who she was. To make things much worse, they were talking with Dr.

and Mrs. Goodling. Ashleigh's dad wore a brown, fairly realistic toupee, and his hair was unnaturally dark for his wrinkled face. Mrs. Goodling looked about twenty years younger than him, though it was hard to tell because her face had been stretched into Barbie doll smoothness by plastic surgery, and her hair was many layered shades of dyed blonde. She wore diamonds at her ears, neck and fingers, outdazzling the restrained pearls and gold worn by Mrs. Barrett.

Jenny tried to avoid them with a sharp turn, but Mr. Barrett must have noticed the lost, panicked look she'd been trying to hide.

"Hey there, young lady," Mr. Barrett said, and his wife frowned. "Can I help you?"

"Oh, hello, Mr. Barrett," Jenny said, making herself smile. "And Mrs. Barrett, you look so lovely." Jenny hoped this was the appropriate kind of thing to say.

"Why, thank you," Mrs. Barrett said. "I think that dress is just adorable. I do apologize, but I'm having a little trouble with names tonight. Forgive me."

It took Jenny a few seconds to realize Mrs. Barrett was asking Jenny's name. She panicked again. If she said the truth, they would know she was Darrell Morton's daughter, someone they hadn't invited. Fortunately, Mr. Barrett spoke before Jenny could think of anything to say.

"No, let me guess," he said. "Luke Bamford's daughter. Liza May. Am I right? Liza May Bamford?"

Jenny smiled very wide.

"I knew it," Mr. Barrett said. "She looks just like Darlene, doesn't she, Iris?"

"Is that right?" Mrs. Barrett eyeballed Jenny. "We haven't seen you in, well, it must be six years? Eight?"

"I'm not really sure, ma'am," Jenny said.

"Listen to that," Mrs. Barrett said. "There are a few polite ones left."

"Well, she's a gorgeous young lady now, isn't she?" Mr. Barrett drank from his whiskey, ignoring his wife's arched eyebrow. "Have you met my son, Seth?"

"Our daughter Ashleigh is Seth's girlfriend," Mrs. Goodling told Jenny, in a pleasant, honeyed voice that Jenny found uncomfortably familiar. "More than three years now. They're very serious, aren't they?" she asked Mrs. Barrett.

"I believe so," Mrs. Barrett said.

"To be honest, I'm still looking for Seth...and Ashleigh and everybody...I only just arrived," Jenny said. "Are they nearby?"

"The kids are upstairs on the back veranda," Mr. Barrett said. "They think we don't know they're getting drunk up there."

"Jon!" Mrs. Barrett gave the preacher's wife an apologetic look. "How is your mother, Liza May?"

"Oh, just fine, ma'am. She's never been better. She loves the holidays." Jenny made herself shut up.

"That is amazing," Mrs. Barrett said. "I heard she was confined to her hospital bed not three weeks ago. Well, you know how people get things wrong. Don't you?"

Jenny wanted to slap herself with both hands. Dr. Goodling, who hadn't said a word, now looked openly suspicious of her.

"So I just go upstairs, then?" Jenny pointed her finger off in a random direction. She gave Mr. Barrett a big smile, since he was the only one who seemed to like her. Thank God for strong whiskey.

"You'll want to head on out through that door and down the hall," Mr. Barrett said. "You can't miss the back stairs. Get yourself a drink first."

"I already have one, sir, thank you," Jenny said.

"Then get another one. You need it with this crowd." He finished off his whiskey. Mrs. Barrett looked mortified and shook her head.

Jenny followed his directions, past little clumps of people. A waiter offered glasses of plump shrimp with cocktail sauce, and Jenny shook her head. Her stomach was a knot of nerves. It felt like she would never eat again.

The back staircase was built in two flights, the walls hung with framed black and white photographs, some of them with that sepia color of very early photography. They were family pictures, stern elders, frowning adults, moping children in ties or puffy silk dresses. The family had never been particularly large in number, and many of them had a sickly look.

The stairs brought her to a second-floor gallery, with more paintings, some very large urns, bookshelves displaying sculptures and leather-bound volumes. There were antique, uncomfortable-looking chairs. She saw a wooden table with a chessboard painted on it and black and white armies set up for a new game. One corner of the gallery held a harp and a piano.

Two hallways led into the depths of the house, and two pairs of French doors opened out to the back veranda. The outdoor lights were turned off, and a few tabletop lamps outside provided low illumination. A stereo had been set up out there, playing Mos Def at a loud, thumping volume.

She saw Cassie and Ashleigh, both in dark cocktail dresses. They drank wine as they stood at the veranda railing, looking down on people in the back yard. Then she saw Seth.

Seth sat at a table with Everett and a couple of guys she didn't recognize. There were several people like that on the veranda, probably the high school and college age children of party guests. Nobody looked exceptionally happy to be there.

Seth wasn't saying much, just sipping his glass of whiskey while the guys at his table made bets with each other about the upcoming bowl games. His eyes looked distant, not focused on anything.

Jenny stayed in the gallery and watched. She didn't yet have the courage to go outside. She didn't know how Seth would respond to her presence, but she knew how viciously Ashleigh and Cassie would react. This was her last moment of safety, before her presence was known.

She took a deep breath and stepped toward the nearest French doors—only to see two guys coming inside, walking straight toward her. She didn't recognize either of them, the taller one with freckles, or the handsome, tanned guy who was looking her up and down. They were college age, and both of them wore suits, but without ties.

"Hey," the tanned one said to Jenny, "You know where the bathroom is?"

"Uh…" Jenny picked one of the two hallways and pointed. "Down that way."

"Maybe you should show us the way." He glanced behind him, then lifted out a plastic bag, twisted and tied closed, filled with a fine white powder that probably wasn't a half-cup of sugar. "You look like you could use some of this."

"Bet we could use some of her! Ow!" the freckled one said. He reeked of bourbon.

"Shut the fuck up, Kevin," the first boy said, and handed him the baggie. "Why don't you go warm up the bathroom or something?"

"More like *blow up* the bathroom! Ow!" Freckled, drunk Kevin staggered down one of the halls, not the one Jenny had indicated.

"Don't worry about my stupid cousin," the boy said. "We can ditch him. He'll probably pass out, anyway. Hey, let's go up to the third floor, I heard it's haunted."

"No, thanks," Jenny said.

"Don't tell them we have any, okay?" he said, with a nod towards the people on the veranda. "I didn't bring enough for the whole class."

"I won't."

As he walked away, Jenny gathered her nerves again and looked out through the veranda doors. There had to be some way to get Seth away from Ashleigh and Cassie. Maybe she could hide somewhere and wait for him to come inside. Or maybe Ashleigh and Cassie would come in and leave him out there alone. Or maybe—

"Hey, boy!" Jenny called after him. "Wait!"

He stopped in the hallway and turned. Jenny walked over to him, trying her best to do a sexy smile.

"Change your mind?" he asked.

"No, I'm good," she said. "But you know who would love it? Did you see those two girls out there, the blond and redhead, in the tight black dresses?"

Now she had the boy's attention. "Yeah. I think we noticed. Isn't one of them Seth's girl or something?"

"Not that much," Jenny said. "But they're pretty friendly about the…" Jenny nodded at his coat pocket. "They're actually kind of slutty about it. But don't tell them I said that!"

Jenny was inventing all of this. Years of being picked on by Ashleigh and trying to figure out what Ashleigh might do next had apparently taught her to think like Ashleigh. She was becoming her enemy.

"Really?" He looked back out at the veranda, his eyes on Ashleigh's rear. "They look kind of stuck up."

"They are," Jenny said. "But they'll get friendly. I heard them complain about how they were fiending for it." As far as Jenny knew, Ashleigh might get offended at the offer of hard drugs, even run downstairs to narc him out to the police chief. It was worth a try, though. And the guy was kind of a douche, anyway.

"Cool, thanks. What's your name?" he asked.

"Liza May."

"Nice to meet you, Liza May. I'm Davis."

"Okay, see you, Davis." She pointed down the hall in which they stood. "I'm going to the other bathroom now. By myself. For the normal reason."

He grinned as he returned to the veranda, looking cocky, betting on a sure thing with a big payoff. Jenny watched him swagger toward Ashleigh and Cassie, who remained at the railing, talking to each other.

Davis whispered in Ashleigh's ear. Ashleigh immediately put her hand on his and turned her face toward him, so that their noses were only an inch apart. She clearly liked what she saw, and gave him a big smile. The boy seemed suddenly enchanted by Ashleigh, staring at her with profound admiration.

Jenny felt her heart leap. Maybe she'd done more than she hoped. Maybe Ashleigh would get interested in this rich, handsome college guy and leave Seth alone.

Ashleigh whispered in Cassie's ear while tightening her grip on Davis' arm. Cassie brightened and nodded. She stepped forward, introduced herself to Davis, and shook his hand. Ashleigh's PR department.

The three of them turned and crossed the veranda, going inside. Ashleigh cast a quick, narrow-eyed look at Seth, who still stared into the distance, holding his glass, while the guys talked around him. Seth didn't seem to notice Ashleigh, or anyone else, at all.

Then Jenny realized that Ashleigh and Cassie were walking through the French doors, heading straight towards Jenny. They hadn't seen Jenny in the dark hallway yet, but she had only a few seconds to hide.

Davis followed them in. He laid his hands on both girls'
backs as soon as they were inside and out of everyone else's sight.

Jenny turned and dashed down the hall. The first door she
tried was locked; the second, a closet crammed full of boxes and
coats, no room for her. The third door was open and lighted—the
bathroom, where Kevin would be chopping out white lines to snort.
Jenny dashed past that door. The fourth door opened without a
problem. She hurried inside and closed it most of the way, without
letting it click into place.

She was in a bedroom, with a huge four-poster bed and very
heavy antique dressers and mirrors. The walls were hung with
posters of supermodels in skimpy underwear, hip-hop artists,
professional football players, and one picture of Albert Einstein
sticking out his tongue. There were socks and boxer shorts and
jeans scattered all over the carpet, a heap of big trophies thrown
carelessly in one corner, and the smell of boy-sweat everywhere.
There was a picture of Seth and Ashleigh on one dresser, and next to
that, a picture of a younger teenage boy Jenny didn't know. She had
to be in Seth's bedroom.

Jenny realized she wasn't safe yet. The light in this room
came from the open closet door. On the far end of the walk-in
closet, instead of a back wall, there was a door open to the
bathroom. The closet served as a small, private hall between the
bedroom and bath. In the bathroom, Kevin bent over the marble
countertop, scraping around with a razor blade. If he looked up, he
would see Jenny in the mirror.

"What's up, Kev?" Davis said. He and Ashleigh and Cassie
trooped into the large marble bathroom. Davis locked the hallway
door behind him. "This is Ashleigh and Cathy."

"Cassie," Cassie said.

Kevin snorted a line and stood up, pinching his nose, his
eyes squeezed shut. He blinked a few times and looked the girls
over. Ashleigh was quick to grab onto his bare arm. Kevin lit
tensed up like he'd been electrocuted, and then he smiled at
Ashleigh.

"Well, all right, ladies," Kevin said. "Hey there, blonde girl.
Bend over and snort this fat one."

Jenny eased open the door to the hall. With her shoes in her
hands, she jogged past the bathroom door. She stopped in the

gallery to replace the shoes, and she retrieved her wine glass from the 19th century rosewood table where she'd placed it without so much as a coaster. Then she strolled onto the veranda with her head high.

Seth was in the same chair, at the table with the guys. Jenny smiled as she walked toward him.

"Hi, Seth," she said.

He looked up at her, his eyes blurry.

"Oh, hey," he said. "It's Jenny."

Seth did not look surprised to see her. He did not look upset that she had crashed his party. He did not look worried that Jenny's presence might upset Ashleigh. He did not stand up and sweep Jenny into his arms. He did not seem very aware of anything. His eyelids were low, his mouth slack.

"Merry Christmas," Jenny said. "How are you?"

"Merry Christmas," he echoed.

Jenny sidled up next to his chair. She peeled off one of her long black gloves. Then she touched his hand, wrapping her fingers around it. It felt good to touch him, to touch anyone at all.

He took her hand, but it felt like an automatic reflex.

"Zeth," she said. "I vant to zuck your blood."

He just looked at her, his mouth open.

"Don't you remember me?"

"Oh," he said. "Jenny. I'm glad you came. I didn't know you were coming."

"It's a surprise," Jenny said. "Are you feeling okay, Seth?"

"Oh, sure," he said. "I'm okay."

One of the two guys Jenny didn't know stood up from the table.

"Take my chair, I need another drink anyway," he told Jenny, then noticed her empty glass. "You want anything at the bar? Egg nog?"

"You wouldn't mind getting me a whiskey sour, would you?" Jenny asked.

"Whiskey at Christmas," the guy said as he walked to the doors. "My kind of girl."

Jenny sat down beside Seth and rubbed his hand. She was directly across the table from Everett Lawson, Cassie's boyfriend.

Everett paused his conversation with the other guy, and stuck his right hand across the table, smiling wide at Jenny.

"Hi," he said. "Everett Lawson."

He didn't recognize her at all. The liquor probably helped. Jenny's right hand was still bare, so she held out her left instead. There was an awkward moment, then he changed hands.

"Hey," she said. "I'm Jenny." *You killed my dog*, she thought.

Everett looked her up and down, gave her another big smile. He looked like he wanted to say more, but then, happily, his companion started talking and pulled him back into their conversation, which sounded like it focused on the relative hotness of female cartoon characters.

"You look pretty," Seth said.

Jenny blushed a little, caught off-guard by his compliment. His eyes seemed more focused now, looking at her.

"Thank you, Seth," Jenny said. "So do you."

"Yeah," he said. He sipped his glass, where all the ice had melted. He didn't seem drunk, but doped up some other way. Jenny leaned close to him and whispered, her lips brushing right against the delicate, warm skin of his ear. She raised her bare hand and lay it against his face while she whispered.

"Seth, were you telling me the truth that day? Does Ashleigh really have something, like you and I do? Something that makes people love her?" Jenny thought about how quick Ashleigh was to touch both the college boys, like something she had to check off when she talked to new people. Jenny had always thought Ashleigh was just one of those aggressive-touching types who always wanted to clap your shoulder or sock you in the arm, the type Jenny had to avoid.

All her life, she'd seen people work for Ashleigh's attention and approval. She'd seen how they lit up when Ashleigh favored them with a word, and especially a small touch or hug. Jenny just thought they were stupid for adoring Ashleigh. She didn't notice the pattern until now, looking back. Ashleigh was as obsessive about touching people as Jenny was about avoiding contact. It all fit. Jenny would probably be the same way, if her touch made people love her, instead of giving them a horrible, deadly disease.

"Ashleigh…" Seth sighed. "I don't know, Jenny. I forgot."

"Maybe I can help you remember," Jenny whispered. She stroked her fingertips along his face, and looked him right in the eyes, their lips at kissing range. "Look at me, Seth."

"Jenny?" He touched her hand. A smile broke across his face, the first emotion he'd shown tonight. His fingers traced up along her arm, then he lay his hand on her side. "I can't believe you're here," he whispered. "Thank you."

"Are you awake now?" Jenny asked. "Or still under her spell?"

"I don't know." Seth looked nervously at the French doors. "Is she gone?"

"She'll have her hands full for a minute." And her nose, Jenny thought. And maybe more, if the college guys got their way.

"It's addictive," Seth whispered. "She fills you up with it, and the world is perfect. Then it fades and you want more. I wish I could stop."

"You can stop, Seth," Jenny said. "I can help you."

"What do I do?" Seth whispered.

"I don't know," Jenny said. "You tell her we're together now. You're not going to be with her anymore."

"Oh." Seth gave the French doors a frightened look, as if Jenny had advised him to jump in a cage with a hungry tiger, and pour a little steak sauce on himself, too. "Now? Tonight?"

"You're killing me, Seth." Jenny stood up and held out her hand. "Okay, then let's take a break from this party. You can walk me outside and show me all your trees and crap."

"That sounds good." Seth took her hand. They walked in through the French doors. As they approached the stairs, Ashleigh and Cassie emerged from the hall, clinging to Davis. His cousin Kevin trailed behind like a clumsy puppy who desperately wants to be part of the pack.

When Ashleigh saw Seth, she stiffened and put on a self-righteous face. Then her eyes shifted to Jenny. Coke-fueled self-righteousness ignited into coke-fueled outrage.

"Oh, my God!" Ashleigh said. "Seth? Not Jenny Mittens again. Come on!"

Davis, seeing Ashleigh's boyfriend with another girl, apparently decided he was at a swingers' party. He dropped his hand down Ashleigh's lower back, spreading his fingers along the tight curve of her ass in the black cocktail dress. Ashleigh ignored him.

"We're going for a walk," Seth said.

"You are not! Why is she even here?" Ashleigh moved toward Seth, holding out one hand toward him. Seth and Jenny both stared at Ashleigh's hand, and Jenny felt very suspicious. Davis reached after her, and when she was out of range, he turned the other way and embraced Cassie instead. Cassie rolled her eyes, slipped away from him, and went to stand at Ashleigh's side.

"Don't touch him," Jenny said. She moved herself in front of Seth, blocking Ashleigh's access to him.

"Get out of my way, Jenny Mittens," Ashleigh said. "I can touch my own boyfriend."

"Try it." Jenny raised her own bare hand. "I'll scratch your face open, Ashleigh. Remember how that turned out last time?"

Jenny couldn't remember the last time she'd seen Ashleigh scared, but at that moment, Ashleigh looked terrified and confused. Ashleigh's jaw rubbed from side to side, working the muscles in her face.

"Let's kick her ass right now," Cassie said, bouncing on the balls of her feet, full of new energy. Her jaw was making the same weird, grinding movements. "I am so ready for a fight or something exciting to happen."

"No," Ashleigh warned Cassie. "Don't touch her. Don't let her touch you."

"Why not?" Jenny asked. "Cassie, bring it on. I can take you."

"No!" Ashleigh threw an arm across Cassie's stomach to block her. "Listen to me, Cassie."

"What's your problem?" Cassie asked Ashleigh. "It's only Jenny Mittens."

"Why don't you tell her?" Jenny asked Ashleigh.

"Why don't you?" Ashleigh countered.

"Is there something dangerous in my touch, Ashleigh?" Jenny asked. "Or is there something dangerous in yours? Something that makes people love you, even though nobody should?"

Ashleigh froze. She was looking a little pale.

"But that's your secret, isn't it, Ashleigh?" Jenny said. "Everyone thinks they like you because you're just *so* lovable and *so* perfect. But you enchant them. It's your big secret, isn't it? You touch and they love you. Maybe, after all these years of doing it, you even believe all these people really do like you."

Jenny stepped towards Ashleigh, raising her bare hand towards Ashleigh's face. Ashleigh screamed and ducked behind Cassie, using her best friend as a shield.

"That's why you hate me so much, Ashleigh Goodling," Jenny said. "Because I'm the one person you can't control. You do remember. You know you'll get Jenny pox."

"Shut up, Jenny Mittens!" Ashleigh lunged forward on the balls of her feet, then stopped herself and swayed back. "You're such a bitch. A crazy, crazy bitch. Doesn't she sound crazy?" she asked Cassie.

"Totally," Cassie agreed automatically, but her face looked dubious. Maybe it didn't sound completely, entirely crazy to her.

"All three of us have it, Ashleigh," Jenny said. "Different kinds of it. Now we all know it. And you know what I can do to you." Jenny batted her open hand at Ashleigh's face, and Ashleigh recoiled.

Jenny took Seth's hand and they started down the stairs. Ashleigh stood and watched them with her fists clenched at her hips. Cassie gave Ashleigh a confused look, and so did Davis and Kevin.

"Man," Davis said. "What have y'all been smoking?"

"And do you have any left? Ow!" Kevin added.

Jenny and Seth continued down the stairs with their hands together. Jenny's touch actually seemed to help him, like giving a strong cup of coffee to a sleepy drunk. His eyes became clearer, and he walked straighter as they reached the bottom of the stairs. It was the first time her touch had ever helped anyone.

Jenny led him through the central hall, which widened into the front receiving hall, with her eyes on the open front doors and the driveway and the night beyond. They only needed to get through that doorway, and they'd be free.

They passed the monumental granite chimney under the stern glares of Seth's grandfathers. Jenny accepted a wine glass from a passing waitress, drank it down, replaced it on the tray.

A loud commotion sounded from the ballroom. Ashleigh and Cassie charged into the front hall, followed by the Barretts, the

Goodlings, and curious onlookers trailing after them to see why their hosts were running.

"There they are!" Cassie shouted. She and Ashleigh both pointed at Jenny.

"Stay put, you two," Mrs. Barrett ordered. "Liza May, I am disappointed in you. Where are your parents?"

"Her name isn't Liza May, ma'am," Ashleigh said. "Her name is Jenny Mittens. Morton."

Jenny couldn't remember another time when Ashleigh had said her last name correctly.

"Is this true?" Mrs. Barrett asked.

"Yes, ma'am," Jenny said.

"She wasn't invited," Ashleigh said. "She's a country grifter."

"No, I invited her," Seth said. "I told her she could come over anytime. Right, Jenny?"

"She wasn't on the invite list," Ashleigh said. "You can check."

"I don't think I know any Mortons," Mrs. Barrett said. She turned to her husband. "Honey, do we know any Mortons?"

Mr. Barrett looked at Jenny very carefully with his bleary, drunken eyes. Jenny knew the look well—he was trying to solve a problem that would have been very easy, had he been sober. He took a long drink. He sighed a little. Then he said, "Mr. Morton. Business associate of mine. I probably invited them. Sorry, honey."

"We're going for a walk now," Seth said, still pretty doped. "I like Jenny."

"I don't think so, Jonathan Seth Barrett," Mrs. Barrett said. She opened her hand. From her fingers, she dangled the plastic baggie of cocaine that had once belonged to Davis Jordan, sophomore in the pharmaceutical school at the College of Charleston. The amount was much diminished, no more than a thimbleful.

"Ashleigh tells me you brought this into my home," Mrs. Barrett said. "And gave it to Seth and the other kids."

"I did not!" Jenny said. "Ashleigh and Cassie were doing it in the bathroom with some random guys—"

"We happen to know Ashleigh very well," Mrs. Barrett said. "And I don't believe she would lie about this."

"Why would we bring it to Mrs. Barrett if it was ours?" Cassie asked. "Duh."

Mrs. Barrett raised her eyebrows, as if to say that Cassie had just made a very astute point.

"Ashleigh's a manipulative liar," Jenny said. "She makes Dick Cheney look like Mr. Rogers."

"That is an ugly thing to say about Dick Cheney!" Dr. Goodling snapped. "And my daughter, as well."

"I didn't know anybody had coke," Seth said in his doped-out voice. "Who has coke?"

"It's a little late to pretend, Seth," Ashleigh said. "Heaven knows you're obviously all druggied up." Ashleigh darted in and seized Seth's other hand, the one Jenny wasn't holding. Jenny was already too stunned at the drug accusation to react. She didn't register the importance of Ashleigh's sudden grab, or the need to stop Ashleigh, until it was too late.

Seth's eyes drooped, his pupils dilated, and he gave Ashleigh a big, relieved smile. Ashleigh pumped the energy hard to take control of him, and an enormous wave of it washed through Seth and into Jenny. Jenny felt a sudden, painful, physical urge to strip off her clothes and jump in bed with both Ashleigh and Seth, but especially Ashleigh. Jenny's heart bloomed, and she really could feel it open up like a delicate, many-petaled flower in the middle of her chest. She didn't know how she could ever have disliked Ashleigh at all. The girl was magnificent. She was angelic. Jenny longed to be close to her, and felt sad that her touch would only hurt Ashleigh.

"Let go of her," Ashleigh said. Seth released Jenny's hand. The bright, glowing adoration of Ashleigh faded quickly inside of Jenny, but left her with a happy, drugged afterglow. After all, Ashleigh was still nearby. Maybe Ashleigh would do it again.

"Come on, Seth," Ashleigh said. "Let your mom sweep up the trash." Ashleigh steered him up the front staircase. She kept her shoulder under his arm as if he were drunk, which he wasn't, and she were supporting him, which she wasn't.

"Where were you and my son going?" Mrs. Barrett asked.

"Nowhere," Jenny said. "Just for a walk."

"She told Ashleigh she planned to drug him up more and have weird drug sex with him." Cassie spat the words out, fast as machine-gun fire. Her eyes were very bright, her jaw grinding hard now. "She wanted to have weird drug sex with everyone."

"I didn't say that," Jenny told them. She was still buzzing with Ashleigh-euphoria. Too bad Ashleigh was out of the room.

"Are you calling Ashleigh a liar?" Mrs. Barrett said.

"Oh, no," Jenny said. "Ashleigh wouldn't lie. Not without a good reason."

Cassie seemed confused by this.

"Then you admit it," Mrs. Barrett said.

"Okay," Jenny said. She was a little dazed. What was she admitting to? The whole room had a warm, weird glow to it. Seth's dead ancestors leered down on her like funny zombie puppets.

"I think it's best you leave," Mrs. Barrett said. She put the cocaine in her own purse. "And we'll be holding on to this, in case we need to contact the police."

"Okay," Jenny said. More than twenty people were looking at her now, some of them amused by the minor scandal.

A college guy emerged from the ballroom, carrying a glass of beer in one hand and a whiskey sour with the other. He saw Jenny, raised his chin upward in a greeting, and winked at her. It was the boy who'd given up his chair to Jenny on the veranda.

"One whiskey sour for the pretty lady," the guy said. He sauntered towards Jenny, but none of the crowd moved to let him through. Twenty heads turned to stare at him with disapproval.

He stood there, perplexed, for a long minute.

"Oh-kay..." he finally said. He headed for the stairs, keeping both drinks. The faces all turned back to Jenny.

"You'll want to go that way." Mrs. Barrett pointed at the door.

Jenny followed her finger. She turned her feet in that direction and wandered outside. Dr. Goodling stood with her while the valet fetched her car.

"Young lady, you seem troubled," Dr. Goodling said.

"Actually, I've never felt this happy," Jenny said. She had eventually learned that her dad didn't call Dr. Goodling a "carnie-booth crook" just as a slur. Dr. Maurice Goodling had, decades ago, been an actual game-booth operator in a traveling carnival.

"But that's just the drugs, isn't it?" Dr. Goodling asked. "How would you like to feel high all the time, without any drugs?

Do you realize how wonderful it feels to be born again, to be part of a new covenant with God through His Son?"

"I'm okay," Jenny said. She watched for her headlights on the driveway. She wanted to leave. Something had gone wrong inside the house and she had to leave, but she couldn't remember exactly what. The details were fuzzy and wouldn't sharpen in her mind.

"Have you studied the Word of God?" Dr. Goodling said.

"No," Jenny told him.

"You should come by my office," he said. "Call the church and schedule an appointment. We can talk about the way to righteousness."

"Okay." Jenny watched her car arrive and she drifted toward it. The valet smiled and gave a joking little bow as held the door for her, and then he closed her inside.

"Thank you," she told the valet.

"Yeah, thanks for the tip, lady," he muttered as she drove away.

Jenny swerved down the long brick driveway, occasionally slipping off the road into the lawn. She made it out the gates and onto Barrett Avenue, then pointed the car towards town. The Barretts owned a buffer zone of farmland around their house, so it was an empty drive for a few minutes. She felt good inside. She drove slowly through the night, thinking delicious thoughts about Seth and Ashleigh, images and fantasies full of longing and need. She wondered when she could see Ashleigh again.

CHAPTER SIXTEEN

The day after the party, Seth's father called him into the office, a spacious room located at the back of the first floor. Seth had never liked the office. It was well-lighted, but by small rectangular windows near the ceiling, giving the lower part of the room a stuffy, shadowy feel. As a boy, Seth had been frightened of the collected trophies of past generations: the lion head mounted above the fireplace, the stuffed dead falcon perched on a lacquered limb jutting out from the wall, the big buffalo-hide rug, and the row of heads that looked down on you from the wall as you sat on the visitor side of the desk: jackal, hyena, jaguar, grizzly bear, snow leopard, a big black wolf that always reminded Seth of the Three Little Pigs. Great-grandfather had been quite the skilled hunter, if by "skilled" you meant "able to hire a gang of men with high-powered rifles."

Below the heads were a row of old photographs like the one in the back stairwell, depicting Seth's grandfathers going back several generations, the same men immortalized in oil around the front stairs. He didn't know what scared him more as a boy, the dead animals or the stern looks of his ancestors bearing down on him and casting their judgment from beyond the grave.

The rest of the room was dark wood paneling, like too much of the house. One entire wall was taken up by rows of pigeonholes and wooden file cabinets. In the back corner sat a liquor cabinet that looked like it came from an Old West saloon, every bit of it handmade, with no two pieces exactly alike: the rough-hewn drawers and shelves, the iron handles, the thick cloudy glass doors in front of the bottles. Seth's father stood there now, pouring amber whiskey from a bottle with a faded, illegible label into two 19th-century drinking glasses that had a primitive, not-quite-circular look.

"Did you still want to talk?" Seth asked.

"Close the door and have a seat," his father said. Seth took one of the chairs, which had wide arms and a hard back, upholstered in leather pinned by brass tacks. The ancient material creaked under Seth, and it smelled like drunk old men.

Seth's father eased into a taller chair across the big black slab of the desk, which was carved entirely from petrified wood. A blue iMac sat on top of the desk, as incongruous in the office as a Roomba sucking up bone fragments and rock chips on a Neanderthal cave floor. They had a satellite on the roof for high-speed internet, since the TV and phone companies still didn't offer that in Fallen Oak.

His father placed a glass of the old whiskey, neat, in front of Seth. Then he raised his own glass.

"To another year gone," he said.

Seth clinked his glass against his father's, and drank a sip. It was smooth and smoky on the way down. In his belly, it turned into a fire that burned up his esophagus and into his brain. He wondered what whiskey became if it aged too long.

"So," his father said. "Are you still thinking about medical school?"

"I never was," Seth said. "I think physical therapy is about my speed."

"We looked into that. It sounds like you're just a nurse and a personal trainer. We don't think you're setting your sights high enough, Seth."

"You didn't break out the good whiskey to have this talk again," Seth said.

His dad looked at him for a minute. He opened a wooden box, lifted out a cigar, and lit it with a match. He offered Seth one, and Seth shook his head. Whiskey and cigars, he thought. The big guns.

His dad eased back in the office chair and smoked. Eventually, he said, "You're right. This isn't that talk again. This is a bigger talk. This is about responsibility."

"Okay," Seth said.

"It's not a pleasant word, is it?" his dad asked. He gestured at the row of dead men behind and above him. "When you look at those old pictures, you see it in their faces. Makes them all sour. Like they've been carrying a load of bricks on their backs."

"They don't look happy," Seth said.

"You can feel the weight of them in this house, can't you? The old generations pressing down on you. I never liked it here as a kid. Don't like it now."

Seth smiled. "Me, neither."

"We've been in Fallen Oak a long time," his dad said. "The last of the great families, that's what my father used to call us. Most people who could leave, already have. The horse market's long ago abandoned. The cotton exchange is just a roofless shell full of weeds. The textile mill—you probably don't remember that, either. And this town really started dying when they built the federal highways. We're not any kind of crossroads anymore.

"Your great-grandfather didn't keep all his eggs in this henhouse. He put money out in New York and London, kept the family diversified--he didn't build this house with just farm mortgages and loans to haberdashers. Now, we're seeing some good things in Shenzhen and Bangalore. That's where you'll want to focus during your life, China and India." His father looked at him carefully, making sure this sunk in.

"Okay," Seth said. He took another nip of whiskey, letting it burn him inside. "China and India."

"Now, we have a lot of legacy investments in this town, a lot of assets bringing in bad returns. There's negative growth. There's falling property values. There isn't much future. So why do we stay here, with the old Merchants and Farmers Bank?"

"Um," Seth said. He took another burning sip, stalling for time, but his father kept looking at him and waiting for an answer. "I don't know, Dad. So we can squeeze the last few pennies out of the people that are left?"

"No." He puffed on the cigar, regarding Seth intently. "We could sell out to a national banking chain, if we wanted. Wash our hands of all this bad debt, all the headaches. But we don't, and we won't. Because if we did that, one-third of this town—that's not an exaggeration—would lose their homes or businesses tomorrow. Most of them, within a few years. The people would leave, property values would hit rock bottom, the town would implode. There'd be nothing.

"There's a lot of leverage in this town, backed by shrinking assets. The Merchants and Farmers Bank keeps the town alive on float, month to month, year to year. We rework credit terms all the time. We take what they can pay." His dad puffed the cigar for a minute. "Now, tell me why."

"Because we're such generous, kindhearted people," Seth said.

"No." He flicked his cigar into a big, wrinkled ashtray made out of a rhinoceros foot. "Because we settled this town. My great-great-great-grandfather cut down the giant oak at the crossroads to make way for his farm and store. He left it there as a landmark. All that is forgotten now. You don't even learn about it in school. No respect for your own history, no knowledge of it. These kids all think everybody came over on the Mayflower. And you remember why we moved you from Grayson Academy to Fallen Oaks High in ninth grade?"

"Because it used to be Barrett Hall," Seth said. He remembered that talk very well, too, though it had been hot chocolate instead of whiskey. "The school we built for the town children, back in the ye olden days—"

"Back in 1873," his father said. "The state didn't take it over until 1941."

"But nobody at school knows that," Seth said. "I doubt Principal Harris even knows."

"This town is our legacy," his father said. "Whether the town remembers it or not. Whether they think of us as just the mean old loansharks up on the hill. We have a common history together, all the families, that nobody knows."

"So now we keep the town as a wildlife preserve for drunk rednecks," Seth said.

"We owe a lot to the families in this town," his father said. "Their ancestors provided our first fortune, through hard work and diligence. And suffering. My grandfather, J. S. Barrett number one, extracted a lot of blood from a lot of stones. He had his own effective ways of collecting debts."

"Sounds like a great guy," Seth said.

"Don't be sarcastic. We aren't hunters and killers anymore. We are investors who look for opportunities in emerging technology and international cost disparities. But the world of global capital flow is full of con artists, bad information, and every kind of political intrigue. It takes brilliant minds to cope with the complexity, and with the personalities. You'll face that across the world. And you'll still have to carry this town on your back. And that's why we need to talk."

Here it comes, Seth thought. He drank more whiskey to steel himself.

"These two girls you're seeing," his dad said, and Seth knew the conversation was about to get a lot more uncomfortable. "Look at Ashleigh. Smart, ambitious, she knows how people work. She's crazy about you. She would be a powerful ally at your side, a person who knows how to carry responsibility. And beautiful, on top of that. God doesn't make many women like her. You'd be foolish to throw her away."

Seth thought of Ashleigh, and immediately the pangs began in his heart, and gut, and pelvis. He thought of how her body felt in his hands, how her lips felt against his. He thought of his fingers inside her, while she made Cassie give him head, and he shuddered. He tried to push those feelings down, because if he let them rise, he would ache and burn to touch her, and he'd be calling her in an hour. He wanted to call her now.

"But she's manipulative," Seth said. "She's all about controlling people and making them do what she wants. That's her talent."

His dad sighed, then drank, then smoked. "That's just it, Seth. That's what you need. Someone manipulative, because there are people to be manipulated. Someone who can be ruthless, because there are ruthless choices to make."

"I don't know," Seth said. "I might meet someone else."

"That's true," his dad said. "But that's what you need to look for. Good human material. People who can go far with you. Someone like Ashleigh can be useful. And there won't be many like Ashleigh. Believe me, I've met a lot of women. You shouldn't be so careless with her.

"Now, this Jenny Morton," his dad continued, and Seth looked down at the buffalo-hide rug. "She's cute, all right. And she's from a good family. Small, tragic family, but a good one. Her father's probably the nicest, most honest, most hardworking man in this town. I'll bet a thousand dollars she's the same way."

"She is!" Seth sat up, finally getting a chance to smile. "That's what I'm saying. Jenny's a good person. Ashleigh isn't."

"That's the trouble," his dad said. "You don't need nice and honest. You need smart and manipulative. You need a thinker and a ball-breaker. Not a wife who's just going to be a little pet in your bed. You can have pets on the side, if you need them--but watch for danger there, too. Jenny Morton. What are her plans? Is she going to college?"

"We haven't talked about that stuff," Seth said.

"Then she must not be very serious. Is she strong enough to be a Barrett?"

"We're not even talking about that!" Seth said.

"There's something else to consider," he said. He was already refilling his own drink. "When we talk about the future of the family, we don't just mean finances. There's also the next generation of children."

"I know," Seth said. "So there's a Jonathan S. Barrett the Fifth, and the Sixth...and one day, Jonathan S. Barretts underwriting farm credit on the moon. And it's all up to me and my magical Barrett sperm." The strong drink had loosened Seth up, and he kept talking, when he normally would have stayed quiet. "Why couldn't Carter have been the Fourth? He was ahead of me. Then we'd be done with it. Why did you wait for me?"

His dad was quiet for a long time. They never discussed Seth's older brother. "Your mother wanted to name our first son after her father," his dad said. "Old Carter bailed us out of a lot of tight places here and there. So we had Carter Mayfield Barrett." He smiled thinly at the name, and poured more whiskey in both their glasses.

"And all you had to sacrifice was your firstborn son, huh?" Seth asked.

"That's not funny."

"Who said it was?" Seth drank some of the freshly poured whiskey.

"I don't appreciate your attitude. These things are important. They matter."

"I believe you," Seth replied.

"So now it's just you," his dad said, and he was slurring badly now. "That's my point about breeding. We've had a lot of illness in this family, miscarriages, crib death. And bad luck. We don't pass on well. You need to think about that. Because, to me, Jenny looks awful pale and skinny. That's not a good type for having kids. You need a woman with strong, healthy breasts and hips. Like Ashleigh."

"Dad, you're grossing me out right now," Seth said. "I'm not kidding."

"You won't get strong children out of a weak woman. That's all I'm saying." His dad puffed on the cigar. "You want to think like a horse breeder."

"No, I don't."

"So that's what we need to do," his father said. "We need to keep hold of Ashleigh. And we need to let good little Jenny Morton go free, so she can find someone more suited to her."

"Is that your final verdict, Your Honor?" Seth asked. Now, he finally did reach for one of the thick cigars. He struck a match, and coughed several times as he lit it. The smoke was thick and harsh, and Seth hated smoking.

"That's what will happen," his father said.

Seth blew a long plume of smoke in the air.

"But what if I love her?" Seth asked.

"Ashleigh?" his father asked.

"No."

J. S. Barrett III poured yet another drink, and filled Seth's cup to the top, emptying out the decades-old bottle.

"Let me tell you something even more true than this tired old horseshit I've been repeating from my father and grandfather," he told Seth. "If you really decide you're in love with Jenny, then, for God's sake, don't damn her to a life in this family. Let her go find some happiness."

His father sat back in his chair again, drinking deep, like the vintage whiskey was Kool-Aid.

" Maybe we Barretts ought to go on and die out anyway," he said. "We seem determined not to survive. Maybe that's what God wants. Maybe we should let the locusts and the buzzards come and

178

take all we've accumulated. What good did it ever do for any of us?"

"Is that our last toast?" Seth raised his glass and swigged. He was completely plastered now. He had to go to the bathroom, but wasn't sure if he could walk.

"You're going to do as we say," his father told him.

"Oh, is that what 'we' say?" Seth asked. "You and the ancestral spirits?"

"Yeah, that's right, Seth."

"How do you speak to them again? Séance? Drum circle?"

"The grandfathers are in me," his father said. "By the time I'm dead, they'll be in you. And I'll be there with them."

"Because of little chats like this," Seth said, with a bitter note in his voice.

"Because of little chats like this," his father agreed.

Seth drank. He snarled at his father, who did not respond. There was a dark, empty void opening inside him, a painful hollowness, and only one way to fill it. He imagined Ashleigh spread out naked on his bed, wearing only her jewelry, diamonds gleaming on her anklet. Her bare toes. Her thighs. The curly blond patch between her legs. Her navel—and in his mind, that was pierced, too, with another diamond. Her large breasts, her wide pink nipples. Her red fingernails. Her rich blond hair, spilling around her shoulders. Her inviting smile. Her haunting gray eyes.

Seth took the cell phone from his pocket.

"You want me to call Ashleigh?" he asked his father. "Will that end this talk? Will that send you back to Florida?"

"It will, if that's what you want."

"It's what I want." Seth dialed Ashleigh's number, and under the eyes of his father and his dead ancestors, he invited her to his house.

CHAPTER SEVENTEEN

Jenny received the panicked phone call from Mrs. Janet McNare late in the afternoon, three days before Christmas. Her husband, Ellis McNare, had spent the last two days plowing up and clearing out the weedy, overgrown dirt roads crisscrossing his farm. Yesterday, the tractor had bogged down and quit, and Mr. McNare couldn't get it started again. This morning, Jenny's dad had gone out to the McNare farm to have a look and see if he could tinker it back to life.

Her dad had called Jenny from his cell phone and told her there was hope for the tractor, and not to expect him until after sunset. He'd been running to a scrap yard in Vernon Hill to look for parts.

Jenny had put together a thick venison chili, since someone had paid her dad for a plumbing-repair job with ten pounds of frozen deer meat. She browned the meat, then she combined the tomatoes, beans, peppers, cumin, vinegar and some garlic and hot sauce, and left it on a low boil all day.

Then she worked at the dining room table, which was now splattered everywhere with bits of dried clay, on top of the layers of paint streaks and grease stains left by her father. She had a new inspiration. She wanted to sculpt a mask, like the elaborate tribal masks she'd seen in a copy of *National Geographic*. But she wanted it to represent her, everything hidden inside that she could never let out. She would give it a white glaze, then illustrate it with acrylic paint.

She wanted to start with a cast of her own face, which meant driving to Apple Creek for plaster. Before leaving, she'd picked up the phone and thought about calling Seth. She'd gotten him on his cell phone two days after the party, but he was back to his slow, drugged self, barely able to string words together.

Jenny now knew that Ashleigh did have the power Seth claimed, a power like theirs. She also knew Ashleigh had control over her power and knew how to wield it to her advantage. While Jenny had spent her life trying to restrain and hold back, Ashleigh had played and practiced with her own power. Jenny could dampen Ashleigh's influence on Seth temporarily, but only when she was touching Seth. But even then, Ashleigh could strike at Jenny through Seth. Jenny was still having erotic dreams about Ashleigh, which left her feeling dirty and disgusted in the morning.

Until she could figure out what to do, Jenny sculpted. First, she slathered her face in petroleum jelly. Then she closed her eyes and covered her own face with strips of paper dipped in the wet plaster. It was a difficult process to do alone—you were really supposed to have someone put it on for you. She worked entirely by sense of touch, layering on more and more of the strips until she had a good, thick mask. Then she waited for a long fifteen minutes, breathing through straws in her nostrils while lying on her back on the dining room floor. The plaster against her face gradually grew powdery and itchy. She carefully peeled it off, then left it to dry in a dish rack on the table.

Jenny checked and stirred the simmering chili, and added some peppers. She went outside to the shed to check Rocky's food and water, and discovered a light rain had begun to fall. She was washing the plaster from her face, and thinking about running a bath, when the phone rang in the living room.

At first, Mrs. McNare didn't make much sense at all.

"What's wrong?" Jenny asked. "Mrs. McNare, slow down."

"Jenny, it's your father," she said. "They were working on the tractor engine, and we don't know—some of the earth slipped away. Jenny, the tractor fell over, your father is trapped—"

"Call 911!" Jenny screamed.

"We did, honey. They're coming, but your father, he's...it's awful, Jenny. You'd better get here in the next few minutes. You may not get another chance." Mrs. McNare broke down into sobs, and Jenny slammed down the phone.

She ran in a wide, frantic loop around the house, grabbing the jacket with the gloves stuffed in the pocket, the car keys, her shoes. She ran to the front door, opened it, ran down the steps, opened the door to the Lincoln, then turned around, ran back up the steps, into the living room, and picked up the phone. She dialed Seth's cell phone.

He didn't answer on the first try. Or the second.

The third time, he finally picked up the phone.

"Hel-lo?" Seth sounded heavily sedated.

"Who is that?" Ashleigh's voice asked in the background.

"Seth, it's Jenny. Where are you right now?"

"It's Jenny," Seth told Ashleigh.

"Hang up!" Ashleigh ordered.

"Seth, tell me where you are!" Jenny screamed.

"Huh?" Seth said. "Oh, hey, yeah, we're just chilling over at Ashleigh's—"

"Give me that!" Ashleigh shouted, and the phone disconnected.

Jenny was out the door again. She started the Lincoln, kicked up spatters of mud as she raced backward out of the driveway, then squealed as she straightened out on the paved road, leaving smoldering rubber tracks behind her. Jenny stomped the accelerator, swerving wildly to pass a slow pick-up truck, running through stop signs. When she crossed through town, she ran the red light, causing a truck to swerve aside and honk.

The sky darkened and the rain picked up. Hail stones pelted the Lincoln's roof, hood and windshield. Jenny accelerated into the storm, hoping the tires could handle the running mud and the slick road.

She flew across town, to the west side subdivision where the Goodlings lived. Jenny jumped the curb on her way to Ashleigh's driveway, then squealed to a stop, turning the car slantwise. She barely avoided the rear bumper of Mrs. Goodling's Chrysler Suburban.

Jenny jumped from the car, leaving the door open. Rain and hail pelted her as she ran up the cobblestone walk to the tall peach-and-yellow house with the big picture windows. Electric candles glowed in every window. In the front yard was an entire lighted

Nativity scene, complete with life-size glowing plastic wise men and shepherds, and even electric sheep.

She dropped her jacket on the front porch and pushed open the front door without knocking. Her shoes squished out water with every step across the foyer.

"Who's that?" Dr. Goodling emerged from the kitchen, trailed by Mrs. Goodling in a cooking apron that showed a cartoon Jesus holding a cartoon Fallen Oak Baptist Church in his hands and smiling down on it. The apron also had the Fallen Oak Baptist logo and web address. They were part of a limited series made for a fundraiser bake sale three years ago, available for a suggested donation of only $40.

"Where is Seth?" Jenny snapped.

"I imagined he's up in the media room with the other kids," Dr. Goodling said. "Now, you don't just come barging into my house, dripping water everywhere—"

Jenny stripped off her sweatshirt and left it like a wet towel on the foyer floor. She ran upstairs in only her small tank top, with a maximum amount of skin exposed.

"What on Earth?" Mrs. Goodling gasped. "Who is that?"

"I think it's the druggie girl from the Barrett party," Dr. Goodling said.

Jenny ran along the upstairs hall, pushing open doors to every room until she found the one where Seth, Ashleigh, Cassie and Neesha watched a movie on a big screen in a darkened room. Cassie and Neesha swung in the hanging chairs, while Seth lay on the couch with his head in Ashleigh's lap. Ashleigh's jeans were down to her knees, so that his head rested on her panties, pulling Ashleigh-energy from her bare thighs.

Jenny stormed into the room, still dripping, her black hair smeared down across her face. She flipped on the lights.

"Seth, get up!" Jenny yelled, and everyone jumped.

"What the hell?" Ashleigh pushed Seth off her, and he rolled drunkenly off the couch and onto the carpet. She stood up, fastening her pants around her waist. "Jenny Mittens? What are you doing in my house? Daddy!"

Jenny stalked toward her, holding out her cold, dripping, uncovered hands, staring at Ashleigh between the dark, wet strands of hair over her eyes.

"Ashleigh, move," Jenny said. "If you get in my way, I will give you such a deadly case of Jenny pox, you'll be nothing but a rotten corpse on your daddy's carpet. I'm taking Seth."

Jenny never stopped walking. Ashleigh screeched and ran out of her way, and Jenny continued straight ahead to Seth. She lifted Seth's hands in hers.

"Seth, get up!" she said. "Now!"

"Okay. Just a minute." He lay with his eyes closed, his fingers opening and closing at random.

"What did you do to him?" Jenny yelled at Ashleigh.

"I just filled him with love," Ashleigh said. "He's so in love, he can't even think right now. Too bad."

Jenny squeezed Seth's hands.

"Seth, please. My daddy's hurt. He's going to die, Seth."

With what looked like great effort, Seth managed to push his eyelids halfway open.

"Jenny," he said. "Are you friends with Ashleigh now?"

"Seth, up!" Jenny said.

"I will. Give me a few minutes." He closed his eyes.

"I'm calling the police," Ashleigh said. Then she screamed, "Stop!"

Jenny looked up at Ashleigh's sudden cry. She followed Ashleigh's gaze, and discovered Cassie and Neesha sneaking up on her, ready to pounce on Jenny's bare shoulders and arms. Ashleigh was yelling at them to stop.

"Try it," Jenny said. "I'll kill you both."

"She will," Ashleigh said. "She can't touch anyone..." She realized Jenny was gripping both of Seth's hands. "Why isn't he getting pox?"

"He's my opposite," Jenny said. "I kill and he heals."

"He heals?" Ashleigh sounded genuinely surprised. "So that's it. Little bastard can keep a secret."

Jenny could picture her father, pinned in mud under the tractor, the big machine sinking lower with every second that passed, crushing the life out of him. She needed to focus. She needed Seth awake and functioning.

Ashleigh had tremendous control of her powers. She could give people just a little, enough to entice them and make them her followers, or she could give a lot, like the tidal wave she'd sent through Seth at the Christmas party, so much that it conducted into Jenny and made her a grinning, horny idiot for the next twelve hours. Jenny hadn't known the powers could conduct through one person into another. If she had, she would have been even more frightened of herself.

But this wasn't the time for fear. She knew her touch could wake Seth a little from Ashleigh's trance. Maybe if she intended it, and focused her mind, and pushed her power out instead of trying to hold it in, she really could accomplish something.

Jenny imagined Ashleigh's power woven through Seth like golden thread, a net that bound him to Ashleigh. Now Jenny imagined a terrible black cloud forming in the pit of her own stomach. It was the way she had always envisioned the pox, swarms of tiny flies that passed through her skin into other living things. Now she focused on them, and told them they had one single purpose: to eat the golden thread laid down by Ashleigh. Jenny couldn't heal people, and she couldn't make people love her, but she could by God unleash destruction.

Jenny saw this slithering, buzzing cloud of oily-bodied flies fly up through her chest and concentrate around her mouth. She felt the skin on her lower face bubble and pop as bleeding sores formed on her lips. Pustules cracked open on her face, extruding curls of pus like tiny white worms.

"Gross!" Ashleigh said. "Everybody get back."

"That is really, really sick," Neesha said. She was absently clicking pictures with her cell phone.

Inside Jenny's mouth, her tongue swelled and deformed as sores bloomed all over it. She straddled Seth, pushing her hands down on his. She leaned in toward his face and stuck out her swollen tongue, which dripped blood, and creamy yellow pus, and a thick, clear fluid.

"Do not do that," Ashleigh said. Her parents were behind her now, watching in shock and disgust from the doorway.

Jenny opened Seth's mouth and pushed her tongue all the way inside, stretching it as far as she could, infecting him with her fluids. She imagined the cloud of flies swarming out, down into Seth, chewing away at the golden bonds Ashleigh had woven.

"I'm gonna be sick," Cassie said.

Jenny came up after a minute and looked around her. No one had attacked her while she worked on Seth. She saw fear in all of them now. For the first time, Jenny felt more than dangerous. She felt powerful. She could use what she had, and she could direct it, just like Ashleigh.

Jenny stood up and held out her bare arms. At her wish, boils erupted up and down the length of them, spreading to her hands, where sores cracked open and bled. She looked at Dr. Goodling and decided to blow his mind. She held up both her palms toward him and willed the broken sores to run together into one big, open wound in each palm.

"Behold," she said to him, and the voice that came out of her was not anything she had heard before. It was her, but more than her. It was Jenny with power, Jenny laughing at those who defied her, Jenny the ancient and terrible spirit. "Behold, priest, the markings of Christ."

Mrs. Goodling screamed and grabbed his arm. Dr. Goodling looked like he would pee himself.

Jenny laughed, and the laugh was not exactly hers, either. It had a truculence, a deep enjoyment of the man's fear and suffering. It was even a little Ashleigh-like, but even sharper and colder.

At her feet, Seth rose on all fours, coughing and sucking for air. She put an arm under him and helped him up.

"What did you do?" Ashleigh asked.

"I undid your work," Jenny told her.

Seth looked around the room, blinking, and still coughing. He looked pale and shaken, like a bad fever had just broken, but his eyes were open and clear.

"Jenny?" he asked. "What's happening?"

That snapped Jenny's mind back into her dad's emergency.

"My dad's hurt," Jenny said. "Maybe dying. We have to go."

"Really?" Seth said. "Let's go!"

They ran out of the room. Dr. Goodling stepped forward, as if he meant to block their way, but Jenny held out one hand full of open sores towards him.

"Daddy, no!" Ashleigh yelled, but it was unnecessary. Dr. Goodling recoiled from Jenny's leprous fingers.

They ran down the hall, the front steps, and out the front door. Everyone else came after them, but kept their distance.

"Take my car," Jenny said. When she was in the driver's seat, and Seth had the passenger door most of the way closed, Jenny punched the gas. She didn't want to waste time with straightening out the crooked car and backing up. Instead, she made a sharp turn through the Goodling's rain-soaked front yard, turfing it deeply. She flattened a flower bed. Sheep and shepherds skipped off her windshield, trailing broken wires. Then she plowed through the wall of the nativity stable, scattering plastic boards and plastic hay everywhere.

She punched through the white picket fence and fishtailed out into the road, scattering broken picket slats all over the street. A plastic manger fell from the Lincoln's roof, followed by a plastic baby that bounced head over feet down the length of the hood, shedding the white plastic sheets that swaddled it, before landing in the street.

"That is really disturbing," Seth said.

Jenny fought the car's fishtailing, straightened it up, and accelerated again.

Behind them, Ashleigh, her two girlfriends, and her parents all piled into the Suburban. The Goodlings pulled out of the driveway to chase Jenny.

Jenny roared through town, the hail thick enough that it cracked her windshield and windows in a few places.

"This weather sucks," Seth said. "What happened to your dad?"

"A tractor rolled on top of him."

"Oh, Jesus," Seth said. "Is he okay?"

"No, Seth, why do you think I'm acting like this? Mrs. McNare says he's dying." Jenny's voice hitched a little, and she rubbed tears from her eyes and forced herself not to cry. "You're going to save him."

"Okay," Seth said. "But only if we survive the trip there."

Jenny didn't slow down. She swerved and hydroplaned their way out of town, to Hog Willow Road, nearly losing control of the car three times. She shot down the road, past the fields of humped earth and cows huddled together in the sudden rain, her accelerator flat on the floor mat.

Blue lights strobed inside her car, blinding her in the dark weather. A town policeman was on her rear bumper. Behind the cop was the Goodlings' SUV.

Jenny ignored the cop and sped past Merle Sanderson's house. They were surrounded by the McNare fields now. Ahead, an ambulance was parked on the side of the road, flashers blinking, both doors open.

"Right there." Seth pointed to the field closest to the ambulance. In a back corner, on the far side from them, several pick-up trucks had gathered, their headlights providing illumination in the storm.

Jenny turned off the paved road and onto the dirt track, which was choked with weeds and pockmarked with deep, muddy holes. Obviously, Mr. McNare hadn't cleared this one before his tractor died.

The mud slowed them down and the police car stayed right behind her. Eventually the old Lincoln had slogged as far as it was going in the mud and weeds, and its coated tires wouldn't turn. Jenny kicked open her door and jumped out. She and Seth ran across the field toward the truck lights. Lightning broke across the sky above them, followed quickly by a loud smack of thunder.

The scene at the overturned tractor was chaotic. Men shouted, threading ropes through the tractor and tying them to their truck bumpers. The paramedics stood uselessly to one side, since they couldn't reach Jenny's dad to help him.. Obese, bucktoothed Deputy Guntley, who had left his car to chase them across the field, had momentarily lost interest in pursuing Jenny. He caught his breath while the paramedics filled him in. Janet McNare and her daughter Shannon, usually a happy minion of Ashleigh's Christian group, stood nearby under an umbrella, their arms around each other, crying.

Jenny found her dad and knelt beside him. She didn't dare touch him, with her upper body so bare. She planted her knees in the mud and looked down on him.

The tractor had fallen on his legs, abdomen, chest, and the lower half of his right arm. Hail batted his exposed face. He was clearly not going to live, not even when they raised the tractor off him. Jenny couldn't believe they hadn't done that already.

"Daddy," she whispered.

His eyes, which were mostly closed, may have moved toward her, or it could have been splashing rainwater.

"Daddy, you just have to hang on for one minute. I brought Seth." She took Seth's hand as he knelt beside her. "He can help. Like I can hurt, he can help. Just don't go. Please."

Jenny was crying. Shannon McNare ran toward her, arms wide, clearly wanting to wrap Jenny in a hug.

"Don't touch me, Shannon!" Jenny snapped. "You'll get hurt, I'm serious."

Shannon flinched like she'd been punched and stopped where she was. Jenny looked past her, to Mrs. McNare with her big blue umbrella.

"Bring me that umbrella!" Jenny yelled at Shannon. The girl turned uncertainly to her mother, who gasped and handed it over. Shannon ran to Jenny's side and held the umbrella over Jenny's father, keeping the rain and ice from his face.

Finally the men, all of them farmers who'd come when they heard about the trouble, pulled on the ropes and decided they were satisfied. They piled into three different pick-up trucks tied to different parts of the tractor. They threw it in reverse, and tall geysers of mud erupted from their tires. Slowly, they inched back, and the tractor raised up off of Jenny's dad, and continued to rise.

Jenny cried out when she saw him. It looked like most of her dad had been replaced by shredded meat. Everything was crushed. She wondered if he could even be alive.

Then the tractor crashed down, and the ground shuddered. It landed on its tires, standing upright, shuddering from the impact. Her dad was free. Seth was already at his side, his sleeves rolled up.

"Out of the way!" a paramedic shouted at Seth, as the two EMT workers ran towards Darrell Morton's pulverized body. "Kid, move!"

"Both of you stop!" Jenny blocked the paramedics, while the remaining farmers and Mrs. McNare yelled at her and Seth to clear off. Jenny held out both her hands towards the paramedics, making them bubble with bleeding sores and strange blisters that wept a dark fluid like tree sap.

"Oh, sick," one of the paramedics said. "What is wrong with you?"

"I have the plague," Jenny said. "It'll kill you. Stay there."

Seth lay his hands on her father's crushed body. He pressed down and closed his eyes, and he concentrated. In front of everyone, Darrell Morton's crushed chest inflated as if filling with air. Then his abdomen, with clicking and clacking sounds as his shattered ribs fit themselves back together. Seth shuddered in the cold rain while his skin turned gray. So did many strands of his hair. His teeth gritted together in pain. He pressed down harder.

The onlookers had stopped yelling at Jenny and begun staring at Seth. The deputy, the paramedics, the farmers, the McNare family, Ashleigh and her parents, and Cassie and Neesha all stared as Darrell Morton's ruined legs straightened, puffed up, and regained their natural shape inside his muddy jeans. His left foot rotated and locked into place.

Jenny's dad gave a long, loud groan, and Seth fell over and splashed into the mud. Jenny hurried to Seth and pulled his torso into her lap and supported his head with her hand, since she couldn't touch her dad at all.

Her dad coughed several times, then he sat up, blinking. Gradually he stood, then stretched, as if his spine had been compacted a little. Then he noticed that everyone was staring at him.

"What happened?" he asked the crowd.

"That was a miracle," Shannon McNare breathed. "Wasn't it, Momma? A real miracle from Jesus."

Most people looked to Dr. Goodling, but the preacher just stared at Jenny's dad. Slowly, he turned to look at Jenny, who sat in the red mud with Seth's sickly, unconscious form laid out across her.

"Witchcraft," Ashleigh hissed, and that drew people's attention.

"What do you mean, Ashleigh?" Shannon asked.

"Jenny Mittens used witchcraft to save her father. Look, she sucked all the life out of Seth."

The farmers looked to Dr. Goodling on this, but the preacher hadn't gathered enough wits to talk. He was just staring at Jenny and Seth, his expression unreadable.

"Would somebody just tell me what's going on here?" Jenny's dad asked.

"Seth saved you," Jenny said. "Now help me pick him up, Daddy. We got to take care of him."

Nobody moved while Jenny and her dad lifted Seth to his feet. Seth roused a little.

"Sleep," Seth moaned. "Food."

"Where's your truck?" Jenny asked her dad.

"This way," he said. They carried Seth away across the field, supporting him on both sides. Nobody else moved to help. Nobody offered to give them a ride in one of the trucks. They trudged across the field, through hail and rain and sucking mud, toward the McNare driveway where he'd parked the rusty old Ram that morning. Her fingers and arms itched as the open sores closed themselves and were absorbed back into her skin.

At home, Jenny and her dad eased Seth out of the truck. He was barely conscious and couldn't walk without their help. They trudged through the hail and mud, one step at a time. Rocky yowled at them from the shed doorway. His tail was wagging, but he was not coming outside in this weather.

"Careful!" Jenny's dad said as they reached the porch steps. "You're touching him all over!"

"I can touch him, Daddy." Jenny helped Seth raise a foot onto the first step. "He's the only person."

Her dad just looked exhausted. They got Seth up the steps and into the house. They brought him to Jenny's room and laid him across her bed. He was drenched and still gray, his eyes closed.

Her dad went to his room and brought a thermal undershirt, flannel pajama pants, a pair of wool socks.

"I can take care of him," Jenny said. "I left some chili on the stove. Maybe you can save it."

Her dad's face looked drawn and tired as he stared at Seth. Finally, he walked towards the kitchen, and Jenny closed the door behind him.

She pulled off Seth's wet socks and touched his cold, damp feet. She thought of what she was about to do, taking off everything, and she felt a little excited. Then she felt guilty for feeling excited.

She pulled off his sweater and t-shirt, throwing everything onto her closet door to hang dry. She unbuckled his belt, then hesitated a little, feeling her face turn warm, before she unzipped him and pulled off his mud-soaked jeans. His shorts were plastered to his skin. Those had to go, too. She gently took them down, and she couldn't help but look.

That's it, she thought. That's his dick. She smiled.

Jenny found it easy to pull the wool socks down over his feet. It was more of struggle to get the pajama pants on, but she eventually managed that. His skin felt terribly icy to the touch, and his pulse was faint.

Jenny looked at him, then came up with another way to warm him up, the way you actually were supposed to do it when someone was freezing. She made sure the door was closed and turned the lock as quietly as she could. Then she stripped out of her own cold, sopping clothes, until she wasn't wearing a stitch. Jenny straddled Seth, as she had before giving him the pox-infested kiss. Then she lay down on top of him, her bare chest on his, her face against his neck. She pulled the blanket over her and wrapped it completely around them like a cocoon.

She laid her face against his and started kissing his cheek, then worked her way over to his lips. She didn't have any thought that the kissing would help him. It was completely selfish. She wanted to touch him, she could touch him, and she had a lifetime of loneliness to make up for.

He awoke a little, and his hands found their way to her.

"Jenny?" he whispered.

"It's me," she whispered back. "Are you feeling better?"

"Starting to," he said. Then he slipped a hand into her wet hair and pulled her face down to him, so he could kiss her again. She felt his skin grow warmer against hers. His hands slid up to her breasts, and she shivered, and not just because his hands were cold. His fingertips brushed her nipples, and she thought she would die of pleasure.

He grew hotter, recovering from the icy rain. It was the second time her touch had ever helped anyone.

After a minute, one of his hands caressed its way down her back. His eyes widened when he realized she was completely naked. Jenny felt something stir and push against her thigh.

"My dad's in the next room," she whispered. "And you need food. You've had enough strain today."

Jenny slid out from the covers and got to her feet. Seth gazed at her. His eyes seemed to tickle her, making her skin tingle wherever he looked. She wanted to giggle and cover herself, but she didn't. She kept her hands at her hips and let him see her.

"You know," Seth said, "I could handle a little more strain…"

"Ha." Jenny slung the thermal shirt to him. She dressed herself in dry jeans, sweatshirt, and gloves. She scrubbed her hair with a towel, and watched herself in a mirror as she tied it back. Seth came up behind her, dressed now, and wrapped his arms around her. One hand just happened to land on her left breast, near her heart. He kissed the side of her neck. He was hard against the back of her jeans.

"You better put that away," Jenny said. "We're fixing to have chili with my dad."

"Then give me one more." He turned her head and kissed her until Jenny's dad knocked and announced they should come eat.

Some of the chili had scalded against the bottom of the pot, since Jenny hadn't moved it from the hot burner in her panic to leave. Her dad had salvaged most of it. All three of them sat at the kitchen table with steaming bowls of venison chili in front of them. Jenny was too nervous to eat with Seth so close to her. Her dad stirred his chili again and again, looking somber.

Seth, on the other hand, tore through three full bowls of it, spooning it fast, not talking until he was full.

"That was really good." Seth sighed and leaned back. "Best chili I've ever had. Thank you, Mr. Morton."

"Huh?" Jenny's dad looked up. His eyes were a thousand miles away. "Oh. Jenny made it." He went back to his slow stirring.

"Really?" Seth looked at Jenny and raised his eyebrows a couple of time, which made her laugh.

"Jenny," her dad said without looking up. "I think I died."

"Almost, Daddy," Jenny said. "Seth brought you back and healed you up. So, can I date him now?"

He raised his eyes to look at Seth, who was scraping his spoon around the bowl for stray sauce.

"How'd you do that?" he asked Seth.

"I always could," Seth said. "Whenever I touch people. They just heal." He dropped the spoon in the bowl. "I've never done it like that, where everyone could see it. It's always been secret."

"He's just like me, Daddy," Jenny said. "He's my opposite."

"Healing." Her dad shook his head. He lifted out a spoonful of chili and tilted it, letting it drizzle back into the bowl. "That sounds a lot more useful than what you got."

"I don't know," Seth said. "You should have seen Jenny today. She was ferocious."

Jenny rolled that word in her mind a little. Ferocious. She liked it.

"I do thank you, Seth," he said. "I guess there's no way I can ever repay you." His eyes shifted to Jenny. "And I guess I know what you want for it."

"Daddy, don't say it like that!" Jenny said.

Her dad looked at Seth a long time. Seth straightened up in his chair, aware he was being inspected.

"You just be good to her," Jenny's dad told Seth. "You treat her like she ought to be treated."

"I will, sir," Seth said.

Jenny's dad set his spoon down in his chili. He looked very tired.

"Jenny, can you clean up?" he asked. "I think I need to go to the bed for a while."

"Sure, Daddy! I'll take care of everything."

"I guess you already did." He stood and walked back to his room, shaking his head. He closed the door behind him.

"Good-night, Daddy! I love you," Jenny said. She took Seth's hand. Their fingers curled together. She looked at him, and she couldn't stop smiling.

CHAPTER EIGHTEEN

Seth's parents returned to Florida the day after New Year's. Until then, he could only sneak out to see Jenny for a couple hours at a time. When they talked on the phone, Seth sometimes had to pretend he was talking to Ashleigh instead of Jenny, if his parents were around. He had told Jenny about his father's decree. He'd also called the phone company and blocked Ashleigh's cell and home numbers from his home phone, as well as Cassie and Neesha's numbers, to reduce any chance Ashleigh would talk to his parents and give the game away. Jenny couldn't wait for the Barretts to go back to Florida. Jenny had thought Seth's dad was nice, since he'd covered for Jenny at the party, but apparently he was a real tyrant in his own way.

Jenny drove the Lincoln, which she hadn't yet returned to Merle, up the wide brick driveway, past the old dogwoods. Last time, she'd been scared to make this drive up to the house. Today, she was giddy.

There was no valet service this afternoon, but Seth directed her down a side spur of the driveway so she could park in front of the four-car garage, which was as wide as her entire house. He opened her car door for her and held out his arm, which she accepted.

The door in the garage led to something Seth called "the mud room," where apparently you took off your dirty shoes and raincoats to hang them up. There was a big laundry room here, too, and a narrow staircase to the upper floors.

Another door took them through a pantry, where there was a deep freezer as tall as Jenny's waist, and into the kitchen. Jenny stared at the vast sub-zero refrigerator, the vistas of tiled countertop. All the cabinets looked antique, with elaborately molded door pulls, but the appliances were sleek and black, with digital touch screens.

"Is this where you'll be cooking for me?" Jenny asked.

"No, I promised you a *nice* dinner," Seth told her. "I'm having something delivered later."

"Oh, just having something delivered, huh?" It sounded like an insane luxury to Jenny, though they had ordered pizza a few times, on special occasions like her birthday.

"Until then," he said. "What do you want to do? The place is ours."

Jenny liked the sound of that.

"Just show me around," she said. "So I don't get lost in here."

Seth took her to the dining room, where the table seated twenty-four, and big portraits of Colonel Ezra Barrett and Jon Seth Barrett I glared down from either side of the massive brick fireplace. They crossed the receiving hall, the scene of Jenny's latest humiliation by Ashleigh. There was also a library with floor-to-ceiling bookshelves and its own fireplace, and probably the only antique chairs in the house that actually looked comfortable. There was a billiards room. There was the office, which was frightening and sad at the same time, with all the dead animals. The whole house was dark, not only because of all the black and brown wood, and the dour paintings and photographs, but also because the windows were narrow and stingy. If they had intended to create an oppressive, melancholy home, the designers had succeeded.

They reached a gallery at the back, where French doors opened onto a giant porch with two swings and a row of rocking chairs. Nearby were the stairs leading up to the second-floor gallery where she'd spent so much time watching the people on the veranda, and now Jenny learned that upstairs gallery was called the "music room."

Seth opened one of the doors and took her out to the porch. The back yard sloped away below them, filled with rows of peach trees that faded into pine woods on either side of the orchard. Another hill rose beyond the peach trees, and Jenny thought she could see little buildings there.

"What's that?" she asked Seth, pointing to structure on the far hill.

"Oh, that," Seth said. "You want to go there? It's not a long walk."

"Just a second." Jenny unlatched her black high heels. After a moment's reflection, she removed her gloves, too. She stepped barefoot onto the cold grass.

"Don't you worry about snakes?" he asked. "Spiders?"

"Never have. They don't live long enough to hurt me. Only you can do that." She took his hand and let him lead her into the orchard. She loved the feeling of even a little of their skin rubbing together.

In January, the trees were just skeletons, looking dead to the world, their life slumbering in hidden places inside their roots. The rows of bare trees made her feel a little wistful as she passed among them.

They crossed a footbridge over a small irrigation canal.

"This whole area used to be orchards," Seth told her. He gestured at the pine trees rising up on either side. "My grandfather said any land that could be put to use, should be. My dad doesn't care as much. He just keeps a few trees for tradition and all that."

"I bet it's pretty in the spring," Jenny said.

"Good peaches, too," Seth said. "Did you know South Carolina actually produces more peaches than Georgia? They totally ganked our title as the Peach State."

"You are full of fascinating information, Seth Barrett," Jenny said.

"Come on. I want to show you something."

They reached a clearing with knee-high weeds, fenced off by wooden rails, some of which were broken or rotten. At the back of the clearing was a long two-story structure, the bottom floor divided into little compartments with rusty gates.

"That used to be the stable," he said. "We haven't had horses since I was little. You can also find barns, if you look around the woods. And there's a house with tree grown up through it, used to be my grandfather's cottage."

"We should make a horror movie," Jenny said.

"My house would be enough for that," Seth said. "You should see the third floor."

"Then we'll make the sequel out here."

"This way." Seth led her along a trail up the hill. It grew steep near the top, and several giant stairs had been placed in the ground here. They looked hewn from the same slab of dark gray granite as the big chimney in the house. They also looked intended for beings much larger than humans, and Jenny had to take a huge step up each one, then a few steps across to reach the next one.

At the top stair, a wrought-iron gate opened into a high brick wall. Through the gate, Jenny could see rows of dark granite megaliths. Seth took out his Audi key ring and found an iron key inscribed with elaborate scrollwork.

"What is this place?" Jenny whispered.

"The Barrett burial ground." He slid the key into the big lock, and it squealed as he turned it. He pushed the gate inward on heaving, grinding hinges.

"You carry the key to your family's graveyard around with you?"

"Oh, yeah," Seth said. "It's tradition. My father carries one, too."

"That's kind of..."

"Creepy?" Seth asked. "Check this out. Turn around."

Jenny turned. Behind her, the gloomy house rose on its hill above the bare orchard.

"You can see the cemetery from any bedroom in the house," Seth said. "My great-grandfather designed it that way. It's supposed to remind you of your mortality, and death, and all that. I guess it's to encourage you to hurry up and make money quick."

He stepped through the gate.

"That's so weird," Jenny said. "I'd have nightmares."

"It gets weirder," he said.

Jenny stepped over the threshold into his graveyard. A crushed-gravel path led the way ahead, through rows and rows of identical granite slabs, all of them blank. At the very back, Jenny could see a little church, complete with a steeple and bells, just large enough for a couple of people to stand inside, crowded together, or for one person to kneel and pray. The sun was setting behind it.

"There aren't any names," she whispered as they walked past the rows of stones.

"There are some back here." When they were only a few rows from the miniature church at the back, he stopped. He brought her to a stone on the left side of the path. "Here's my grandfather. Look."

The inscription on the left side of the stone read:

JONATHAN SETH BARRETT II
1923-1995

"Now, look at these." Seth led her back across the path, to the same row, on the right side of the path. He touched an inscription on the left flank of the first stone. It read:

JONATHAN SETH BARRETT III
1962-

"That's my father," Seth told her. "And my mom's here." He pointed to the inscription on the right flank of the same stone:

MATHILDA IRIS MAYFIELD BARRETT
1965-

"Wow," Jenny said. "That would be crazy to see your name like that, wouldn't it?"

"Over here." Seth moved to the next stone in the row and reached for the name inscribed on the left flank of it. His fingers curled back at the last second, not wanting to touch it.

JONATHAN SETH BARRETT IV
1992-

"This is where I end up," Seth told her. He moved his fingers to the right flank of his gravestone, which was smooth and blank. "And over here...some lucky girl."

"Is this why you brought me here, Seth?" Jenny asked. "To invite me to your grave?" She meant it as a joke, but he looked at her solemnly for a moment. Then he laughed a little, but it was forced and cold.

"No, I actually wanted to show you this." Seth took her to the third stone in the row. "This really should be mine. It's for the second-born son of the third J.S. Barrett. Crazy old great-grandpa got ahead of himself with the inscriptions, though, because my dad named his first son Carter."

Seth wore a deep, serious frown as he touched this inscription. It read:

CARTER MAYFIELD BARRETT
1986-2000

"I didn't know you had a brother," Jenny said.

"He died in a car crash," Seth said. "Riding with a friend's family on the way to the beach. He was trapped for a while before he died. If I'd been there, I could have saved him."

Jenny held Seth's hand tighter. Then she decided to go ahead and embrace him. It was the third time her touch had ever helped anyone.

"It was hundreds of miles away," Seth whispered. "I didn't know he was in trouble. That's why I never told my parents about how I can heal people. By the time I really figured it out myself, Carter was already gone, and all I could think about was how I could have saved him."

"Seth, that's not your fault."

"We kept it quiet around town. Otherwise everybody wants to get involved, go to the funeral, make a big production of it. Because, you know, the Barrett family."

"They want to pay respect," Jenny said.

"Like hell. Every time a Barrett dies in this town, everybody just thinks, 'There's one more bastard I don't owe money to. The rest drop dead and we're free and clear.' That's why they like our funerals."

Jenny was quiet, not sure what she thought of that.

"I've saved a lot of people," he said. "Did you know that? Anytime I see an accident on the road, I pull over, and I heal anybody who's hurt. Then I just get in my car and drive away while everybody's still freaking out. When I saw you by the road that day, I thought there'd been a wreck."

"There was," Jenny said. "My dog was wrecked."

"I'm glad I stopped."

"You didn't run away when you finished, either."

"I had to rebuild his whole leg," Seth said. "That sucked out everything I had. I never felt anything like that, until I healed your father. That was a big one."

"A very big one." Jenny kissed him.

Seth showed her the older rows of graves, including the original J. S. Barrett. The very back row was a little different. Indentations had been carved out of the megaliths, and older, much smaller gravestones had been cemented inside to provide identification. These ran back to Elijah Samuel Barrett, 1803-1849. The night was falling, and Jenny could barely read the eroded inscriptions.

"My great-grandfather had his ancestors disinterred and moved here," Seth explained. "He wanted everyone to be part of the same plan. Up there, all those empty rows we passed? I'm supposed to fill those graves with generations of future Barretts."

"Is this where you take all your girlfriends?" Jenny asked.

"No." Seth gave another humorless laugh. "I don't tell people about my great-grandfather's personal death cult. I kind of keep that to myself."

"Then why did you want to show me?"

Seth looked at her, gathering his thoughts.

"I wanted you to know this is really me," Seth said. "I'm not doped up on Ashleigh anymore. This is who I really am, part of my weird family." He shrugged. "You probably think we're crazy."

"No," Jenny said. "But can we leave the creepy graveyard before it gets dark?"

"Yeah, good idea," Seth said. "We don't want to run into Great-Grandpa's ghost."

"Why did you have to say that?"

"I vant to vrite you a mortgage..." Seth said in a ghostly voice, "...on a mortuary!"

"Seth!" Jenny shrieked. Seth ran after her, arms raised. Jenny raced up the path between the gravestones, her bare, callused feet slapping the gravel.

"Interest rates are spookily low!" he said in the same voice. Jenny ran faster, laughing and shrieking at the same time. He chased her out of the cemetery, bounding after her down the steps.

He caught up with her in the orchard, picked her up, and slung her over his shoulder. He continued running, holding her legs while she hung upside down behind him, clinging to his back, laughing uncontrollably.

Seth finally set her down on the back porch, and he kissed her. She looked over his shoulder, past the orchard, to the brick wall on top of the hill. In the moonlight, she saw the open gate gleaming.

"We left the gate open," she whispered. "Won't the ghosts get out?"

"They're already out," he whispered back. "They're everywhere."

The Italian food was delivered all the way from Vernon Hill, so Seth tipped the driver a twenty. Seth carried the bags into the kitchen, and insisted that Jenny sit at the dining room table and pretend he was cooking everything.

"One house secret," he said. "Forget the head of the table. It's drafty. You want to sit right in the middle, facing the fireplace."

Jenny sat where he recommended, and he brought a bottle of wine and a pair of glasses. He opened the bottle and handed her the cork.

"What am I supposed to do with this?" she asked him.

"Like at a restaurant. You sniff it."

Jenny sniffed. "It smells like wet cork."

"No, you're just supposed to nod your head, like it's all beneath you."

"Okay." Jenny put her nose in the air and nodded once.

"Perfect." Seth smiled as he poured a tiny splash in her glass. "Now, you taste it."

Jenny tasted the wine. It reminded her a little bit of cherries. She gave the same snooty nod.

"You've got it." He poured full glasses for both of them and left the bottle on the table.

He brought the courses out one at a time, after transferring them from the disposable aluminum pans in which they'd been delivered into a set of the Barretts' good china. He brought salad, then spaghetti—which Jenny didn't really want, since she'd eaten venison spaghetti three times this week, but she didn't say anything--then manicotti, then lasagna. At some point she noticed that she was using forks and knives made of gold, and eating off plates inset with the same metal. When she mentioned this to Seth, he laughed.

"Don't think my ancestors were extravagant," he said. "They outlawed gold in the Great Depression, but you could own it for industrial use. So Great-Grandpa had all his gold coins melted and made into tools. Upstairs, there's still a few golden hammers and screwdrivers in a safe. It's kind of hilarious."

Though Jenny was stuffed, Seth insisted she try the tiramisu, claiming he'd worked all week on it. She'd didn't regret it. She had three spoonfuls of the chocolate, cake, and cream before she really couldn't take anymore. She'd had half the bottle of wine, which was a lot for her. She wasn't drunk, but everything had a warm buzzing feeling, a lot like what she'd felt when Ashleigh had enchanted her and Seth at the Christmas party. No wonder her dad liked to drink.

After she was done, Jenny stood up and collected her purse from the chair beside her.

"That was great," she said. "Now I want to see the rest of the house."

"Okay," Seth said. "Except for the third floor. We never go up there."

Seth reached an open hand across the table. Jenny took it, puzzled. They could barely reach their arms across it, and it was a long walk to either end of the table.

"Come on over." He tugged on her arm. Jenny climbed up on the table, and laughed as she walked with bare feet among the dishes and empty wineglasses. He took her in his arms as she came down on his side, and kissed her as he set her on her feet.

She drew back after a few seconds. "Now, the rest of the house."

"It's all the same," he said. "Just pictures of dead people, furniture used by dead people. A museum of who we used to be."

"I want to see."

Seth took her upstairs, where it was indeed more of the same. She'd seen the music room and much of one hall. There were multiple guest rooms, bathrooms, sitting rooms. Seth skipped his own bedroom, she noticed.

"This is my favorite," he said as he pushed open another guest room door. On the wall was an eight-spoked wooden wheel from an old sailing ship. There was a model frigate on the mantel, and an iron anchor in the fireplace for holding logs. Paintings of the ocean and sailing ships hung on the walls, filling the room with morose blues and grays.

"These are made from actual sails." Seth touched the thick canvas bed curtains that encircled the bed. "They're a hundred and ninety years old. Been all over the Americas. When you open the windows, these snap against each other and it sounds like you're on a boat. We used to pretend the bed was a pirate ship."

"It's too cold to open the windows," Jenny said.

"That's true."

Jenny parted the curtains and climbed up on the bed. It was huge compared to hers at home. She liked how the curtains and canopy turned the bed into its own little soft-walled room. She sat down in the middle, stretching out her legs, and tossed her purse all the way to the foot of the bed.

Seth climbed in beside her. He pointed up at the canopy frame.

"Those timbers come from the same ship," he said. "The whole bed does."

"If you were a pirate," Jenny said. "And you boarded my ship, what would you do to me?"

"I'd keep you for booty."

Jenny turned to face him. "And what if I fought back?"

"Then I'd capture you." He grabbed both of her wrists and pushed her back on the bed.

"And then what would you do to me?"

He looked at her, then he lay across her, his arms on both sides of her, and he kissed her. Jenny pulled him close and opened her mouth, letting his tongue inside her. She put her hands under his shirt and slid it up, and ran her fingers along his muscular belly. He had to raise up so she could pull his shirt up over his arms and off his head.

He took off her shirt, and she unclasped her bra for him. He threw that aside and scooped up her breasts in his fingers, then brought his face down and surrounded one with his mouth.

Jenny cried out, her hips pushing up against him. Her hands clenched down on his head as he licked and sucked at her. She let him do it until she couldn't take the agony of that pleasure anymore, and then she pulled him toward her face and kissed him hungrily.

She slid her hands down over his smooth chest, across his stomach, to the buckle of his belt. She tugged the leather strip out of the buckle, then unbuttoned his pants and slid them down, along with his underwear. She took him in her hand, feeling an incredible heat well up inside of her. She rubbed her fingers along the erect length of it, exploring him, and he gasped a little.

Then Jenny unzipped her own pants and pushed them down. He let her look at the lacy black panties she'd picked out for him, and then she pushed those down, too. She kicked all of their clothes off the bed, momentarily puffing out the sail-curtain.

He kissed her again, and when he was done, she took him in her hand again.

"Come on," she whispered.

"Are you sure?"

"You don't want to?"

"I haven't since ninth grade," he said. "And that was just a couple times. And then Ashleigh would only do it with her hand—"

"Sh," Jenny said. "I'm not Ashleigh. And if you ever say her name again when I'm naked in front of you, I'll break your mouth."

"Okay," he whispered. "But you still want to, right?"

"Look in my purse," Jenny said.

He found the black purse where she'd tossed it across the bed, and took out the red pack of Trojans Jenny had bought at the gas station.

"You already thought about this," he said.

"Hurry," she whispered.

He tore it open. When he was ready, Jenny spread out her knees and let him lay between them. She put her hand between her legs, rubbed him for a second. Then she eased him into her.

It hurt, and she gripped the blanket as he broke through. She pressed her thighs inward against his hips. He moved slowly inside her, either because he was gentle or because he was still figuring out what to do. He gradually went faster, and Jenny pressed herself upward to take him, grunting with mingled pain and pleasure. Then he said her name and she felt something hot punch against the condom inside her.

It only lasted a couple of minutes. When they were done, she lay against him, kissing him. Then she just looked into his eyes, her hand on his cheek.

"I love you, Jenny," he whispered.

"I think I love you, too," she whispered back.

They let that hang in the air for a while, while she lay with her eyes closed, her face against his chest, his arm holding her.

Much later, he whispered, "I need to ask you a favor."

"You picked a good time for it."

"You know how they have that stupid Easter egg hunt in the square every year?" he asked. "For the kids?"

"Yeah?"

"My dad says we need a representative there, since we sponsor it. He's too busy getting ready for a regatta. Mr. Burris, the bank manager, will be out of town. So I'm the cheapest he could find."

"That's a lot of people," Jenny said.

"Will you come with me?" Seth asked. "The boredom will kill me without you."

"I don't know."

"You can cover up. It's Easter. It's like a mini-Halloween. Ladies wear gloves and hats." He looked in her eyes. "Come on, Jenny. It's not that scary."

"Who said I was scared?"

"So you'll go."

"I don't have anything to wear."

"I'll buy you the biggest hat in the county."

Jenny laughed. She rolled on her side and then laid back against him. He embraced her across the stomach, and that one hand just happened to end up on her left breast again, over her heart.

"Will you keep me safe?" she whispered.

"I promise."

"Then I'll go anywhere with you."

CHAPTER NINETEEN

Ashleigh couldn't get Seth on the phone for several days. He didn't answer his cell, and when she called his house, she just got a recording saying the number was "not available." For a while she was paranoid that he'd put her on call block—probably Jenny Mittens' idea—but then she tried from Cassie's cell and got the same result. She even had Neesha try from her house, and the same thing happened.

Ashleigh was desperate to know what was happening with him. She was cautiously excited to learn about Seth's power, but she resented learning about it from Jenny Mittens. When Ashleigh saw Seth heal Jenny's dad, she realized she'd missed plenty of opportunities to make better use of Seth. Ashleigh could even stab and torture people if she wanted, and make Seth erase the evidence, so her victims would sound crazy if they told anybody. There was a lot of fun to be had there.

The real problem was Jenny Mittens. Apparently, the creepy girl had gotten control of her own powers, and was ready to wield them against Ashleigh. She shook with anger when she considered how Jenny had stormed into *Ashleigh's* house, stuck her tongue down the throat of *Ashleigh's* boyfriend, and broken *Ashleigh's* spell over Seth. What right did Jenny have to interfere in Ashleigh's life?

Ashleigh needed to know if Seth was still on her side, or if Jenny Mittens had him. Now that she'd seen how powerful Seth really was, she wanted him even more. And Ashleigh feared Jenny Mittens more than ever. One thing that could not be allowed was for Jenny and Seth to combine against Ashleigh. Together, they might be more powerful than Ashleigh, and they would be a threat to Ashleigh for the rest of her life.

Ashleigh had only one question: did she only need to destroy Jenny, or did she need to destroy them both?

Seth finally called her cell phone on the first Sunday in January, the last day of winter break.

"Seth!" Ashleigh said. "I'm so glad you're okay! I've been worried sick about you!"

"Kill the bright and chipper, Ashleigh," Seth told her. "Things aren't going back to how they were. I know you've been using your power against me, and you've used it more and more since I met Jenny. I could barely even think. You tricked me into believing that I loved you."

"Seth...that is just crazy talk. Nobody can cast spells!"

"And I can't heal people who've been crushed by tractors. And you run screaming, for no reason at all, whenever Jenny holds up her empty hands."

Ashleigh panicked. She felt like she'd been stripped open and exposed. Soon the whole world could know about Ashleigh's secret. She changed tactics.

"Seth, I love you," she said. "You know that. I've given you years of my life."

"You mean you've taken years of mine."

Ashleigh gasped as if hurt by this.

"Seth, we belong together," Ashleigh said. "Isn't that obvious? With my abilities and yours, we could do anything. We could rule the world, Seth. Seriously."

"I don't want to rule the world." His voice sounded angry over the phone.

"Then what do you want?" Ashleigh snapped.

"I want you to leave us alone. Jenny knows how to break your spell now. You won't trap me again. Just leave us alone and mind your own business, if you have any clue how to do that."

"Seth, that's it," Ashleigh said. "I'm coming over."

"You're not. I don't want to see you. And I definitely don't want to touch you."

"Seth!" Ashleigh made herself sob. It wasn't hard to fake, since she was terrified of losing control of this whole part of her life. "You're just going to leave me? You're going to crush me like that?

208

That's heartless, Seth. You're my one true love. I don't think I can live without you."

"Ashleigh," he said, "You can trick people into thinking they love you. And you can act like you love other people. But I don't think you understand real love at all."

"Seth, don't do this to me. I need you so bad." She was whimpering now, reduced to playing for his pity. If only she could touch him, she could sort this out fast. "Please let me see you just one last time. I'm going to die if you leave me like this. I'll come over, and we can just talk."

"Good-bye, Ashleigh." Then Seth, the self-important bastard, hung up on her.

Seething, Ashleigh grabbed her car keys and ran outside. She raced across town to Seth's house, but the front gate was locked. She stood there and pressed the buzzer, again and again, but got no response. She held down the buzzer and screamed a long tirade of insults into the speaker, not entirely sure whether he could hear her, but it made her feel better.

Ashleigh stepped back and looked at the fence. It was tall, at least twelve feet, and topped with sharp iron points. The gate was solid. The two stone lions perched on the columns mocked her with their distant, knowing stares.

"Fuck you, Seth!" she screamed at the top of her lungs, up toward the house. Then she kicked her car, before getting inside and driving away.

When spring semester began, there were two big subjects of gossip in school. One concerned the fact that Seth Barrett and Jenny Mittens had arrived at school together and were seen holding hands, even kissing. Ashleigh was quick to tell everyone that she had dropped Seth, not the other way around, but it was a hard tide to turn. It didn't help that Seth was with someone new, while Ashleigh was alone. The implications were obvious.

Even if Ashleigh had left him because he was with Jenny, that was only a minor detail. Jenny Mittens had been preferred over Ashleigh Goodling by the boy who could have anyone. In the world of Fallen Oaks High, it was the equivalent of the French Revolution—with Ashleigh as the beheaded Marie Antoinette. Everywhere, people were looking at Ashleigh, whispering, pointing, trying to figure out why Seth had dumped her. It was humiliating. Seth and Jenny had to be punished good and hard.

There was opportunity in the second rumor, the one about Seth and Jenny doing some crazy witchcraft over at the McNare farm, healing Jenny's dad after a tractor accident. This rumor was quieter and didn't spread so well, since many people who hadn't been there refused to believe it. This rumor had the seeds of something useful in it, Ashleigh thought.

Monday, Ashleigh caught a glimpse of the new couple at Jenny's locker, though Ashleigh didn't look too long, because she didn't want people thinking she was at all interested—or worse, that Ashleigh was jealous of Jenny Mittens.

Seth and Jenny talked very close to each other, looking into each other's eyes with secret, knowing smiles. While Seth and Ashleigh had sometimes gotten grabby with each other, maybe a little too passionate in public, there was something deeper and quieter between Seth and Jenny. It took Ashleigh time to figure out what it was: intimacy. That diseased slut had already put out for him. No wonder he was so smitten. Well, that would wear off, Ashleigh thought.

As Ashleigh passed them, one more thing made her ill. When Seth put his arm around Jenny, she saw he was now wearing little cloth gloves, just like Jenny. Somehow, that made Ashleigh furious.

Ashleigh immediately started shopping for a new guy as she walked down the hall, but her options were terrible. She wanted an athletic boy, but the majority of them were black, and Ashleigh certainly did not date black guys. Among the white guys, most were dumb hick boys who dipped tobacco and listened to David Allen Coe and would eventually die in bar fights or meth lab explosions.

Lunch period, when Ashleigh, Cassie and Neesha were on their way to the picnic tables, someone tapped Ashleigh's shoulder. Her head was so full of Jenny and Seth that she whirled around glaring, expecting one of them. Instead it was Darcy Metcalf, who looked on the verge of tears. Ashleigh quickly remembered she had bigger things going, more important than stupid issues with Seth. She made her face kind and concerned.

"Ashleigh," Darcy whispered. "I need to talk to you."

"Gosh, what is it, Darcy?" Ashleigh put a hand on Darcy's arm and let just enough juice seep out that Darcy would feel relieved to be talking to her.

"It's private," Darcy whispered.

"Okay." Ashleigh waved to Cassie and Neesha. "Catch up to you later, ladies."

For Darcy's privacy, they had to go out to the deserted football stadium and sit on the bleachers. Darcy leaned on Ashleigh's shoulder, weeping, and Ashleigh's lip curled. It felt like the girl was leaking snot onto Ashleigh's sweater.

"Come on, Darcy." Ashleigh eased Darcy's face away from her. She opened Darcy's panda-bear lunchbox and lifted out a Capri Sun. She even punched the straw into place before handing it to Darcy. "Hey, have some juice."

"Thank you." Darcy sipped the straw, and at the same time, snorted back a wad of snot and swallowed it. Ashleigh shivered with disgust.

"Now, nothing can be that bad, Darcy. Just tell me what the problem is."

"Ashleigh…I'm pregnant. With a baby." Darcy broke down crying again. "Momma's gonna kill me!"

"Oh, Darcy." Ashleigh covered her own mouth in pretend shock and horror. "How did this happen?"

"It was Bret Daniels," Darcy sobbed. "That night, at the library? He said he knew a pretty spot to hang out at Barrett Pond. We went there…and we started drinking tequila…" Darcy sobbed harder. "And we got carried away and we did it. Twice. And a third time when we woke up in the morning. Oh, Ashleigh, you shouldn't have set me up with him! You ruined everything."

"Come on, Darcy. I was doing you a favor. You wanted to get with Bret. You asked me to do it. You can't blame me for your irresponsible choices."

"But I just wanted him so bad—and he wanted me—"

"That's why I always say women need to lead the way on abstinence, because boys won't," Ashleigh said. "You failed in your responsibility. Now God has given you this sin child to punish you and force you to learn responsibility."

"But what do I do?" Darcy wailed.

"Are you going to eat those?" Ashleigh pointed to the yellow and orange Cheetos bag in Darcy's lunchbox. Darcy shook her head, and Ashleigh ripped them open and started snacking. One good thing about her power, and the constant energy drain that went with it, was that Ashleigh could eat like a cow and never gain weight.

"Well," Ashleigh crunched, "I know you aren't thinking about abortion. You're not that wicked."

"No, of course not!" Darcy breathed. "I would never."

"Good. And what does Bret say?"

"We're not together anymore!" Darcy put her face in her hands. "He's dating some sophomore girl from the swim team."

"Well," Ashleigh said, "Now he has to marry you."

"What?" Darcy looked frightened. "I don't want to marry him! I want to go to college and meet a nice Christian guitar player—"

"Those are your plans, Darcy. Now you have to give those up and let God's plan take over. If Bret is good enough to impregnate you, he's good enough to marry you."

Darcy laid her arms across her knees, and her face in her arms. She was sobbing very hard now, her whole body shaking, and Ashleigh could even feel it through the bleachers' bench seating. Ashleigh snacked on Cheetos while she waited.

"The good thing," Ashleigh said as she tilted up the Cheetos bag and shook the last orange crumbs into her mouth. "Is God's will is so clear." She chomped on the Cheetos remnants and talked with her mouth full. "He wanted this baby born, and He picked you and Bret as the parents. Submit yourself to God's will and everything will be fine." Ashleigh dropped the empty Cheetos bag down between then bleachers and licked the orange cheese powder from her fingers. Then she took Darcy's hands and looked deep in Darcy's eyes. She pumped her enchanting energy deep into Darcy—and through Darcy, into the little developing fetus inside her. "But I want to tell you something now, Darcy."

Darcy raised her eyes and gave Ashleigh full attention.

212

"I want you to know," Ashleigh said. "That I'll always be there for your baby. And you. From now on, you're a very important part of my life, Darcy. And I'll take care of you."

"Oh, thank you, Ashleigh!" Darcy threw her arms around Ashleigh and cried into her shoulder again. "You're my best friend in the world. I love you, Ashleigh."

"There's just one thing." Ashleigh plucked up Darcy's left hand and tapped Darcy's abstinence ring. "You have to give this back."

"What? No!" Darcy shrieked.

"Come on, Darcy. How would the Crusaders look, with pregnant teenagers wearing abstinence rings? What would people say about my daddy's church, Darcy?"

"Oh, wow." Darcy's eyes were very wide now. "I didn't think about all that. I've disgraced the Crusaders. And Christians Act!" Her voice fell to a whisper. She slid the ring from her finger and stared at it. This was clearly breaking her. It was tedious to watch. "I've disgraced Fallen Oak Baptist. And my family!"

Ashleigh took the ring and pocketed it.

"You're a sinner, Darcy," Ashleigh said. "And you acted like a tramp. But God forgives, and so do I, if you do the right things from now on."

"I will, I promise," Darcy sniffed.

"Come here, baby." Ashleigh embraced Darcy, and then she surprised herself. She slipped one hand under Darcy's shirt and laid it on Darcy's skin, against the new bulge in Darcy's chubby belly. She bathed the unborn in hot, glowing Ashleigh-energy. She didn't know what this would do. The idea had only just occurred to her. "I love you, and I love your baby," Ashleigh said in a deeper, huskier voice that didn't sound quite like her own. "Stay with me and obey, and you both will thrive."

"Oh, thank you, Ashleigh!" Darcy kissed her cheek. Ashleigh would need a stack of Handi-Wipes to clean up the snot. She nudged Darcy away, and fortunately the end-of-lunch bell rang. Ashleigh stood and gathered her books.

"We'll stay in touch," Ashleigh said, and she was back to her normal voice again. She wasn't sure what had come over her. She stood and gathered up her books. "You just take good care of that baby. He—or she—has a very special purpose in life. You'll see."

As they were leaving school from their last class, Ashleigh and Neesha passed Shannon McNare in the hall. Shannon was talking animatedly to three other juniors, two girls and a boy. She waved her hands around, talking faster as the three of them grew more skeptical. Ashleigh slowed down to listen, and Neesha slowed with her.

"—and then his bones all fitted back together, and it was like it never happened!" Shannon said. "The whole time, Jenny Mittens is keeping everybody away with her hands—"

"How did she do that?" one girl asked.

"She—you had to see it—she made all these big cuts and infections open up all over her hands. I mean, they were opening and closing like little mouths, and all bloody and black. She told everyone she had the plague. It was so scary and gross!"

"Whatever, Shannon," one of the junior girls said.

"Shannon!" Ashleigh called out. She circled back to Shannon and hugged the younger girl tight, even pressing her cheek to Shannon's, as if they were long-time best buddies. The other juniors were impressed now, seeing that Shannon had somehow become one of Ashleigh's elect, the chosen few. Shannon herself was overwhelmed and delighted.

"What are y'all talking about?" Neesha asked the three juniors.

"Shannon says a bunch of crazy supernatural stuff happened at her farm," the boy replied.

"Oh, yeah," Ashleigh said, dropping into her stage whisper and looking around suspiciously. "We were there. It was the craziest I've ever seen. I knew Jenny Mittens was into witchcraft, but I didn't take it seriously, until that day at Shannon's. Jenny is completely with the devil now. And she brought Seth Barrett over to her side."

This brought gasps all around. All this, from no less an authority on both God and Seth Barrett than Ashleigh Goodling.

"Shannon," Ashleigh said. "How are you getting home? Driving?"

"I'm riding with Leslie." Shannon indicated one of the girls, who smiled at Ashleigh.

"Hi, Leslie." Ashleigh touched her hand, letting off some energy. "I'm going to need to borrow Shannon today, 'kay?"

"Oh, sure!" Leslie said.

"Come on, Shannon," Ashleigh said. "Say bye to your buddies."

"Bye!" Shannon said, elated as Ashleigh took her hand and pulled her up beside her as they walked.

Ashleigh took a long, critical look at Shannon. The girl had dark auburn hair, pinned back with barrettes, and fresh, enthusiastic green eyes. Ashleigh knew Shannon had the energy of a hummingbird. She was a little too farm girl, with the plaid shirts and the zero makeup, but that could be mended. The aw-shucks eagerness on Shannon's face was annoying to Ashleigh, but it would be useful. It was nearly impossible to believe Shannon would lie to you. There was some definite potential.

"Shannon," Ashleigh said. "Have I told you what a great job you've done as abstinence coordinator this year? A lot of people signed up and got buddies, more than I expected. You show real leadership. I'm proud of you."

"Wow!" Shannon beamed at her with that annoying/adorable face. "Thanks, Ashleigh!"

"And we think you're so cute," Ashleigh said. "Don't we, Neesha?"

"The cutest," Neesha agreed. She tousled Shannon's hair, and Shannon giggled and blushed a deep red.

They reached the parking lot. Neesha hugged them both good-bye, in front of all the students walking to their cars, announcing publicly that Shannon McNare was now in the club. As she hugged Shannon, Neesha gave Ashleigh a half-smile. To control the story of what happened at the farm with Jenny and Seth, they needed to control Shannon. That had proved incredibly easy.

Ashleigh led Shannon to Ashleigh's Jeep. Once they were inside, with the doors closed, Ashleigh said, "Shannon, tell me something. I need you to be honest."

"Okay." Shannon looked up at her with a serious, earnest look.

"Are you a virgin?"

Shannon gasped. "What? Of course! Why would you even ask that?"

"Never had one in you? Not even at a party? Like a Halloween lock-in party?"

"Oh." Shannon blushed. "I guess you saw me there. I did make out with these two guys, and they wanted to take my pants off, but I didn't let them. I kind of wanted them to, a little, but I didn't let them. I actually ended up hiding alone in a closet most of the night. Wow, I've never told anyone about what I did! A lot of people got way crazier than me. Want to hear about them?"

"It's okay, Shannon," Ashleigh said. She didn't believe the girl's story. Why would this little country brat be so resistant to Ashleigh's power? "You did the right thing. Will you lift up your shirt so I can see your belly?"

"Uh…"

Ashleigh held Shannon's hand. "Just for a second."

"People will think we're lezzing out." Shannon cast nervous looks among the students who were still coming out to their cars.

"Please." Ashleigh pushed more energy as she said it.

Shannon bit her lip. She pulled up her sweater, revealing a very flat, lightly freckled stomach. She didn't look pregnant. Ashleigh laid her hand across Shannon's belly and pumped the love-energy hard. There was no extra drain, as far as she could tell, no extra life force sucking down Ashleigh's energy.

"Ashleigh!" Shannon was giggling her head off, her face the color of tomato sauce. "Now we really look lezzie!" But Shannon touched her fingers to the back of Ashleigh's hand and caressed it. She leaned back in her chair, spread her knees a little, and gazed at Ashleigh's face. She lay a tentative hand on Ashleigh's thigh. Suddenly, she was more serious than giggly.

Ashleigh felt relieved. Shannon wasn't resistant to Ashleigh's power. She was just resistant to boys. Perfect.

Ashleigh took her hand back from Shannon and cranked the car. They were one of the last cars to leave the student lot.

"What are we about to go do, Ashleigh?" Shannon whispered.

"We need to talk," Ashleigh said. "First, you should know I've been looking at you for a long time."

"Really?" Shannon smiled. "Me, too."

"Next year, I'll be gone, and we'll need new leaders for the Crusaders. You've worked hard and I know you're devoted. What do you think about joining Leadership Committee?"

Shannon's smile fell, but only a little. "Really? Me?"

"Definitely. But listen, and this is top secret: Darcy Metcalf is pregnant."

"No!" Shannon was mortified. "Not her!"

"Right. So we need someone to jump into a leadership role right away. What do you think?"

"Me, on Leadership Committee with you and Cassie?"

"It would be effective immediately," Ashleigh said. "Someone has to take Darcy's place while she focuses on her new purpose in life. Are you up to it, Shannon?"

"Gosh, yes!" Shannon said. "Whatever you want, Ashleigh, I can do it."

"That's my girl."

Shannon turned away to hide her smile.

At the McNare farm, Ashleigh stopped at the field where the tractor had overturned and asked Shannon if they could look at it. Shannon was happy to show her.

They left the car on the paved road and walked up the clear, freshly plowed dirt road leading into the field.

"When the ground dried up," Shannon said, "Mr. Morton came back and finished repairing the tractor. It was weird. He and Daddy didn't speak one word to each other. It was so creepy to see him again, after I just about watched him die. Oh, and here's what else." Shannon pointed to a particularly gouged-out part of the road. "Jenny Mittens left her car stuck here in the mud, and they had to come back and tow it. I don't know if they got it working again. That was a whole lot of mud. One time, my uncle did that, his truck got caught in the mud over by Excel, Alabama and he had to stay in a Motel 6 and share a room with this biker guy he knows and then..."

Ashleigh let Shannon chatter until they reached the back corner of the field. With the dirt roads freshly plowed, there wasn't much evidence of what had happened, just an indentation next to the road, inside the field, where the tractor had lain on its side with Mr. Mittens underneath.

"It's strange to think about, isn't it?" Ashleigh said, interrupting Shannon, who had somehow gotten on the topic of how her cousin was into cross-dressing. Shannon looked around.

"Oh, yeah," Shannon said. "I have bad nightmares about it. You know what else gives me nightmares? Guinea pigs. We had one in our second grade class, with Mrs. Lessing, and his name was Bubba Boy, and he smelled like--"

"You know what gives me nightmares, Shannon?" Ashleigh turned to face her. "I worry people will hear about what happened, and they'll think witchcraft is cool and makes you powerful. I'm kind of an expert on witchcraft, you know."

"Right." Shannon's forehead crinkled as she thought this over. "So, we shouldn't tell people what happened?"

"No, people should know," Ashleigh said. "As scary as it is, they really should know." Please, Ashleigh thought, please blabber up and down every room in school for the rest of your life. "But what's important, Shannon, is that people understand it was evil. Jenny has been into Satan a long time, I mean since she was a kid. Some people are just born evil. Demons disguised as people, really. They get born as people, but they're evil inside. And Seth has been doing evil with her, but he kept it secret from me. That's the real reason we broke up."

"Oh, wow." Shannon's eyes had become huge. "I didn't know that!"

"So, anyway," Ashleigh said. "Make sure people understand it was evil. And if you can't remember something, just make up something if you have to. Just remember that Satan was present that day. People have to learn to watch out for Seth and Jenny's black magic."

"Okay," Shannon said. "But I can talk about it, right?"

"Oh, you have to talk about it, Shannon," Ashleigh said. "We all have to talk about it. It's the only way we can heal."

Ashleigh hugged Shannon close, giving her another big boost of love. Shannon kissed her cheek, and Ashleigh tolerated it.

Ashleigh started walking back to her car. When she was several yards away, she turned and said, "Oh, you can walk to your house from here, right?"

"Sure," Shannon said. "Bye, Ashleigh! Thanks for everything!"

"Bye, honey!" Ashleigh turned away and started towards her car again.

She wore a tight little satisfied smile. Shannon was under control. Darcy was pregnant. And for Seth and Jenny, Ashleigh was planning a sharp little counterattack. Not the kill move, not yet, but definitely the first step.

CHAPTER TWENTY

Jenny spent Friday and Saturday nights at Seth's house. It was the longest time she'd ever spent away from home. She called Saturday to check in with her dad, who wasn't exactly thrilled to hear she was spending the weekend at her new boyfriend's house-- but he didn't order her to come home.

Jenny couldn't keep her hands off Seth. She felt more alive than ever before, sated and deliciously hungry at the same time. She had never expected to fall in love, and certainly never expected to be loved back. She'd never thought anything could feel as good as falling asleep in Seth's arms.

When she finally went home on Sunday, she found the kitchen at her house unusually bare. Her dad sat at the kitchen table, drinking iced tea and reading the newspaper.

"You cleaned up the kitchen," Jenny said.

"Got started."

Jenny looked around a moment, then got out the Pine-Sol and a rag and started cleaning the counters and cabinets. She was bursting with extra energy and didn't know what to do with it.

"Have a good time with Seth?" he asked. She turned to see his face, to determine what he meant by the question, but he was just giving her a tired smile.

"I did, Daddy. He's so good to me. He's sweet."

"Jenny, I need to tell you about something. After that tractor fell on me, it hurt like nothing ever hurt before."

"I bet!"

"But that only lasted a minute. Next thing I know, I'm just kind of laying there all calm and peaceful, and didn't feel nothing.

And I wasn't afraid of nothing, not even dying. I was just looking up at the sky."

Jenny nodded and sank into the chair across from him. She wiped down the table and chairs while she listened.

"And I started to see things, up above me, in all that lightning and rain. Your momma's face smiling down at me, looking just as pretty and happy as I remember her. And then I could see my whole life up there, every second of it, like a bunch of pebbles spread out across the beach." He wore a distant, thoughtful look, his glass of tea forgotten halfway to his mouth. "I never drank so much when I was young, you know that? Not in the mornings, never during the day. Not until she died."

"When I was born," Jenny whispered.

"Don't think like that. I drank for losing her, not for gaining you. You was the only thing kept me alive all these years."

Jenny felt like crying, but somehow it wasn't an altogether bad feeling.

"When I could see all the moments of my life like that, all at once, I realized something," he said. "All the moments I spent drunk was just a rotted black color. They wasn't worth nothing. They was all wasted moments, time I could have spent with you, love I could have given you. I messed things up for myself, Jenny, and so I messed things up for you, too."

"You did fine, Daddy," Jenny said. She stood up and embraced him with her gloved hands, keeping her bare head away from him.

"I could have done a lot better. And when I was laying there, seeing this, I wanted nothing but more of those moments. I thought, if I had just a few more to spend, I'd spend them on Jenny, and I wouldn't let another one rot like that. And I wished to God I just had some more moments to spend, even though my body was wrecked and couldn't live no more."

"But Seth healed you."

"And that's how it all fell together," her dad said. "I asked to live, and I lived. So I poured it all out, Jenny. There ain't nothing left."

Jenny looked around the kitchen—no liquor bottles by the stove. No case of Pabst on top of the fridge. No empty cans and bottles scattered all over the place. He'd cleared out everything to do with drinking. No wonder the kitchen looked so bare.

"Daddy, that's great!" Jenny said. She poured her own glass of iced tea from the pitcher, then sat by him. "That's amazing. I'm really proud of you."

"Funny thing is, I don't miss it. I ain't even really been able to drink since I died. I've poured a few, and look at 'em, but I never wanted to drink 'em. I'd always end up pouring them out."

"Maybe it's too late," he said. "But I still want to try and be a good father to you. If there's any time. If you ain't all growed up already."

"There's plenty of time, Daddy." Jenny covered his hand with her glove. Her eyes were full of tears now, but not the bad kind. "Just cause I'm about grown up don't mean I don't need a daddy. I'm going to need you for a long time to come."

"And I'm gonna be here for you," he said. "I promise you." He looked at her a long time, and it looked like there were a lot of thoughts wheeling in his brain. "It's amazing what that boy Seth can do, ain't it? You sure he's immune to what you got?"

"I guess he heals himself," Jenny said. "Or it just don't bother him."

"And you're happy with him?"

"Yes, Daddy. Happiest I've ever been." Jenny couldn't resist the chance to talk about Seth. "He's the most amazing boy, Daddy. There's nobody else like him. He understands me. And I feel like, this is strange but, I feel like we can learn a lot from each other."

"You think you could stand living in that big old mansion? Dressing in them fancy clothes?"

"Daddy! Why are you so serious? I'm just happy to know him right now."

"I guess I saw how fast time really goes, when I was out there." He snapped his fingers. "All your life goes just like that. Then it's over."

"Now you sound like Mrs. Sutland," Jenny said.

"She knows what she's talking about, then."

"I know I love Seth, and I know he loves me," Jenny said. "Does anything else matter right now?"

222

"Nothing does, Jenny." His eyes got teary, and Jenny knew he was thinking about her mother. "Don't listen to nobody who tells you different."

They were still in the process of fixing up Jenny's car so they could return it in decent condition to Merle. Seth picked Jenny up before school on Monday, and she surprised him with a breakfast of salty country ham on homemade biscuits. She noticed he was wearing gloves, though it was a mild January and not too cold during the day. He said it was to control how much healing energy he lost during the day, but Jenny wondered if it wasn't just to make her feel more normal.

When they arrived at school, they drew a lot of surprised and confused looks in the parking lot and hallway, but nobody avoided Seth except Ashleigh and her closer friends. Jenny wasn't used to any kind of popularity, and she was spooked to be surrounded by so many people everywhere they went. More than twenty people sat around them at lunch, talking with Seth and even making tentative conversation with Jenny. People who'd always been cold and distant to her were turning into friendly faces. Jenny wanted to cringe and wait for the hostilities to begin, but nobody was cruel to her. Even Ashleigh and her gang just avoided them altogether, though Jenny got very cold eyes when she passed them in the hall. During P.E., they whispered among each other and glared at Jenny, but didn't say anything directly to her.

Jenny noticed something else strange happening around her. By the end of the first week, many other students, especially in lower grades, started wearing gloves all day. By wearing gloves himself, Seth had turned the symbol of Jenny's isolation and general freakishness into a new fad. Within days, kids were competing to wear the brightest, flashiest, most unique gloves. Jenny saw satin gloves, bowling gloves, fingerless motorcycle gloves, soccer goalie gloves.

Now that Jenny was a trendsetter, lots of people were approaching her and striking up conversations, especially the younger girls, in search of what made her cool enough for the coolest boy in school, so they could emulate it.

At home, Jenny and her dad got to work on the new fence Jenny had designed months ago. Seth usually brought her home from school, then stayed until dark, helping to dig post holes and nail up the boards, scrap wood, and shingles from which they built the fence. Jenny's dad couldn't help developing a little grudging respect for the rich boy who wasn't afraid to get his hands dirty and scraped with hard work. Her daddy, true to his word, never touched a drop of alcohol again.

During the late night hours, Jenny gradually finished the mask she'd molded from her own face. She'd glazed it white, and now she decorated it with designs in purple, indigo and black. She painted skull-and-bones "poison" symbols on the cheeks, and big stylized biohazard symbol on the forehead. She painted little spiked balls representing virus spores, and oily-bodied little black flies, the imaginary ones that she pictured spreading Jenny pox from her to other people.

The clay mask was too heavy to ever wear, but it made a striking, frightening little decoration. Seth hung it on the wall of his bedroom. He said he liked having her face to look at, and to look at him, when she wasn't there.

On the third Monday of the semester, Jenny and Seth arrived at school to discover that they suddenly had a new power: dispersing crowds. People gave them disgusted looks and hurried to get away from them, even Seth's best friends. A group of freshman girls actually ran screaming at the sight of them.

When Jenny opened her locker, she discovered a bright yellow flier someone had slipped in through the vent slits in the locker door. Around them, everyone was pulling bright yellow fliers out of their lockers, showing them to each other, whispering, pointing at Seth and Jenny. A couple of girls, and one boy, made barfing sounds and ran to the bathroom.

"It's something Ashleigh made." Jenny took the folded yellow paper from her locker and handed it to Seth. "You look first."

Seth unfolded the paper. There was a moment of shock on his face, then dismay, and finally a growing, simmering anger.

"What is it?" Jenny whispered.

Seth frowned as he turned the flier towards her.

Emblazoned across the top, in blazing red letters, was the warning DON'T GET JENNY POX! Under this was a row of three clip-art biohazard symbols, not nearly as cool as the one she'd painted on her mask.

Most of the flyer was a full-color photograph that had been taken at Ashleigh's house the day Jenny's dad died. It was a close shot of their heads, with Jenny on top of Seth. Seth was semi-conscious, his eyelids low, while Jenny opened his mouth with her fingers. Her chin and lips were full of leaking blisters and broken pustules. Her tongue was fully extended, reaching down towards his mouth, dripping pus, blood, and clear fluid onto Seth's lips and face.

There were smaller words at the bottom of the flyer: STAY AWAY FROM JENNY MITTENS & SETH BARRETT OR YOU'LL BE INFECTED!!!

Jenny hugged Seth and buried her face in his chest, while hundreds of students made disgusted sounds and spat out the words "Jenny pox" up and down the hall. At least there was someone to share her suffering this time.

"I'm sorry, Seth," Jenny whispered. "This is my fault. Because Ashleigh hates me."

"Like hell it is." Seth lowered his mouth to her ear and whispered, "Hey, let's make them stop."

Jenny looked up at him, an eyebrow raised. "How?"

"On the count of three," he whispered, "We charge them and run them off."

"Who?"

"Everyone."

Jenny thought about it for a second, then smiled. Why not?

"Okay," Seth said. "One, two…three!"

Jenny and Seth charged the largest group of gawkers making disgusted faces at them.

"Everybody gets an infection!" Seth yelled. "Come on, baby, who's first?"

The resulting stampede cleared out the hallway, leaving flyers, notebooks, and pencils all over the floor.

After that, gloves were no longer fashionable at Fallen Oaks High, and neither were Seth Barrett and Jenny Morton.

By February, it became obvious there was a pregnancy epidemic at Fallen Oak High. There were usually a few each year, but this year it was dozens of girls pregnant across all grade levels. Ashleigh could trace many of them to the Halloween lock-in. Others, like Darcy, she had arranged personally, enchanting pairs of individuals until they were overcome by desire. She'd even arranged a few by picking two people at random at a party or football game, then holding their hands until they couldn't resist each other.

Ashleigh delighted in how so many girls came right to her for their first advice. Ashleigh would put her hand under their shirts and pour her energy into the fetus, and naturally some spilled over into the girl, and she would love Ashleigh even more. She would advise them to keep the baby and stay close to her.

Ashleigh and Cassie quickly organized a Girls' Outreach Ministry based out of her father's church, with weekly meetings for all the new mothers. Shannon McNare's first big duty was the unpleasant task of collecting abstinence rings from any pregnant girls who wore them. She brought them to Ashleigh in a big Ziploc freezer bag.

Most important, though, were the press kits.

Ashleigh, Neesha and Cassie spent the first weekend of February at Ashleigh's house getting the press kits together. They even split a large pizza, which was a very big indulgence for Cassie and Neesha. It was nothing for Ashleigh, who could probably burn off a hundred thousand calories in a day just by touching people, if she really wanted to.

Late Saturday night, Cassie called Neesha and Ashleigh over to Ashleigh's computer desk.

"Is it ready?" Neesha asked.

"Y'all tell me what you think," Cassie said. "This is what I've got so far. It's still rough."

Ashleigh put a hand on Cassie's shoulder and leaned over to read the monitor. Cassie was designing the press release for the kit. Each kit would also include a DVD of the Neesha-produced video *Abstinence is Power!* along with a sample anti-abstinence poster,

226

plus pictures of the pregnant teens of Fallen Oak. The kits would go to conservative and Christian media outlets across the country.

TEEN PREGNANCY SOARS 1000% AFTER PRINCIPAL REJECTS ABSTINENCE CAMPAIGN

At Fallen Oak High, more than 90 students are pregnant after their principal rejected a faith-based abstinence campaign early in the school year. The school had never seen more than six pregnancies in one year before the fiercely anti-abstinence Principal Dwight Harris pulled the plug on the student-led movement.

"It really changed the culture here," said Ashleigh Goodling, president of the Christians Act! prayer group that organized the abstinence push. "If your leaders tell you abstinence isn't important, what do you expect teens to do?"

The group wanted to provide student-designed posters, literature and a video to explain the benefits of abstinence to their peers, with the theme "Abstinence is Power!" The campaign encourages girls to consider the impact of sexual behavior on their future careers.

Principal Harris, who describes himself as "spiritual, not religious," rejected the proposal without explanation. Some say that his strong rejection of abstinence encouraged the outbreak of sexual experimentation among the student body.

"I know religion offends our principal," Goodling said. "But we believe abstinence is the right choice for all girls."

To help the many confused teen mothers, Goodling and her friends have started a special girls' outreach ministry at church, which counsels them to choose life and to return to morality.

"We don't just have these girls to consider," Goodling said. "Now we have their innocent babies, too. I believe that every last soul can be saved for God, if we try hard enough. Most of these girls regret their choice, and want to set things right."

Donations to help the young mothers and babies can be made to Fallen Oak Girls' Outreach Ministry, by mail or through their website.

"What do you think, Ash?" Cassie asked.

"This is great!" She squeezed Cassie in a hug and gave her a generous dose of love as a reward.

"I think this is the best picture to go with it." Neesha turned her laptop toward them. She'd gathered the ten most pregnant-looking girls in school and taken them to the football field for pictures. Each of them looked sad, or somber, or ashamed, some of them turning their faces away from the camera as if they couldn't bear it.

"They know this is going to national media, right?" Ashleigh asked.

"They all signed a release," Neesha said.

"Sweet. Good job, Neesh!" Ashleigh hugged her.

"One more thing, Ashleigh." Neesha turned her laptop back around and tapped at it. "I think we should include these pictures, too."

The first picture on the screen showed the three of them in bikini tops at Barrett Pond, with Ashleigh in the middle. They hugged tight, their three faces squished together, grinning like loons, just three innocent best friends from a good old small town. Another showed Ashleigh in stylish glasses and a professional black blazer, a picture from her student council campaign.

"But we're not pregnant," Ashleigh said.

"Duh, Ash," Neesha said. "This isn't about them, it's about you. You want reporters to interview you, right? More will do it if they know you're hot."

"Good thinking," Ashleigh said. "That'll probably help."

"Probably?" Neesha rolled her eyes. "Come on. A hot girl talking about naughty, forbidden sex?"

Ashleigh and Cassie both laughed.

"I bet they'll put you on TV," Neesha said. "You're really that pretty, Ashleigh."

"Aw, thanks, Neesh." Ashleigh hugged both girls close to her, much like the pose in the swimming photo. "I'm so glad you guys are my best friends. We're totally powerful together! Let's never split up. Promise?"

The other girls promised such a thing would never happen.

On Monday, Ashleigh, Cassie and Neesha skipped first period to visit the Fallen Oak post office. They mailed two hundred and thirty-one press kits to a carefully selected list of newspapers, magazines, radio talk shows, and television programs.

CHAPTER TWENTY-ONE

On Tuesday, the second week in February, Jenny discovered that someone had used a knife to carve lots of little crosses all over her locker. They'd gouged through the pasty yellow paint and scratched into the metal underneath. They also carved two words, right at eye level: WITCHES BURN.

Someone had gone after Seth's locker with more of the little crosses. They'd also taken the time to etch a pentagram into the metal, and then scratched big, fat "X" on top of that. More words were scratched on his locker: EXODUS 22:18.

The next day, the Christians Act! group stood in a circle around the flagpole, holding hands for morning prayer before homeroom. A clear majority of the girls were pregnant. Ashleigh and Cassie were noticeably absent. Neesha Bailey was leading the prayer.

As Seth and Jenny walked past them from the parking lot, the whole group turned to look at them. They then reached into their pockets, purses and bookbags and brought out small, blue square objects. The group began yelling and chucking them at Seth and Jenny.

"Ow!" Jenny said, when one smacked into her forehead. She caught it and looked at it. It was a pocket-sized Bible, bound in blue pleather. More of the books pelted her arms and chest.

"Whore!" Darcy Metcalf screamed at Jenny. Her stomach protruded under her shirt. Apparently Darcy was no longer a group leader now that she was with child. "Devil slut!"

"You're the one who's pregnant, bitch!" Jenny yelled back. "Who's the slut?"

This brought a lot of red-faced shouting, especially from the other pregnant girls in the group. "It's your fault!" one of them cried. "You put a spell on us!"

"How does Satan's cock feel, Jenny?" sneered pale, acne-cursed Larry DuShoun. "You like that big black devil dick?"

"Excuse me?" Neesha asked Larry, with an arched eyebrow.

"I mean, that big red devil dick, you slut?" Larry corrected himself.

"Call her that one more time, Larry," Seth said. "I fucking dare you."

"Seth, relax," Jenny whispered.

"I'm not scared to say the truth!" Larry yelled. "I read all about witchery on a website. I know how it works. Jenny Mittens is the Devil's tramp, his concubine, his harlot—"

Seth dropped his bookbag and charged directly at Larry. Larry screeched and ran away, across the grassy lawn, towards the parking lot. He ran as fast as he could, but Seth had been a starting running back since middle school.

Seth grabbed Larry's bony shoulders. Larry whirled around and brandished a full-sized black Bible at Seth, as if he expected Seth to shrink from it like a vampire.

"Get thee back!" Larry screamed, his voice breaking.

"Don't hurt him, Seth!" Jenny yelled. Larry was gangly and narrow, and Seth could do real damage to him without much effort, even by accident.

Larry slapped the Bible against Seth's face, and Seth rolled his eyes. He snatched it from Larry's hands, and Larry shrieked. Seth returned the book to him by slamming it into Larry's abdomen, and Larry doubled over and staggered back a few feet, clutching the Bible to his gut. He finally lost his balance and fell backward in the grass.

Seth stalked toward the flagpole, eyes blazing. The prayer circle had broken up, and now people pulled together into little defensive clumps. Seth glared among them, waiting to see if anyone would dare approach him. He flipped over the card table that Christians Act! set up every morning. An open box of Dunkin Donuts Munchkins, a stack of pamphlets, and a paper donation cup full of change all tumbled to the ground and spilled out across the grass.

"Get out of here!" Seth said. "All of you!" He ran towards the largest group of boys, who scattered, screaming. The other little clumps broke apart, and everyone ran towards the safety of the school building.

Seth stood by the overturned table, still angry and ready to fight, but there was nobody left. Jenny picked up his bookbag and brought it to him.

"That was stupid, Seth," Jenny said. "Really sweet. Super sweet. Like, amazing. But stupid. You haven't been dealing with this crap all your life. Now they just get angrier. Who knows what they'll do next?"

"Whatever they do, I'll take care of it," Seth said. "No one treats you like that. I promised to keep you safe, remember?"

"I remember." Jenny kissed Seth, then held him for a minute, her head against his thumping heart.

"We should report them to Principal Harris," Seth said.

"He'll take their side," Jenny said. "Everybody takes Ashleigh's side. Come on, let's get to class."

Friday night, Jenny rode to Vernon Hill in her dad's Ram, sitting between her dad on the driver's side and Seth on the passenger side. She felt very safe between the two of them, safer than she'd ever felt. These were her people, her family.

They spent more than an hour at Lowe's, a place that her dad never left without buying more than he'd originally planned. He picked up some lumber, tarpaper and shingles for the shed extension he wanted to build. Together, they'd completed the fence between the house and the shed, and painted it with half a dozen old paints, which her dad had sealed and saved from jobs over the years. The front side of the fence was red, white and blue, while the back was orange, purple and green.

Seth bought Jenny all the plants she picked out for her front yard, now that all the junk had been moved behind the fence. She wanted azaleas, a couple of baby willow trees, and a Knock Out rosebush. After they'd carted everything out and loaded it into the back of the Ram, Seth glanced furtively back towards the store. Then he reached into his shirt and pulled out a big blue forget-me-not blossom he'd stolen from a plant inside.

"This reminded me of your eyes," Seth said as he handed it to Jenny.

"Oh, Seth, a forget-me-not!" Jenny sniffed it and twirled it in her fingers. You know what these are? Ladies wore them to show they were thinking about their lovers."

"Uh, yeah," Seth said. "I totally knew that."

Jenny rolled her eyes. She tucked the flower into her hair, then lay her hands on Seth's face.

"Thank you. It's beautiful," she said. And they kept looking at each other.

Her dad cleared his throat. "Y'all want to stop at the Waffle House on the way back? I'm getting kinda hungry."

"Okay, Daddy." Jenny forced herself to turn away from Seth.

The Vernon Hill Waffle House, like most of its species, was a low brick diner under a big yellow sign, with glass walls overlooking the interstate below. There were a few old men at the counter, a black family with little kids in one booth, a very white gang of darkly-clad teenagers in another. The book pile in front of the teenagers indicated they were into the role-playing game Vampire: The Masquerade.

They took an outside booth, with a window, and a waitress appeared and laid out their napkins and silverware on their table. She was fortyish, a little plump and very sunburned, her frizzy yellow hair tied back from her face.

"Hey, honey," she said to Jenny's dad. "Nice to see you back. Bringing the kids this time?"

Jenny lifted an eyebrow at her dad.

"This is my daughter, Jenny," he said. "And her boyfriend Seth."

"Hey there, Jenny and Seth." Her gaze lingered on Seth. "I guess some girls have all the luck."

Jenny blushed.

"I'm June," the waitress said, and the yellow nametag on her pin-striped shirt confirmed it.

"That's pretty," Jenny said. "Like June Carter."

"That's right! My daddy named me for her. I still listen to my Carter Family albums. You never hear them on the radio anymore."

"Me, too," Jenny said. "My momma left with me a bunch of their old records."

"Didn't have to say 'old,'" June said, with a laugh. "All right, what y'all drinking?"

After she left, Jenny turned to her dad and whispered, "What was that? Do you have a secret Waffle House romance, Daddy?"

"Naw, she's just waited on me a couple times, when I come to Lowe's."

"She remembers you, though," Jenny said. "And she called you 'Honey.'"

"It's Waffle House, Jenny. They call everybody that."

"She's kind of hot," Seth said. "Why don't you ask her out?"

"That's not a good idea. Waitresses get tired of that," he said. The way he said "idea" rhymed with "mighty."

"She won't get offended," Jenny said. "It's kind of a compliment, if you think about it."

"I don't know." He watched June lift a slice of apple pie from the display by the cash register. "Been a whole mess of years since I dated anybody, Jenny."

"There's only one way to change that," Jenny pointed out.

"Maybe I'll ask her sometime, when it ain't so busy."

Jenny looked around. Most of the tables were empty.

"Daddy," she said. "Somebody told me that life goes by just like that." Jenny snapped her fingers, though the effect through her blue wool gloves wasn't quite what she wanted.

"Want me to hook it up, Mr. Morton?" Seth asked. "I bet I can."

"He could, Daddy," Jenny said. "Ladies can't say no to Seth." Her dad gave Jenny a sharp, questioning look, and she ducked her head and took a sudden interest in her silverware.

"I appreciate it," he told Seth. "But I don't think so."

"Do you like her?" Seth asked.

"So far as I know," he replied. "But you can't just ask a lady on a date when she's working."

Seth dug around in his pocket. "Somebody give me a quarter. I'll pretend I'm just going to the jukebox, and I'll talk to her."

Jenny found one and flipped it to Seth, who winked at her and got to his feet.

"I thought I said no," her dad said, while Seth walked away. "You kids don't listen too good."

"Too late now," Jenny told him. She watched Seth step slowly toward the jukebox, which was behind her dad and out of his line of sight. June passed the table to drop off their drinks, and Seth stopped her on her way back behind the counter. He lay a hand on her arm, and June immediately straightened up and smiled as any aches and pains in her body dissolved.

"What do you recommend?" Seth held up the quarter.

"54B," June said.

"Listen…" Seth leaned in and whispered to her, and Jenny couldn't hear him. June's eyes widened and she looked at the back of Jenny's dad's head. They whispered to each other for a minute. Then June circled back behind the counter, while Seth dropped in the quarter.

The Waffle House was filled with "Black Velvet." Seth wore a cocky smile as he sat down.

"I think she's interested," Seth said. "She said as long as you don't drink. She's had enough drinkers."

"Never touch it." Her dad smiled at Jenny.

June seemed extra friendly when she brought their food. She managed to ask Jenny's dad three times if he wanted anything else.

When she eventually dropped the check by the table, Seth flipped it over and tapped it. On the back of the yellow paper, she'd signed her name in big cursive letters. There was also a smiley face. And a phone number.

"I should have bet somebody money on this," Seth said.

"What did you say to her?" Jenny's dad asked.

"I told her you raised your daughter by yourself," Seth said. "Instant melt. You should use that one."

"It's kinda personal," her dad said.

"It's kinda going to get you laid," Seth told him.

"Seth!" Jenny clapped her hands over her face, wishing she could turn invisible. That, at least, would be a useful power.

But her dad was looking over at June, who pumped vanilla flavoring into a glass of Coke. She saw him looking and gave a sly little smile.

"Sunday is Valentine's Day," Seth said. He slid the ticket closer to Jenny's dad. "And she doesn't have anybody. I'm just saying."

"Maybe I should go and pay," her dad said.

"Maybe you should," Jenny agreed.

They spent Saturday straightening up the front yard. Seth and Jenny raked pine straw from the woods, while her dad chopped down the high weeds and grass with a push mower. They used the straw to turn the bare, oil-stained patches of yard into little islands. They planted an azalea in each island, the rose bush by the front steps, the willows further out from the house.

Later, when her dad was ready for his first date in more than twenty years, Jenny cut some flowers from her new rosebush so he could give them to June. Jenny and Seth stood in the driveway and waved as he drove away in the freshly-washed truck. He would be taking his new lady friend to The Catfish House in Apple Creek. If she wanted to come back with him, he had coffee and a little chocolate cake waiting.

"They grow up so fast," Jenny said, and Seth laughed. "And what are you and me doing for Valentine's?" she asked.

"You said you were cooking for me."

"Did I say a thing like that?" Jenny teased. "Okay. But we have to go by Piggly Wiggly. And you have to give me money. And wait in the car while I shop."

When they eventually reached Seth's house, she banned him from the kitchen while she cooked. He filled the first story of the house with Patsy Cline, which made her smile as she worked for the next two hours.

She brought him supper in the dining room: shrimp and grits, cornbread that was a little on the sweet side like Jenny liked (and her father hated, preferring his cornbread as rough and dry as Brillo pads), green beans she'd flavored with pieces of bacon and crushed red pepper, and a simple fruit salad with melons, cherries and coconut to sweeten up the Valentine's meal.

Seth had set her place at the table with a vase of assorted roses, a box of Godiva chocolates, and an envelope printed with red and pink hearts. Jenny's own heart fluttered at the sight of all this. It was really her first Valentine's Day, she thought.

As they ate, they tried to guess how her dad's date was going. Jenny made sure he had Seth's phone number and told him that if he didn't call, she would take it as a good sign.

For dessert, they had strawberries dipped in a chocolate sauce Jenny had purchased at the store, but allowed Seth to believe she had made from scratch.

She gave Seth his present, which had been first manufactured as a brown wool hunting jacket sometime in the 1960s. She'd sewn some new black material at the collar, pockets and wrists, and remade all the buttons with vintage bottlecaps and old coins she'd picked from a box at the Five and Dime.

He paraded around in front of her, striking poses, flipping up the collar. "Nobody has a coat like this!"

"You like it?"

"Love it, Jenny." He kissed her, then put the envelope in her hands. "Now you go."

Jenny carefully peeled the envelope open without ripping any part of it. The card had a picture of two baby lambs nuzzling together. The inside read I WOOLY WOOLY WUV EWE! When she opened the card, a folded slice of blue-tinged paper tumbled out and landed on the table.

"What is that?" Jenny asked.

"It's your present," Seth said. "Open it."

Jenny eyed him while she unfolded the sheet. It had a thick blue border veined with white, and a golden seal with a palmetto tree in the upper left corner. The page's header read:

State of South Carolina
Certificate of Title
Of A Vehicle

The paper identified Jenny Morton of Fallen Oak, SC as the legal owner of a 1975 Lincoln Continental.

"Seth? What did you do?"

"Nothing," Seth said. "I just went by Merle Sanderson's house and paid him for the car, so you could keep it."

"You're kidding."

"He really didn't charge that much. He said he couldn't decide between giving a Morton discount and charging a Barrett premium."

Jenny laughed. Then she held the page and stared at it for a while. It was really her car now. She and her dad wouldn't have to share the truck. She could go where she wanted, whenever she wanted, without asking anybody. She felt her eyes sting.

"Seth, this is amazing." She sat in his lap and wrapped her arms around his neck. "God, I'm actually crying. You bastard. That was way better than my coat."

"Nah," Seth said. "I didn't make the car or anything."

She kissed him. She brushed his lower lip with her finger. "I want one more thing. Can you guess?"

"I think I can." Seth smiled.

"I want to see the third floor. The haunted part."

"That wasn't my guess," he said.

"Come on, Seth. What's up there?"

"Just my great-grandfather's room." His smile shrunk away. "They had to move all of it from the second floor, because of the all the racket his ghost made after he died."

"Shut up," Jenny said.

"That's what my uncle told me," Seth said. "He never visits. He says he still has nightmares about this house."

"Seth, that's not cool," Jenny said. "I have to sleep here."

"Yeah, so do I," Seth said. "Which is why I stay away from great-grandpa's stuff. They say he's territorial about it."

"Come on," Jenny said. "You haven't ever seen a ghost. Have you?"

"No."

"I knew it."

"I've heard his footsteps up there. And his adding machine clacking."

"When?"

"When I was a kid," Seth said.

"That could have been anything." Jenny stood up and held out her hand. "Take me."

Seth stood up, but he looked reluctant. They had to go to his father's office to find the third-floor keys, which were buried in the back of a file cabinet drawer.

They followed the curving front stairs to the second floor. Seth unlocked a tall door by the head of the stairs.

"Are you sure?" he asked her.

"Stop being dramatic," Jenny said.

The door opened onto a steep, very dusty staircase. Seth flicked on the single electric bulb hanging from a string.

"Ladies first," Seth said.

"Still not funny," Jenny told him.

"Scared?"

Jenny scowled at him. She elbowed him aside and started up the stairs, sneezing as the dust puffed up under her tennis shoes.

The steps widened and grew less steep, and began to curve along the wall. Jenny realized it had once been part of one continuous staircase spiraling from the first floor up to the huge windows and skylights of the third floor, all of which were now filled in or boarded up. It must have been a breathtaking entrance hall in its time.

The stairway flattened into a balcony that curved around to the third-floor gallery. Looking over the balustrade would once have given a sweeping view of the entrance hall below. Now the big, empty space in the center was sealed with unpainted boards. Layers of spiderwebs filled the rafters, hiding the ceiling.

"Why did y'all cut it off like this?" Jenny asked.

"My grandfather did it," Seth whispered. "He was scared of his father's ghost. He moved my great-grandfather's room and personal things up here. Then he had workers demolish all the staircases to the third floor and seal them off. He left this part as the only way up. Then he moved his own bedroom down to the first floor, to get away. The last years of his life, he lived in an old servant cottage out back to escape the main house."

"That's crazy," Jenny said.

"He wasn't crazy." Seth said it quickly, automatically. Then he added, "I mean, not if it's haunted."

"And what if it isn't?" Jenny worked her way down the hall, which was cluttered with old furniture, stacks of framed daguerreotypes, glass cases with their contents hidden by thick dust. Dust and cobwebs covered everything. The dry floorboards creaked under her feet.

"Doesn't it feel haunted to you?" Seth asked.

"It feels like it's full of spiders."

"Come on. I'll show you his room." He led her forward. The hallway turned to the right for a while, then made a U-turn and sent them back to the left. Seth pulled the chain on another hanging light bulb. They faced two doors.

"Uh, hold on." Seth flipped through the ring of iron keys he'd taken from the office. "I think we need...the left door." He tried a few keys, until he was able to unlock the left door. He walked in and pulled another hanging light. Another passage snaked away to the left, this one cluttered with dusty shelves, where Jenny saw rows of arrow heads and broken pottery shards.

The twisting passage eventually ended in a T-intersection. Seth turned to the right, but he didn't look very sure about it.

"Do you know where we're going?" she whispered.

"I think so. It's been a few years."

"Why's it so..."

"Difficult?" Seth suggested. "My grandfather again. He had the halls and rooms chopped up into a maze. It's to confuse my great-grandfather's ghost."

"Your grandfather was really serious about this."

"Very serious," Seth said. The hallway ended at a wall of dust. Seth wiped the dust with his fingers, revealing glass that reflected a murky shadow of his face. "A mirror. We should have taken the door on the right. Let's go back."

"That's the whole hallway?" Jenny asked. It was only about twelve feet long.

"There's lots of dead ends with mirrors," Seth said. "Grandpa thought mirrors could trap ghosts."

Eventually, through narrow passageways, and with a few false starts, they found the double doors to his great-grandfather's room. Seth unlocked them.

"I haven't been in here since I was a kid," he said. "Are you ready?"

"Seth, you've got me expecting a skeleton to jump out or something," Jenny said. "What's in there?"

"Just a bedroom." Seth pushed the doors open with a loud, rusty screech.

The interior was full of cobwebs, and very dark until Seth ignited a glass lamp on a tabletop. There were no windows, not even boarded-over windows, so they must be somewhere towards the center of the third floor, away from any of the four exterior walls. As she looked into the gloomy space, she realized one of the brick chimneys passed through this room, but the fireplace was plugged with cement.

Rugs that Jenny couldn't see very well were scattered over the raw floorboards. She saw a roll-top desk with a big mechanical adding machine, which had circular ivory buttons set into an ornate wooden box, with a big brass hand crank on one side. Gold and silver coins were scattered in no particular order around it, as if to keep the ghost busy.

An antique sideboard held a porcelain washbowl with a pitcher, a straight razor resting on its leather strop, and several brown medicine bottles lined up in a neat row. There was a wall of grainy photographs, including one that Seth thought was his great-grandfather shaking hands with Woodrow Wilson. In that picture, Jonathan S. Barrett I was a thirtyish businessman, in a stiff felt homburg hat and overcoat, his jaw tight, his eyes like circles of cold iron.

The bed itself was spartan, a simple iron frame and a thin mattress covered with a quilt, not particularly large. A servant bell with a rope was mounted in the wall by the head.

"I don't see any ghosts," Jenny said.

"Maybe he's resting tonight."

Jenny looked at Seth, and thought about him growing up underneath all of this, with the strange family stories about ghosts and obligations to the dead, passed on through his grandfather and his father. The thing about money was that it really gave you a chance to express your insanity.

Jenny pushed Seth back onto the bed, and the rusty springs underneath groaned.

"What are you doing?" he whispered.

Jenny crawled on top of him, and began kissing Seth's lips.

"We can't do this here," he whispered, after a minute. "Let's go to the navigator room."

"We have to show the ghost this is your house now," Jenny said. "He can't rule it anymore." She lifted away her sweater, then unhasped her bra.

"This is really scary for me, Jenny," Seth whispered.

"That's why we have to do it."

He closed his eyes while she undressed him.

It was hot, sweaty work, but Jenny did her best to exorcise the ghost of Jonathan S. Barrett from Barrett House.

CHAPTER TWENTY-TWO

Ashleigh watched out the airplane window as the city of Atlanta fell away below her. Ahead of her was New York City and her future.

The right-wing media outlets had gone bonkers for her story, as Ashleigh had planned for them to do. It had everything— Christians suppressed by the secular public schools, kids in danger, and lots and lots of sex. Ashleigh had already done more than twenty interviews with magazine writers, call-in interviews with radio shows around the country, and a few appearances on local TV. She'd been featured on the very popular "RighteousRight" website. Tens of thousands in donations had poured into the PayPal account tied to the Fallen Oak Girls Outreach website. But now she was finally reaching the big time.

Chuck O'Flannery, one of the most-watched pundits on TV, had caught wind of her story. There was plenty to get morally outraged about, and O'Flannery specialized in angry tirades, for which he needed a constant flow of new targets. Ashleigh had hoped he would call, since he had a pattern of obsessing over stories about child pornography or teachers having sex with underage students, often bloviating for weeks over a single allegation of it anywhere in the country. He'd already done some reporting of Ashleigh's story, complete with the pictures of pregnant teenagers, and of course the one of Ashleigh and friends in swimsuits at Barrett Pond.

Originally, a producer from The O'Flannery Overview Hour had called to arrange for Ashleigh to visit a local Fox affiliate in

Columbia, where she would appear on the nationally broadcast program via satellite uplink. Later, O'Flannery himself had called Ashleigh, and Ashleigh was just as charming, flirtatious and sweet as she could be. She giggled at his jokes, and she told him her friends said that he was sexy when he got angry—which wasn't remotely true, since O'Flannery was least a hundred pounds overweight, and only had a fringe of hair left, and anyway none of her friends watched the news or anything close to it.

The following day, the producer had called back and invited Ashleigh to New York. She'd been upgraded to a live "special guest" and would actually be in the studio with O'Flannery, at his famous interview desk, where he sometimes grilled and insulted his guests without ever allowing them to speak. Ashleigh didn't think hers would be that kind of interview.

Ashleigh had the window seat on the airplane, with Cassie beside her. Ashleigh's dad sat several rows ahead of them, since neither Dr. Goodling nor Mayor Winder were about to send their teenage daughters into the legendary sin and temptation of New York without a responsible adult.

When the pilot announced that electronic devices were now permitted, Cassie opened her laptop and connected to the plane's wireless hotspot. She downloaded the email from the Girls Outreach website into her Outlook Express.

"Radio show in Tennessee," Cassie told Ashleigh as she clicked through the messages. "One in Texas, one in California, all want interviews. Tons of new PayPal donations. Volunteers who want to help the girls. A guy in Rhode Island who wants to date you. You're invited to give talks to groups at Liberty University and Bob Jones University. Lots of churches, too. And some groups want to use *Abstinence is Power!* in their own churches and schools."

"Up the recommended donation to fifty dollars for the video," Ashleigh said. "Let's do all the radio shows. I want to do appearances, but I only want to talk to big groups where I can reach a lot of people. Smaller groups of important people are okay. Is there anything from The Covenant yet?"

Cassie checked. She gave Ashleigh an apologetic smile. "Nothing yet."

"Goddamn it!" Ashleigh said. "What the fuck do I have to do to get their attention?"

"Maybe the O'Flannery appearance will take care of it," Cassie said.

"It better. I'm not putting my hands on that fat piece of shit for fun."

When they reached LaGuardia airport, there was a driver waiting with Ashleigh's name on a sign. He stacked their luggage on a rolling rack and carted it out for them, then loaded them into the trunk of a black limousine. He held the door while the three of them piled inside.

"Ashleigh, this is impressive," her dad said as the limo rolled away from the airport. He'd worn his best suit, and now he was looking out the window and shaking his head, either at the vast crowds or the amazing scale of the city. "Your mother and I couldn't be prouder of you."

"Everything I know, I learned from you, Daddy," Ashleigh said.

"I don't know. I've never pulled anything on a national scale like this."

"Maybe we can get you a TV show," Ashleigh suggested. "Televangelists make buttloads of money."

"That's not a bad idea, sweetie," her dad said.

"Want me to look into it?" Cassie asked. "I've got producers calling from all over. I bet you could at least get a radio show, to start."

Dr. Goodling looked between Ashleigh and Cassie, smiling like he was at the pulpit and getting ready to pass the collection plates.

"You girls are brilliant," he said. "I really will be surprised if you two don't end up ruling the world one day."

"We're working on it, Daddy." Ashleigh winked at him.

They arrived at the studio building, a huge black skyscraper, with an hour to spare before the live broadcast. The O'Flannery Overview Hour started at eight PM Eastern time every weekday.

Ashleigh was whisked into a make-up room, where a girl with spiky blue hair and a nose ring went to work on Ashleigh's hair. A slender, handsome young man did her makeup. Ashleigh was pretty sure he was a gay, and she was glad her dad wasn't in the room to make remarks. She didn't want a single enemy at this cable news channel.

She watched the show's intro segment on a monitor in the green room with Cassie and her dad. O'Flannery went on an angry rant about the deteriorating morals and lack of patriotism among kids these days.

"But there are exceptions," he said. "I've been telling you folks about a disgraceful situation down South, where a loony lib high school principal decided to ban a student abstinence campaign. Well, these kids learned their lesson from him. They started humping like wild monkeys, all over the place. Nearly a hundred girls pregnant, and that's a fourth of all his students.

"Tonight's special guest is Ashleigh Goodling, the pretty young lady who wasn't allowed to teach her peers about abstinence. She's become the face of Christian teens in this country and their struggle against the left, so you know she's getting persecuted by all the usual moonbats. Well, we don't persecute young Christian girls here on the Overview, we embrace them. She'll take us behind the scenes of this national scandal, after this quick commercial break."

A production assistant led Ashleigh out to O'Flannery's interview desk, which was shaped like a wide "V" with his massive, reinforced chair on one side and three guest chairs on the other. The P.A. directed her to the chair closest to O'Flannery, since she was the only guest. O'Flannery was already in the opposite chair to face her. The studio lights made him sweat profusely, and two ladies were hurriedly mopping his face with towels and touching up his makeup.

Ashleigh felt very confident and calm as she approached the huge man. She wore her favorite black blazer, now with a flag on the lapel for her TV appearance, and under that, a new white blouse with a neckline that let Ashleigh seem modest while letting America know she had a great rack. She also wore a golden necklace with a cross pendant, with three little diamonds on the crossbar. Her abstinence ring was freshly polished. Extra tanning bed sessions had turned her skin the color of dark honey, and now the studio staff had done a great job with her hair and makeup. She looked professional and sexy.

O'Flannery saw her approaching. He placed both hands on the desk and heaved himself to his feet. His eyes bounced up and down her body a couple of times, and he smiled over his triple chin and held out one meaty paw towards her.

"Welcome to my kingdom, Miss Ashleigh," he said.

Ashleigh ignored the offered handshake and instead hugged him tight around the neck, squishing her body against his monstrous gut, and sighed as if meeting him fulfilled some lifelong dream.

"Oh, thank you for having me, Mr. O'Flannery," she gushed. "It means so much to me, and to the kids back home…"

"Save some of that for the show," he told her.

"Thirty seconds, Mr. O'Flannery," a producer announced.

"Gotcha." O'Flannery smacked Ashleigh's ass. "Have a seat."

Ashleigh clung to him, pumping her love out through her fingers and into his neck folds. She put her mouth to his ear to sink an extra last-second burst into his brain.

"I'm so nervous," she whispered. "I've never done anything this big before."

"You'll be fine, baby." He patted her ass again, and this time gave it a squeeze. Ashleigh gave him her best smile as she took her chair.

"Welcome back to The O'Flannery Overview Hour," he said. "My special guest is Ashleigh Goodling of Fallen Oak, South Carolina, population nine thousand. Thanks for coming today, Ashleigh."

"Thank you for having me, sir."

"Let's start by telling the Overviewers at home a little about you. You're the head of the Christian club at your school, is that right?"

"Yes, sir. I'm also very active in cheerleading, and I'm our student council president. Next year, I hope to be a freshman at Georgetown." She held up both hands with fingers crossed, and gave her most nervous-looking smile.

"You're a very well-rounded young lady."

"Thank you, sir." Ashleigh giggled.

"Ever been to New York before?"

"Oh, goodness, no. I didn't know cities could be so big! I hope to see the Statue of Liberty while we're here, because she's so inspiring, and also Ground Zero, because such important things happened there."

"We hope you enjoy your visit. Now, for the Overviewers at home, give us a little background on this teen abstinence story."

"Gosh. Well, teen pregnancy is such a major problem, even in little towns like mine. Our group decided to promote the only moral choice, abstinence, at our school. We thought teens would listen to other teens. We planned to reach them through posters, brochures, and a video we made with kids from school."

"But this loony lib principal rejected all of that. He's obviously a liberal, right?"

"Oh, sure. I mean, he hates abstinence. He'd rather see his students having sex instead of learning Christian values. That doesn't sound very conservative to me."

"It absolutely does not!" O'Flannery thundered. "Would you say his rejection encouraged all this crazy sex the kids were getting into? I've heard there were after-school sex parties."

"Yes, sir. Definitely. It's hard enough to say 'no' when you're a teen. I mean, I'm not perfect. I get tempted all the time. Your body wants it. That's why you have to rely on your mind, and on prayer. When adults set the example, and they say abstinence is bad, it just tells us to go ahead and give in to our urges." Ashleigh made herself look very agitated while she talked, as if she were craving sex right now, and gosh darn those strong religious values that kept getting in the way.

"We actually have a clip of this Principal Harris. This is from the press conference he didn't want to give." O'Flannery pointed at the camera with a pen.

On a monitor, they could see what the viewers at home were seeing. Principal Harris stood at a podium in front of the school, shifting nervously on his feet, his eyes big and cartoony behind his glasses. Reporters pushed in toward him. He looked sick.

"...the truth is," Principal Harris said. "I supported the abstinence campaign initially, and only rejected it when I saw the content. The particulars were disturbing..."

While the clip rolled, Ashleigh grabbed O'Flannery's hand and squeezed, pushing energy into him. His eyes glazed and his lids began to sink, and she released him. She didn't want him so enchanted that he became too stupid to do the show.

The video clip ended, and the monitor cut back to them.

248

"So he was for it before he was against it," O' Flannery said. "That makes him the O'Flannery—" A picture of Principal Harris appeared on the monitor, and then a pink cartoon beach sandal appeared over his face with a *thwack!* sound. "—Flip-Flopper of the Week."

Ashleigh giggled, and O'Flannery turned to face her.

"So of course the left has unleashed the crazy hounds," O'Flannery said. "I've seen awful things about you on the web, Ashleigh. Just hateful bile. Cartoons and Photoshop pictures that aren't suitable for this program. Even The Onion has attacked you. All this attention must be hard on a kid your age."

"I think it's sad the left has to resort to attacking little girls," Ashleigh said. "But you know what? My daddy's a preacher, and he always tells me no matter what I suffer, it's nothing compared to what Jesus and the Disciples suffered. Christians get persecuted, but God takes care of us. I don't care if everyone hates me. I have my faith." She touched the cross pendant, as if seeking strength from it. She released it, and as she dropped her hand, her fingers just happened to trace along the partially exposed curve of her right breast.

"I think you must have incredible strength to cope with all this vitriol," O'Flannery said.

"All I ever said was teens shouldn't have sex," Ashleigh said. "How is that controversial?"

"Never underestimate the sheer hatred of the left," O'Flannery said. "The truth makes them howl. In fact, I think it's time to call out the Liberal Moondogs."

A sound effect of several barking dogs played in the studio. On the monitor, four cartoon dogs paraded across the screen: a limp-wristed pink poodle, a big black pit bull wearing a do-rag, a Chihuahua in a sombrero, and a sheepdog in a tie-dyed headband and a "Save the Jackelopes" t-shirt, giving a peace sign with his shaggy fingers. Ashleigh giggled.

"Now let's look at the victims of this radical atheist principal," he said. On the monitor, there was a slideshow of Neesha's photos, with the pregnant girls looking depressed and ashamed. The producers had turned them black and white, and added slow, sappy music, like it was an ad for starving African children or homeless pets.

"These are the faces of girls who weren't allowed to hear Ashleigh's important message," O'Flannery intoned. "Look at them now."

Ashleigh made sure she looked sad and pouty when the cameras came back to them. O'Flannery shook his head at the tragedy of it all.

"What's going to happen to those girls, Ashleigh?"

"Unfortunately, college is out of the question for most of them," Ashleigh said. "We've started a special Girls' Outreach Ministry to guide them back to a moral life and help provide for their babies. I'm proud to report that we haven't suffered one abortion in our school." She doubted this was true, but who cared?

"And what about the boys who got to enjoy all this wild sex?" O'Flannery said. "Are they stepping up to the plate?"

"We're encouraging all the girls to get married. I'm helping my daddy put together a big marriage ceremony for everybody at once."

"That is just great, Ashleigh." He jabbed his pen at the camera. "How can the O'Flannery Overviewers out there help these poor girls?"

"They can donate through our website, and they can send any kind of baby supplies. We're a poor church in a poor little town. We need all the help we can get."

"Put that website up there," O'Flannery said. On the monitor, it appeared in fat letters at the bottom of the screen: fallenoakgirls.org.

"Help out those girls if you can, Overviewers. I donated. These are innocent victims of the loony left's loony agenda." He turned to Ashleigh. "Ashleigh, we didn't tell you this, but we have a special treat for you today. We can't make this loony-moony principal show your abstinence video at school, even if your classmates clearly need it. But we can show it to millions of O'Flannery Overviewers across the country, right now, tonight."

"Oh, wow!" Ashleigh said. "Thank you! Maybe it will help some kids, after all!"

"We hope so." He turned to the camera. "Get ready, folks. Here comes the controversial video the left doesn't want you to see—after these messages."

They cut to commercial, and O'Flannery's two sweat-swabber ladies ran out with clean towels and fresh makeup. As they patted his face, O'Flannery's eyes appraised Ashleigh, and he laid a meaty, sweaty hand on top of hers.

"Ashleigh," he said, "Let me take you to Sparks while you're in town. They have the best steaks in Manhattan."

"Sure!" Ashleigh said. "My daddy will love that. He never misses your show. Oh, I can't wait to tell him, Mr. O'Flannery!"

O'Flannery frowned.

"That's a lot of people on short notice," he mumbled. "Maybe some other time."

"You bet! I'll call you next time I'm in New York. Without my daddy." Ashleigh winked. Flirting with him gave her the urge to yarf in the nearest trash can.

Then they had to shut up and wait for the cameras.

O'Flannery set up the video for viewers just tuning in, and then it played on the monitor. Ashleigh watched it with her tight little smile.

It started with some jazzy music, and then the *Abstinence is Power!* logo spun out from the center of the screen, in a Comic Sans font, electric purple letters outlined in yellow.

The first sketch starred Erica Lintner, the freshman girl who believed she'd invented the slogan "abstinence is power." She wore pigtails and glasses, and she smiled around her braces. She also wore a white lab coat with a stethoscope and held a clipboard. The Goodlings' Welsh Corgi, Maybelle, stood on a table in front of her. The dog wagged her tail.

"Abstinence was the right choice for me," Erica said. "Becoming a veterinarian took a lot of school and a lot of studying. If I made the wrong choices, I wouldn't have gotten where I am today." She petted the dog.

The next clip featured Brenda Purcell, the girl who'd acted as DJ for the lock-in while dressed as the Bride of Frankenstein. Now she wore a straw cowboy hat and held a guitar across her lap.

"Abstinence was the right choice for me," Brenda said, though in real life Brenda was five months pregnant. Fortunately, they'd made the video back in the fall. "You can't succeed in country music without a lot of dedication and practice, and tons of hard work." She strummed the guitar and sang a few bars of Dolly Parton's *9 to 5*.

There were a few more. The last one was Ashleigh herself, in a blue suit, at a podium with the American flag behind her.

"Abstinence was the right choice for me," Ashleigh said. "Becoming President of the greatest country on Earth takes a lifetime of planning and public service. If I hadn't practiced abstinence before marriage, I wouldn't be where I am today. Abstinence really is power!"

The original posters that had actually hung in the school, featuring the "sexy abstinence" campaign, had all been burned up long ago in Ashleigh's fireplace after the Special Activities Committee secretly collected them for her. Neesha had created alternative posters, derived from the video that Principal Harris had prohibited without seeing, the one now being played to cable news viewers around the country. This alternative campaign, about which Principal Harris knew nothing, was the one featured in their press kits.

When the video clips finished, Chuck turned to Ashleigh, still smitten from his doses of Ashleigh-love.

"What is wrong with that?" O'Flannery asked. "Your principal calls that 'disturbing.' I find him disturbing, to be honest."

"We thought it would be okay because we weren't preaching our religious beliefs. We knew Principal Harris would never allow that."

"Because he's a loony lib. I thought it was harmless and very valuable, actually. Overviewers, you can find the full video on the O'Flannery Overview website." The web address popped up on the monitor. He turned back to Ashleigh. "Ashleigh, was that you as the President of the United States up there?"

Ashleigh giggled. "I do hope to go into public service. But my personal favorite is my little buddy Erica as the veterinarian."

"Let me tell you, Ashleigh..." O'Flannery put a meaty hand on top of hers, and gazed into her eyes. "If you ever became President, the men in this country would be very happy."

"Is that an endorsement, Mr. O'Flannery?" Ashleigh giggled.

"You can count on my support, Ashleigh." He gave a goofy smile.

"Well, bless your heart," Ashleigh said. "Thank you, Mr. O'Flannery."

"Thank you, Ashleigh." He looked at her for several seconds before remembering it was a live show. He turned to the cameras. "When we come back: Ashleigh takes questions from viewers. After this short break."

"Turn it off," Jenny said. "I can't listen to her anymore."

"The DVR's recording it, anyway." Seth flipped over to Comedy Central. He and Jenny slumped towards each other on the couch, his left shoulder against her right, a roach smoldering in the awful rhinoceros-foot ashtray on the coffee table. Where did Seth get these things?

They were in an upstairs sitting room in Seth's house with the French doors open to a warm April night. Jenny hadn't smoked much pot in recent months, since it really hadn't occurred to her. She felt good most of the time with Seth, and even when they argued, they eventually found peace, usually through laughing.

To prepare herself for Ashleigh on national television, though, Jenny had snagged a half-quarter of her dad's stash of homegrown. That seemed a little dry and stale, too, probably because of all the time her dad was spending with June.

"Light a second one," Jenny said. "I need it."

Seth struck it up, puffed a few times, and then passed it to her once it was burning well. Jenny filled her lungs with smoke, then coughed.

"Do you think Ashleigh's behind the pregnancies?" Jenny asked.

"How could she be?" Seth asked, while his fingers stroked her cheek.

"Think about it, man," Jenny said. "She can make people love her. But can she also make people fall in love with each other? Like Cupid? Or is that stupid?"

"I wouldn't know," Seth said. "She never admitted having any powers to me. And I don't understand mine all that well."

"But we do know about ours," Jenny said. "Let's figure this out. We can't turn them off, right? That's one thing."

"But we can turn it up," Seth said. "I can pump out more if I want, like when I healed your dad. When Ashleigh turns it up, you're basically her slave. When she turns it way up, your brain stops working, and you're just her pet animal."

"God, I'd hate to see what mine does when I turn it up," Jenny said. "But I know I can focus it. Like when I infected you to burn out Ashleigh's influence. I can tailor it. So maybe Ashleigh can make two people go for each other. Maybe if she touches them both at the same time."

Seth remembered, with some embarrassment, the time Ashleigh had made Cassie perform on him. Ashleigh had put her hands on both of them at once, and Seth felt a sudden burning desire for Cassie. Obviously, Cassie had felt something similar for him.

"I think maybe she can do that," Seth said.

"So she makes all these pregnancies happen, and then she gets on TV," Jenny said. She sat up against the armrest, still puffing on the joint. Seth took it from her. "Wait. First she has to get her abstinence thing rejected by Principal Harris. So she does all those sexy posters. Right? Remember?"

"Yeah, those were good," Seth said, exhaling smoke.

"No, they were crazy," Jenny said. "Using sex to sell abstinence. So of course Principal Harris cancels it. Then Ashleigh has to make all the girls pregnant in time to blame the principal. Do you see it, Seth? She's been planning this all year!"

"I guess if anyone is capable of that, it's her," Seth said.

"But what's the point?" Jenny asked. "She just wanted to screw with people? And get on TV?"

Seth reflected on this as he smoked. "I bet it's part of her flowchart."

"What's that?"

"Did I never tell you? She has a flowchart on her wall. Floor-to-ceiling, posterboard, Magic Marker. Been there since like ninth grade, okay? As long as I've known her. And it's her whole map of her future."

"Seriously? What's on it?"

"Georgetown for undergrad. Law school, preferably Yale. Then a job with a major lobbying firm, preferably oil or defense.

Two years. Then she comes back home and runs as a small-town girl for state office. Next step: governor, House or Senate, depending on what's available. Next step: the White House, maybe somewhere in the Cabinet, maybe Vice President, maybe...you know."

Jenny broke down laughing, and there was a small, panicked tremor inside her laugh. "President Goodling! What a nightmare. No way."

"I used to think it was funny," Seth said. "That she wanted to get inside the White House so bad. Not that she couldn't, maybe, possibly do it, but it just seemed like a silly thing to want. Like being an astronaut. Hardly anybody gets to do that.

"But think about it now," Seth continued. "With her enchantment. Shaking hands. She can't help but make people like her, all the time, wherever she goes. She only needs a little bit of access to power, doesn't she? And then she can charm her way to the top. Can you imagine Ashleigh with the access to touch people in the Senate? Or the White House? The Pentagon?"

Jenny felt dizzy. Too much smoke. She crammed out the joint, with a grimace at the rhino foot, then stood up and walked out to the balcony. She looked out over the budding life in the orchard, the wildflowers in the stable yard, the blooming vines creeping up the walls of the graveyard on the next hill. She thought of her ride to school after her first date with Seth, how life in the trees crawled underground in the winter, resting in the roots like a corpse in a grave, but it always came back with a new eagerness to live again.

"That's it," Jenny said. "It's all about getting access to powerful people. She's too impatient to wait. She wants to climb high and fast."

"It could work," Seth said. He came out to join her. "Old Chuck there can probably introduce her to some people. She'll have him enslaved by the end of the show."

"And then she graduates and moves to Washington, DC to start school," Jenny said, "Seth, we have to stop her!"

"What? Why? Maybe she'll leave town for good."

"But nobody else knows about her power," Jenny said. "And they wouldn't believe us if we told them. And nobody else has powers like us, to fight her with."

"We don't know that," Seth said. "If there's three in Fallen Oak, there must be others in the world."

Jenny paused. She had never really thought of that. She wondered how many were out there, what they were doing, if anyone else had a curse like hers.

"Okay," she said. "But they aren't focused on Ashleigh. That's our responsibility. She's from our town."

"Now you sound like my dad," Seth said. "'Ooh, responsibility's such a tough word, isn't it? Breaks your back, doesn't it?' Whatever."

"You know I'm right, Seth."

"What can we do?" Seth asked. "Should I go heal her? Or do you want to infect her with something?"

"I don't know."

"Do you want to kill her?" Seth asked.

"No!" Jenny turned on him. "Why would you say that?"

"It's something you could do," Seth said. "You wouldn't go to jail, because it would be death by disease, not murder. No one would believe a person could do that."

"You've thought about this?" she asked.

"Haven't you? Haven't you ever wondered what would happen if you killed someone on accident? Or on purpose? If there's a witness, do the police believe him? Or whether you could even go to jail for Jenny pox? Would you be considered a biological weapon? You never thought about it?"

"No, Seth," Jenny said. "I've always just pretty much tried to avoid killing people. That's plenty to worry about on its own."

"If you wanted to kill Ashleigh—"

"I don't!"

"—now's the time," Seth continued. "Before she has powerful friends. Before she's working in secure areas that we can't reach."

"We can't just do that," Jenny said.

"What else could we do?" Seth asked.

Jenny tried to think of another idea, but nothing came to mind.

"Anyway, we've got bigger things to worry about," Seth said. "The Easter egg hunt thing on Sunday. Do we need to go shopping?"

"You've got closets and closets of things upstairs," Jenny said. "I'd rather go shopping right here."

"Help yourself. Some of those closets haven't been opened in ages, mwah-haha-haha. There's all kinds of jewelry and everything."

"Is there any I can borrow?" Jenny asked.

"You find it, you dust it, it's yours."

Jenny gaped at him.

"What?" he asked. "I'm not wearing it."

"Do you have a sewing machine?"

"Maybe an antique. My mom's not the knitty type."

"My favorite kind. And, so what do we have to do at this Easter thing?"

"I have to give a speech that the bank manager wrote for me," Seth said. "Which I will shorten. And then we sit on the bandstand with the mayor and the preachers, the town council."

"Dr. Goodling's going to be there?" Jenny said.

"And Rev. Isaiah Bailey from New Calvary Church." New Calvary was the black church, located on the southern outskirts of the town, not too far from Jenny's house.

"Yeah, but back to the Goodlings. Is Ashleigh going to be near us?"

"We can try to avoid her," Seth said. "Anyway, the mayor talks, and the white preacher and the black preacher give a blessing together. And then the kids hunt for eggs all over the square. The police block off the roads."

"What do I have to do?" Jenny asked.

"Just sit by me until the hunt is over."

"How long does that take?"

"One year it took three hours."

Jenny shook her head. She got to her feet. "I'm going closet shopping. If Ashleigh's there, I want to look twice as good as her."

CHAPTER TWENTY-THREE

Ashleigh sat with her family on the front row of the white folding chairs arranged on the bandstand. Cassie was beside her, and then Mayor and Mrs. Winder. She watched as the people of Fallen Oak trickled out into the grassy square after church. Cars parked around the square, and black families in colorful Easter clothes emerged, having brought their kids to the square from New Calvary Church to participate.

Ashleigh watched little knots of people come together to greet each other, shake hands and hug. Kids in their Sunday best ran everywhere. Lots of teenage girls were looking very big with their pregnancies, and they didn't seem terribly happy about it. Ashleigh liked looking down on these little peasants who had done so much to advance her in the world. One day, some of these people would staff her first campaign for state office. Ashleigh had enchanted all of the unborn. She believed they would be of use to her when they grew up. When she eventually reached high office, she would have a devoted young staff to serve her.

She was feeling cheerful and cocky from her string of victories. She'd strolled into the principal's office on his last day and acted surprised to see him loading his pictures and framed degrees into a cardboard box.

"Principal Harris, why on Earth are you packing your office?" Ashleigh had asked him. "It's only April."

He had glared at her for a moment.

"You know very well why, Ashleigh," he said. "I've been suspended. Mrs. Varney will be acting principal for the remainder of the year."

"Oh, goodness, no!" Ashleigh said. Principal Harris just stared at her.

"Ashleigh," he asked. "Why do this? Why ruin my life? What did I ever do to you?"

"Gosh, Principal Harris," she'd said. "I guess I wasn't thinking about you at all."

Then Ashleigh took a strawberry lollipop from Mrs. Langford's desk on the way out. Ashleigh didn't care about Harris one way or the other, though she enjoyed crushing somebody who had tried to stand against her. Of course, if he hadn't done that, Ashleigh wouldn't be where she was today. She was glad some people were so predictable.

Most important, the real reason Ashleigh felt like a queen as she looked down from on high on the bandstand, was that Ashleigh had gotten the call from The Covenant.

It had come, appropriately, on Good Friday, just two days ago. A lady named Beth Underwood, who called herself an "event coordinator" for The Covenant, reached Ashleigh at home to make the invitation. They wanted her to give a presentation in May, at the big monthly dinner meeting, not just a little prayer breakfast or a lunch seminar. Ms. Underwood, who didn't sound much older than Ashleigh, offered to send a private jet to meet Ashleigh at the Greenville Downtown Airport. She said Ashleigh's family was welcome to stay in the Magdalene Suite at Covenant Hall, or the plane could take them home after dinner.

Ashleigh asked to stay. Covenant Hall was a beautiful forty-room Colonial Revival mansion in Georgetown, originally built in the early 20th century by a member of the Mellon family. It had later been an expensive hotel, before it was acquired by the private, tax-exempt religious organization known as The Covenant. She would be giving her presentation in the small theater there, then eating with the members in the dining hall. Staying meant more time to network. Maybe she could even stretch out the visit a few days. It would be Ashleigh's first visit to Washington, DC, and she wanted to see everything. She especially loved the idea of touring around the center of world power with Cassie at her side.

"Here is what our members will expect from you," Ms. Underwood had said. Ashleigh had grabbed a pen to take it down word for word. "First, they want a full presentation of the abstinence program you created. They will want a recap of your tribulations. Finally, they will ask for your input on possible federal abstinence programs aimed at your age group."

"Okay," Ashleigh said. "I can do that."

"Additionally, everyone in your party will sign a confidentiality waiver regarding all discussions and events inside the building. This simply allows everyone to speak his mind freely."

"Of course," Ashleigh said. She was trying not to jump up and down, trying not to let out the excited squeal that so badly wanted to escape her. "Will I be able to meet people and shake their hands?"

"Yes, at the reception," Ms. Underwood said. "Several of our members are eager to meet you, Miss Goodling."

"Tell them I'm eager to meet them, too," Ashleigh said.

Afterward, Ashleigh had run excited, screaming laps around the house, frightening their dog Maybelle, who opened and closed her mouth uselessly, since Ashleigh's mother had long ago grown sick of the dog's occasional barking and instructed the veterinarian to cut Maybelle's vocal cords.

Ashleigh had spent months laying out the bait to attract an invitation inside The Covenant's locked and guarded doors.

The Covenant was a small, very specialized ministry, focused on makers of law and policy. Among its members were eight Senators and thirty-four Representatives, as well as assorted top officials, all of them men. Their main focus was promoting war against Muslim countries—any war, any country, as far as she understood. Ashleigh didn't know much about foreign policy, but she had a simple strategy for that. She would simply agree enthusiastically with whatever they said.

The Covenant sometimes took an interest in domestic policy, including abstinence education on religious grounds. When Ashleigh had read about them, she recognized this as an issue where her power could work for her, and she could actually portray herself as an expert on current teenage behavior, which was forever a mystery to most adults, anyway. She simply needed a scapegoat to oppose her abstinence campaign, someone to blame for the rash of pregnancies that Ashleigh could create. Principal Harris had been a perfect mark and walked right into it. Her daddy had taught her how to recognize a sucker.

Now she looked forward to putting her hands on the Congressman and Senators at The Covenant's May meeting. She would have the chance to talk to a room full of powerful men. She would enchant each of them, handshake by handshake, and a thousand opportunities would open up for her. She did not plan to leave Washington without job offers for the summer. She wanted to be somewhere she could shake a lot of hands, so that she would already be her own little power center by the time she started at Georgetown in the fall. The first door was wide open and waiting for her, and that was all she needed.

From the bandstand, Ashleigh watched the brightly dressed crowd grow larger. They were like toys in her sandbox, and playing with them had helped prepare her for the world. Now it was time to leave her toys behind.

Her mood darkened when she saw Seth and Jenny approach the bandstand. She studied the dangerous couple. Seth wore a simple black suit, with a tie and pocket handkerchief the color of a robin's egg. Jenny had clearly gotten into the Barrett closets: her vintage cloche hat had a bouquet of red silk roses stitched on one side, and she wore a long blue dress that nobody in Jenny's family could afford.

Ashleigh had gone for the simple look, with a white boater-style hat wrapped in a single purple ribbon, which matched the purple trim on her white dress. She found herself comparing herself to Jenny Mittens, and she resented that. Jenny had worked a pretty good scam of her own, taking Seth from Ashleigh so quickly. Seth had betrayed Ashleigh, after she'd invested so much time making Seth into who he was. He'd dropped Ashleigh cold. Ashleigh didn't know who she hated more, Seth or Jenny. Her hate for Jenny was lifelong, etched deep into her identity. Her hate for Seth was recent and hot, a freshly opened wound she hadn't expected.

She smiled and waved her pastel handkerchief at Jenny and Seth as they made their way up the steps. They sat in the back row of folding chairs, as far as possible from the Goodling and Winder families. Boo-hoo. Seth ignored Ashleigh, but Jenny gave her a worried little frown. This brightened Ashleigh's heart a little, knowing that Jenny Mittens worried about her, maybe even feared Ashleigh's coming revenge.

The white choir and black choir assembled in the shade of the gnarled old trees in front of the courthouse, where, Ashleigh had heard, men had once been lynched. Her family wasn't local; her father was from Arkansas, her mother from Texas. Her father had moved to Fallen Oak over two decades ago, after completing his six-month "accelerated learning" theology doctorate from McGimmell Bible College, P.O. Box 2038B, Tampa, Florida. Ashleigh's mother, who'd been some kind of dancer, wanted to settle down somewhere nice. The old Fallen Oak preacher had died, and there was hardly anybody willing to work for the meager salary—except her father, who had heaps of cash to launder but open arrest warrants in three states, under the name Waylon Humphries. The statute of limitations had since expired on those, and anyway it was no longer his legal name or Social Security number.

Ashleigh had not learned all of this information directly from her father, but she had learned it.

The event opened with the joint blessing by her father and the Rev. Bailey, Neesha's father. The churches in Fallen Oak were segregated, but the preachers got along well, and had supper together frequently. Between themselves, they viewed segregation as a matter of not poaching on each other's territory.

The white choir sang "The Old Rugged Cross" and the black choir sang something upbeat that Ashleigh didn't recognize, but judging by the frequent refrain, she would guess its name was "By the River Jordan."

Then the event turned secular when Seth Barrett took the podium with Jenny Mittens at his side. Ashleigh had finagled a copy of the speech prepared by the bank manager. There was nothing unusual or threatening in it, just platitudes.

But Seth did not give that speech.

"Hundreds of years ago," Seth said, "Our ancestors arrived in this wilderness and carved out a place to live. Our families share a common history. Nobody remembers it now. We have suffered together. And survived together. And here we are, a great town of thousands. Our ancestors would never have believed it. That was a big city in those days." There were a very few chuckles.

"Our families have built a great place to live together. People in big cities dream of living in nice little towns like this.

And we owe a great debt to all our ancestors, who made this town for us."

Ashleigh wanted to snicker. When people saw Barretts in public, the last thing they wanted to hear about was debt they owed. Big mistake, Seth.

"And I think we will continue to grow in the future. This is the great settlement built by our ancestors. And I think we should keep working together, to keep making this a better place to live. And I was supposed to say some words on behalf of the Merchants and Farmers Bank, but I'm not going to bother you with that. Happy Easter, everybody."

There was a little smattering of applause as Seth and Jenny returned to the back row on the bandstand, but not much. Ashleigh saw a lot of stony faces in the crowd, especially among the regular religious crowd. Little rumors about devil worship and black magic had actually spread, thanks to a bored, willing audience and a preacher with time to fill. Ashleigh's father hadn't had much choice but to thunder about the immorality of the young, given the outbreak of pregnancies among his teenage congregants. And the young in question were happy to point to Seth and Jenny as the source of their corruption, the instigators of the "sex parties" that the media had invented, and the parents had consequently believed and interrogated their children about. Gabby little Shannon McNare had rapidly spread the rumor that Jenny and Seth did such things as part of their witchcraft, that some other kids she knew had definitely gone to one. So when the parents grilled their kids, everyone knew who to finger. There was a lot of blame to go around, and not many targets beyond Principal Harris. People needed more.

All of this had evolved without much effort from Ashleigh. It was just the beautiful way things came together sometimes, and you got the sense that you were secretly one of God's favorites, and that's why He bestowed such great powers upon you.

Then it was Ashleigh and Neesha's turn. They went to the podium together.

"Hi, I'm Neesha Bailey, from New Calvary Holy Land Church—" Neesha said.

"And I'm Ashleigh Goodling, from Fallen Oak Baptist Church—"

"—and we're seniors!" they said together, and embraced each other, to laughter and applause.

"The town Easter Egg Hunt was officially desegregated in 1983," Neesha read from her stationary. "By Mayor Jebediah Lowrence Guntley."

There was applause. Deputy Guntley, the obese nephew of the late Mayor Guntley, raised his hand and waved, grinning with his big buck teeth. He wore a peach suit with a pink tie, which made him look larger than ever. His pregnant teenage daughter Veronica rolled her eyes.

"Since then," Ashleigh said, "Fallen Oak has a proud tradition of both churches coming together for Easter. Last night, the police blocked off the roads around the square. The teen groups from both churches hid plastic eggs full of candy, dollars and toys. This year, there are also five American Eagle coins made of real gold, donated by the Merchants and Farmers Bank."

The children oohed and aahed over this. Some of the adults, too. Ashleigh flipped her hair as she turned her head to look at Seth. She blew Seth a kiss, and much of the crowd laughed, as did most of the people on the bandstand around them.

"But there is one problem, before the hunt can begin," Ashleigh said. "And here to take care of that is Mayor Hank Winder." Ashleigh and Neesha stepped back and applauded while Cassie's dad took the podium, then they returned to their seats.

"Ever since 1921," Mayor Winder said, "All forms of hunting are illegal within the town of Fallen Oak proper, except by special decree of the mayor or his authorized deputy. Therefore, as mayor of Fallen Oak, I declare Easter egg hunting season open!"

This was the cue for all kids aged six to twelve to run around screaming, waving their empty Easter baskets, and spread out across the square. They stormed in all directions, looking for eggs among the roots of trees, the bandstand, the courthouse lawn and steps, the church gardens, the narrow sunken windows of the bank, the shops and benches, the potted flowering plants that had been brought out to decorate the square.

Gradually, the crowd on the bandstand began to break up, going off to speak to their relatives or watch their grandchildren hunt.

Ashleigh waited until the crowd trickled out, then she stood. With Cassie and Neesha behind her, she strolled to the back row, where only Jenny and Seth remained. Jenny and Seth were whispering to each other and smiling, as if oblivious to how much the town hated them.

"Hello there, Mr. Barrett," Ashleigh said. "And Miss Mittens."

They both looked up at her. Jenny glared right into Ashleigh's eyes.

"It looks like somebody helped themselves to the Barrett closets," Ashleigh said. "I never gave into the temptation myself. A little too Seth's-mom for me, you know what I mean?"

"You look lovely, Ashleigh," Jenny said. She said with just the right inflection, the one that made it an insult, which Southern ladies could do.

"As do my friends," Ashleigh said, and Cassie and Neesha snickered behind her. Ashleigh turned to them. "Go ahead. I'll catch up." Cassie and Neesha left, with suspicious looks at Jenny.

"Seth, congratulations on completely demolishing your own reputation," Ashleigh said. "It was almost a work of art how you brought yourself all the way down. Even with all that money." She tsk-tsked. "Or maybe because of it, am I right, Seth? A little something there for everyone else to resent. You know?"

"School's almost over, Ashleigh," Seth said. "We don't have to worry about this stuff anymore. The world isn't high school."

"Maybe it isn't," Ashleigh said. "But we're all still tied up together by this town, aren't we? You own it. And little Jenny the pauper isn't going anywhere without you—because she can't, can she? Because you're the only person she can touch, in the whole world." Ashleigh looked at Jenny and laughed. "You're stuck with his bumbly little ass for life, aren't you? Because it's him or nobody. No matter how he treats you. Good luck with that. Just wait and see how he really is."

"I'm not interested in your advice, Ashleigh," Jenny said.

"And I still have my girls to think about," Ashleigh said. "And my little babies. My little army. I can't just abandon them. No, the three of us are stuck together. I think we all understand each other now. So why should we fight? We each have our separate lives. Why can't we have a truce?"

"Have we had a war?" Seth asked.

Ashleigh scowled.

"A peace agreement," Jenny said. "You don't bother us and we don't bother you. Let's agree to that, Ashleigh."

Jenny held out her hand. It was sheathed in a cream-colored, elbow-high glove, but Ashleigh still didn't want to touch it. The girl was a bag of pestilence.

"We can do that," Ashleigh said.

"That's not a fair agreement, Ashleigh," Seth said.

"What?" Ashleigh asked. Jenny asked the same thing, turning on him.

"Look at what you do," Seth said. "Look at all these girls. And it's just so you can get yourself close to powerful people. Isn't it?"

"That's ridiculous, Seth," Ashleigh said. "I am trying to help them—"

"After you put them in this condition," Jenny said. "And pretended to be their friend while you did it."

Ashleigh didn't like this new, defiant Jenny, the manipulative boyfriend-stealing Jenny. Ashleigh had felt in control so long as Jenny was the hopeless reject, walking with her hair in her face and her eyes on the ground, laughed at by everybody. Jenny had woken up and gotten control of her powers and taken Seth at the same time. With Seth under her thumb, Jenny had even more power at her command, power she'd taken away from Ashleigh. It had been a bold and brilliant move by Jenny, who had laid low for so many years Ashleigh had nearly forgotten what she could do. But it was time to remember.

"You do dangerous things," Seth said. "You hurt and manipulate people. We can't just leave you alone. First you have to promise to stop doing it."

Ashleigh looked around. She spoke in a low whisper.

"I cannot stop doing it!" she whispered. "I can't turn it off. I can turn it down, but not off. Okay?"

"You can block yourself off," Jenny said. "Think about it."

Ashleigh's eyes fell to Jenny's gloves.

"Oh, no," Ashleigh said. "I am not going to be some mitten-wearing freak."

"Just stop pushing people around," Jenny said. "Try to be a normal person. Don't try to be powerful."

"And try to be a good person, and help people," Seth said.

"Oh, well, fuck you," Ashleigh whispered. "Fuck you both in the head. I am not going to be some worthless little nobody just so you two can laugh at me."

"That's what we have to do, Ashleigh," Seth said. "All three of us. It's the right thing."

"I don't even know what you're talking about." Ashleigh stepped back from them. "And I don't care. You two are not standing in my way." She turned her back and walked down the bandstand steps.

So the war was on. Ashleigh liked to think she could escape to Washington, and leave all this small-town nonsense behind her. But she knew they would pursue her. Jenny hated her. Besides, Ashleigh needed the option of coming back to Fallen Oak to open a political campaign office, to be staffed and partly funded by the town that adored her. She needed to stay in close touch to oversee "Ashleigh's Girls," as some of the media now called the pregnant teens, and see that the unborn children into whom she'd invested so much power were raised the right way, by the group that she would bind together in marriage.

There was no breaking away from Fallen Oak, or Seth and Jenny. And Seth and Jenny would only grow strong together and more in command of their powers. They would never be any weaker than they were today. The time to strike was now, while they were young, before they became any more of a threat.

When Ashleigh, Cassie and Neesha were in Ashleigh's car, with the windows up and doors closed, Ashleigh said it.

"I want them dead," Ashleigh said. "I'm not kidding. I want them to die today."

"Whoa!" Neesha said. "Somebody needs to hit the pond, get stoned and relax."

"No," Ashleigh said.

"I know you hate them," Cassie said. "But you're too stuck on this Seth and Jenny thing. We've got bigger projects going now."

"They have to be dealt with," Ashleigh said. "They're the last obstacle."

"And you have a plan to get away with it?" Neesha asked.

"Hell yes," Ashleigh said. "We aren't going to do it ourselves. We get the town to do it for us."

"How do we do that?" Cassie asked.

"First we go to my house and get ready," Ashleigh said. "My parents have brunches and teas and crap. They won't be home for hours. Have somebody we trust keep watch on Seth and Jenny."

Cassie took out her cell phone. "Shannon McNare?"

"Anybody but her. And somebody with a car."

"Brenda Purcell?" Neesha suggested.

"Perfect," Ashleigh said. "She's pregnant, Jenny won't mess with her. She just needs to see where Jenny and Seth go, make sure they're not leaving town or anything crazy. Hurry up and call! Everybody's leaving."

Cassie dialed Brenda's number.

Ashleigh pulled out of the church parking lot, into the alley by the church. She glared up at the window with the temporary black plastic panel, where some jerk had smashed the pane with a rotten apple. It looked ugly. Her dad needed to hurry up and replace it. He'd fundraised for a replacement window three times already.

As she drove to her side of town, a cold, calm mood fall over her. Her brain was spitting out calculations, plotting how to make this play out her way.

CHAPTER TWENTY-FOUR

Jenny and Seth returned to Barrett House after the Easter egg hunt. They made fun of each other for their fancy clothes, but kept wearing them anyway. It was like being in a Halloween costume, just as Seth had said.

She worried about how the town had responded to Seth with cold silence, and about their confrontation with Ashleigh. Jenny could have told Seth that Ashleigh's offer of peace was a ruse, that if Ashleigh was being friendly, it meant she was plotting something. Jenny had just accepted Ashleigh's offer because it seemed like the best thing to do at the time. She'd fully expected Ashleigh to be insincere, but Seth had gone ahead and called her on it.

It was interesting, and troubling, how Ashleigh spoke in terms of war and peace, as if they were competing nations instead of just three people. Maybe Ashleigh had interpreted Jenny's liberation of Seth from Ashleigh's control as an attack by Jenny. Maybe it was, technically, but Jenny hadn't thought of it like that.

Ashleigh was right about one thing—the three of them were linked together, like it or not. None of them could pull free, not if Ashleigh had plans for all the unborn children. Ashleigh had called them "my babies" and "my army." The idea that Ashleigh could be thinking so many years ahead gave Jenny chills.

It was long since noon and they'd never eaten, so Jenny went to work in Seth's kitchen. She wanted something quick but Easter-y, and ended up making scrambled eggs and French toast, plus some cantaloupe. They ate at the kitchen table now, using the normal flatware and some *Gilligan's Island* collectible plates.

"Thanks for doing that," Seth said as he ate.

"Which thing? Going to the stupid egg hunt or making you breakfast for lunch?"

"All that. You're great to me."

"Yeah," Jenny said. "If you can get around the whole pestilence and death thing, I'm not so bad."

"What's a nice girl like you doing with an evil power like that, anyway?" Seth said, and she laughed. "Seriously. Why couldn't you have a nice power, like making people fall in love?"

"And what if Ashleigh had my power?" Jenny asked. "She'd kill everyone she didn't like, and she'd get away with it."

"At least she finally admitted she has it." Seth shook his head. "What are we, Jenny? And why three of us in one little town?"

"I don't know." Jenny poked at her French toast, feeling her appetite suddenly fade. "Something in the water? If I try to think about it, my mind just goes in circles until I stop."

"Maybe if we understood it, we'd understand how to stop Ashleigh. Keep her boxed in."

"But there's nobody to ask," Jenny said. "Nobody can explain it to us. I don't think there's even a word for what we are." She put down her fork, her appetite completely gone now. "Maybe there aren't any answers, Seth."

"There are answers," Seth said. "There must be."

When they finished, Seth put away the dishes. It was almost four, and they had school the next day. They made it a lazy afternoon. Jenny called her dad, who was at June's in Vernon Hill and planned to stay there, unless Jenny needed him. Jenny told him to stay. June got on the phone to wish Seth and Jenny a happy Easter, and to tell Jenny about the cute chocolate rabbit she'd received from Jenny's dad.

The call for Seth came later, after they'd nearly dozed off in their favorite upstairs sitting room. It was just after dusk. Seth's cell phone erupted on the end table, rattling around and startling them both awake. It vibrated to the edge of the table, danced over the side, and fell silent as it hit the carpet.

Seth stretched and picked up the phone from the floor.

"Who is it?" Jenny asked.

He looked at the screen.

"It was Dave Trenton. He's our kicker. Was our kicker, I guess, since we're graduating."

"Is he a good friend?" Jenny asked. She was already thinking about Ashleigh. "How well do you know him?"

"He was, before the…"

"The Jenny pox pictures," Jenny said. "When I cost you all your friends."

"Shit happens," Seth said. The phone began buzzing in his hand. "It's Dave again."

"Don't answer." Jenny had a cold, knotty feeling in her stomach. "He can leave a voice mail."

"He could be in trouble." Seth answered the phone. He immediately looked perplexed. "Oh. Hey, Shannon."

Shannon McNare? Jenny mouthed. Seth nodded, and Jenny began shaking her head vigorously. She pantomimed hanging up the phone.

"Okay, slow down," Seth said. "When did it happen? How bad?" Seth listened for a minute. "I'll be right there." He clicked the phone off and jumped to his feet, grabbing up his Easter dress shoes, the only ones in the room.

"Seth, what's happening?" Jenny asked.

"I have to go," Seth said. "There was a car crash at the square. Dave's hurt. So's Franny Blackfield, and she's only eight."

"But that was Shannon, right?" Jenny followed him out of the room, toward the front stairs.

"Dave's unconscious. He's bleeding from his head." Seth raced down the steps, and Jenny hurried to keep up with him. Seth opened the front door, and Jenny followed him towards his car. "Shannon took his cell phone to find my number. She remembers what I did at the farm, and she thinks I can help. She's right."

"Wait!" Jenny yelled, as Seth climbed into the car. "We need to talk about this!"

"Then get in." Seth slammed his door and cranked the engine.

Jenny huffed and ran around to the passenger door. Why wouldn't he stop for a second?

As soon as she was inside and closed the door, Seth turned his car and raced down the winding brick drive, toward the gate.

"Shannon is one of Ashleigh's," Jenny said. "She's in all her groups. We can't trust her."

"I don't have to trust her," Seth said. "I just have to help these people."

"Seth, there might not be anyone who needs help," Jenny said, as Seth peeled out onto Barrett Avenue.

"What do you mean?" he asked.

"It could be a trap," Jenny said. "Ashleigh threatens us, then we get a call from her little minion? We'd be stupid to walk into that."

"What if it's not?" Seth asked. "What if somebody dies because of me? Dave's a good friend."

"Too good to talk to you," Jenny said.

"This isn't the time to be petty."

"No," Jenny said. "It's the time to be suspicious."

Seth gave her a worried look, but he continued accelerating towards town.

"Ashleigh can't be behind everything, Jenny," Seth said. "You can't live in fear of her."

"If you're me, you have to." Jenny watched out the window as the world streaked past.

When they reached the square, it was dark enough that the corner lamps, designed to look like old-timey gaslights, had come to life. A large mob milled around on the lawn, concentrated near the courthouse.

"There's Dave's truck." Seth pointed. They could just see the cab of a white pick-up truck that had stopped slantwise in the middle of the road, right in front of the courthouse. They couldn't see much through the crowd. If there was another car involved, the crowd was blocking Jenny's view of it. Many of the people were still in their Easter clothes, like Jenny and Seth, while others had changed over to jeans and boots.

"Why are so many people here?" Seth asked.

"Maybe Shannon McNare called all of them, too," Jenny smirked. "We should leave. All these people hate us."

Seth parked in front of the Five and Dime, since the crowd was blocking the roads. They couldn't safely park anywhere closer.

"I'll just check," Seth said. "If nobody's hurt, I'll be right back. Okay?"

272

Jenny unfastened her seatbelt. "You're not walking out there alone."

Jenny left her high heels in the car and walked across the grass in her bare feet, annoyed at herself for not grabbing her sneakers. But she'd been too busy keeping up with Seth.

Several people turned to face them, and their mouths dropped in surprise. They smacked the arms of the people around them, murmuring, and soon everyone was looking at them. They whispered to each other. Jenny was ready to run away, but Seth kept plodding ahead, determined to help people even if it killed him.

They made their way toward Dave's truck, and the crowd pulled back and let them through. Jenny saw revulsion and hate on every face. She took Seth's hand and clung tight.

When they reached the truck, both truck doors were closed. It didn't look damaged. Seth looked in the window, but there was nobody inside, no sign of injury.

"Dave?" Seth turned back to face the crowd. "Where's Dave?"

"Right here, buddy." Dave emerged from the crowd, along with Everett Lawson and a few other guys from the team. Shannon McNare trailed behind them, obviously wanting to be close enough to watch without getting involved.

Dave carried a hunting rifle. So did all of the other guys, except for Everett, who had a pump-action shotgun.

There was a ripple of movement through the crowd, and lots of people raised their weapons. Besides guys from the team, there were guys from Ashleigh's groups, Coach Humbee and a few other teachers, a gang of random men from McCronkin's, the entire Women's Steering Committee from Fallen Oak Baptist with their husbands, and assorted men and women from all over town. They were people from her school, people who hired her dad for repair jobs, people Jenny saw at the gas station and the Piggly Wiggly. They were armed with rifles, pistols, crowbars, hammers, and the occasional broken chair leg.

Even Chief Lintner was there, and Deputy Guntley, and Mayor Winder. They stood with the crowd.

The entire crowd was eerily silent, just staring at Jenny and Seth.

"Dave, what's going on?" Seth whispered. He looked at Shannon, who turned her eyes to the ground. "I heard you were in trouble."

"You're the one in trouble, asshole," Dave said.

"What did I do?"

Dave snorted.

"You know what you did," Everett said. "Everybody here knows."

The crowd closed in on them from every side. Jenny cast a panicked look in the direction of Seth's car, but the mob stood directly in the way. Jenny and Seth backed up, but the crowd kept advancing, one step at a time, like a herd of zombies. Jenny and Seth backed across the road, under the gnarled oaks, up the courthouse steps, until they were against the courthouse doors. The crowd stopped at the bottom step and grew denser as stragglers caught up. It was a wall of people. There was nowhere else to go.

"I told you it was a trap," Jenny said.

"Okay," Seth whispered. "But how could Ashleigh do all this?"

"She's an amazing girl," Jenny said. "You should date her."

"Somebody tell me what's happening!" Seth yelled at the crowd.

"You went too far this time," Earl McCronkin said. He held a large revolver in one hand, against his hip. "You Barretts think you can do anything to anybody. Took my granddaddy's farm away. You think you own this town." Several men and women shouted their agreement.

Jenny looked to the police chief, but the man had his arms folded, just keeping watch without interfering.

The front doors to the church opened, and Cassie and Neesha stepped out, their eyes down, looking upset. They waited on the front stoop of the church, letting the crowd notice them and whisper to each other to look.

When the crowd's attention was on the open church door, Ashleigh came out, looking awful. Her hair was dirty and wild, but pinned up to reveal her face. Bruises covered her face and neck, one eye was black, a lip was swollen, and her left cheek looked cut up and mangled. She wore only a lace dressing slip, and she was barefoot. More wounds and fresh bruises were visible on her shoulders, arms, and legs.

The crowd gasped and grumbled at the sight of her. Many angry looks were cast at Seth and Jenny, who just looked at each other. Either Ashleigh had accomplished the world's most incredible make-up job, or she'd had her friends pound her with blunt objects until she bled.

Ashleigh descended the church steps slowly, her eyes on the ground. Her two friends followed at a careful distance, like bridesmaids, or mourners.

The crowd's voice fell into low, urgent whispering as Ashleigh crossed the street, then became silent as she stepped on the lawn. The people parted for her, creating a wide grass avenue toward the courthouse. Ashleigh walked along the center of it, looking at no one, keeping her eyes down. It was the way Jenny had walked in public for most of her life.

Ashleigh walked all the way to the first courthouse step, while her two friends lingered back in the crowd. She looked up at Seth. She pointed her finger at him.

"He did it," Ashleigh said.

The crowd erupted in chatter, and a few angry shouts. Mayor Winder and the two police now made their way through the crowd, to stand behind Ashleigh, looking up at Jenny and Seth.

"She told me about it," Cassie said. She glanced at her father, the mayor. "Seth invited her over after church. He said he wanted to make things right and get back together with her. So Ashleigh went, because the truth is, she never stopped loving Seth."

Some of the crowd found this whisper-worthy.

"But it was a trap," Cassie said. "He assaulted her. He…" Cassie shook her head.

The crowd muttered, and there were a few more shouts.

"That's crazy," Jenny said. "I was at Seth's. Ashleigh never came over."

"She helped!" Ashleigh jabbed a finger at Jenny. "She beat me. And she tore off my abstinence ring." Ashleigh held up her empty left hand, to some gasps.

"She's lying," Seth said, which only seemed to anger the crowd. Ashleigh's condition seemed to speak for itself. "It's what she does. She manipulates everyone."

"Shut up," Jenny whispered.

"Why? It's true. Isn't it, Ashleigh? Tell them the truth. Tell them I didn't do this. Tell them how your friends Cassie and Neesha beat you up so you could frame me."

Many outraged voices spoke up in the crowd, and somebody shouted "Get him!"

"I don't think the truth is working," Jenny whispered.

"How can you just let them stand there?" Ashleigh wailed. She looked to the crowd on her left, the crowd on her right. "Look what they did! Somebody do something!"

Some of the mob shuffled forward. Everett and two older armed men in hunting jackets got as far as the third courthouse step, with seven steps left to go. They looked at each other, waiting to see who would go first. Nobody volunteered. They were attacking unarmed teenagers, hometown kids.

"Please!" Ashleigh screamed. "Somebody! Somebody!"

There was some more shuffling forward, but not as much. Ashleigh turned to face them.

"Won't anyone protect me?" she asked. She stepped toward the crowd, extending her hands out, palms up. She seemed befuddled, as if the intense head bashing by Cassie and Neesha had, just possibly, affected her head. "Come on, everybody. Touch me. Touch me!"

They whispered among each other, not sure what to make of this. Even Cassie and Neesha looked worried and whispered to each other. Ashleigh wasn't doing it right. Her head was too mixed up.

"Fuck!" Ashleigh said. Then she screamed it: "Fuck you all!"

She whirled towards Seth and stalked up the courthouse steps.

On the fourth step, Ashleigh snatched the pump shotgun from Everett's hands.

On the fifth step, she raised it.

On the sixth step, she pointed it at Seth.

"Ashleigh," Seth said. "Put it down. The police are right behind you."

Jenny looked. The police were still on the sidewalk, watching, waiting for the mayor to give an order. Cassie gripped her father's forearm and kept whispering in his ear, distracting him.

On the seventh step, Ashleigh squinted an eye and took aim at Seth's gut.

"Ashleigh," Seth said. "Don't."

Jenny couldn't speak, and didn't even know if she should. The sound of her voice might set Ashleigh off. If she moved fast enough, she could kill Ashleigh. But Ashleigh's finger was already on the trigger, and Jenny didn't think she could make it. She'd probably just startle Ashleigh into shooting. Better to let Seth talk her down.

On the eighth step, almost to the top, Ashleigh stopped. Her eyes locked onto Seth's.

"Go to hell, Seth," she said. "I have a heart, too."

Then she pulled the trigger. Seth's heart and ribs exploded through his back and spattered across the courthouse doors.

Seth stumbled backward. He slammed against the locked door, then slid down along it. He stopped in a sitting position on the lip of the door sill, and remained there a second, his eyes bulging in surprise. Then he flopped over on his side, and his hand smacked across Jenny's bare foot. Jenny screamed.

She sank to her knees beside Seth, laying her hands on him, unable to do anything at all. She checked his pulse at his neck and his wrist, but there was nothing. There wasn't a heart left to beat.

Ashleigh approached her, fiddling with the slide on the shotgun.

"Seth," Jenny whispered, unable to believe what Ashleigh had done. Her hand passed over Seth's face. No life remained in his eyes, just a fading echo of the shock in which he'd died. The loss of him seemed too enormous to understand. No more touching. No more love. No hope for the future. The rest of her life would be as lonely as the first eighteen years, but worse, now that she'd glimpsed what could have been. She would never recover from losing him.

Jenny looked up.

Ten seconds, she thought. Ten seconds ago, she could have killed Ashleigh and saved Seth. Just ten seconds. Maybe she wasn't fast enough, but she should have tried.

Jenny rose unsteadily on her feet. She held out her hands to Ashleigh. Ashleigh was grunting, still trying to work the slide on the old gun. It wasn't budging.

"Come," Jenny said. "Come on. Let me touch you."

Ashleigh's gray eyes looked down at Jenny's. Ashleigh gave the slide a final useless try, then dropped the gun. She turned and ran away down the courthouse steps, through the wide avenue the crowd had made for her.

"Stop!" Jenny yelled. "Somebody stop her!"

But nobody did.

Jenny looked down at Seth and dropped to her knees again. She touched his head, and a deep, sudden sob tore through her. But she didn't cry, not yet. There was just the one wrenching sob.

She pulled him into her lap, holding up his head the way she had done the day he'd almost put too much into the healing. The day he'd brought her father back to life.

But there was no one she could call to bring Seth back. The only person with the power to do that was gone.

Ashleigh jogged on foot through the church, not sure where Cassie and Neesha were now, not really caring. She found Neesha's car keys. Neesha had driven, since Ashleigh was supposed to be too traumatized. Ashleigh was feeling a little traumatized. The girls had really whacked her with the cooking pans. And the meat tenderizer. And then she'd lain back on the floor while Cassie and Neesha kicked the shit out of her.

And still she'd screwed it up, even with dedication like that. Her head felt thick. She hadn't activated the crowd right. She'd never made anyone kill before. Usually she had them give her things, or do stupid little favors for her. Maybe it took a special approach. Maybe she hadn't dialed it up enough. Maybe she'd been relying too much on the influence she'd pumped out earlier in the day, shaking hands at the church and the Easter egg hunt, and it had faded.

The plan had seemed so clear earlier, sometime before her multiple head wounds. Neesha and Cassie had resisted the plan at first, but everybody eventually agreed with Ashleigh. She'd had them spread the word about what had supposedly happened, calling everyone they knew. They told everyone that everyone was meeting on the square to deal with it and everyone was bringing a gun just in case.

She'd meant to trigger an incident, but she'd ruined it. The crowd wasn't agitated enough. She thought they were on edge, that maybe if she took the first shot, that would do it. But instead she'd broken her first rule, gotten blood on her own hands. And her second rule, in front of witnesses. She'd been impatient. She'd just wanted to see Seth and Jenny die.

Ashleigh climbed into Neesha's Acura and cranked it, adjusted the seating to her body. Neesha and Cassie were still back on the square. Oh, well. If they didn't keep up, they were too slow. Neesha had annoyed Ashleigh, anyway. Ashleigh had wanted a very mixed crowd, because she thought a crowd with lots of black people would be scarier, but it looked like Neesha had called mostly white people. She deserved to lose her car for a while. Ashleigh drove out into the alley and pushed the accelerator.

But it wasn't a complete loss. Seth was gone, and that was half the battle. She didn't know what to do about Jenny. She'd screwed up there, gotten over her head. The gun had jammed or something. She'd ended up standing in front of Jenny Mittens, basically unarmed, with nothing but Jenny's murdered boyfriend between them. She had to get out of there.

Ashleigh couldn't turn her power off, but she could turn it up. She could make someone like her, love her, adore her, worship her, put them in a state of complete bliss. She could instigate all kinds of romantic encounters between anyone, make them lose control. When she turned it up, really let the power flow, she could enchant and ensorcel anyone, even a crowd, if she could touch them.

She had a feeling Jenny Mittens was about to turn it up. And Ashleigh did not want to be near that. It was time to retreat and let Jenny burn herself out, if that's what she was going to do. Maybe she would die in the process. There were a lot of armed guys out there, experienced hunters. If they'd been too chicken to shoot for Ashleigh, maybe they would shoot to save themselves. If they had the chance.

Ashleigh had her fallback plan ready to go. On her cell phone, she dialed Darcy Metcalf, already waiting at Ashleigh's house.

Jenny held Seth across her lap, rocking back and forth, completely stunned. The crowd was quiet, with only an occasional whisper. Then the whispering became louder and faster. Jenny saw Dr. Maurice Goodling, in his Easter suit with a lily pinned to the pocket. He was climbing into the flatbed of Dave Trenton's white truck, the one parked slantwise in the middle of the road, the decoy that had drawn Seth into the crowd. People whispered and nudged each other, and he straightened his coat while he sized up the crowd.

"People," Dr. Goodling said. "Good people of Fallen Oak. I feel it is my duty, on behalf of the Lord, to speak to you at this time. I feel the presence of the Spirit here today. And I feel the presence of another, fallen spirit here tonight."

There were gasps from the crowd, and some heads bowed to pray, eyes closed.

"There are times, we are told, when we must render unto Caesar what is Caesar's," he said. "And times when we must render unto God what is God's. We know all about rendering unto Caesar—" A few people chuckled, but others cut them off with sharp looks. "—but, now and again, we are called upon to render unto God."

Heads nodded as people took this in.

"We have heard information," he said. "About illicit activities up at Barrett House. Full moons, mostly. The practice of witchery, also known as witchism. Drugs. Sexualization. Our children. We have seen our town flipped inside out. Our poor high school girls, so many drawn in by this witchdom.

"I thought y'all were a little off when you started bringing me stories about witchcraft," he said. "Thought I had to be the cool-headed one. The one that kept everybody else from worrying. But now I realize that sometimes, occult things do happen. Darkness does move upon the earth, and we must strike back against it."

More heads nodded, and there were murmurs of agreement.

"The girls tell me," Dr. Goodling said. "There was great witchery again today at Barrett House, because of Easter. They have their own kind of Easter ritual, you see." He turned to look at

Cassie and Neesha, evaluating them for a moment. "Cassiopeia," he said. "Did Ashleigh tell you about seeing any black magic today?"

Cassie looked around nervously as hundreds of faces turned toward her.

"Yes," she said. She cleared her throat. "Um, yes, Dr. Goodling. That's why they did it, for their Easter ritual. Because, uh, you see, the devil, they celebrate a different Easter. Right? So, they need to...I'm sorry, this is hard to say. They need to sacrifice a virgin."

The entire crowd gasped. Even Dr. Goodling looked surprised.

"Yep, sacrifice a virgin," Cassie said. "They knew Ashleigh was a virgin, right? So they lured her in. I mean, Ashleigh is a major get for Satan, right? Only she escaped. And she made it all the way to church. And so...here she was, and then. Well, and then..." Cassie glanced at Jenny. "Then Jenny and Seth came to chase her. That's why they're here."

Then Cassie buried her face in both her hands. She looked like she was sobbing, but Jenny believed she was hiding laughter.

"Scripture is very clear," Dr. Goodling's voice boomed. "'Thou shalt not suffer a witch to live.' Exodus...well, Exodus."

Jenny watched this unfold. Her mind was completely numb. Had Ashleigh really planned everything?

"However," Dr. Goodling said. "Did you know that black magic, witchcraft, and devilry are not felonies in South Carolina?"

The crowd murmured, surprised and mystified by this.

"It's not illegal," Dr. Goodling said. "On account of...it's freedom of religion."

Many an outraged cry went up from the crowd.

"On the other hand," Dr. Goodling said. "We have God's law. We have the Book. And it tells us, 'thou shalt not suffer a witch to live.' Say it with me, folks."

They said it with him.

"That's from the Bible, folks," Dr. Goodling said. "Now, we all know my daughter Ashleigh. She's about as close to an angel as I can imagine. And to think, what they did, and tried to do. Of course the Lord will give us a sign. Of course the Lord will send an angel to strike the first witch, to show us what to do. The signs are here. This is a test of faith.

"We are way out beyond human justice," Dr. Goodling said. "Ain't that right, Chief Lintner?"

The police chief looked at Jenny, then at Dr. Goodling, and nodded his head.

"Tonight, we have to rip the evil from this town, root and branch," Dr. Goodling said. "Tonight, we're going back to the Old Testament, and the original law. Tonight, we are gonna see God's justice."

Shouts went up from the crowd.

"Traditionally," Dr. Goodling said, "Witches are killed in two ways: by hanging, and by burning. I recommend we start with one and finish with the other. Hang the girl-witch. Burn both bodies and bury them in unmarked graves on unblessed ground. And, uh, cover the graves with salt!"

Many voices rose in support of this.

Dr. Goodling walked to the cab of Dave's truck, leaned against it, and waited.

Gradually, people came together, a thick nylon rope was found, a lynching party picked out, including Everett Lawson, Deputy Guntley, Larry DuShoun, and a fat guy in a denim jacket named Arbie Blackfield, who owned an old gas station on the south side of town, and had just come from drinking at McCronkin's. His eight-year-old daughter had allegedly been hurt in the accident with Dave Trenton.

Jenny watched all of this in disbelief. Then she happened to catch a look between Dr. Goodling and Cassie. Cassie raised her eyebrows, and Dr. Goodling winked at her. Jenny realized this wasn't all one big, intricate plot arranged by Ashleigh. They were adapting. Dr. Goodling's carnie-booth con man instincts kept the show going his way, and obviously Cassie had learned a few tricks from the Goodling family.

They were improvising.

Jenny needed to improvise, or they were going to kill her. Arbie was twirling up a nylon noose. Why did they want to kill her?

She blinked, and the meaning of Dr. Goodling's speech clicked into place. She'd spent a lot of time thinking like Ashleigh, for her own defense. That meant she knew at least a little about how Dr. Goodling worked, too.

Jenny stood up, and many people quieted, looking at her.

"Can't you see what he's doing?" Jenny asked. "He's just trying to protect his daughter. Ashleigh Goodling is a murderer. She killed Seth. And now he wants all of you to share her guilt. He wants you to burn our bodies? Think about it. You'll be part of both crimes."

There was angry muttering and some unfriendly shouting.

"If you do what he says," Jenny shouted, "You're all guilty! Don't you understand? He's a con artist. Like his daughter."

This brought a lot of angry shouting, and the crowd surged toward her. Dr. Goodling stood upright in the pickup bed again.

"Be mindful of the devil's deceptions," Dr. Goodling said. "Is there any here among you who would defy God? Is there any here who would speak on behalf of this girl, who has brought only curses and evil upon us through her witching? Think of all the innocent girls who suffered, all the strange pregnancies. The horror and death we've seen today. Who wants it to continue? Who speaks for the child of hell?"

Jenny looked out on the silent crowd.

"Please," Jenny said. "Somebody?"

There was whispering, and Jenny thought she heard hissing. But nobody spoke up in her defense.

Dr. Goodling said a special blessing over the four members of the lynching party. They walked up the courthouse steps together, towards where Jenny stood by Seth's body. Seth's blood coated her dress, her gloves, her face. It was already starting to cool. She could smell it everywhere.

Deputy Guntley dangled the noose.

"Y'all hold her," he said as they approached. He smiled around his buck teeth. "I'll rope her."

Everett seized her left hand and Albie Blackfield grabbed her right, both of them insulated by Jenny's long gloves. Larry DuShoun got behind Jenny and clapped his hands to the front of her hips, which just seemed unnecessarily perverted to her.

"You just hold still," Deputy Guntley said. He raised the noose over head. Jenny watched his fat, jiggling forearm moved into striking distance. "Hold still…"

Jenny lunged her head forward and sank her teeth deep into the deputy's arm. Guntley screamed and tried to pull free, but

Jenny bit down with all her strength. A dark red rash spread up his arm and into his sleeve. It appeared again on his neck, then spread across his face like kudzu overtaking a tree. His whole body shivered, and ropy saliva sputtered from his mouth.

Jenny opened her mouth and pulled away, and thick strings of dissolving flesh came with her, clinging to her lips like hot mozzarella. She left a mouth-sized hole in his forearm, open all the way to the bone. Guntley collapsed as seizures racked his body.

Jenny tried to pull her hands free. Everett was quick and clamped down tight, but Albie Blackfield was not as quick, and he only managed to catch the fingers of her glove. She pulled her right hand free. She wouldn't be needing the glove, anyway.

She clapped her hand onto the back of Arbie's and pressed down, willing the Jenny pox to spread. Arbie's hand dried and cracked, weeping blood. The same happened to his bristly, unshaven face, the skin shriveling and breaking to scales and flakes like mud drying in the sun. Arbie hyperventilated, then fell to his knees and puked up blood and bile.

Jenny slapped her free hand against Everett's face, and it immediately broke into the flaky scales, with blood leaking out between the cracks. More blood seeped from his nose, his ears, and his eyes. He fell aside, dead by the time he toppled down the steps.

Larry DuShoun wrapped his arms around her waist and pulled her back against his hips. It really felt like he was dry humping her, trying to get one last nut before he died.

Jenny twisted around in his arms, her face uplifted as if she expected him to kiss her. She put her hand under his chin and gripped his pimply jaw. Larry's acne began swelling and bursting, with a sound like popcorn, and Larry howled in pain. The burst pimples opened into ragged holes, which revealed rotting face muscles beneath his skin.

She shoved him back into one of the courthouse's big front columns. Larry bounced off, leaving red smudges all over it. Then he fell on his face, and he never moved again.

It had taken less than thirty seconds to kill the four of them. Jenny looked out at the crowd. Some were screaming, but most just stared in shock and horror.

She leaned down to touch Seth's face one last time. He was already getting cold and stiff, the memory of life leaving his body.

That boosted her anger. She stood up and faced the crowd. She lifted the ruffled skirt of her bloody Easter dress as she started down the steps, one bare foot at a time.

"You're murderers," she told the stunned crowd. "You killed him. He was a miracle, and you killed him. Now you've just got me. And I'm a curse."

The crowd eased back as she took one slow step down after another, keeping her eyes on them. She'd tolerated these people long enough. They had always made her life hell. And tonight they'd taken her only love from her, the only one she could ever love. Then they'd tried to kill her.

And so they were all going to die. Every last one of them.

One of the middle-aged hunters, Gus Lotrie, who worked the meat department at the Piggly Wiggly, raised his deer rifle and fired. The shot tore through her left side, just below her heart, tearing out a lot of meat. She stumbled and fell to her knees. She caught her balance on the step with her hands, but she slumped forward anyway. She wanted them to think the one shot was fatal. It certainly felt fatal. It felt like someone had poured burning gasoline down the left side of her body.

She pictured the swarm of black flies in her gut, always eager to escape and spread the pox. She imagined them sprouting big, sturdy dragonfly wings. She told them they were attracted to human flesh. She told them they were hungry for it.

Jenny pushed herself to her feet, slowly raising her head. The crowd muttered and whispered, trying to figure out what to do.

It felt like a large, invisible hand reached into her back and squeezed her lungs. Her nose and throat swelled. Then coughs racked her body, and she hacked out what felt like a lungful of sand. Grainy black spores spewed out of her and expanded into a cloud, which drifted down to the armed men at the front of the mob. Jenny watched in amazement. She'd never known she could do that, but she seemed to have an instinctive understanding of her powers when survival was at stake.

She'd created airborne Jenny pox.

The men dropped their weapons as coughing fits ripped through them. They sneezed out blood and little gray flecks of brain. One football player, the junior with the flattop who'd made fun of Jenny's "pancakes" and pretended he was trying to lick his own nipples, way back on the first day of school, looked up at her through bloody eyes. His jaw dropped open, and it kept dropping, the bone splintering away from the rotten skull, the decaying flesh of his face ripping open all the way to his ears.

His jaw bounced off his chest and landed between his shoes. Gurgling, gagging sounds escaped his open throat hole. Then his blood-rimmed eyes rolled back into his head, and he toppled to the ground, his arms and legs kicking out at random.

Jenny had infected the row of armed men at the front, plus several people behind them. These included Police Chief Lintner, the school receptionist Mrs. Langford, and a man in a matching kitten sweater who had to be her husband. All of them lay in a heap, jerking and twisting as the Jenny pox ate through their muscles and nerves, looking like a clump of ants drenched in a good dose of Raid.

Mayor Winder had been near the front with the police, but now walked backward through the crowd along with Mrs. Winder and Cassie. Dr. Goodling still stood in the pickup truck bed, his eyes wide in horror. Clearly, his theological studies had not prepared him for this.

The whole crowd was creeping backward, but nobody wanted to be the first to break and run. All eyes were on Jenny. She snarled back at them.

Jenny reached both her hands behind her neck and found the zipper tab for her Easter dress. She pushed it down as far as she could reach. Then she grabbed both sides of the dress and pulled them out, ripping the dress all the way open. She pushed the torn dress down off her hips, and it puddled on the stairs around her.

She eased her right foot down to the next step, then her left. Only her underwear and bra remained, all of it originally white, but now stained dark red with Seth's blood. If anyone else tried to grab her, they would die.

She raised her arms high above her head and extended her fingers, as if surrendering. Then she turned her palms inward to face each other, following her instincts, and suddenly she knew this pose was ancient, it had been engraved somewhere on Babylonian clay or Egyptian stone thousands of years ago.

The surface of her skin rippled from her fingertips to her feet, and then dark, bloody sores broke open everywhere. Weeping rashes spread all the way down her legs. Dark lesions bloomed all over her stomach and breasts. Boils opened on her feet and hands. Dark tumors sprouted along her jaw and forehead, distorting the shape of her face. She smiled, and her teeth were coated in blood and thick, black fluid. She felt like she'd just put on the clay mask of her face, the scary one Seth hung on his bedroom wall.

"Come on," Jenny said to the crowd. "Who else will lay their hands on me? Who's next?"

Then the crowd screamed and broke, running away from the courthouse. But it was too late for that. They'd made their choice. Above Jenny, on the relief carved into the courthouse pediment, farmers brought offerings of wheat to the goddess Justice. She was blindfolded, and in one hand, she held a pair of scales.

But in her other hand, she held a sword.

Jenny ran after the crowd.

She reached Coach Humbee first, as the obese man huffed and plodded his way across the street, trailing behind the crowd, which was already spreading across the grassy square. Jenny grabbed a thick fold in the back of his neck, and his skin sizzled at her touch. He howled.

"You let him alone!" Mrs. Humbee turned back and began swatting Jenny with her purse. She was a heavyset woman with a pretty face, an ex-cheerleader who'd taken in a lot of beer since then, and now kept the face preserved in layers of makeup. "You stop it!"

Jenny shoved Coach Humbee into her, knocking Mrs. Humbee to the ground. Her giant husband crashed on top of her. Jenny pushed the pox, trying to pass it through Humbee and into his wife. She needed to know if her power conducted through the people, the way Ashleigh's had conducted through Seth and into her. The coach howled again, then burbled, as if drowning in his throat, then he was quiet and still.

With a great effort, Jenny rolled Humbee's corpse onto his back. His face was peeling away into wide, curling strips. Dozens of bloody red polka dots appeared on the white dress shirt stretched over his vast stomach.

Mrs. Humbee tried to crawl away through the dirt with horribly blistered hands. Pustules covered her face. She was infected, but still alive. Jenny would have to push harder next time.

Jenny hurried over and stomped her bare foot onto the back of Mrs. Humbee's neck, shoving her face in the dirt. She had a quick, bloody seizure before dying.

Jenny saw Dr. Goodling, who'd just told the crowd to kill her, still in the back of Dave Trenton's pickup. Dave himself climbed in through the driver's door, and Dr. Goodling sat on the wheel well in the back, looking very pleased to find himself with a ride.

Jenny ran towards Dr. Goodling, and he saw her. He slapped at the rear window of the cab, and Dave slid it open.

"What is it, Dr.—" Dave began.

"Drive! Drive now!" Dr. Goodling shouted.

Dave cranked the truck, and immediately a Kid Rock CD blasted over his sound system. The crowd was everywhere, all over the street, and Dave could only creep slowly along.

Jenny leapt into the truck bed, landing on her feet. She felt fast and nimble now, as small and light and deadly as a single virus cell floating on the breeze.

Dr. Goodling gasped and backed away from her, but she grabbed his tie and pulled him close. She put her left hand on his face and traced her fingers down the center of it, from his forehead to his chin. In the wake of her fingertips, streaks of skin decayed and ruptured open. She grabbed the hair on the back of his head.

"Priest," she whispered, in the throaty, gravelly voice that only came out of her when she was deep into using her power. "I'm going to kill your family tonight. Especially your daughter." Jenny laughed. Some part of her delighted in messing with his head. "I came all the way from Hell to collect her."

Dr. Goodling whimpered. His scalp sloughed off in a bloody tangle, bringing his walnut brown toupee with it. Foamy pink saliva leaked from his mouth.

Jenny shoved him. He landed on his back, his spine slamming across the edge of the truck bed, then he spilled over and landed in the street.

Jenny looked into the cab, where Dave Trenton still attempted in vain to steer through the crowd. Dave, who'd let them use his phone and truck to trick Seth, then confronted Seth with a rifle when Seth arrived to save him.

She reached through the open window into the cab, and she curled her blistered, leaking fingers around his throat. Dave screamed.

He stomped the accelerator, no longer worrying about the crowd. He ran over people, and the crowd screamed and started running onto the grassy lawn. Dave made a sharp turn, slinging Jenny from one side of the truck bed to the other, but she held onto him. Then he drove up over the curb, onto the grass lawn, alongside the rest of the fleeing mob. The impact on the front tires knocked Jenny's hand loose, and the following impact on the back tires threw her on her back, banging her head against the floor of the truck bed.

She felt dazed while the truck accelerated. Jenny blinked a few times, hissing at the pain in the back of her head. She pushed up to her hands and knees, then crawled to the cab window. Dave's head slapped against the driver-side window, blood from his ear smearing against it. His blistered, rotting hand lay across the center armrest. He was dying, or dead, but his foot was still on the accelerator.

Jenny looked ahead through the windshield. The two-story brick building, home to the Five and Dime, rushed toward her at a frightening speed.

Jenny turned and crawled to the tailgate. She kicked it down, then rolled off the back. She smacked into the sidewalk, just one second too late to land in the grass.

Behind her, Dave's truck flew across the street, jumped up the curb on the far side, and smashed into a dusty, whitewashed shop window framed in brick. The engine died and, thankfully, so did the Kid Rock CD.

Jenny looked the other way, into the square. Her short truck ride had put her ahead of the mob, and now they were running towards her. Jenny smiled.

She pulled herself up, rocking unsteadily on her bare feet. She stepped into the grass and spread her arms wide, as if ready to embrace them all.

People at the front of the crowd saw her, but when they tried to stop or turn back, they got trampled by the people behind them.

Jenny took a deep breath, then hacked out another dense cloud of grainy spores. They spread out over the mob. The spores were drawn to people's eyes, noses and mouths, like a handful of iron filings thrown among magnets.

The front half of the group collapsed, coughing and puking up blood and gore as their skin blistered. The rest of the people trampled over them as they pushed forward, not understanding that they were charging towards the danger instead of away from it.

Jenny ran to meet the rest of the mob, skipping over the screaming infected people writhing on the ground. She spotted Ashleigh's mother and grabbed both her hands.

"Die quick," Jenny whispered, her voice deep. "Everybody dies."

Bloody sores split open all over Mrs. Goodling's arms. Her face blistered and decayed—except, oddly, her forehead, nose, and chin, which were mostly plastic. They managed to stay smooth and intact, like pieces carved from a mannequin, while the rest of her face corroded.

Jenny released one of Mrs. Goodling's hands and pushed her back into the crowd. Jenny held onto Mrs. Goodling's other hand and pumped into it, spreading the pox through her, deep into the remaining mob, skin to skin. They screamed and cursed as leprous ulcers bulged out through their faces, and bloody blisters appeared all over their heads.

Earl McCronkin approached Jenny with his pistol raised in his right hand, which shook a little. He aimed it at Jenny's head.

Jenny dodged under his arm, then grabbed his forearm with both hands and squeezed tight, willing the pox to eat it up. He howled and pulled back from her. His desiccated right arm came apart at the elbow, and he fell backward into the twitching, groaning, bleeding crowd. Jenny was stuck holding his forearm and hand, his fingers curling and wiggling even as the pox ate through them like acid. She threw it to the ground in disgust.

She grabbed one person after another, trying to push the pox all the way through the mob. A small group broke and ran away across the lawn, towards a gray Cadillac sedan parked on the street. Mayor Winder, Mrs. Winder, and Cassie. Jenny was not going to let them escape. She ran after them, feeling like she was gliding, her feet barely touching the grass blades.

She reached Mrs. Winder first and seized the back of her neck.

"Help!" Mrs. Winder screamed. Blood and loose teeth fell from her mouth. "Hank, she got me!"

Mayor Winder looked at her, looked at Jenny, then continued what he was doing, which was unlocking the door to his car. He clearly had no intention of going back for Mrs. Winder, and neither did Cassie, who jumped into the passenger door and screamed at her father to hurry. He pulled the door open, the keys still hanging in the lock.

Jenny threw Mrs. Winder's corpse aside and leapt onto Mayor Winder. Her knees landed in the center of his chest, knocking him backward. He sprawled on his back across the pavement, and Jenny pinned his arms with her shins.

"You're supposed to protect us," Jenny whispered. She pressed both her hands down on his face, and he convulsed beneath her, dark fluid bubbling at his lips. "You're a bad mayor."

She kept pressing her hands down, until his face caved in like a rotten pumpkin.

A car door slammed beside her. Cassie had snatched the keys and closed the driver door. She cranked the engine, and Jenny sprang to the Cadillac and slapped her hands against the closed window. Cassie cringed, her face stark white and terrified, then she punched the accelerator. Jenny stumbled back as the Cadillac screeched away down the street. Cassie had escaped.

Jenny turned back to the dispersing clumps of mob. She saw Dick Baker, lawyer and realtor, stumbling with Bret Daniels, the father of Darcy Metcalf's baby. They were both infected, trying to hold each other up as they limped along. Middle-aged women from the Women's Steering Committee and their husbands, crawled along after them, coughing and sneezing.

She spotted Neesha, squatting alone and bewildered near the center of the lawn, abandoned by her friends. Jenny walked toward her. The grass died under Jenny's feet, leaving dead white footprints in the grass behind her.

"Neesha," Jenny hissed.

Neesha looked up, her mouth wide in shock, eyes full of tears.

"I tried to stop them," Neesha said. "I told Ashleigh she was going too far. She wouldn't listen to me!" Her voice turned into a wail.

"Next time, try harder." Jenny laid her hand on Neesha's head as if blessing her. Neesha didn't resist, and she shriveled and died instantly. Jenny kicked her squatting corpse onto its side.

Jenny turned to the escaping group led by Dick Baker. She sucked in a gut full of air, then blew a thick cloud of spores at them. They toppled over, writhing, their skin breaking and blistering.

Jenny blew her pox toward each of the four corners of the square, infecting the remaining few who were still trying to escape.

Jenny walked among the fallen. She found those with lighter infections, and those who had only been trampled by the mob. She lay a bare foot on each face until they were dead.

In the street in front of the courthouse, she did the same to those who'd been hit by Dave's truck. Among them, she found Shannon McNare, who bled from the corner of her mouth and had a bent spine. Dave had driven right over her.

"Jenny," Shannon breathed. "I'm sorry."

"Shut up," Jenny said.

"No, it was..." She gasped for air. "Ashleigh. She tricked me. She said she loved me."

Jenny knelt in the street beside her. A grain of pity had formed inside her, murking up the righteous clarity of her fury. It bothered her.

"That's Ashleigh," Jenny said. "That's why I'm going to kill her. You have to die, too, Shannon. If Seth was here, he could heal you. But you get me instead. That's your fault."

"Seth was good, wasn't he?" Shannon breathed. "A good person?"

"Yes, he was."

"He was from God. I knew it. I knew it before...Ashleigh tricked me..."

"You have to go now, Shannon," Jenny whispered.

"Will you..." Shannon's chest hitched, and more blood trickled from the corner of her mouth. Her eyes glazed. "Will you kiss me good night?"

Jenny looked at her. The girl was losing her mind. She nodded.

Jenny kissed Shannon's cheek. Shannon sighed, her lips kissing at the air, and then her face ruptured open into three rotten slices, filled with pestilence and decay.

Jenny stood up as a cool breeze passed through town, and her long black hair streamed over her face. It was very quiet with everybody dead. The square smelled like rotten meat. She tasted blood on her lips—her own, Shannon's, countless other people's.

There was a little more to do tonight, while she was still on her rush. Jenny stepped onto the road that led west out of town, and she started to walk.

Behind her, more than two hundred plague-infested bodies littered the square.

Jenny limped through the woods. Her left leg, and everything on her left side below the gunshot wound, had turned stiff and hard. She stumbled over a thick tree root and caught herself on a trunk.

Root and branch, she thought. That's what Dr. Goodling had said. Rip out the evil, root and branch. Jenny had hacked away all the branches. There was still the root to deal with.

Jenny was past tired, past exhausted, into delusional hallucination territory. She'd turned it up and poured it out, and now there was nothing left. Almost nothing. She would push it out one more time, for Seth, even if it killed her.

She urged herself forward. She climbed over a barbed wire fence and found herself in a cow pasture. She stayed very wide of the slumbering herd.

She eventually emerged into Ashleigh's subdivision. She limped down the middle of the street, passing through the stark white circles under the streetlamps. Sweat, blood and gore matted her hair into clumps and coated her from her face to her feet. Her skin was turning gray. Her ribs were unusually prominent, her stomach sunken, as if she'd burned up all the fat in her body, and some of the muscle, too. She looked like a walking corpse, and she felt like one. It didn't matter. She didn't need to last much longer.

There were extra cars parked in front of the Goodling house. Jenny recognized Neesha's Acura, Darcy Metcalf's old Honda Civic, Brenda Purcell's rusty Nissan truck, among others.

Jenny limped up the driveway, up the cobblestone walkway, up the stairs to Ashleigh's front door. The door was locked, so Jenny made a fist and bashed it through the colored-glass window, oblivious to any new pain. She found the deadbolt knob and turned it. Then she opened the door.

In the foyer, Ashleigh's Welsh Corgi made a silent barking motion, then ran and hid her head under the couch in the front parlor. Jenny ignored her and headed upstairs. Ashleigh would be up there. Jenny could sense her. She was drawn to Ashleigh's energy like a homing beacon. She could smell Ashleigh's skin and jasmine perfume in the air.

In the upstairs hall, three pregnant sophomores stood by an open, lighted door, whispering to each other. They fell silent at the sight of Jenny.

Jenny approached them. Her dark hair was smeared down into her face. Open sores dripped blood and black fluid all over her body. The girls made no move to stop Jenny from walking into the open door beside them, into Ashleigh's room.

The pregnant girls from school had crammed into Ashleigh's room, wall to wall, each girl very visibly pregnant as they entered their third trimester. More girls were packed into the little sitting room off Ashleigh's bedroom, and others had crowded into her bathroom. There was nowhere to walk, just a solid mass of pregnant girls, and the air was stifling and hot.

Ashleigh sat on her bed, on the far side of the room from where Jenny stood. More pregnant girls sat around her, like Darcy Metcalf and senior cheerleaders Alison Newton and Ronella Jones, who'd been part of the original abstinence campaign, and were now the furthest along in their pregnancies. The closet girls would be conducting Ashleigh-energy from her out into the rest of the dense crowd, skin to skin. Jenny could sense that energy rippling outward from the bed.

Ashleigh was still in her slip. Her gray eyes peered at Jenny through the curtain of filthy blond hair that concealed her face. She gave a cold, deep laugh when Jenny stepped into the room, nothing Jenny had ever heard from her before.

"Oh, little Jenny Pox," Ashleigh said. "I didn't think you'd make it."

"I'd walk any distance to find you, Ashleigh."

Ashleigh laughed again. "You look like a skeleton, Jenny Pox. Except there. There, you look like raw hamburger." She pointed at the chunk of missing flesh on Jenny's left side, and some of the girls close to Ashleigh giggled.

Jenny held out an empty hand. New blisters bloomed and popped on her palm and fingertips, seeping sticky black fluid.

"Come on, Ashleigh," Jenny said. "Come to me. We belong together."

"Why don't you come to me?" Ashleigh asked. "Do you want to touch me bad enough to kill these girls? And their babies?"

Jenny looked around the room. There was no way to Ashleigh without touching dozens of girls, and Jenny was hardly wearing any clothes.

"Oh, Jenny," Ashleigh sighed. "How long can you stand there? It looks to me like you'll fall down and die just about any time. What a mess. I mean, who would clean it up, right? Who'd want to touch it?"

"I can wait," Jenny said.

Ashleigh gave her cold laugh. She leaned forward and spoke in a stage whisper, her filthy blond locks puffing out around her mouth.

"Want to know a secret, Jenny Pox?" she asked. "Just between you, me, and the famous sluts of Fallen Oak High?" None of the girls took offense. They were all doped on Ashleigh-love.

"What is it?" Jenny asked.

"Look at me." Ashleigh tucked her hair behind her ears. Her left cheek looked mangled, and Ashleigh cleaned it off with a Handi-Wipe. Then she brushed her fingers across it. "Do you see that, Jenny Pox? Look close. Look at my scars."

Jenny looked. She could see four sunken, pockmarked streaks down Ashleigh's cheek.

"That's you," Ashleigh said. "Your fingernails, from first grade. The scars didn't heal, you bitch. Do you have any idea how early I have to get up, how much concealer I have to wear, just to make my face look decent? Did you know you're the first thing I think about every morning, little Jenny? Can you see what you've done to me? You filled me up with hate. If I seem wicked to you, it's because you made me that way, Jenny Pox."

Jenny thought this over for a minute.

"No," Jenny said. "You were already a bitch in first grade."

Ashleigh hissed. Then she lifted her head and cocked it a little, hearing something. Jenny listened. Footsteps crossed the foyer to the stairs.

"Who is that?" Ashleigh asked Darcy Metcalf. Darcy shrugged.

"It's not your parents," Jenny said. "I killed both of them."

"You whore!" Ashleigh snapped.

"They tried to kill me first," Jenny said. "Fair's fair."

"Well," Ashleigh sighed. "At least I won't have to beg Daddy for his money anymore. So glad I didn't let them have any more little brats."

Jenny edged further into the room as the footsteps approached. Cassie burst into the room, then stopped when she saw all the girls blocking her way.

"Ashleigh!" Cassie screamed. "Jenny Mittens is flipping out! We have to get out of town…" Then her gaze fell on Jenny, less than a foot away from her, and she gasped.

Jenny gave her an apologetic smile, while Jenny's hand darted out and seized Cassie's bare upper arm. Cassie screamed, but Jenny held the pox back this time, turning it down as far as she could, to a bare trickle. White lesions cropped up on Cassie's arm on either side of where Jenny gripped it. More appeared slowly, like the footprints of a small invisible tortoise, creeping down toward her elbow, up toward her shoulder. Cassie shouted and tried to break free, but Jenny held on tight.

"Come on, Ashleigh," Jenny said. "It's Cassie. Your best friend. Come to me and I'll let her go. Or stay there and watch her die."

Ashleigh looked agitated, baring her teeth, but she didn't move.

"Ashleigh, please!" Cassie begged. White lesions appeared on her neck.

"I'm not very good at holding it back," Jenny said. "It wants to spread, Ashleigh."

The lesions appeared faster, popping up on Cassie's lips and cheeks. One swelled on her eyelid and forced it closed. Cassie's stomach heaved, and thick spittle bubbled at her lips.

"Look, everyone," Jenny said. "Ashleigh's best friend in the world, and Ashleigh won't help her. Ashleigh won't protect you, either. She can't protect you. She can only use you."

There was whispering around the edge of the room, among the girls furthest from Ashleigh, probably getting the weakest doses of her power.

"Last chance, Ashleigh," Jenny said. "You can save her. Just come here."

"Fuck you," Ashleigh spat back. Her voice was dark and husky. "I can get another one of those."

"Ashleigh!" Cassie wailed, and Jenny pushed. All the lesions on Cassie's body ruptured and oozed black fluid. Blood ran from Cassie's nostril, and her red hair began to slide and fall from her head. Spasms jerked through her body, and Jenny released her just before she crashed into a pregnant freshman girl. The pregnant girl shrieked and backed up a few inches, but couldn't go any further.

Cassie crumpled to the floor, her nerves whipping her body one way, then the other. She vomited black liquid down her chin, over her dress, and onto Ashleigh's carpet, and then she died.

"How dare you!" Ashleigh snapped. "She was mine."

"I warned you," Jenny said. Her voice was as dark and gritty as Ashleigh's. "I'm feeling very murderous today. It must be the witch in me. You can ask your father about it when you're together in hell. Tonight."

Ashleigh bared her teeth again and growled like a wolf. She seized the arms of the girls closest to her and squeezed. Jenny could feel Ashleigh's energy pushing out into the crowd, conducting from girl to girl, skin to skin. The room grew even hotter. It was starting to feel like an oven.

"Get her, bitches," Ashleigh said through gritted teeth. "Tear her to pieces."

Pregnant girls advanced on Jenny from every side. The three pregnant sophomores in the hall sealed off the doorway.

"No!" Jenny screamed. "You'll die!"

"We're not scared of your threats." Ashleigh smirked.

Jenny ignored Ashleigh. She closed her eyes and imagined the little flies in her gut, only a few left in the hive now. She told them they had one purpose, to eat up Ashleigh's power. She imagined the golden thread of Ashleigh's influence woven among the girls in the room. She pictured the black flies eating the thread. And then she pictured them with big dragonfly wings.

Jenny's mouth and nose swelled, with blisters breaking all over them. She opened her eyes as a dozen girls laid their hands on her bare skin.

She sneezed and coughed all at once as the grainy little spores exploded out of her head. At the same time, her power flowed into and through all the girls grabbing at her, and all the girls behind them trying to get at Jenny, conducting in a giant ripple through the room, draining Jenny's depleted body.

All around her, faces erupted—eyes watering, yellow liquid drizzling from their noses and ears. They coughed, and some of them puked, spattering the awful-smelling yellow fluid everywhere.

"What?" Ashleigh asked. "What are you doing, Jenny Pox?"

"I'm setting them free." Jenny threaded her way among the sick girls. Ashleigh's room smelled like the sick ward at a hospital, with no air conditioning, in the middle of July. The stench of disease and body fluids thickened the air.

Jenny reached the foot of the bed. Ashleigh crawled back to the headboard, while Darcy Metcalf vomited yellow all over Ashleigh's pink-checkered quilt.

"Now it's your turn, Ashleigh," Jenny said in her deepest, darkest voice. "Your time to go free."

Ashleigh grabbed the window and shoved it all the way up. She threw her bare shoulder against the window screen, and there was a cracking sound as it bent outward. She bounced back from it with red hash marks all over her shoulder.

Jenny stepped up on the bed and over the hiccupping, puking, hiccupping Darcy Metcalf. Jenny approached Ashleigh, leaving dirty, bloody footprints on Ashleigh's sheets. She held out her hands, bubbling with blisters. She was filled up, with one last big dose of the specially-tailored Jenny pox.

"Leave me alone!" Ashleigh screamed, and her voice was dark and full of gravel. "I'm sick of you hunting me!"

Then Ashleigh threw herself against the screen again, and

this time it broke free of the window frame and fell out into the night. Ashleigh tumbled out after it, over the windowsill.

Jenny seized Ashleigh's foot as it went over. She wrapped both hands around the captured ankle. Ashleigh was heavier than her, so Jenny had to brace herself against the headboard.

Ashleigh dangled upside down above the cobblestone walkway.

"Let me go!" Ashleigh screamed.

"I have something for you," Jenny said. "I made it to eat your power out of people. I want to see what it will do to you. I call it...Ashleigh pox." In Jenny's mind, the last little flies were going to eat the golden thread out of Ashleigh. But Ashleigh was mostly golden thread.

Ashleigh screamed. Fat tumors formed on her legs, in her ankle joints, and inside her toes, bending and twisting her feet. Veins of black rot spread over her calf, through her knee, up her thigh. Where veins of rot crossed each other, great oozing holes opened up in her flesh, down to the bone. It looked like an invisible hand was punching circles with a giant cookie cutter up her stomach and back. The veins of black reached her face, and the skin began to decay.

Ashleigh twisted and jerked, still trying to kick free. Jenny squeezed her fingers through the mush of Ashleigh's muscle and tendon, and she gripped the wet bones of Ashleigh's ankle.

Ashleigh screamed and curled up at the waist, swinging her hands wildly toward Jenny. Her fingertips had decayed, revealing points of bone, and now her fingernails loosened and flaked away.

Jenny had a glimpse of her face that she would always remember. Ashleigh looked up at her, screaming her head off, long blond hair fanning out below her. Her eyes and nose were just raw, empty red holes. Her lips were gone. Her remaining teeth dangled loose, attached only by their nerve fibers, and a fragment of her tongue wiggled at the back of her rotting throat.

Then Ashleigh fell back, and she kept struggling, even though it was hopeless. All the soft tissue was now shriveling against her skeleton and turning black and crumbly, as if she had been dead and in the ground for months. The skeletal Ashleigh gasped through her mummified face, and kept jerking against Jenny's hand.

The Ashleigh pox ate its way through her bone marrow, and the ankle bones in Jenny's hand turned brittle. She dropped Ashleigh's remains into the cobblestones below. It shattered from skull to pelvis with a wet, splintering sound. After a few seconds, Ashleigh's remains stopped struggling.

Jenny stared at the broken pieces for a minute. She had done it. She had killed Ashleigh Goodling.

She felt the sense of a duty done, a purpose fulfilled. It was a serene feeling, but a cold and bitter one.

Jenny turned back from the window. Most of the girls had left the room, eager to escape the wretched smell and body heat. The few that remained just stared at her. They looked sick, but nowhere close to dying. None of them seemed to be having any trouble with their unborn children, either, at least not right away. Maybe she had been successful, attacking only the Ashleigh infection and nothing else.

Jenny hobbled through the room, keeping away from everyone. She didn't have the energy or the focus to make only Ashleigh pox right now. Anyone who brushed against her would die of plain old Jenny pox. Losing the dose of energy it would take to transmit that Jenny pox would kill Jenny. She was teetering on the edge.

Fortunately, it was mutual, and nobody wanted to come close to her. She saw herself in Ashleigh's mirror, which was framed with real seashells. She looked emaciated. Her eyes were sunken, her cheeks sucked in and gaunt. There were gray streaks in her hair. She could see the shape of her teeth through her lips. Where she'd been shot, the loose fat and muscle tissue had all been eaten up to fuel her power, and she could actually see her own ribs. She looked like death. She was death.

Jenny made her way past more girls in the hall. The front steps were crowded, so she went down the back way, through the kitchen, onto the back terrace. Everywhere she went were little knots of pregnant girls, whispering to each other, looking for food, looking for the way out, looking for answers.

She passed some more on the terrace, including Darcy Metcalf, who was taking a drag from freshman Veronica Guntley's cigarette.

"Hey, Jenny," Darcy said as she passed. Jenny turned her head to look at her but didn't say anything. She felt nothing but pain, and the desire to crawl somewhere dark and let it end.

"What happened?" Darcy asked. "What happened to us?"

"Ashleigh Goodling put a spell on y'all," Jenny said. "She was a witch. I killed her."

Jenny kept walking, off the terrace and into the sweet, cool grass, which soothed her blistered feet.

"Hey," Darcy called after her. "What are you?"

Jenny stopped walking. She looked back at Darcy.

"I don't fucking know," Jenny said. "But I guess I'm fixing to find out."

Then she walked again, across the Goodling's manicured lawn, and through an island of daffodils, leaving a trail of dying plants behind her. She felt sad for them. She normally got along pretty well with plants, as long as she wasn't scared or excited.

She followed the gradual slope down to the centerpiece of the Goodlings' back yard, the duck pond, which was big enough for a little fishing dock and deep enough to float a rowboat.

Jenny walked out along the dock and looked into the black water, where moonlight framed her death's head reflection. She didn't have much time left. She'd eaten herself up to get to Ashleigh.

She jumped into the water.

Brackish water flowed into her mouth and nose. Her body fought against it, choking and thrashing, but she didn't have much strength. The water forced its way in. She panicked, ready to change her mind, but it was too late now.

Her flooded body sank like a stone into the darkness. She landed in cold, slimy mud and sharp underwater weeds. And then Jenny died there, at the bottom of the pond.

CHAPTER TWENTY-FIVE

She floated in darkness for a long time. The pain was gone, and the cold, and the anger, and every other feeling.

In time, patterns of light glimmered somewhere below her. She sank down to them, or they floated up to her.

She drew close to them. She discovered that each bit of light was a memory, and each memory contained a cluster of memories, a lifetime of them.

She saw herself on a low square tower of stone and mud, in gloves and a coarse linen cloak made from flax. She watched an army of men in copper helmets approach her walls. She was planning to spread a plague among them in order to protect her city, which was mostly mud houses inside an earthen wall.

She saw herself in a rough wool tunic, again with gloves, seated on a bench in the back of a galley rowed by fifty men, across salty, choppy, cold water. She'd been sent to an enemy city on a mission to spread pestilence there.

She saw herself in the head and skin of a lioness, looking out through the eye holes. She sat on a raised wooden throne inside a large, boxy building of simple clay bricks, on the bank of the Nile. In war, she slew the king's enemies. In peace, those accused of injustice were brought before her for judgment, and sometimes execution. She was worshipped and feared, and many tried to influence her with gifts. They called her *Sekhmet*.

She saw herself a thousand years later, in fine woven cotton and gold jewelry, in a vast limestone temple complex devoted to the memory of her earlier incarnation, since elevated to a goddess. There were hundreds of black granite statues of the lion-headed goddess *Sekhmet*, and a sacrifice was made to a different statue each day.

She saw herself with dreadlocks to her waist, deep in the Central African rainforest. She led a band of rebels armed with spears and slings, determined to drive the invaders from their land. She was fearsome in battle and her people loved her. They called her *Nyabinghi*.

There were hundreds of lives. In most of them, she had warred ceaselessly against others of her kind. For tens of thousands of years, through one incarnation after another, they had made their wars on each other. Though they were born into humanity, humans were their pawns, the world their game board. They delighted in destruction.

They had not been human souls, originally. They had been wild, primordial spirits, wandering for eternities in darkness and desolation in the wastelands of the universe. They found their way to this tiny, hot, bright pocket of life, and they learned the trick of incarnating as humans. They found themselves with special powers when in human form, powers normal humans did not have. And they found that power attracted great interest from other humans.

Their first wars were fought by clans of humans, grunting a simple language and wielding stone hand axes. In time, these became spears, arrows, swords, cannons, ballistic missiles. They hunted each other down the millennia, and their armies grew larger, the game more complex. She saw that most of history was lost, there had been great civilizations and sprawling empires now long forgotten.

There were others out there, not just the three of them. There might have been a hundred or more spirits of her kind who'd found their way to this world. As spirits, they were immortal, but also invisible, voiceless, and powerless, with a very limited range of emotion and communication. Incarnation gave them the richness of sensual experience and the power to act and speak.

When incarnated, they were so dazzled by the drama and spectacle of life they did not remember their true nature. Discarnate, between lives, they could not help but remember their true selves, and they yearned to return to the warm pulse of flesh, the brilliant senses, the pleasures and pain, the storms of feelings, impressions, ideas. The mental focus needed to enter human life left them with a near-total amnesia while alive, but the experience of being alive was worth that. So she had decided, hundreds of times.

She'd grown more careful about trying to prepare her human mothers so that her birth was not fatal to them. That could take years. The most recent time, she'd been in a hurry to find a vessel, and gotten reckless.

She had known Seth and Ashleigh, or the spirits behind them, countless times. She had a memory of killing Seth, when he was a bearded man in bear skins, by nailing him to a pile of logs and kindling with iron stakes, then setting the pyre ablaze. She remembered killing Ashleigh, and being killed by Ashleigh, more times than she could count.

Through the ages, they had styled themselves as gods, demons, angels, holy men and women, magicians and witches, fae and djinn, according to whatever myths existed at their place and time of birth. When they took on such roles, they truly believed in them. When incarnate, such legend and folklore provided her kind with the only available explanation of their powers. She had spent lifetimes genuinely believing she was a goddess.

Discarnate, she saw clearly and coldly. Ashleigh's soul had been eager to try the new weapons, the ones that could incinerate cities and annihilate millions. It would be a new achievement for her, the largest number ever killed at a single stroke.

Ashleigh had tried to hide herself from the other spirits by getting born in a tiny out-of-the-way place. She was normally attracted to the largest cities, where she could make the greatest use of her powers. She wanted to get ahead of the game years before the others knew she had incarnated again.

The souls of Jenny and Seth had tracked her down and hurried to incarnate nearby, so they could keep watch on her and stop her before she gained access to the city-eater fire weapons. They had succeeded. Jenny had discarnated Ashleigh before she could unleash the death and destruction she craved.

Jenny had almost lost it, had totally forgotten her purpose in the overwhelming, hypnotic spectacle of being alive. If she'd waited much longer, it might have become difficult to get close to Ashleigh. Ashleigh had known instinctively that Jenny and Seth were her greatest threats, and taken great measures to neutralize

Jenny and control Seth. When they found each other, Jenny and Seth had begun to awaken.

There was another purpose to her life. Only in life could she and Seth touch each other and experience their depth of feeling for each other. They could engage each other in the passion and drama of being human. As spirits, they were isolated within themselves. As humans, they could be together.

Already, she ached to return to the nerve and sinew of flesh, to find a body and live again. Incarnate, she forgot her true nature. Discarnate, she could hardly imagine the terror and ecstasy of human emotions. She needed to be alive to feel them.

There was a sense of loss. After a lifetime of suffering, she had found him again, only to lose what they'd begun to yet another war with Ashleigh. As Jenny and Seth, they had started to build a good life together. Ashleigh, still playing the old game, had ruined it for them.

For a long moment, she was just a feeling of sorrow. They could incarnate again, born into new little bodies, but there was the risk they would get lost and never find each other in their new lives. As ever, the risk would be worth it, but she still felt cheated. This time around, she'd had the long pain of being alone, then the delight of discovering him—which never got old—and then, after only very brief togetherness, the inevitable loss and death. It was unfair. She wished for a second chance.

She mourned for Jenny and for Seth, the lovely little people they had been, with their lives cut so short.

After an unknowable amount of time passed, she felt the vibration of a distant signal. It was him, calling to her through the endless dark. They could be aware of each other, but they could not talk or share themselves in a very meaningful way, if they were discarnate. They could signal intent in a general way.

She signaled back, and moved toward him through the dark inverted space of the discarnated.

CHAPTER TWENTY-SIX

Sensation slammed into her from every side. She felt cold, hunger, sickness and extreme pain all through the core of herself. It was almost delicious. It was glorious to be alive.

Then the pain really took over, blotting out her thoughts. She coughed, and someone turned her on her side. She puked dark water that tasted like duck crap. She caught her breath, then coughed up more water. Her lungs and stomach were competing to empty themselves out.

A hand patted her bare wet back, helping her cough some more. Then it slid up to rub her affectionately on the back of the neck, while she coughed up the rest of the water.

"Feeling better?" he asked.

"I can't see." Her voice was a wet croak. "It's so cold." She was naked and shivering hard.

"Here." He wrapped something like a blanket around her. It helped a little, but it was open and drafty in both the front and the back.

He pulled her close to him, into his lap, and his skin was as hot as open flames. She wrapped her arms around his neck. He lay one scorching hand on her drenched head. He lay another across her bare stomach, and rubbed, creating more warmth through friction. She realized he was wet and mostly bare, too, except the soggy boxer shorts under her ass.

"Seth?" she whispered. Her eyes itched. They were starting to work, but so far it was all dark, fuzzy streaks.

"Now you ask? Would you just climb naked into anybody's lap?"

"Right now I would." Her teeth chattered. "It's really, really cold."

"Next time, don't drown yourself in a pond."

"I was already dying," she said. "I just wanted the pain to end."

"You made it a lot harder on me," Seth told her. "I didn't think I could do it, after I pulled you up and saw you."

She could see the pale, fuzzy shape of his face now. She lay a hand on it.

"Is this real?" she whispered, then coughed. Her windpipe and lungs felt very sore. "Am I dreaming? Am I dead?"

"You were. Now you're not."

"Why?"

"Because I can't live without you." He turned her head and kissed her. Her vision cleared up.

"But, seriously," she said. "What happened? What day is it?"

"It's still tonight," Seth told her. "I woke up on the courthouse steps a couple hours ago. It took a while for me to finish healing. Then another while to look around, because I woke up surrounded by dead bodies as far as I could see—"

"Sorry," Jenny said. "But they were all guilty."

"—yeah, so I remembered about the plague-goddess girlfriend," Seth said, and his choice of words startled her. "Then I had to find you. Ashleigh's body wasn't on the square, so I thought you might be here."

"In the pond?"

"That was easy. You left dead white footprints all the way from the house." Seth grinned and held up her lacy, dripping wet panties. "And these float."

Jenny snatched her underwear from him. Then she touched his pale chest, where the bullet had entered his heart. There was only a scar.

"She got me pretty good," Seth said. He reached into the gaping, tattered hole in the back of the coat he'd put around Jenny, and his fingers touched her skin. "Ruined my best suit, too. Almost want to resurrect her so I can kill her again. Have you seen her body in the driveway? Looks like chicken bones and charcoal."

Jenny was still concentrating on his new scar.

"Does this mean you can't die?" she asked.

"I'm sure I can," he said. "Just not that easy. Besides, I had to come back and take care of you."

"And I didn't really die, either," Jenny said, her voice full of wonder. "I survived the drowning."

"Nah, you were totally dead when I pulled you out," he told her. "I mean you were the color of a fish, no pulse, muddy, skin rotten, weeds in your hair, totally bloated up with water—"

"Okay!" Jenny said. She touched her left side. Seth had erased her gunshot wound, too.

"I've never healed anybody that dead before," Seth said. "I'm very impressed with myself."

"I'm impressed with yourself." Jenny looked at him carefully. "But I bet you would die if I nailed you down with iron and set you on fire."

"Yes!" Seth recoiled. "That would probably do it! That's the worst thing I've ever heard. Why would you even think of that? I think I've had nightmares about that."

"I think I already…I just had some crazy dreams down there."

"When you were dead?"

"Don't laugh."

"I had some, too," Seth said.

Jenny looked him in the eyes. "Really?"

"You first," he said.

She told him what she could remember of what she'd seen, though it was all getting murky and jumbled. They had past lives together. They made war on each other, and on the others who were like them, since prehistoric times.

"I saw some of that," he said.

"Don't screw with me, Seth."

"I'm not." His eyes looked into the distance toward the first pale shade of blue in the east. "And something else. Before we were human—I know that sounds weird, but listen—before we were human, we came from this dark, empty place. Not…wherever normal humans souls come from."

"The wastelands," Jenny said, nodding.

"That a good word for it. A great word. Wastelands." He frowned deeply, as if remembering a little of what it was like. Jenny had a few memory-impressions of it, too. Deep cold, darkness, an urge to scream in a place with no sound. Trying to think about it filled her with horror.

"When we first tried being human," Seth said, "We didn't understand people at all. We were powerful, but we were wicked and brutal. We loved destruction."

"Sounds like Ashleigh." Jenny laughed a little.

"Exactly like Ashleigh. But some of us, or maybe just you and me, we started learning from all these human lives. There's a lot more available here, in this world, than just power and pleasure, but that's all we could see at first. We laughed at everyone else for their weakness. But really the weakness is important. Pain and suffering can teach compassion. And love. You and I have been learning about love for several lifetimes now. We learn about it from each other."

This struck Jenny as painfully sweet, and she gave him a long kiss. Suddenly, she couldn't get close enough to Seth.

She hugged against him.

"I don't think I understand love yet," Jenny whispered. "But I want to keep trying. With you. I know I love you, Seth."

"I know I love you, too," he whispered.

The sky was brightening above them. They were sitting in the back yard of the deceased Goodling family, from which about ninety pregnant girls had recently emerged under inexplicable circumstances. The broken pieces of Ashleigh's body lay on the front walk. Before long, someone would be here to investigate. Someone would also be investigating the mysterious plague that left bodies all over downtown.

Seth wore only his wet boxers. The rest of his clothes were scattered on the grass, where he'd left them when he dived into the pond to get her. Jenny was naked except for the coat, which was missing a lot of its back.

"We should go," Jenny said.

They dressed as much as they could. Jenny wore Seth's bloodstained black pants. Seth put on his bloodstained dress shirt, with the back blown out by shotgun. It was hard to share one set of ruined clothes between two people.

"We had another reason for being born this time," Jenny said. "To stop Ashleigh."

"We did that," Seth said. "I mean, you did. She pretty much stopped me."

"But there are others," Jenny said. "I got the feeling there could be a lot of others. Won't they try to do the same kind of thing? Won't Ashleigh be looking for another chance to get herself born?"

"Then we'll watch out for the others." Seth took her hand, and they walked towards the front yard. Both of their backs were exposed to the rising sun. "Today, I don't want to think about anyone but you."

Jenny smiled.

"What are we, Seth? Before, we always had something we could believe. Something we could pretend to be. I actually spent a whole lifetime thinking I was Arabian death angel. It was kind of cool. But we always let other people tell us what we are," Jenny said. "Now we have our memories of other lives. Now that we remember, what do we do?"

"We make it up as we go," Seth said. "That's what we've always done."

"But how should we—what do we—should we try to—" So many questions filled her up that she couldn't begin to focus on any particular one.

"We have forever to figure that out," Seth said. "Right now, let's just think about living this one lifetime together."

"Then we'd better get started," Jenny said. "One lifetime goes by like that."

Jenny snapped her fingers.

THE END

ABOUT THE AUTHOR

Jeffrey L. Bryan studied English literature at the University of Georgia and at Oxford, with a focus on English Renaissance and Romantic period literature. He also studied screenwriting at UCLA. He lives in Atlanta with his wife Christina and assorted pets.

Visit him at: **JLBryanbooks.com**

1287113R00179

Made in the USA
San Bernardino, CA
06 December 2012